STEALING CINDERELLA

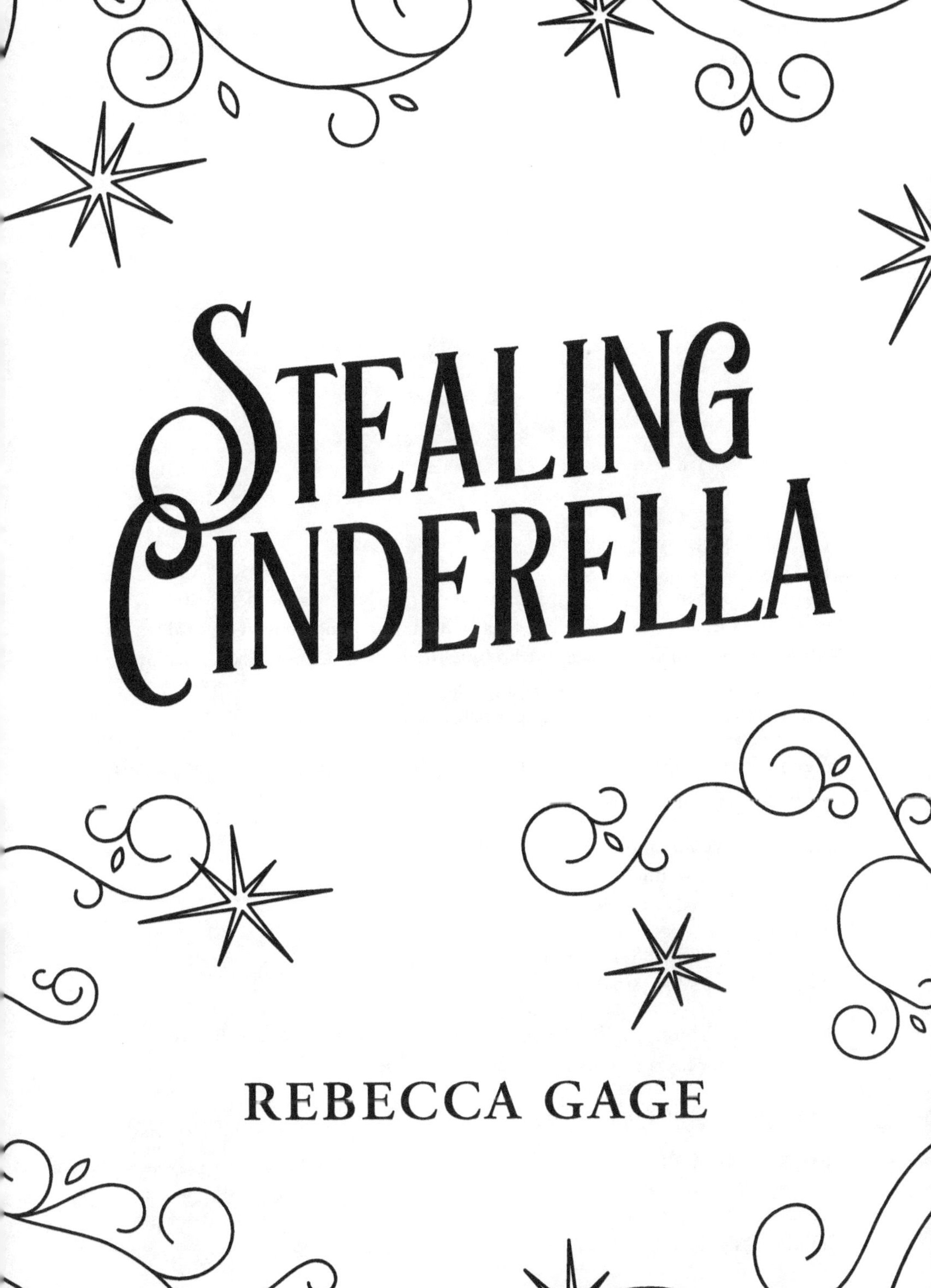

Stealing Cinderella

REBECCA GAGE

Publisher's Cataloging-in-Publication data
Gage, Rebecca, author
Stealing Cinderella / Rebecca Gage.

ISBN: 979-8-9880888-4-4 (paperback)
ISBN: 979-8-9880888-5-1 (digital)

1. Fantasy—Fiction. 2. Fairy Tale—Fiction. 3. Medieval—Social life and customs—Fiction. I. Gage, Rebecca. II. Stealing Cinderella.

Printed in the United States of America

10 9 8 7 6 5 4 3 2 1

Cover design: L1graphics
Interior design: Suzanne Uchytil

For the brave hearts who fight against the dark,
you are not alone

Content Warning

This book contains mild depictions of parental abuse (physical and emotional), a second-degree burn injury, dealing with grief and the death of a parent, sexual harrassment, and intense kissing.

1

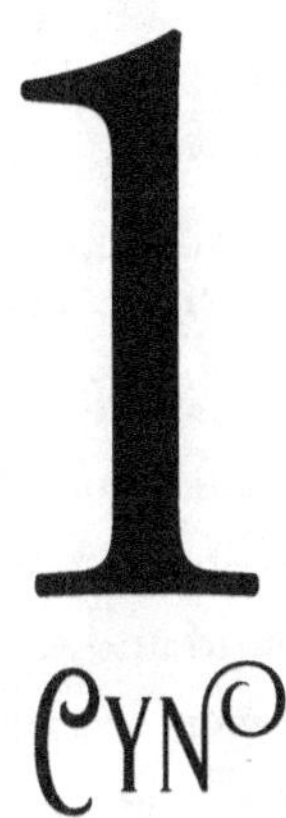

CYN

Arguing with my house fairy while crouching behind a rose hedge in the middle of the night was a really bad way to start a burglary. "Stealing is wrong, m'lady," Shar said, her light turning from pale yellow to a disapproving brown.

"We've been over this. I'm not stealing." I motioned her lower, lest one of the four standing guards see her over the estate's hedge. Then I reached into my satchel, double-checking I had all of my equipment. "I'm trading."

The moonlight glinted off the two large silver candlesticks ready to be exchanged and a large burlap bag of soot. Shar's palm-sized light—the only visible aspect of the fairy—hovered a few feet from my face.

My fingers drifted over the packets of loosely tied spices, the smell of cinnamon and ash lifting into the chilly air. I stopped at the grainy texture of two small terra-cotta pots—left over from when Papa traded with Shiangsu.

Cold tickled the back of my hand as I placed the apple-sized *bombe fumigène* on the wet grass, my joints popping as I shifted slightly. The pot had a fuse the length of my forearm sprouting from the top. I nestled the explosive deep within the hedge. The bristles from the fuse peeked out from the bush like a braided mule's tail.

Keeping close to the hedge and the ground, I moved ten feet away, then concealed the second pot with an equally long fuse.

Time to set the stage. I scattered handfuls of ash along the length of the hedge, the smokey smell filling my nose.

I wiped my hands on my pants, knowing there was ash on my face as well. *Blast, I never manage to stay clean.*

"Shar," I said, gesturing to the *bombes*.

"Lighting things on fire to steal something is wrong," she whispered.

"Can't conduct a proper Magpie trade without my signature flair." I gave a small flourish with my hand and dipped my head in a tiny bow.

She sighed but dropped lower, her light deepening to a rich orange, and flew to the first fuse. "*Brûler*," her tiny voice hissed.

A minuscule spark jumped from Shar onto the thin braided rope, which caught fire easily. She moved to the second and did the same, then joined me.

"It will be a beautiful explosion, don't you think?" I said.

Shar's light turned a flat yellow, and she flew in an equally flat line to the other end of the hedge.

I sighed, grabbing my bag and following her. I had only a few moments to assess my next move. My eyes darted from hedge to flower bed, gathering my options.

It was a long dash to Lady Eline's darkened mansion. Her manicured garden stood to my left with two guards at attention near the house. Water spouted from a sculptured fountain, next to which two more guards were surveying the estate. The *bombes fumigènes* would distract them, but what then?

A sprawling lawn grew from the outer hedge to the house with a sparse offering of rosebushes between me and the building. *Beasts, not a lot of cover.* I'd have to sprint from bush to bush, then race to the base of the balcony. With Lady Eline at court for the festivities before the masquerade, most of the staff would be away—though there would still be a skeleton staff and hopefully no more guards.

A muted thud echoed against the estate's walls, followed by the patter of falling dirt.

The guards near the fountain raced toward the sound and away from the chateau. Their cries in the distance quickly followed. The attention of the two guards near the house was fixed on the noise.

I raced for the next rosebush.

"Mistress, there are too many guards," Shar hissed behind me. For such a small creature, she certainly made a big fuss.

I stopped behind a rosebush pruned into the shape of a swan, white roses blossoming from its folded wings.

The shouting continued. Shar's light joined me, now a dull red.

"The masquerade is only four weeks away," I hissed, "and I'm still missing the *pièce de résistance.*"

"A firm moral foundation?"

"No. Shoes, silly. Stepmother wants me at the masque, and we don't have the money to buy anything new."

Shar's light dimmed and dropped close to my shoulder. "Why are we doing this?"

"Because I can't show up to the ball in these." I pointed at my black clothing.

Several more shouts of alarm rose, this time closer to the house. Good. If the staff helped with the fire, there would be less for me to worry about once I was inside.

"That's not what I meant. Why do you let Stepmother treat you like this? You deserve better."

I whipped my head around, my voice hard and flat. "No. I don't."

Shar took a breath, but thankfully the second pot exploded, cutting off her reply. Shouts of "smoke!" and "fire!" pierced the night.

I peered around the swan's leafy back and checked the house for movement, satisfied to see the last two guards leave their post and race toward the smoke. "Time to trade for some shoes."

Shar sighed and her light bobbed lower. "I am merely trying to protect the rightful heir of the Manette household from being arrested and jailed." Her now-dirt-brown light bobbed disapprovingly.

I rolled my eyes, then I sprinted for the next bush with Shar following behind.

Armand 2

There was no saving my dignity, not with thirteen marbles in my mouth. I, Prince Armand Paul de Lyon, was acutely aware I looked ridiculous—and that I was drooling on my second-best dinner jacket.

A dull noise like a dropped sandbag sounded outside. That was odd. Lady Eline's estate was not remotely close to the palace or shipyard.

"Once more, Your Royal Highness," said my speech tutor, continuing as if nothing had happened. *Monsieur* Parler stood next to a small claw-footed side table upon which sat a tray of instruments designed to cure my speech—attempts that had lasted fifteen of my eighteen years. The study, decorated with rich wood furniture, deep burgundy damask, and soothing colors, was usually relaxing, but tonight it felt like a circus with me on display.

Father sat in an overstuffed orange satin chair directly across from me. I hated that chair. I had once gotten sick on it. Lady Eline had cleaned it, then reupholstered it carrot orange. Just looking at it made my stomach turn.

After a tortuous dinner with Father, lessons had begun at sundown. The stars now glinted mockingly. Father had visited two days ago and I'd made no progress since then. Why was he here again?

Another thud from outside. An explosion?

As muffled shouts from the guards reached my ears, I glanced at Father. His frown lines deepened. His message was clear: *We are not done here.*

I gripped my armrest and held Father's gaze. He would not approve of eye-rolling even with a mouthful of marbles—or under possible attack. Father wouldn't move until he was satisfied with my "progress." Very well.

I lifted the small book in my hand and breathed through my nose lest the marbles slide down my throat. The print stood neat and orderly and I willed the words to form properly in my mouth. Around the marbles.

"Gew see duh wibberwy."

The tutor automatically handed me a handkerchief to wipe the spittle from my mouth. Instead, I filled it with the wretched marbles.

M. Parler raised his fleecy white eyebrows.

"N-no m-more." My jaw muscles ached.

"Your Royal Highness, your impediment shall remain without proper diligence." The man rolled his *r*'s and crisped his *t*'s with precision.

"I have t-tried everything with p-proper d-d-diligence." I gaped like a dying fish. *Out, words!*

Even from inside, phrases such as "Put it out!" and "More water!" could be clearly heard from the guards.

I leaped from my seat so quickly, the chair teetered on its legs. "I'm going t-t-to investigate."

Father leaned forward. "Hermann." My shoulders tightened at the sound of my given name. I much preferred the nickname Luc had given me. I moved away from the table. "The guards will attend to it." His thick voice carried a note of warning. He stood and the orange chair creaked. "My son will resume lessons tomorrow."

The aged tutor bowed and took his infernal tray of instruments with him, casting a backward glance over his shoulder.

The cords in my neck coiled. I hated that pity-filled look—the same pity I saw in Mother's eyes. Though it was better than Lady Catherine's laughter. I winced inwardly. I'd only meant to inquire after her sister, the Duchess of Cowley, but I'd stammered so much I'd asked about the duchess's cow.

I strode toward the glass-paneled doors leading to the balcony. Billows of gray smoke poured from behind a corner of the garden's outer hedge.

Four guards and a few staff members with buckets and blankets were working to douse the fire.

My hand gripped the handles.

"Hermann—" Father joined me on my right, his barrel-shaped frame so large that the room seemed to shrink.

My grip around the handle tightened. "Armand. C-call me Armand." Something I'd asked him to do for years. Both Luc and Mother complied—easily. When would Father listen to me?

I turned the handle, but Father placed his hand against the doorframe, stopping it from opening completely. The smell of ash filled the room.

"Father. Smoke. F-fire." What could possibly be more important than a fire? The activity around the smoke had died down, and the guards and staff seemed to be a little confused. Was it out? I squinted. Smoke, but no flames. What was going on?

Father turned his back on the garden. "It is being taken care of." There was a finality in his voice that brooked no argument. He pressed against the door until it closed.

The handle slipped out of my grasp and my chest tightened. Trapped. "Yes, F-Father." I stepped backwards from the door when something caught my eye.

I focused on just next to where the movement had been. My muscles tensed. There. It shifted again. A figure peeled away from the rosebushes and shot across the lawn with a tiny muted red light trailing close behind. Both stopped behind a cone-shaped topiary.

I pressed my arms to my sides at attention but continued to watch the garden, my mind racing. Smoke with no fire. We were at Lady Eline's house. It had been a while since the last theft . . .

"Hermann."

It couldn't be, could it? Father hated any news of the burglar who kept evading arrest; it only elevated the man in my eyes. What else did the gossips say? That he only stole an odd assortment of women's accoutrements? I snorted. What thief only steals women's clothes?

I crossed my arms. Lady Eline was known for her shoes. Was the smoke the Magpie's distraction so he could steal them?

"You must announce your marriage at the upcoming masquerade."

Father's words crashed through my thoughts, and I whipped around to face him. He placed a hand on my shoulder, his countenance like a judge passing a gallows sentence. "I came to tell you this in person—it only seemed fair."

My heart beat faster. That was in a few weeks' time. I knew I had to give a speech, but *marriage*?

"I b-beg your p-pardon?"

Father winced and retreated a few steps. "Speak clearly." His brow clouded. A painting of a lion in a rose garden dominated the wall of the study and he walked to stand beneath it. "You will announce your marriage at the ball in three weeks' time."

"T-to whom?"

"Does it matter?"

My chest heaved with anger. Luc had warned me Father would try something like this. Leave it to my stupid brother to be stupid right. "T-trying to get rid of me?"

He turned from the painting and grasped his hands behind his back. When he spoke, his tone was conversational, as if he were speaking of how he preferred his eggs cooked. "Not necessarily. The kingdom looks weak. Especially with you as next in line and no heir."

The urge to fight those words sprang within me, snarling like the lion in the painting. I turned to face the garden again. The smoke in one portion was now half of what it had been. "You really think so l-little of me?"

Father grunted noncommittally, but the truth was as plain and ugly as the pumpkin-colored chair.

The shadowy figure peeled away from another topiary, sprinting from bush to bush toward the chateau. I lost sight of the shadow when it stopped just under my balcony. Desperation clawed in my chest. I could stop the Magpie. Arrest him.

The urge to apprehend the thief, to escape—to be done—launched words out of my mouth.

"I w-will choose who I m-marry."

"You? You can barely speak, let alone choose a suitable bride."

"N-nevertheless," I said, "I will—I will choose."

Father's nostrils widened and he snorted.

I crossed my arms. There was no way I would cede this point.

"You have until the masquerade to find someone. If you don't, I'm choosing for you and we'll be done with this."

I opened my mouth to shout. But all the thoughts crashed on me and only a whimper escaped.

Father's hopeful look soured and he glared at me. "Two weeks."

I gave a quick nod, then a jerky bow, every muscle taut.

Was the Magpie still out there? Was I too late?

Father's hands clasped together, disapproval etched across his features. He nodded once and left, the door to the study closing with a click.

I charged out onto the balcony, air rushing into the study and out of my lungs.

I was free—for now.

My back pressed against the cold wall and I checked in the garden for movement. No groundskeeper. He should still be prowling the front of the mansion with a *bombe fumigène* of his own. Above me, the balcony jutted outwards like a stubborn chin. It was even higher from up close.

Ivy covered the wall. I'd have to be careful not to rustle the leaves. Shar had placed *les charmes du silencieux et attaché,* and they had never failed, but a girl couldn't be too cautious. Turning, I pressed my hands against the wall, pleased as they stuck fast. I pulled my feet up, and they also stuck. *Le charme attaché* made climbing easier, although Stepmother's brutal strengthening exercises did their part as well.

Halfway up, I stopped and pulled one hand off the wall, shaking it to warm my stone-chilled fingers.

A faint breeze carried the earthy scent of decaying leaves. Shar looped in the breeze, then froze, then zipped back to me.

"Guard," she hissed.

I glanced down, my mouth going dry. A guard stood directly below, scanning the garden. Had they found the pots and put them out already?

As I pressed tighter against the wall, my heart pulsed in my fingertips.

With one hand, I reached behind me into my satchel, feeling for the rough burlap. As I pulled out the lump, a tiny trail of ash escaped, bits of charcoal dropping.

Shar's light turned a nervous gray.

The guard whipped to his left. If he looked up . . .

In one motion, I flung the bag of ash, watching it arc away from me and the estate and then crash into a rosebush to my far right.

The guard took off to investigate.

I exhaled and pressed my forehead to the cold stone, then I continued to climb.

Soon my muscles were screaming in protest. *How tall is this beastly wall?* I gritted my teeth, pushing past the fire burning in my arms.

Shar's light stopped in midair and turned a dark, agitated gray. She flew directly at my head, nearly colliding with me.

"M'lady," she whispered, "*le charme attaché* is fading."

My eyes widened and my stomach fell to the ground. Where was that ivy? I glanced to my right. The ivy, instead of growing perpendicular up the wall, had followed the wall's curvature—away from me. *Petite bêtes!* Why hadn't I stayed closer to the vine?

"Are you sure?"

"Yes," she hissed, her light now a ghostly white.

I looked down. The ground seemed miles away. My palms slicked with sweat, and my breath caught in my chest.

I clenched my teeth and pulled myself up. Three more feet. Muscles shaking, I reached one hand as high as I could. Almost there. My fingers stretched over the balcony, seeking purchase. If I fell, I'd be lucky to break only a leg.

I poked my head over the ledge, then quickly ducked back down. *By the Beast's beard!*

Shar's light dimmed and flickered a confused purple.

"There's someone on the balcony." I cursed. The house was supposed to be empty. "Hide," I mouthed.

Shar flitted under my collar.

I gripped the baluster, pulling my knees to my chest, then pushed myself over the railing. I crouched in the balcony's corner, as far from the man as I could.

The dark-haired young man, looking to be the same age as me, stared out over the gardens. His large frame stood straight and immovable, like someone who was used to following the rules. I sighed. He'd arrest me in a heartbeat.

My gaze darted to the door. Large draperies billowed on either side. If I could get to them, I could hide and wait, maybe even get inside—*facile*.

I crept toward the door. The man remained still, as if carved from stone.

Step. Step. Almost there.

ARMAND 4

Where are you, thief?

I rushed to the edge of the balcony and gripped the sand-colored balustrade. When no sign of the Magpie appeared, I turned and faced the house, leaning against the railing. Four immense limestone columns sprouting decorative tops covered the facade of the estate. Large topiaries carved into the shapes of lions flanked both sides of the door. Smaller rosebushes clustered around the lion.

My fingers curled, missing the familiar grip of my sword. If only I could conquer my stammer as easily as I did an opponent.

Marriage? And just weeks away? I rolled my eyes. How did Father expect me to impress the court, visiting dignitaries—my future wife—if I could barely speak? Curse my defective speech. Never mind that I'd successfully integrated new conditioning methods for the military or that I was one of the most skilled swordsmen in Lyonelle.

I rolled my shoulders, rooting myself firmly in the present, and tried to work out a knot in my neck. It was bigger than those infernal marbles.

The breeze picked up, and I turned to lean forward again on the cold balustrade, watching the straggling thread of smoke rise and the remaining guards returning to their posts.

"No fire, sir."

I turned. A servant stood in the doorway, yellow light pouring from the study behind him.

I nodded, and the man disappeared back into the house.

My boots scraped on the pavement as I moved to get one last glimpse of the garden. My face twisted in disgust. What a terrible night. No fire, no clear speech, an arranged marriage, and now no thief.

Something shifted behind me. I froze. From the corner of my eye, the lion topiary on the left bobbed slightly.

Ah, very sneaky. You almost made it past me.

I rotated slightly to the right to get a better view but not so much as to alert whoever was hiding behind the topiaries.

The lion stopped swaying, and for the first time in a long while, a grin fell on my face. If I couldn't speak, at least I could catch a thief.

Was he smiling? Why was he smiling? Maybe he was crazy.

I pressed myself against the foliage. *Blend in, Cyn.*

Then the young man lunged and caught my wrist.

"Ha!"

I wrenched my arm, my satchel swinging wildly, but I had no strength left.

"I think not," he said. He tried pinning my arm behind my back, but I twisted and dropped low to sweep his legs from under him. But he raised my wrist and I couldn't get the leverage. Blast. Fighting wasn't an option. My muscles hadn't recovered from the climb.

Reaching for my bag with my free hand, I fumbled for a spice packet. *There.*

Taking a deep breath and closing my eyes, I flung it at his face. The finest cinnamon and spices this side of the Andal Mountains filled the air. The man coughed and hacked like he was losing a lung. I almost felt sorry for him.

I yanked back on my hand, but his grip only tightened. I moved to kick him, but he pulled me off balance while he rubbed at his eyes. Why hadn't I covered more self-defense in training? I kicked again, and he yelped as my foot connected with his shin. I brought my heel into the top of his foot, digging deep.

His hand remained clamped onto my wrist. Beasts. I needed to change tactics.

"Unhand me at once." I hoped I sounded commanding—not like a girl terrified of imprisonment.

"A l-l-lady?" he coughed, continuing to hold onto my wrist.

I straightened my jacket and trousers, gathering as much dignity as I could. "Indeed. And I will excuse your brutish behavior provided it never happens again."

His dark hair was ruddy with cinnamon, and white lines furrowed around his eyes where he had squinted during the spice attack. His dark eyes were bleary and filled with tears as he looked at me.

"N-no," he wheezed. "I'm not letting the Magpie escape."

Panic swelled in my heart—he knew. My blood burned with an icy fire. What should I do now? Every muscle coiled, ready to escape. Should I scream?

Logic rescued me. *Remain calm, Cyn.* Resisting the urge to thrash again, I stood tall and narrowed my eyes. If looks could kill, perhaps I'd get lucky and my escape would be easy.

Still gripping my wrist, he continued, "You are f-fond of exchanges. Therefore, I have a proposal for you. I p-propose I let you go."

I cocked my head. He'd just caught the Magpie, Lierre's most infamous burglar. This man must be an idiot. "In exchange for?"

"Your help."

"With what?" My muscles tensed and I waited for him to spring a trap.

A slow smile broke across his face, reflecting what he clearly thought was a brilliant idea. "Meet me here each night until the b-ball to speak with m-me. Then you may d-do as you wish and n-never return."

He'd release me. That was a relief, but he wanted conversation? With that stutter? And with me, a criminal? He really was an idiot.

"We're negotiating for your silence? Not much of a bargain. You can hardly speak at all."

"M'lady, insulting the man who is responsible for your possible arrest is unwise," Shar whispered from under my collar.

The man's angular jaw pushed forward, and he clenched his hands. "And the shoes, of course," he added. "That is why you c-came tonight."

I raised my eyebrows.

"It's c-common knowledge that Lady Eline has a healthy appetite for f-fashionable shoes."

A smart idiot. I looked up into his dark, serious eyes. His features softened. Under different circumstances, I might have even said they were handsome features. My heart tripped over itself. Was he letting me go? I tugged at my wrist, and he released his grip. I folded my arms and stuck out my chin.

"How do I know you won't arrest me tomorrow night?"

"I g-give you m-my word," he said, his intense gaze holding mine.

All of Stepmother's lessons said I shouldn't trust him—couldn't. My eyes locked on his, and I felt my resolve weakening. He wasn't lying. Something about him was too genuine, too honest.

"B-besides, you intrigue m-me." He took a small step toward me, and a corner of his mouth quirked. "And it will annoy the k-king."

My head cocked to the side. Avoid arrest, get the shoes, and annoy the king? The rewards abounded.

He ran his fingers through his thick hair. Cinnamon dislodged itself, and he sidestepped to avoid inhaling the tiny cloud of spices. What were my options? I still needed those shoes. I could steal different shoes, but Lady Eline's were the best. And just this once I wanted something for myself. Beasties, there *was* only one option.

I groaned. "Give me your name."

"My n-name?" He swallowed hard. "Why?"

"So I know who to curse if I'm arrested. And whose family to wreak vengeance upon once I escape prison."

His lips curled up a tiny bit and he rubbed at his throat. "Armand."

"Hermann? Wait—" My eyes narrowed. I thought the prince was a shut-in, never left the palace—but a stuttering young man? It wasn't probable but it was possible. "Are you the stupid prince?"

"N-no. Not Hermann. Armand. With a *d*." He shifted his weight and brushed his vest, smearing cinnamon from chest to waist.

"Then what are you doing in Lady Eline's house?" I balled my hands.

"My f-father works for the k-king. T-trades in t-textiles. Staying here is a b-bonus. While Eline is at c-court. We've had a p-profitable year."

They must have, judging by the expensive clothing he wore. He leaned on the edge of the balustrade, resting on his elbow, clearly striking what he thought was a saucy pose. The effect was ruined by his spice-covered face, the lighter smile lines stretching awkwardly.

I rolled my eyes at his stance. "Your family works for the king? You don't even like him."

He stood straight again and tugged at his jacket. "He's a d-difficult person to like."

I relaxed a bit. "What does your father do?"

Armand swallowed hard, as if building the words in his head before speaking them. "He's head of d-d-domestic t-trade. Very important."

My stepsister must have courted at least a dozen swaggering peacocks disguised as noblemen, but this man didn't seem to have even half the ego of one of those narcissists. And he was bargaining like a back-alley trader. There was no way this man was the prince.

"So you're the son of a trade minister?"

He executed a grandiose bow, spices raining down and setting off a coughing fit—complete with flecks of spit. "I am who you say." He wiped his mouth as he stood.

I almost laughed. How could I have thought this young man was the heir to the kingdom? If he was, we were doomed.

"Now that you know w-who I am, d-do we have an accord, *mademoiselle* . . . ?" He raised his eyebrows, waiting for my name.

I smiled and shook my head. "You already know it. I'm the Magpie."

I leaped off the balcony, twisting in midair and sailing over the balustrade. My fingers reached forward, gripping the strong vines that climbed against this side of the wall. Their leaves rustled noisily. Apparently, *le charme silencieux* was also gone. I scrambled down and reached the bottom, my heart racing. *Leave as quickly as you can, Cyn.*

The two guards turned, raising their halberds. "Halt!"

Energy snapped through my body and I crouched, reaching for the remaining spice packet.

"Leave my g-guest alone," Armand's voice shouted from above. "Return to your p-post."

The guards looked puzzled but reluctantly followed their orders.

I nodded my thanks to Armand. I was lucky there was someone here to call off the guards—even if he was only the son of a trade minister.

I raced back across the lawn with my heart in my throat and climbed over the outer wall. Papa's horse, Pumpkin, stood by the tree, contentedly munching on grass. I clambered onto his back, then tapped my heels to his side. Pumpkin's hoofbeats thundered through grassy fields toward the Manette mansion.

What would Stepmother think of this ridiculous arrangement? I tightened my grip on the reins. Best not to tell her—but my stepsister, Aimée, was another matter. I couldn't wait to see the look on her face when I told her about Armand.

"What an unusual man," Shar murmured close to my ear.

"Most unusual," I agreed.

6 ARMAND

Cinnamon and pepper mingled with sweat in the chill morning air. *Clear your mind, Armand. You can't fight an enemy if you cannot think clearly.*

My sword sliced through the air as I went through the motions Swordmaster Battaglia had drilled into me day after day.

The Magpie and our deal warred with the Alemanian threat in my mind. Aggressions were growing along the borders—there had already been three skirmishes within the last four months. And there were rumors of new weapons called firelances—but those were rumors Father refused to listen to.

I pulled the sword back level with my eyes. In reality, it was me, his stuttering son, that he refused to listen to. *What if there is another attack before I can speak?*

The gray predawn light diluted the autumn colors of the orchard. During the night, a hazy mist had crept from the lake on the far side of her house and snaked through the orchards. Several lights—probably the last fireflies of summer—drifted among the branches. It had been an hour since

I had started my drills. My shirt stuck to my sweat-slick skin, the wide sleeves billowing as I moved.

I thrust and turned to face the orchard. More lights gathered amid the trees. *Odd for fireflies to be active at such an early hour.*

Slice. The air sang as I spun around to face the chateau.

Clear your mind.

I inhaled, and an intriguing need to see the Magpie filled me. And it was not simply because a cross-dressing woman covered in ash had disabled me with a spice-filled teabag bomb.

The sky lightened from blue to gray and more fireflies gathered. Thirty pale yellow lights now drifted among the trees.

I'd introduced myself as Armand, not Hermann. *What an outdated name.* And she had called me the "stupid prince." That wasn't me—I didn't want to be the stupid prince to at least one person in the kingdom.

I grunted and I thrust my sword. Thin clouds streaked the sky, which refused to lighten though the sun was nearly risen.

Technically, I hadn't lied. I'd strategically bent the truth. I needed someone who didn't bow or simper. Only one other person who knew me as Armand was someone with whom I could be myself, but I couldn't exclusively hang around my brother for the rest of my life—he'd drive me insane long before that.

With her, I could cure my stutter. Even if she was sassier than a wet cat.

Cool air burned at my throat. Sweeping my sword, I glanced across the orchard again, and an uneasy feeling wove through my blood. Hundreds of tiny yellow lights bobbed through the branches.

Slice. Turn. Face the orchard.

Slash. Rotate to the house.

As I turned back to the orchard, I saw a brilliant flash of white and nearly dropped my sword. A woman dressed in a dewy gown stood not three meters away. I blinked and she vanished, a firefly drifting in her place.

I lowered my sword and pressed the heel of my hand against my eyes. It was early. That was all.

In the corner of my eye, I saw another flash.

I whirled. Another woman, this time two meters away.

Fear spiked through me.

A second burst and she was gone, replaced by a firefly.

"*Bonjour? Qui es-t-tu?*" I gulped for air, the sweat chilling my skin.

The lights settled on the trees and the feeling of hundreds of eyes pressing down on me increased.

Wind roared in my ears but no trees stirred.

I gripped my sword tighter and lowered myself into a fighting stance. *Je suis prêt, allons-y.*

With a thunderous roar, the mist gathered around my feet, then rose like an enormous gray wave. It crested into a towering wall that flickered, forming shapes in its depths. Pinpricks of firefly light appeared through the fog, and several danced along the edge of the glowing wall of mist. Some settled on the images in the fog, sharpening them, though how that was possible, I did not know.

Faces I recognized appeared. My breath died in my throat, and the tip of my sword dropped until it sank into the wet grass. Lady Eline's study formed, rich in color. *Général* Sanson burst inside, holding a long metal tube in his hand.

The edges of the mist tinged red, and Sanson's image rippled with heat waves.

"Looks like you don't like the *général* either."

More flashes. *Général* Sanson and his garrison stood in the woods, each man holding torches. Where were they? Lyonelle or Alemania?

Général Sanson and his troops blazed a molten red before collapsing on themselves. Then the Alemanian insignia blazed bright—three stars over two crossed swords. The images changed and reformed, this time glowing like a pearl. A shock chilled my blood.

Qui est-ce?

It was me.

In this field.

With a woman.

I stepped forward, my feet moving of their own accord. Her face was obscured but she glowed like a beacon. We danced, and I could almost feel her in my arms. Hundreds of fireflies surrounded us. I reached to touch the woman, and tiny droplets of mist pricked my skin. Who was she?

Once more the images disappeared, and the edges of the mist burned with an angry red. It was Lierre, the palace close to the sea, overlooking the harbor. But instead of a peaceful scene, Lyonelle's navy was engulfed in flames.

"No!" I raised my sword, slashing through the vision.

One last image burst through the mist, flaring a sunrise orange. A lion and a rose—the symbols for Lyonelle. The vision stopped and the wall of mist collapsed like a waterfall.

The fireflies drifted back to the orchard as though nothing had happened.

I gulped air and sheathed my sword. What had I just seen? It couldn't be the past. *Général* Sanson had never been to Lady Eline's, and I had certainly never danced with a woman in these trees. I scanned the sky for smoke. Nothing. Was that a vision of the future?

My breathing slowed but uneasiness lodged in my stomach.

One thing was for certain: something bad was happening within Lyonelle, and Sanson was involved.

I swallowed. I had to convince Father.

The sun crested the tips of the apple trees.

"I'm l-leaving," I whispered. The long grass swished as I made my way back to Lady Eline's.

The lights—which I strongly suspected were not fireflies—did nothing.

CYN 7

$\mathcal{P}$ale morning light diffused into the bedroom, hitting my back. I carried my load of threadbare linens over to my bed, careful that my feet didn't scrape the pile of firewood my stepsister had neatly stacked.

"Aimée, we've got to get the estate ready for your new suitor, and he'd better be nicer than the last one," I called over my shoulder, hoping she'd hear me—wherever she was. I'd been up for the last hour, and I'd hoped Aimée had already started on her chores even though I hadn't seen her in the kitchen or in the garden.

Shar's light zipped around our shared bedroom, her cheery glow bouncing from surface to surface as she charmed the dust away.

"Thank you, Shar. At least someone here knows where our food money comes from," I muttered. Although, if Aimée kept finding suitors like her last one—Lord Cadieux—I'd rather starve. The pompous man had taken to showing up at the house without any warning at all and had nearly caught me during a Magpie training session.

I scanned the room, my glare landing on an Aimée-shaped lump under the linen covers of her bed. *Petite bêtes!* She was still asleep?

I stormed over to her, the floorboards creaking in protest, when the bed exploded in blankets and pillows and she sat up, fully dressed.

"Surprise!" Her round face shone.

"Aimée!" I grabbed the closest pillow and thumped her with it—then once more for good measure. "Do you want this suitor to know we are poor? If we don't get the estate in shape, he'll cut you loose the minute he sees it." *And Stepmother will do worse once she finds out about the shoes.*

"Then it is good that the sweeping and mopping are *fini*." Her Alemanian accent was less pronounced than Stepmother's, only catching on the "th" sound and changing it to a "z." Aimée clasped her hands over her heart and looked wistfully above her head. "But *M.* Bontour wouldn't care about a thing like that."

I rolled my eyes. "Save the acting for the mark."

She murmured something that sounded like, "I don't need to act with him." I opened my mouth to retort but she pointedly focused on making the bed, her solid frame leaning over her task. Bits of her blonde hair stuck up at odd angles. When she turned, I saw dust smudging her round face, and I pointed her to the table and washbasin.

"Are they beautiful?" Aimée asked. "Can I see them?"

"Are what beautiful?" I moved to my washbasin, and a stale smoky smell followed me. I wrinkled my nose and dipped my hands in the cold water, scrubbing myself clean. I gazed longingly at the large empty bathtub in the corner. I needed a good long soak, and Shar, anticipating that need, hovered over the basin, her light flickering questioningly. I shook my head and sighed. There just wasn't time. So Shar instead flew to my washbasin and spelled the chilled water to a not-quite-scalding temperature. My favorite. We may have had to dismiss the staff since losing Papa, but at least Shar's charms helped stave off the feeling of abject poverty.

"Thank you, Shar," I said.

Her tiny light flashed a sunny yellow and she returned to charming the room. House fairies were exceptionally rare. Once house fairies accepted a family's invitation to stay, they never left and became fiercely loyal both to the home and family—sometimes for generations. Shar was more than a magical maid, though—she was family.

I glimpsed my reflection in the basin and grimaced. I looked terrible and felt worse.

"'Are what beautiful?'" Aimée mimicked my question, then turned back to her own toilette. "The shoes, of course." Splashing accompanied her comment.

My throat tightened. The shoes. The deal. I scrubbed faster. "Nothing makes a better impression than stolen footwear, but you can't see them. Because I didn't get them. And don't tell Stepmother."

"Of course not, but you always get the items."

I sighed, dropping my hands back in the basin. "The house wasn't empty like Stepmother said. I barely got away." And I would have to return if I ever hoped to see those shoes.

Aimée moved from her vanity to gather armfuls of washing, the large pile muffling her voice. "Can't you simply go back?"

"It's complicated."

As I washed and dressed in a light, practical linen shirt and breeches, I recounted last night's events while Shar kept adding bits like "Nearly lost my life," and "Shocked beyond belief."

"Never thought I'd see m'lady captured by a man," Shar said. "And such a handsome man. It may have been dark, but I detected a blush on Mistress's face."

"He surprised me." I turned, tugging on some worn-through stockings. He *was* handsome, but Beast take me if I ever admitted that to Shar.

"He already sounds better than Lord Cadieux." Aimée sniffed, lacing up her shoes. "It took ages to get rid of him."

"Anyone is better than Lord Cadieux," I said, suppressing a shudder. Aimée and I had had to use every weapon in our arsenal to eradicate the pesky man—especially since Stepmother was encouraging him to propose to Aimée. "At least that is over." I sighed, leaning over to lace my own shoes.

Gravel crunched outside and I froze, panic rising in my chest. "Is that your suitor? No, no, no. He's too soon. We haven't even started on the grounds." With the rest of the staff gone, Aimée and I were responsible for the estate's upkeep.

I raced to the window and Shar, who had been about to move to the next room, joined me, her light sharp around the edges.

Aimée threw her hairbrush onto the bed, where it bounced and then clattered to the floor. "*C'est M. Bontour?*" She practically pressed her face to the glass, her golden hair haloing her head.

A man on horseback pulled up to the house, small puffs of dirt billowing in his wake and catching the early morning light.

When I saw the rider my jaw dropped. "Lord Cadieux?" *Petite bêtes. Quand on parle du loup.*

I stared at Aimée. She pulled away from the window, wringing her hands and working herself into a nervous wreck. "I never should have smiled at him."

I dragged my hands down the sides of my face. "You smiled at him? When?"

"At the market, two days ago. I was just being polite." She shrugged. "He simply can't accept my refusals!" Her voice stretched tighter with every turn she made. "If Mother sees him, she'll have us betrothed before five minutes have passed. And what about *M.* Bontour?"

Anxiety twisted my stomach into knots like a well-made croissant.

Lord Cadieux dismounted his horse, far too flamboyantly dressed for a man of his age. His bright-red vest clashed with his green cap, reminding me strongly of a tomato. He removed his hat and smoothed the wispy hairs that bravely tried to cover the balding spot on his head.

My stomach and heart collided with each other. *Think, Cyn. He has to go, but how? Bombe fumigène?* No. I paced, my heels clicking against the floor. Spice packets wouldn't work either. Anxiety twisted in my chest, making it hard to breathe. Stepmother would be up soon and then we'd really be in trouble. We needed help.

Help. *Voilà.* I snapped my fingers and turned to Aimée. "*À l'aide.*"

Aimée sighed. "No need to state the obvious, Cyn."

"No, the game. *À l'aide—*"

Aimée's face lit up in understanding. It was a game we'd played when we were younger. One sister would pretend to be sick from all sorts of made-up maladies while the other went to fetch help.

"Silver scurvy . . . no." I clapped my hands. "Fickle blisters. I can be ready in five minutes."

Aimée pulled her broad shoulders back in determination, then raced for the front door.

"Shar, you'll handle the blisters," I said. Shar's light bobbed in agreement and I scrambled out of my shirt and breeches into a work dress. Together we raced to the kitchen.

Moments later, and with a thin layer of Papa's finest golden-orange *Safran des Indes* tinting my skin, I opened the front door, shuffling outside. The sun's golden light hit my face and I squinted at Lord Cadieux, who was reaching for Aimée's hand despite both of them being tucked behind her back. *Le fou têtu.* The overlay of yellow spice sallowed my olive complexion, but it was Shar's *similer* charm—oozing sores, complete with angry red blisters—that really sold it. I coughed and hunched my shoulders for good measure.

Aimée turned to me, then pressed her lips together in an attempt to hide a smile. "Lord Cadieux, you remember my sister, poor thing." Her voice was overly sweet, and she placed an arm around me, pulling me close.

"Don't overdo it," I hissed.

"He's not the sharpest pin in the box," she murmured, leading me to the gentleman.

I gave a wan smile and coughed in my hands, then held them out to be kissed.

The sides of Lord Cadieux's nose pinched together and he took a step backwards. "Yes, how is your face—erm, health?"

"I always thought I'd have more time," I said, adding a small warble to my voice.

Aimée dropped her voice to a loud whisper as if sharing a shameful secret. "It's the fickle blisters."

Lord Cadieux's throat bobbed in a dry swallow. "The f-fickle blisters?"

Aimée clasped my hands tightly in hers, then stroked my face with the back of her hand. "Yes, very painful." I gave a little groan, and Aimée removed her hands and stepped closer to Lord Cadieux. I dropped lower in my hunch, as if Aimée were my only support. "But do not worry," she continued. "It only comes in spells. You and me? We still have time. Our family is only stricken once they near adulthood."

She advanced on Lord Cadieux, and he backed away, raising an arm like a shield. "Your f-family?"

Aimée waved his words away. "I don't like to talk about their tormented, agony-ridden bodies convulsing on the floor."

I snorted, then coughed. "I'm still far away from that," I said, keeping my voice tight. "Aimée's even farther."

Aimée gave the now-pale and trembling Lord Cadieux a bright smile. "You said you'd come to ask me something?"

Lord Cadieux, wide-eyed, was already reaching for the reins to his horse. "Yes, your family—that's very sad." He scrambled onto his horse. "*De toute façon,* I must go."

Aimée looked up at him, a deep frown on her face, and reached for him with her hands. "Just because it runs in the family doesn't mean everyone will catch it."

Lord Cadieux's face warred between disgust and fear, his mouth twisting as words failed him.

He just needed one small push to leave, but why not make it a big one? *Don't do it, Cyn. You'll send him over the edge.*

But how could I resist?

I wrapped my arms around my stomach and doubled over, gray gravel filling my vision. "It's started, Aimée. It's started." I grunted, reaching for her. "*Ah, la douleur.*"

By the time I'd fallen to my knees, Lord Cadieux was already at the end of the drive and turning his horse for the road back to Lierre.

Aimée dissolved into giggles as she pulled me to my feet. Shar zipped out the front door, congratulating us both, her light a buzzing orange. She then flew around me, spelling off the *Safran de Indes* and the blisters.

I stood and brushed off my dress. The dust from Lord Cadieux's departure was already settling, and satisfaction trickled through me like fresh warm honey. Next, chores, and then the next suitor. Perhaps afterwards I could visit Maman and Papa's trees.

"I am looking forward to seeing those shoes." Stepmother's voice struck my back like ice.

I froze, still facing the road. *Petite bêtes.* Had she seen Lord Cadieux?

I turned, my skin becoming cold, and saw Stepmother standing on the threshold of the door. Shar's light dimmed to a flat blue, and Aimée's smile vanished. Stepmother's graying blonde hair accentuated her steely look, and any remaining nerve I had died in my chest. I chewed on the inside of my lip. If she'd seen us get rid of Lord Cadieux, that would make everything worse. I flinched under her gaze.

"You two"—Stepmother tipped her head toward Aimée and Shar—"have chores to attend to. Inside."

They obeyed, with Aimée throwing a worried glance over her shoulder before the house swallowed her. I held my breath and clenched my hands behind my back.

"The shoes—I'm sure they are spectacular," Stepmother said.

I exhaled steadily. She hadn't seen Lord Cadieux. At least that was one point for me. But the spectacular shoes? They were spectacularly not here. I resisted my impulse to shrink. *Wait it out, Cyn.*

"May I—" I swallowed. "May I start my chores?" Unlike with Lord Cadieux, I had to work hard to keep my voice from trembling.

Stepmother gave a fraction of a nod, and I walked past her, feeling her stare follow me. I entered the house to change into my work breeches and gripped the railing to the stairs. I pressed my fingers into the wood, not wanting to admit how much her sudden appearance had affected me. My heart still pounded in my ears. *Compose yourself, Cyn.*

My foot had just touched the first stair when I heard her speak again, her words falling like a hammer's blows on an anvil. "Don't forget to do the stables."

I turned, unable to stop myself. "But *M.* Bontour won't be in the stables."

"Being prepared is the price of success."

I was about to protest, but a tight knot in my throat stopped me. *Not worth it, Cyn.* Especially since I hadn't gotten the shoes. "Of course" was all that came out.

Stepmother retreated to the dining room and a chair creaked as she sat. *Petite bêtes, Cyn. The Great Beast take Lord Cadieux.*

8 Armand

"T-time for a d-different exercise," I said, leaning back in the chair. I raised my hands to both sides of my head to stop the room from spinning. An hour trying to blow out a candle to strengthen my diaphragm, and the only thing I had to show for it was a splitting headache.

Keep going, Armand. Remember, all of this is for Lyonelle.

Captain Reynaud's latest missive was burned into my memory: *Another border raid. Lyonelle soldiers injured. Two killed.* Anger simmered in my chest. If this kept up, we'd be at war with Alemania before the month was out.

M. Parler placed the cake to the side, his aged hands trembling slightly, and the candle flickered. The man shuffled over to a large black bag, the kind used by doctors—or undertakers. He pulled it across the wooden floor and opened it. If he pulled out a jar of leeches to bleed the words out of me . . . I would do it. For Lyonelle. Parler's hand reached into the bag.

The doors to the room banged open. *M.* Parler jumped and squeaked.

Luc burst into the room and tugged on his offensively bright citron-colored jacket. He looked around the study, taking in the candlelit cake. "Armand,

I didn't know it was your birthday," he said, his blue eyes gleaming. He strode over to the tray, cut himself an enormous slice, then shoved it in his mouth.

Moments later, a red-faced footman came panting into the room. "Announcing the second son and heir, the Duke of Auvergne, Lucien Gerard, Ruler of the—"

"Yes, yes." Luc waved the winded footman away. Crumbs spilled from his mouth onto his jacket. Just two years younger, Luc was every bit as free and debonair as I wasn't.

The footman closed the large gilt doors, wheezing audibly as he retreated down the hall.

I wiped my mouth with my handkerchief, then cleared my throat and stood. "*M.* Parler, you may go."

"Oh, but we've had a very successful afternoon," *M.* Parler said, the loose skin under his neck trembling in disappointment. His hand dove into the black bag again. "I was hoping to have His Royal Highness inflate this pig's bladder." He lifted a rubbery pink sack in the air.

Luc choked, his face turning as red as the harried footman's. Bits of cake dropped onto the ornate rug.

I narrowed my eyes and walked over to *M.* Parler, who clutched his bag, and herded him out of the study. "You are t-too thoughtful," I said, then closed the doors before he could respond.

Luc's laughter pealed through the room. He paused only long enough to hack up more cake crumbs.

"G-glad you're here," I said. "I needed the b-break." I took something out of my pocket and tossed it to Luc. He deftly caught the small wooden chess piece, which had once been part of a rather expensive set. He rolled the familiar king figure between his fingers. The crown on the top was so worn it was little more than a nub. "For ending my session early."

Luc arched an eyebrow as he put the piece in his vest pocket, then he dropped to lounge in the window seat. "Hardly worth surrendering the king."

"You have no idea what I've endured in the n-n-n—" The words flew around in my head. I pressed my fingers to my thumb again, trying to nail the words down. "What I've endured in the n-name of p-proper diction." I exhaled, feeling as if I'd sprinted the length of Lady Eline's orchard.

Luc slapped his knee. "The look on your face when he said 'pig bladder.'"

For the second time that day, the doors to the study burst open. Luc leaped from the settee, brushing crumbs from his clothes.

The footman, still winded, announced the arrival. "*Général* Sanson of Lyonelle's army and Head of the Lierran Guard."

Général Marcel Sanson, recently promoted from Colonel of the Border Patrol, strode into the room. Brass buttons glinted from his red-and-blue uniform, and the epaulettes made his shoulders look larger than they actually were. Sanson focused his muddy brown eyes on me. His aging fair features, though marred by a scar on his forehead, appeared friendly; but I knew better. The man was an oiled snake.

I looked closer. Sanson was carrying something in his hands—a dark metal tube.

Icy fear gripped my heart.

The scene before me was identical to the vision from the orchard. If the images from the orchard were already coming to pass, how long would it be before the dance with the mysterious woman, or before the destroyed navy?

Fear forced the words from my mouth, and I almost shouted them. "What is that?"

Luc's demeanor turned serious as he walked to my side.

Sanson joined us in the center of the study, placing the object in my hand. I turned it over. The cold tube had been split down the middle and sections of it were bent, jutting outward at odd angles. Rust covered the edge where the metal had sheared. A section of blackened wood, shaped similarly to a rifle stock, finished at the end of the metal section. Using a fingernail, I scraped the rust away, easily exposing the iron underneath—it couldn't be more than three months' worth of corrosion.

"Where was this f-found?" I asked, handing the metal to Luc.

"At the crossroads near Ville de Mensonges." Sanson's nasal voice grated in the small study. "By the remains of a campfire not far from the main road."

"Mensonges is right along the border with Alemania," Luc said, giving me the item.

I nodded and my heart rate rose. A firelance. This was a firelance.

My fingers traced the rusting edge. I lifted the barrel to my face and inhaled. *Bien.* Faint traces of acrid smoke remained.

"It is a firelance, *non*?" Sanson dropped his voice to a conspiratorial whisper. "Shall I report this to the king?"

I eyed Sanson. Within the last few years, he had ingratiated himself with Father and had steadily risen in the ranks. He had also never been unsolicitedly helpful to me. There was no reason for him to show me this evidence before anyone else. In fact, it would work more in his favor to keep this information to himself. What was his game?

I glanced surreptitiously at Luc. He shrugged, the corners of his mouth pulling down.

I shook my head slowly, my mind searching for the snare. Just because I couldn't see it didn't mean it wasn't there.

"No, thank you." I grasped the remains of the weapon. "I will p-present this to F-Father." The less time Sanson spent with Father, the better.

"Very good, Your Highness." Sanson's tone was smug, but I couldn't see why. He bowed, then left the study with a slight bounce in his step.

"Why do I feel I've just walked into a t-trap?"

Luc shrugged again. "Perhaps the *général* is turning over a new leaf?"

I pulled my handkerchief from my pocket and cleaned my hands. "Resolutions? And it's n-not even New Year's Eve."

The ghost of the vision still haunted me, and the walls seemed to press inward. Great King Adam's portrait glared at me from the wall.

"Outside," I commanded. I was sick to death of the study.

Shortly, warm sunshine hit my face. My boots crunched on the gravel in Lady Eline's garden, her balcony towering three stories over us. I filled my lungs with as much fresh air as they could hold. I turned left, down the hill leading toward the small lake.

"What are you d-doing here anyway?"

Luc stopped by the edge of the pond, turned, and gave a little bow. "I'm a dog," he said. "Here to fetch you." He imitated a hound begging for scraps. "Woof."

"Fetch me? For what?" I asked. I wasn't due at the palace until the masquerade ball. I'd made sure of it.

"Dinner with the Ambassador of Gallen?"

I groaned. "The Great Beast himself would have to d-drag me back to the c-castle if I'm going to dine with that—"

"And I am also here to deliver the paper," Luc interrupted, pulling a sealed envelope from his jacket pocket. "Letter, actually."

I took it and turned the thick, folded parchment over, revealing the royal seal. "From Father?"

He leaned forward, rubbing his fingers together. "Open it. Maybe it's about the Grand Council. It's only two days away."

Not likely. Father had never asked me to join a Council meeting. Or was Father finally willing to overlook my speech? It would be the perfect time to talk about the attacks on the border and the new Alemanian weapon.

I quickly scanned the document, my surprise mounting.

"What does it say?" Luc asked, stepping closer.

"Father insists I attend the Grand C-Council," I said.

Luc clapped his hands together. "I knew it. He wants you to address them."

Suspicion dampened my surprise. This courtesy was unlike Father.

"Perhaps." I didn't want to get my hopes up. In our earlier years, Luc and I had been forced to stand behind Father during other meetings, no doubt in the hopes that we would learn to conduct affairs of state. More often than not, I suspected we were merely reminders of his power, of his enduring lineage. Mayhaps Father had actually listened to me about the weapons—which would be timely, considering Reynaud's report. However, I still couldn't shake the gloom of foreboding that settled in my chest.

I rolled up the paper and swallowed my trepidation. "So d-dinner at the palace with the ambassador this evening, tutoring here tonight, more t-tomorrow. Then to the palace for the Grand Council a few days later?" I'd lose at least an hour for each round trip. My muscles knotted and I shook my head. This week was going to be terrible.

"You have to go. You know he is temperamental," Luc said. "Half temper and half mental."

"That's not funny," I said, though I couldn't keep from smiling.

"No," Luc agreed, all humor gone. "It's blasted accurate."

It was accurate. Simply speaking of Father could drain the smile off anyone.

I looked at my brother out of the corner of my eye and dropped my hands in defeat. "You'll come with me?" Often, Luc's personality was the best—and sometimes only—buffer between my stutter and Father's fury. Though, in some ways, it was good that I couldn't always speak my mind. I doubted Father would like what he heard.

"Of course," Luc said reassuringly.

"You're not going to stay here and hide?" I narrowed my eyes at Luc's mischievous grin. "Or p-pretend to be sick?"

He placed his hand over his heart. "I promise you, on my honor, I will return to the palace."

My mind raced to find some loophole he could exploit later; I could find none. Nodding my thanks, I turned and we finished our walk around the pond crossing Lady Eline's drive.

Luc clapped me on the shoulder. "Let's get lunch. I'm starving." He rubbed his stomach. "I have a princely figure to maintain."

I picked up a pebble and chucked it at him. He sidestepped it easily.

A magpie screeched from the safety of the trees, its black feathers glistening oil. It was an oddly beautiful bird—not unlike a certain thief I knew. Her green eyes, olive skin, and pert mouth surfaced in my memory. My heart somersaulted as I thought of her vaulting into the air, her dark braid trailing behind.

I almost tripped in the gravel surrounding the entrance to Lady Eline's. *Pull yourself together, Armand.* I shook my head, and the memory of the Magpie vanished, though her stunning eyes refused to leave me entirely.

We walked up the steps to enter the house and hopefully get lunch, when Luc paused and turned, a curious look on his face. "By the by, why do you smell like cinnamon?"

"Do I?" I sniffed my clothes, then snorted. How could I not have noticed? I smelled like our cook's kitchen when apples were in season. It must have been high-quality cinnamon to have lingered through my morning wash and change of clothes. I shrugged, hoping Luc would let it go.

He stepped closer, his nose wrinkling. "You positively reek. Tell me why."

"N-no idea," I huffed. "Let's eat, shall we?"

"Tell me," he pleaded.

"N-no," I said, folding my arms.

"Well, then, you'll never know which lucky lass has captured my attention."

I rolled my eyes.

"This lovely young woman is a humble member of the lower aristocracy with eyes the color of forget-me-nots." Luc clasped his hands near his face, batting his eyes. "As if I could ever forget her—and her hair is like cornsilk. Whenever she smiles, a tiny dimple appears," he said, pointing to a place beside his mouth. "And her pouty full lips simply beg me to kiss them—"

"B-blonde hair, blue eyes. Is she Alemanian?" I asked.

Luc paused, then shrugged. "Maybe. I consider it diplomatic relations." He took a deep breath. "She has a quick and gentle spirit akin to angels—"

"Stop. I'll be sick if you c-continue." I pushed him away, then blurted, "I was attacked with cinnamon."

Luc quirked an eyebrow.

"Last n-night—" My mouth dried. "Last n-n-night—" *Soufre, why now?*

Luc waited patiently.

I bounced on my toes, emphasizing a word each time. "Last."

Bounce.

"Night."

Bounce.

I felt the words and my tongue connect. "I c-caught the Magpie trying to b-break into Lady Eline's. She threw cinnamon at me—"

"She?" Luc said. "Lady Eline?"

"No, stupid, the M-Magpie. And she is one of the b-bossiest, most stubborn women in all of Lyonelle."

Luc snorted. "Didn't see that one coming."

"Neither did I. Then I hired her as my new speech t-tutor—"

"Have you lost your mind?"

"—and I've promised I won't arrest her if she comes each n-night until the ball. I've also promised her a p-pair of Lady Eline's shoes—what else could she have wanted? She's q-quite horrible—the Magpie, not Lady Eline—rude and d-demanding. But she did perform the most amaz-ing acrobatic feat I've ever seen. Swordmaster Battaglia would have been amazed. Of c-course, I didn't tell her who I was—"

Luc coughed into his hand. "You're mad." He folded his arms, settling his weight to one side. "What did this Magpie look like?"

"Mischief with b-brown hair and an inordinate amount of soot."

"What makes you think she can teach you any better than *M.* Parler?"

Why *did* I think she could help? Was I so desperate to cure my stutter that I'd grasp at the slightest, most far-fetched possibility? I didn't want to answer that question. There was something about her, even in the short exchange we'd had. I had been so determined to catch the thief that I'd been caught completely off guard. It also helped that she didn't know my royal identity—that fact alone removed much of the stress brought on by the social expectations and duties associated with being the heir to the throne.

Slowly, I answered. "As long as she doesn't know I'm the p-prince, she will speak to me freely."

"You mean bossily and condescendingly, it sounds like," Luc said.

"At least she didn't simper or treat me like the stuttering shut-in p-prince."

Luc clapped me on the shoulder and smirked. "Your plan is perfect. What could go wrong?"

If my suspicions were even remotely correct, plenty.

The carriage lurched toward Lierre. I folded my arms and turned to stare out the passing window. I hoped Father would be in a better mood today. Conversations with him ranged from humiliating to harrowing. I wiped my clammy hands on my breeches. I'd have to leave the palace as soon as possible or I'd risk missing my meeting with the Magpie.

I cocked my head. If I were absent, would she come back to Eline's tonight or simply vanish?

We were approaching the edge of the city when the carriage stopped. I leaned out of my window and saw a flock of sheep crossing the road. I heard the carriage's other door open and then slam shut. I groaned. I didn't need to see the empty seat to know what Luc had done. *That little sneak.*

Luc's figure, already well past the sheep, gamboled back in the direction we'd come.

The sea of sheep parted and the carriage lurched forward.

I thumped the side of the door. "Driver, stop." I leaned out the window. "T-traitor," I called after Luc.

He turned, shrugging his shoulders.

"You said you'd c-come with me."

Luc, already twenty feet away, grinned mischievously. "I said I'd return to the palace, just not when."

"Where are you going?" I shouted, knowing further argument was hopeless. I should have seen this coming.

"To meet her," he called over his shoulder, jogging farther away.

"K-king goes to me!"

Without looking back, Luc dug in his pocket for the chess piece. Then, holding it up in his hand, he waved over his shoulder. He was soon over the last knoll and out of sight.

I thumped my fist on the seat cushion, feeling the knot in my neck return. The little *canaille* had left me to face two foes at once.

"Your Royal Highness?" the coachman asked.

"D-drive on," I said.

The carriage lurched forward, leaving my stomach somewhere in the middle of the crossroads.

CYN

I pulled my plain beige dress from the wardrobe and held it up, nearly ready for the second suitor of the day.

Aimée sat at the oak vanity once more while Shar wrapped complementary blue ribbons in her curled locks, leaving some to drape over her full shoulders. The ribbons matched Aimée's long gloves, accentuating her blue eyes. Aimée's strong hands and delicate fingers smoothed her gloves, which stretched halfway up her arms. She always had gloves on. I'd never seen her without them. Personally, I never wore gloves—made it easier to pick locks and pockets.

I turned back to my dress and wrinkled my nose at it—one of Aimée's castoffs. Stepmother's orders. The warm-toned, tan-colored dress with its flat elongated torso and drooping shoulders drained my skin of its color. I sighed as I tied the laces. I needed to look unappealing; Aimée was the flower, I was the bee, and together we were the trap. Those poor old fools. While they were distracted by the flower, my sticky fingers helped lighten their pockets. I looked in the mirror. My plain features stared back. Success. I was fashionably unfashionable. I sighed. Ugh. At least my face was clean.

"Just to be clear, you must talk to this Armand for the shoes?"

"And it will be stilted conversation. Literally. He stammers."

"He stutters?"

"Admirably."

Aimée scrutinized me, her hair now done up in a sweeping twist. "This arrangement is good. Yes, I've got that feeling."

"This arrangement gives you a feeling?" I asked as I moved to the washing basin on the nightstand. "That fate feeling? Last time you got that feeling, you were sick in Lord Alton's parlor over the roast turkey."

My fingers gripped the pumice stone. I dipped it into the water and scrubbed my fingertips as per Stepmother's orders.

"This one is different," Aimée said, waving a gloved hand in my direction.

Armand certainly was different. I rested my hands on the edge of the bowl. But he added a hurdle to my already daunting course. How could I talk to him while completing Stepmother's assignments and keeping our family alive?

Aimée stood in front of the mirror, smoothing her pink skirts. "You should have fun with the arrangement."

"I don't have time for fun." I rubbed my fingertips together, feeling each ridge of my print. Perfect—pink and raw. Better for feeling springs in locks falling into place.

"I know you have fun stealing," she said.

"Trading," I sang. I walked over to my bed and put on my shoes. Now I was ready.

She waved the nuance away with her gloved hands, fussing over her already perfect hair. "You get to be free."

Free? I was never free. The only person who held the key to my cage was Papa, and he was gone—because of me.

Guilt washed over me, threatening to weigh me down, but with a practiced mental sidestep, I locked it up, saving it for later. Helping my family—in whatever way I could—atoned for my mistake.

I shook my head to clear it, then clapped my hands and rubbed them together. "Is *M.* Bontour as ridiculous as Lord Cadieux? Overdressed and stubborn as a mule?"

"Not at all. He's the one I met at Lord Rallison's garden party." She perched on the edge of her bed. Her eyes sparkled. "And he's *parfait.*"

"That ragamuffin?"

Aimée's eyebrows knit together. "He's lower aristocracy, same as us."

"Lower aristocracy?" I groaned. "That's simply code for 'poor as a pauper.' Titles don't matter if you're poor, you know that." We had a youngest son of a duke lurking in our family tree somewhere, but that didn't put food on the table. "*M.* Bontour needs to be well connected in the upper echelons of the court, not some pandering gentleman clawing up the ranks. If he claims lower aristocracy, he's probably nothing more than the milkman."

"*M.* Bontour would never pander," she said, sticking out her lower lip. "But he does deliver the most delicious kisses."

My cheeks flushed. "Aimée!"

"Cyn, he makes me laugh." She walked over to my bed and sat on my mattress. "But don't tell Mother," she said, her eyes pleading like a puppy. "She'd never approve." She picked at some invisible fluff on her skirt, avoiding my eyes. "I'm just so tired of flirting with widowers more in the grave than out, and—" She paused, biting her lip. "I like him."

I looked at the ceiling. Seriously?

"He makes me laugh. He's kind." She paused. "He also doesn't care that I'm Alemanian." Her blue eyes blinked furiously.

I sighed. It had been getting more difficult luring suitors—the glaring exception being Lord Cadieux. With tensions between our two countries rising, *M.* Bontour the Milkman may be our only option. I pinched the bridge of my nose. If Aimée really had feelings for the fellow, this could be a way for her to be taken care of—even if it was by a fibbing dairy delivery boy.

"Fine. I won't tell if you won't."

She squealed and bounced on the mattress.

"Aimée. Cinderella. Inspection." Stepmother's strident voice carried from downstairs, and my chest tightened.

"Finish getting ready." I stood, wagging a finger at Aimée and dropping my voice. "Just watch yourself. We'll have to get something from him, or Stepmother will have both our hides. I sure hope your lower-gentry man has expensive taste."

Moments later, Shar, who had been putting the finishing touches on Aimée's ensemble, glanced out the window. "Mistress Manette, Miss Aimée, you'd better hurry. A young man is arriving on horseback."

Aimée took off down the stairs like she'd been stung by a bee, her thudding footsteps echoing through the manor.

I walked to the circular window. The horse's mane and coat looked unkempt, and when the rider turned to follow the drive, a brand from The Salty Lion, the closest tavern, was clearly seen. My shoulders slumped. "He *would* have a rented horse. Figures."

Stepmother waited for us at the first landing with both of her hands clutching her cane. I shoved my own hands in the folds of my dress and stood at attention. I would certainly pass her inspection—I looked terrible.

Stepmother nodded her approval at Aimée, though Aimée hardly noticed; her attention was fixed on the front windows.

You can do this, Cyn. M. Bontour is sure to have deep pockets.

Stepmother's eyes hardened when they rested on me. She stepped closer, and I resisted the urge to back away.

"I don't need to remind you what you owe to this family, do I?"

My blood froze and I shook my head. I needed no reminders.

Stepmother moved upstairs. As soon as the door to her bedchamber closed, Aimée raced to the front door. I took a shuddering breath, making sure everything I was holding under the surface stayed there. Being under Stepmother's evaluating gaze always left me feeling exposed. And with the secrets between Aimée and me piling up, I could feel myself unraveling.

I sucked in air. I just needed a hug from Papa.

M. Bontour pulled his horse to a stop and dismounted.

I concentrated on the air coming in and out of my lungs. *After. You can visit Papa after M. Bontour. If you hurry.* I pasted on a smile and pushed my feelings deeper. I could keep going. For now.

Moments later, as the couple strolled around the estate, I followed behind them as a respectable chaperone should, preserving Aimée's dignity. I hated to admit it, but *M.* Bontour seemed like a proper gentleman. And he did make Aimée laugh. She glowed around him. *M.* Bontour was genuinely amused at something she said, and she drew her arm closer to his, steering him toward the garden path. I almost felt bad for what we were about to do. Almost.

The pond announced its presence long before we reached it. Decay and moisture filled the air, intensified by the afternoon sun. Rotting leaves and an early autumn rain mixed, forming a murky bog rather than a well-kept garden pond.

I eyed *M.* Bontour's well-tailored clothes. A lovely lapel pin glimmered from his jacket. *Tempting.* Knee buckles held up his stockings, but I couldn't very well fumble around his knees. My eyes scanned his torso. Aha! A small coin purse swayed by his hip.

Aimée glanced at me, a pleading look on her face. Seriously? Second thoughts? She'd practically pushed Lord Rallison into the pond herself.

I shook my head. We were doing this. We had to.

I positioned myself so that *M.* Bontour was between me and the muddiest section of the pond. Then, pretending to trip, I crashed into *M.* Bontour.

I collided into his solid frame and grunted. "Oomph." What did this milkman do in his spare time? Thankfully, Aimée put her foot in front of *M.* Bontour's, and over he went.

He hit the pond with a sickening squelch.

"Oh, *Monsieur* Bontour!" Aimée shrieked.

"Are you all right?" I said.

Mud and muck dripped from *M.* Bontour's head, running onto his shoulders. Aimée rushed forward to the edge of the embankment, but he held up a hand to stop her. "Watch your step, *mademoiselle*," he said. "I believe there are exposed roots about."

A wind kicked up, blowing several leaves across the pond. They hit *M.* Bontour and stuck to his face. He stood, somehow still smiling, and glopped his way out of the mess. He held his arms away from his body like a much-abused scarecrow, mud dripping from his sleeves.

Aimée rushed forward, giggling and fussing at the same time.

"*M.* Bontour, oh dear! You aren't hurt, are you?" She removed the leaves from his head, her beautiful gloves getting dirty.

I rushed forward. "*Monsieur*," I said. "*Oh, je suis tres désolé.* Your jacket is ruined—let me help you."

According to plan, Aimée pressed herself shamelessly close to *M.* Bontour while I helped him from his jacket. But this time she was close enough that even I blushed. With the man's attention now wholly on Aimée, I turned to the jacket, scraping the mud off and dipping my fingers into his pockets. There was a small flask, but I tucked it back inside. He'd need that later, when he discovered so many of his personal effects were lost in the pond. My fingers flew about but found nothing.

I managed to stick myself with the lapel pin while trying to remove it, so I moved on. His nice smell was gone, replaced by grime and sludge. I glanced at Aimée, who continued to fuss.

"Are you sure you're unhurt? *M.* Bontour, I am so embarrassed."

Only moments left.

My fingers found a wooden figure and my brows knit together. A chess piece? My scowl deepened. Odd. It was all odd. This man wasn't lower gentry; he was poorer than we were. And what was he doing with a chess piece in his pocket?

I pulled my fingers out of his pockets, put the thin coin purse and chess piece in mine, and shook the coat. Mud splattered everywhere.

M. Bontour grabbed Aimée's hands in his muddy ones and held them to his chest. "Please," he said, "call me Luc."

Aimée lowered her lashes and blushed appropriately.

I raised my eyebrows. A blush? Aimée was not that good of an actress. The Duke Everard had ardently confessed his undying love for Aimée, and she had merely turned her head.

Luc reached up and brushed mud from her cheek with his muck-covered thumb—which merely smudged the dirt more, but her blush rose higher, pinking her ears. She really was taken with him.

"I'm so sorry." Aimée gestured to the coat I held, frowning at its abysmal condition. "Your jacket, your clothes . . ."

Luc stepped closer to Aimée and took the coat from me, slinging it over his shoulder, spraying mud further. "I'm not. It has been an unseasonably warm autumn, and that sun was terribly hot. Now I'm cool and refreshed. You know, I believe my skin will improve from this treatment." He glanced down at Aimée's gloves, and his voice softened. "Though I am sorry about these; I fear they are ruined."

The corners of my mouth turned upward in appreciation. Not bad, *Monsieur*. And pretty smooth to boot. None of the other gents we'd pushed into the pond had been half so amiable.

Aimée grabbed Luc's arm in hers, pulling him toward the house. "We must dry your clothes."

Luc shook his head. "Sadly, I must go. I have another engagement in town."

"You won't be gone long, will you?" Aimée said coyly.

"No," he said, his eyes never leaving her face. He bent and took Aimée's hand, kissing the only clean surface upon her glove in farewell.

Aimée pulled away, blushing further still. "Oh, Luc, your hands are a sticky, muddy mess. Let us at least go to the house to clean them."

Luc looked at his hands, chuckling. He allowed Aimée to pull him toward the house. As he passed me, he paused.

"Looks like I'm not the only one with sticky fingers," he murmured.

My eyes flew to his face, my heart racing. He knew. Was he going to tell? Was this the end? Would he throw Aimée and me into jail?

Luc straightened, then winked at me.

Relief flooded through my body, leaving my legs weak. I trailed behind, my fingers trembling behind my skirt.

We were nearly to the house when we came to a fork in the trail. I couldn't wait any longer. A small path led to two trees—a large cedar towering over a rowan sapling.

I leaned forward and tapped Aimée on the shoulder, and she turned. Luc moved a few feet away to allow us some privacy. "I need a moment." I glanced at the trees.

Aimée nodded. "Don't worry, I know what to do with *M*. Bontour." Her eyes twinkled.

"No kissing," I hissed.

"No promises."

With that, Aimée and Luc continued to the house.

Obviously, I couldn't stay long. If Stepmother saw those two and realized how poor Luc was, we'd be in hot water. But I needed this.

Gathering my skirts, I walked to the trees and a calming silence seemed to envelop me.

"*Bonjour, ma mère.*" I placed my hand on Maman's gray, cracked bark, and the warm smell of cedar filled my nostrils. I traced the ridges in the bark, pressing against Maman's trunk.

After Papa died, it was as if someone had snuffed out the sun. Within six months, Stepmother had found the servants new positions and I was trimming the hedges. It hadn't taken long after that for the most expensive items from our house to disappear—including the music box Papa had given me. Stepmother had sold it without a second thought.

I winced at the memory and turned to Papa's tree, then gently pulled the feathery leaves of the rowan through my fingers. I lowered myself to the ground and inhaled the earthy air, trying to melt this peace into my bones—my time with Maman and Papa.

The finger I'd stuck with Luc's lapel pin throbbed, reigniting my guilt over stealing and my excursions as the Magpie.

"I know this isn't what you wanted for me," I said. "But things will be better. After the masquerade. I promise."

Voices floated along the main path. Time to go. I inhaled, deeply relishing even the brief time with Maman and Papa, the only place where I felt whole again. And then I walked away to join Aimée and Luc.

"*Je t'aime*, Papa," I whispered behind me, and my throat tightened. "I'm so sorry."

Cyn 10

After we'd seen Luc off, I changed into my black breeches and shirt. It was only early afternoon, but exhaustion gnawed at my bones. The bit of bread and cheese I'd nipped from the kitchen did little to fortify me. *Get through this training session,* I thought as I trudged up the attic stairs. My legs protested with each step, stiff from my last round of instruction. I gripped the railing to finish the climb. Sore muscles were nothing compared to an upset Stepmother.

I hesitated on the landing outside the attic room and took a steadying breath. *It won't get easier, Cyn. Just go in.* The door creaked on its hinges, revealing the dimly lit attic.

And remember: you're doing this to save your family.

I opened the door, stepped over the threshold, then gasped. The attic was usually empty except for the three large roof-supporting pillars, a tiny aged desk, and a threadbare chair. Today, gray yarn shot across the room from pillar to pillar, wrapping around the spartan furniture and beams. It crisscrossed the large circular window, which remained shut no matter the weather, and snagged on its corroded hinges. The yarn even snaked its way around the fire irons. It looked as if a giant spider had spun a monstrous web through the room. A bell hung from the center of each strand.

The only place the spider hadn't touched was the top of the desk. Stepmother's small wooden jewelry box rested in the center like an insect afraid to move. The wooden box's inlaid brass and tortoiseshell latticework hinted at a secret. I'd never seen what was inside, and Stepmother had never opened it in front of me.

In the middle of the web, resting on the floor, was the sewing mannequin. Around its neck was a dingy rope necklace.

"Come in, Cinderella," a silky voice said.

I gulped, feeling more fly than spider, and stepped forward.

Stepmother stood a few feet to the side of the desk, near the empty fireplace. Lines of yarn crisscrossed between us. Her deep-blue dress, trimmed with black ribbon, accentuated her gray-blue eyes and her gray-blonde hair. She gripped the raven-shaped silver head of her ebony cane. The bird's beak, frozen in a screech, sent shivers through me.

"You're late." Her eyes narrowed, cold and distant—so altered since her marriage to my father three years ago. Those eyes had beamed as she'd patiently taught me the intricate Alemanian waltz, twinkled softly as I'd struggled making delicate spätzle. But soon after Papa's death, and with money dwindling, her eyes froze—just another thing for which I was to blame. Perhaps after the masquerade job, she'd go back to the way she'd been before. Happier.

"What are we doing this afternoon?" I asked, gesturing to the room at large. Deep shadows lurked in the corners, nestled among the dark wooden beams turning the attic lair-like.

"Report." She thumped her cane for emphasis.

I cringed inwardly. Should I tell her about the shoes? "The delivery went well." Except my deliveries were easily the worst thing about stealing, because it meant I had to interact with two of the slimiest creatures in all of Lyonelle. "I gave Oil—"

She raised her eyebrow at the slip of my tongue.

"I gave Oliver and Theodore the painting. They wrapped it in oilskin," I said. *Please forget the shoes.*

She lowered her chin, her eyes narrowing to slivers, one finger tapping the raven's beak. I chewed on my lip.

"Cinderella, the shoes?" She arched a brow. The sharp ice in her voice cut through me.

Fear snaked through my veins. I would have to tell her the truth. Just not all of it. "A m-member of the household s-startled me." *Beasties, I sound almost as bad as Armand.* "I'll go back tonight."

"Startled you?" She tilted her head, considering me like a hawk would a mouse.

I nodded, my voice caught somewhere between my throat and my tongue. "I—"

"You weren't focused." Her voice raked through my excuses like a scythe. "Are you so incompetent that you need reminders of the importance of this job?" Her knuckles tightened on the raven's head.

"It is our last job. You promised." My eyes fell to the floor, my fingernails digging into my palm.

"If we can rob the gentry blind, and if we don't get caught"—her fingers traced the rim of the table—"and if you remain focused, then yes."

Her words didn't bring the comfort I'd been searching for, but I nodded. I had been distracted—stupid of me, really. "I understand how much this means to our family."

"That is good," she said, her words dripping like water from icicles. "However, not obtaining the shoes is . . . problematic."

I swallowed. She used that word when she was displeased.

Her fingernails clicked on the cane.

"Perhaps I could wear these?" I lifted my faded slippers. A few loose threads dangled from the seams.

Stepmother murmured under her breath, but I caught the words all the same. "You can never see the bigger picture." She walked from the desk to the fireplace, stopping near the crumbling mantel. When she spoke again, her voice was coiled and inflexible. "It is vital you blend in, and to blend in, you have to look the part." She leaned against the desk. "Complete your ensemble for the ball. And make sure it has the ability to hide our take for the evening. We'll need more than we originally planned if war really is coming. And perhaps Aimée should find a more profitable suitor."

I nodded, relieved this was all the reprimand I was to receive. "I'll have it." My heart raced. Our last job. After that, we were free. I was free. No more stealing. We'd have enough to reenter society, reestablish our house-hold. Even with a possible war, we'd be a family again. I locked eyes with Stepmother, the ghost of my smile dying on my face. I shifted my weight and suppressed a shudder.

"One more thing before we begin," she said, turning to the desk. My body stiffened, hyperaware once more. "I need to you steal one of Lord Carte's maps."

"But Papa never traded with Lord Carte." The words were out before I could stop them. My hands flew to my mouth.

Stepmother fixed her eyes on me, and cold fingers of dread wrapped around my chest.

"We steal because it's your fault." She rapped her cane on the floor and it cracked like a gunshot. "Right and wrong are luxuries we can no longer afford."

Something sounded false in her words, but I was in too deep to say otherwise.

Stepmother took a step closer. "You forget why we're here in the first place."

I backed up and realized I was in a corner. I held my breath and pressed my fingers into the grainy wood wall.

"Take the map to the docks."

"Yes, Stepmother." *Keep quiet, Cyn.* These trips to the docks would be over soon.

The yarn around the room looked like a snaring net.

"Time to begin," she said, rapping her cane on the floor again.

I exhaled, relieved her focus was diverted from the shoes.

"Retrieve the necklace," she said.

I glanced at her and nodded. Turning to face the room, I studied the zigzagging lines of gray yarn. I angled my head, planning my route. Jump here, crawl there. *You have to focus more, Cyn.* I couldn't afford to make another mistake. I *had* to do this.

Crouching, I ducked under the first cord of string and climbed over a second by balancing on my toes. Suddenly, a tinkling sound pierced the silence. A third string had caught on my shoulder.

Stepmother thumped her cane. "Again," she commanded. "From the beginning."

I gritted my teeth, determined to reach the necklace.

The web was harder than it looked. Possible gaps between the strings appeared promising, but they quickly closed, intersected with more yarn. Another bell jingled.

I pushed myself harder, as if effort alone could bring Papa back, could make Stepmother and our home happier again. I crouched on all fours and lifted my leg over a low-laying string. My legs screamed from the effort.

My back brushed a string.

Jingle.

"Again!"

Sweat poured off my face. My heart pounded a steady beat. It had broken when Papa died. I'd tried putting it back together, but I didn't know how to. Its warmth had been replaced with a cold weight. I could hear it pumping, echoing the truth I saw in Stepmother's eyes, the words in my head.

I killed him. I killed Papa.

My blood pounded in my ears. My fault. My fault. *My fault.*

11

ARMAND

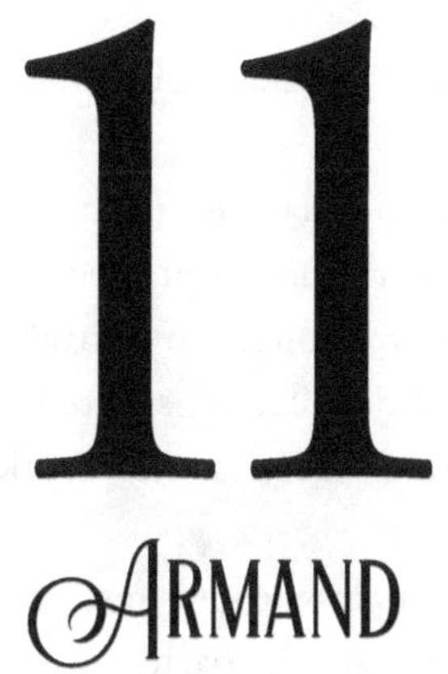

As I walked into Father's study, the afternoon light lingered in warm patches along the maroon rug, but it did nothing to lighten the stern-faced portraits of Lyonelle's past rulers glaring from the walls. Above the mantel, larger than life, was the portrait of the Great Beast himself, founder of Lyonelle, King Adam the First. His stare had silently judged me through the ages.

Don't show Father your weakness. No stuttering.

Curse Luc and his country lass.

Father sat behind his massive oak desk, reading. He grunted a welcome, making the lace spilling from his cravat quiver. A grunt was promising. At least he acknowledged my presence. His shoulders remained relaxed, lines furrowing his forehead. He was concentrating. Not good, but at least neutral.

"Hermann." He stood. "You will join me in two days for the Grand Council." He squared his shoulders and moved in front of the desk, seeming to expand in the space.

I nodded, shrugging off my irritation at the use of "Hermann." Things could change as soon as tomorrow. I'd show Father the firelance and once he was convinced, the rest of the court would fall into place. No more marbles, and Lyonelle would be safe.

"Will *Général* Sanson b-be there?" I asked, hoping Father didn't hear the apprehension in my voice.

His eyes narrowed. "You will be an observer. Nothing more. I trust you will not embarrass me."

I opened my mouth with the rumor of the new Alemanian weapons on the tip of my tongue. Father's mouth pressed into a hard line. The words died instantly. His features mirrored the portraits above, condensed into a single disapproving glare. My collar constricted.

"Sit down, boy," he said. "First some practice, then dinner with the ambassador."

I sat in the stiff armchair without resting against the backrest. For Father. A king must always look the part.

He pulled a piece of paper from within his vest and began reading. His thick voice filled the corners of the chamber. "The Royal Family and all of Lyonelle wish to welcome Their Excellencies, Ambassador Schubert and Baron von Müller, as well as His Excellency, Björgvin Leiffson, and his wife, Lilja."

I gulped. That was a lot of consonants.

Father's eyebrows drew together; he loomed like a gargoyle. My mouth went drier than dust.

"S-sounds very official, but we're not a f-family; we are a firm."

Father growled but otherwise ignored my poor attempt at a joke.

Soufre, I mentally cursed. *Meet me halfway, Father. I can't save Lyonelle unless you listen.* I shoved my annoyance deep. No sense in stepping on a lion's tail. If he wouldn't even laugh, he'd never allow me to address the Council on anything that mattered.

"You think this is funny?" he asked, clenching the paper, wrinkling it in his meaty fist. He strode back to the desk, then turned, and the shadows on his face darkened.

"Once I'm dead and gone, who will stop an Alemanian invasion? Who will stop those high-stepping jackanapes from marching down Lierre's streets?" He paused, his eyes narrow. "You'll have to do." Then he sighed and his voice softened. "Let's hear your progress." He strode back to my chair, his boots thumping on the floor. He shoved the mangled paper in front of my face.

This was my time. *No bouncing or fist-clenching. It's weakness.*

The paper fluttered like a battle ensign.

"It's easy when you know how," he said, his voice tight with strained kindness.

I forced my hand toward the paper.

"Have a go," he said, gesturing to the room. It looked empty but it was crowded with ghosts of my failed attempts, absorbing all the air.

I gulped, then opened my mouth to speak.

"Face the room," he barked. "Stare it down as any decent man would."

My heart hammered against my ribs. I stood, pulling my shoulders back. *Calm. Stay calm.*

"The R-Royal F-Family—" My tongue expanded and my mouth flapped open, a strange click appearing each time I tried to reform the words.

"Get it out, boy," Father said, his voice fracturing. "Take your time."

Anxiety swelled like the words jumbling from my mouth.

"And all of L-Lyon . . . all of Lyonelle . . ." I held the "n" too long.

"Relax." His volume rose, his face reddening.

If only I could.

"W-wish t-to welcome—" A wall instantly dropped between my brain and mouth, and my stomach fell to my heels. No matter how I pounded, once the wall dropped, nothing I did could ever surmount it.

"Just say it."

"Their Ex-Excell—"

"Do it!" He banged his hand on the desk like a gavel—my judge and executioner.

I forced myself to read to the end, knowing a sheen of sweat clung to my temples. I couldn't tell who was more relieved when I finished—Father or me.

He stood and gestured to my lapel. I glanced down to see the familiar pin of a golden lion climbing up a bramble to a rose in full bloom.

"At least you're wearing this," he said. "Then at least people will know you are the prince, even if you can't say it. Follow me."

Numbly, I walked behind him out of his study. A pit formed in my gut as I recognized our destination.

The expansive rectangular ballroom had been cleverly constructed. A large set of curved stairs led downward to the dance floor. The ceiling had recently been painted with images of our family's history, each face now closely resembling Father's.

Soufre. It was impressive. The expense was staggering—money that should have been spent protecting Lyonelle. My self-control barely hid the frustration simmering within.

Workers scurried along, keeping a wary eye on Father. The noise of hammers and men echoed in the hallway.

"*C'est magnifique, non?*" His eyes lingered on the ceiling.

Though it had been two centuries since magic and fairies had existed in Lyonelle, tiny fairy lights still faintly glowed in the candelabras. The palace was one of the only places where one could still conjure them.

My strange encounter with the lights in the orchard flooded my mind. The red-tinged image of *Général* Sanson rose to the surface. Perhaps I should mention it to Father.

"I said, 'Isn't it magnificent?'" His tone was sharp as a hunting knife.

"*Incroyable,*" I whispered.

The ceiling sprouted sixteen new glass chandeliers, replacing the black wrought-iron ones. Several workers hefted a chandelier to the ceiling. Wordlessly, I moved closer. Each chandelier held twenty candles that grew from twenty golden roses. I had never seen any glasswork like this before.

"They were a cursed nuisance," Father said. "Almost didn't get them here. Two of the glassblowers were poisoned last week. *Venenum noix*—terrible stuff."

I shuddered. *Venenum noix* killed men in even small doses.

He laughed. "Apparently the Vénitiens didn't like that I had convinced some of their own to work here in Lyonelle." His hand pressed against his chest. "Even less that they were to be working in Lierre."

"Are they all right?"

"Oh yes. All the chandeliers are in perfect condition. I told the other workers if the chandeliers were not delivered on time, they'd suffer the same fate as their coworkers." He glowered at a passing craftsman.

Leave it to Father to turn attempted murder into a lesson.

Everything was suddenly less glamorous. Time for a change of subject. And not to the vision from the orchard. With Father so pleased with the room, now may be the best time to bring up Alemanian aggressions. I stepped closer to him keeping my voice just loud enough to be heard over the construction but not loud enough to carry to the workers.

"F-Father, the raids on the Alemanian b-border—" I began.

He glared at me.

"C-communities along the b-border are reporting raiding and p-pillaging."

"I also have reports from Parler that you're not making any progress," he said.

"There have been reports of k-killings," I continued.

"The only reports I care about are the ones of your speech improving. Until then, nothing else matters."

"But people are dying," I shouted.

Movement in the ballroom stopped as workers turned in my direction.

Father's face broke into a leering grin. "There we have it," he said, his voice soothing and satisfied. "Maybe I should take over."

What was he talking about? Then realization washed over me like ice water. I hadn't stuttered—and now Father wanted to tutor me.

"Over my dead body," I spat through my clenched jaw, for once hating that the words slipped so easily from my mouth.

"That's no problem. I have a spare who could easily step into your shoes." Father waved to the workers. Noise resumed around us, though a bit more subdued.

I stood straight, pulling down my jacket, ignoring the tightening of my throat.

"Send my apologies to the ambassador. I will not be attending tonight's dinner. I have t-t-tutoring." I emphasized the last stuttered *t*'s, knowing it would irritate him.

The muscles in his jaw twitched. "Just as well. One less embarrassment for me to worry about."

"Is there anything else, sire?" I held the *s* too long. The hiss echoed off the mirrors.

Father turned back to the construction of the hall. I was clearly dismissed.

My fingernails dug into my palms. I bowed and then fled from the palace to the stables. I mounted Gallant and raced toward Lady Eline's, my anger burning with me. I couldn't wait to see Lyonelle's most infamous burglar. See how he liked that. He wanted angry? I'd give him angry.

CYN

I trudged to the kitchen still wearing my training clothes, the stale smell of dried sweat following in my wake. Supper needed to be prepared, and if Shar, Aimée, and I didn't do it, no one would. It wasn't so bad, though. It gave me an excuse to be in the kitchen.

Delicious smells wafted from the heart of the home—my sanctuary. "How does chocolate cake for dessert sound?" I asked.

"*Oui, s'il te plaît*," Aimée called from her table. "How was training?"

"Hard." But without it, where would we be? "But I mastered picking pockets." I gave a weary smile. I gathered ingredients and then chopped some hazelnuts gathered from our tree. When I mixed the cocoa, puffs of it landed on my hands, turning them an earthy brown.

"Excellent," Aimée said, waving a hand in a quick celebration. As I melted Papa's Swizzeran chocolate, sweet steam rose from the double boiler, curling my hair. Soon it would be a frizzy mess.

The cake cooled to the side as Aimée started on the ganache.

Shar flew by my shoulder, an irritated orange tinging the edges of her light. "What does it say about your character that you have a natural propensity for larceny?"

"That I'm a fast learner?" I bit the corner of my lip. As I combined the melted chocolate and hazelnut mixture, the nutty aroma of the chocolate batter sharpened.

Shar's light turned a reasonable cobalt blue. "You should be at court where you belong. Vienne can introduce you."

I snorted. Stepmother would never deign to do that.

"Or you should be running your father's business."

"There is no business," I said, all levity draining. Papa's renowned trade had died with him. I traced my fingers along the edge of the white-and-blue ceramic Delftwijk honey jar. No one else knew the best routes, and even if they did, no one else was brave enough to sail past the northern shoals of Alemania. It's what had made him such a great merchant.

"Mother's not herself," Aimée blurted, slowly stirring the ganache.

Something in her voice made me pause. I stopped stirring the honey and placed it on the table.

Aimée glanced at the doorway. "I've seen her like this before," she whispered, leaning forward.

There was no one else in the kitchen besides Shar, and she knew more secrets about my family than anyone had a right to.

Aimée removed the ganache from the stove, then she turned from the steaming pot and wrung her hands. Unsurprisingly, her gloves were still immaculate. "Before Lyonelle and your father, when Mother and I lived in Dascht with my father." Her voice was strained like fine silk on a needle's point.

I nodded, leaning closer. Aimée and I had become as close as blood sisters since Papa had married Stepmother. I knew everything about her.

"It was just the three of us until five years ago, when baby James was born."

Except that. My brows furrowed. Aimée had a brother? Why was he not here? I racked my brain for any mention of him in the years since Papa and Stepmother's marriage.

Aimée swallowed and her eyes grew distant. "One evening, shortly after James was born, I was out picking berries. Suddenly, Mother came out of nowhere and dragged me into the bushes. She was so scared. I had no idea what was going on. Moments later, a Lyonelle border patrol arrived. They carried torches."

I straightened, knocking utensils against the mixing bowl. "Lyonelle?"

She nodded.

"But why?"

Aimée shrugged. "We never found out. Our countries were supposedly at peace." She shuddered, her slight accent deepening. "We watched from our hiding place while the men stormed our house. Within moments, our home was in flames."

"Aimée." My heart lurched and I put my arm around her, rubbing her shoulder gently.

"We hid, but . . . but one soldier found us. He grabbed Mother and pulled her away."

My hand froze. "What did you do?"

"Me? I screamed," Aimée said, a sad noise catching in her throat. "But Mother, she—she didn't hesitate. She attacked him with a rock. Here." She pointed to her left temple. "There was so much blood. We ran and hid in the woods all night."

My heart raced as I imagined Aimée's nightmare.

"The house was destroyed. Nothing was left. Father and . . . and baby James didn't get out in time." Her voice was small and hollow. Her chin quivered.

"Oh, Aimée." I wrapped her tightly in my arms. "I'm so sorry."

Aimée sniffed fiercely and waved me away. "After that, Mother was . . . different." She hugged her hands around her torso, her gloves a band of white. "Once mother met Papa Manette, though, things were better." Her voice seemed to be reaching for its usual vibrant tone. "Losing your father was hard on her."

She quietly turned and stirred the chocolate. Then, wordlessly, she lifted the pot and tipped it over the cake. Ganache flooded the top, dripping down the sides.

I stood numbly, watching the glaze. Losing Papa had been a deep blow, turning my world upside down. Stepmother's emotionless face swam in my mind. She had lost a husband, a home, and a baby. Then another husband. I could only imagine what that would do to someone.

"I'm sorry, Mistress Aimée," Shar whispered, her light a deep blue.

Aimée set the pot down. I reached over and squeezed her hand, earning a weak smile.

I took the jar of honey and drizzled it over the chocolate-covered cake, truly hoping it might make Stepmother smile.

12 ARMAND

"I'll have some chamomile tea sent up. I believe the stress of our sessions is getting to you."

M. Parler's trembling voice faded and I escaped into the hallway. This last tutoring session had ended with me actually swallowing a marble, and I had only a few minutes to spare before my meeting with the Magpie. There was still so much to do—like get insurance against the Magpie for guaranteed cooperation. My small rebellion against Father fueled my efforts. Meeting with a criminal to talk—and, as an added bonus, to anger Father—was harder work than I'd anticipated. I leaped up the stairs, and then raced down the hall into Lady Eline's room, and threw open her wardrobe.

Rows of shoes lined the walls; Lady Eline's closet was a tiny shrine to her footwear. I stared, bewildered. *Which pair should I take?* One pair rested apart from the others on a satin pillow. I snatched them, tucking them under my arm. I started toward the door but then paused. There were so many other shoes. What if the Magpie came back and simply took another pair and then never returned?

A growl rumbled in my throat. I was going to be late.

Keeping the first pair of shoes under my arm, I grabbed as many others as I could, raced into the bedroom, and shoved shoes under the bed, in the dresser, and behind cushions. Within minutes, Lady Eline's shoe collection had been scattered and hidden within her quarters.

Still clutching the first pair, I raced back to the parlor and threw open the double doors leading to the balcony.

It was empty. Where was she? Perhaps I was early.

The glass beads from the shoes dug into my palm. *Perfect. Now to hide the shoes.* The spartan balcony, two lion topiaries, and a bench offered no cover. I cursed and looked up. A window twelve feet from the balcony caught my eye. A small ledge jutted out from the facade. If I tossed them onto the ledge, I could always retrieve them later from inside.

Taking aim, I lobbed one shoe up, its bright embroidered silk shining in the moonlight. *Ha, first try.*

I was readying to throw the second shoe when a voice behind me made me jump.

"What are you doing, and where are all the other shoes?"

She's here. I turned to face her and shoved the other shoe in the back of my breeches.

"Are you throwing them onto a window ledge?" The Magpie's annoyance flooded the balcony like a rising tide. "Where are all the others?" She folded her arms, her black sleeves bunching at her elbows. Her dark breeches silhouetted her outline against the moonlight.

I swallowed. The masculine clothing she wore pleasantly accentuated her figure in ways dresses couldn't.

"I knew you w-would search inside. Thief."

"Trader." She narrowed her eyes. "Perhaps I should search you instead."

She lunged, and I retreated toward the darkened study doors. As my back hit the cold stone walls, the shoe dug into my spine. I leaned into it, knowing she couldn't get it out even if she did find it. I lifted my arms away from my body.

"Search m-me."

She growled and pressed her hands against my torso, then moved on, frisking me. *Soufre,* she was close. The smell of cinnamon followed her as she patted my chest. Of course she smelled like cinnamon. I was beginning to have very mixed feelings about cinnamon.

"Aha!" She reached around me and hooked a finger around the shoe, tugging. It budged an inch, and I pressed harder into the wall.

"C-can we j-just talk?"

Light suddenly flooded the balcony, throwing our silhouettes across the garden. My eyes grew wide and I froze. *M.* Parler's shadow fell across the balcony. He rattled the doors.

There was no time to hide.

The Magpie sucked air through her teeth and took a small step backwards toward the balustrade, her green eyes shooting accusations.

"N-no, it's n-not what you think."

With a click, the doors swung open, and *M.* Parler appeared with a tea service in his hands. "I thought I heard you practicing. I have often found topiaries to be the best listeners." When he saw the Magpie, he stopped and raised his brows. "Oh, who is this?"

The Magpie and I exchanged glances. If he discovered who she was, he could call for Lady Eline's guards. And report to Father that I'd let Lierre's most notorious thief escape through my fingers.

I swallowed. "M-my d-dance instructor."

"His Españoli tutor," she said at the same time.

M. Parler's brow furrowed. "Which is it?"

"B-both. She is my Españoli d-dance instructor." I wanted to smack my palm against my forehead.

"Españoli dance instructor?" *M.* Parler placed the tea service on the marble bench and settled next to it. "I'd love to see a demonstration."

Blast. Now what? Meeting with a thief to talk and rebel against Father was all good and fine, but I didn't want her to be arrested. Or me to be disowned.

The Magpie smirked, watching me from the corner of her eye. I'd seen that look on Luc before. She was planning something.

"*Bien sûr.*" She stepped forward, pressing her hands together. "The fandango is the most impressive, but we don't have the necessary candles. Perhaps you could—"

"The b-bolero," I said. "We will d-dance the b-bolero." The last thing I wanted was to place a potential weapon in her hands.

"Lovely." *M.* Parler laced his fingers together, his eyes bright with antic-ipation.

I straightened and held my left hand out for hers. She gave me a thin smile, placing her hand in mine. I pulled her close, our bodies inches away. The smell of spices filled my nose.

"The bolero?" she hissed. Her beautiful olive skin and rich brown hair were even more striking up close.

"F-follow m-my lead." I'd had years of dance and cultural lessons. I'd stick to the basics, but I hoped she was a fast learner.

Her hand slid from my shoulder and down my back toward the middle, reaching for the shoe.

I grabbed her hand, then glanced at *M.* Parler, who had lifted an eyebrow.

I forced a laugh. "She is testing me. The woman's hands go here." I moved her hand from my back to my shoulder.

The Magpie smiled. "So glad you remembered." She sounded anything but.

"Actually, *M.* Parler, c-could you—" I handed him the shoe and he placed it in his lap. I returned to the Magpie, pulling her close once more.

That was when something snapped between us. My muscles shivered. *What was that?* Her frame fit perfectly against my own, and the air between us charged like the sky before a storm. I swallowed; my skin was hyperaware of hers. Was this the woman from the vision? We weren't in a meadow, but it was no doubt the Magpie I had seen.

She placed her hands on my shoulder and I stared into her brilliant eyes. She held her breath and her eyes widened. She felt it too. I leaned down, murmuring in her ear. *"Un, deux, trois . . ."*

We moved to a silent rhythm, dragging our feet apart and then together, and our steps scraping against the stone floor. Even without music, our bodies flowed together and I led us through more intricate steps. *M.* Parler and the balcony fell into the background, and all I could see—could feel—was her.

She'd had lessons, that much was clear. As we moved together, her knee brushed against mine, and my heart pulsed in my ears. Perhaps a more difficult move? I pulled her close, using her momentum to pull us into a tight spin. Was she smiling? I dipped her back and her body responded to mine, arching over my arm.

As I stared down her torso, her chest heaving, I swallowed. This dance had been a mistake. Everything inside of me felt like a powder keg, waiting for and wanting her to strike a match.

I pulled her straight and stood, breathing as if I'd been in a race. The night air was sharp in my throat. What the blazes had just happened? "H-how—?"

"You're not the only one who got dance lessons." As she dropped her arms to her side, she let her hand slide from my shoulder to my fingers, leaving tingles on my skin. I moved closer.

A snort to my left pulled me out of my trance. The balcony came into focus and the Magpie stepped away. *M.* Parler was asleep, his white hair falling around his bowed head, the shoe still tucked in his hand.

"You're not g-going to wake him, are you?" I asked, turning back to face her, but she was gone. I whirled back to Parler, but he snored on, the shoe undisturbed in his lap. "Where . . . ?"

Movement above caught my eye. The Magpie hanging on the window ledge twelve feet above me, the palm of one hand flat against the side of the ledge, her other hand reaching for the shoe. It teetered over the edge and fell. In one fluid motion, her foot swung like a pendulum, kicking the falling shoe high into the air. With a graceful flip, she dropped from the ledge, landing confidently on the railing of the balcony. She held out her hand and the airborne shoe fell neatly into it as if I'd dropped it there myself.

I gazed up at her in rapture. "What—? How—?"

She raised a shoulder. "I am the Magpie." With catlike grace, she jumped down from the railing and then tucked the shoe into her belt.

"*Incroyable.* Seeing that was w-worth losing a shoe," I said, shaking my head. "How d-did you do that?"

"I'm legendary." The Magpie pointed at the shoe resting in M. Parler's lap. "Shoe, please."

"'Legendary'?" an indignant voice said.

I pulled back. "Who said that?"

"Shar, what are you—" The Magpie whirled and spoke to her shoulder.

A small, pale yellow light half the size of my palm zipped from under her collar and stopped six inches from the Magpie's face.

"Dancing the bolero is one thing, but bragging?" The light flared orange. "Where is your modesty?"

I tensed. What was this?

"With my other morals, no doubt," the Magpie said. "Shar, Idiot. Idiot, Shar," she added, gesturing between me and the light.

"A fairy," I breathed.

The orchard. The fireflies.

"A house fairy," Shar said.

"I thought they didn't exist anymore." I rubbed my chin. Wild fae had shown me a vision of the future?

The Magpie gestured to the light, now tinged sky-blue. "Shar, you don't exist."

I spluttered, my jaw flapping.

The small light—house fairy—hovered close to my face. "We may be rare, but we're not extinct—"

I edged backwards slowly, my eyes wide with concern. Magic could be extremely dangerous; just ask King Adam about how his experience with the sorceress had gone.

"—and I'm not dangerous. House fairies are still rare. Extremely rare, but it's the wild fae you need to watch out for."

"Very t-true," I said.

My eyes scanned the garden and settled on the orchard, which was as dark as the rest of the landscape. Relief washed over me; at least I wasn't in any immediate danger from Shar. And the fairies in the orchard hadn't harmed me.

My gaze fell on the petite black-clad figure in front of me, her arms crossed and her sharp eyes taking everything in. Shar might be safe, but the Magpie, I wasn't so sure about.

"Now you know," the Magpie said, then held out her hand. "Shoe."

Shar flew to the Magpie's face, her light a triumphant blue. "I told you not to be stubborn."

The Magpie stuck out her tongue.

I turned to Shar. "Is she always like this?"

Her light flushed a smug red. "You don't know the half of it."

The Magpie groaned, rubbing the bridge of her nose. "You know I can't wear one shoe to the ball."

"Of c-course not. You'd dance in circles." I moved between her and the snoring *M.* Parler. "This one you'll have to earn by c-coming back."

Shar flew a bit closer to me and hovered near my face, a brighter section of her glow flared toward the Magpie, almost as if Shar had crossed an invisible line coming to my side. "M'lady, you did agree to return each night until the ball."

The Magpie threw up her hands in defeat. "Curse you and your morals, Shar."

My gaze turned to the fairy, my brow raised. "You were here the f-first night as well?

Shar zipped to my face, six inches away, then she zoomed back to the Magpie, leaving bright spots in my vision. The fairy bobbed, seeming to shrug. "Under her lapel. You really are much more handsome up close."

"Shar," the Magpie hissed, and the fairy flew back to her mistress.

"You said he was handsome, but you didn't mention his eyes are such a marvelous shade of brown."

"*You* said he was handsome," the Magpie hissed.

The fairy light bobbed again. "You never denied it."

Heat crept up my neck and I coughed. The Magpie's face darkened in the pale moonlight. Was she blushing too?

"Shar. Collar," she said, glaring at Shar and pointing to her neck. The fairy zipped and landed on the black upturned collar, like a firefly with its light stuck on.

"I was only telling the truth," Shar said. "It's really for your own goo—"

The Magpie turned down the collar and muffled the rest of Shar's comment.

The Magpie looked at me. "I'll be back tomorrow night. Make sure the tutor is asleep next time."

I couldn't tell if she was happy or not.

She leaped off the balcony with a flourish, and seconds later, her shadow disappeared into the night.

I ran my fingers through my hair. "What have I g-gotten myself into?" I asked aloud.

Nobody heard me but the topiaries.

"Shar, why did you say he was handsome?" I said once we were over Lady Eline's wall.

"Because he is," she said. "A fact you still haven't denied."

I walked over to Pumpkin and harrumphed at the fairy. "Maybe if he weren't so insufferable," I hissed, even if it were only partly true.

What had happened during that dance? What if I had met him under different circumstances, in a dress? *Me in a dress, not him.*

It had been so long since I'd been in feminine attire around other people. It was hard to believe that just three years ago, I'd preened daily for trips to the marketplace with Papa. He had even promised me an excursion to the palace to see the imperial gardens. Now I was forced to "trade" for formal wear; the Manette coffers were nearly depleted.

I murmured a greeting to Pumpkin and freed the reins from the tree I had tethered him to. I reached into the saddlebags and pulled out an apple. As he snacked on his treat, I pulled the shoe from my belt and held it up. Papa would have bought dozens of pairs and then sold them for twice the price in Delftwijk.

My fingers traced the interlacing floral pattern that ended on the delicate square heel. *Parfait.* I tucked the shoe in the saddlebag. The evening hadn't been a total loss—in footwear or conversation. Perhaps meeting with Armand wouldn't be so bad.

The look on his face when I'd caught the shoe. I barked a laugh.

Shar's light bobbed closer, a scrutinizing granite-gray. "You actually enjoyed that."

I chewed on my lip to stop my smile from spreading. "Not in the slightest. This is all for the shoes. For the masquerade." Clever Armand, knowing I'd search the house.

Shar hummed, her tone ending on a hard note. She didn't believe me at all.

I climbed atop Pumpkin, grasping the worn leather reins. A warm, fluttery feeling spread in my chest, and I inhaled, savoring the moment.

Shar's next words turned my insides to lead.

"Must we go to the wharf tonight?"

I touched my heels to Pumpkin's side and turned him away toward Lierre. "Stepmother's orders."

Shar's sickly gray-green light rippled, looking exactly how I felt.

The half-hour ride into town was short, but it was plenty of time for my stomach to twist into knots. Stealing and possible imprisonment aside, these meetings at the wharf were the worst. The smell of fish and salt grew stronger with each step Pumpkin took. The aroma had once been a welcome one. I used to stand for hours on the dock, watching for Papa's ship to berth.

Pumpkin's hooves thudded on dirt and sand; the grass was growing sparse. We stopped by the last patch of it before the docks, and I tethered Pumpkin to the hitching post. As I rummaged through the saddlebag, my fingers brushed Lady Eline's shoe. At least I had one shoe. I pushed deeper to the stolen papers.

I turned to the docks, which were outlined in cold moonlight. A dirty shed crouched in a filthy corner of the wharf—our meeting place. I couldn't see Oil and Toad yet, but I knew they were there. My hands turned clammy and the skin between my shoulders crawled. I shrugged the feeling away, but it lingered like the smell of fish.

"C'mon," I said, swallowing my growing dread. "We're late."

I stepped onto the dock, the wooden boards creaking in protest.

Shar rested on my collar just below my ear, her words piercing. "Why? *Messieurs* Oliver and Theodore are miscreants and liars."

I snorted. "I'm a thief, remember?"

"Trader," said Shar. My lips twitched at her automatic correction as she continued. "Isn't there another way to earn money?"

The moon, high in its nightly arc, washed out the dock. Waves lapped the moorings.

"Quiet," I said. "You ask too many questions."

We were twenty paces from the shed and still no sign of the two men Stepmother had set up for exchanges.

"At least someone is inquiring," Shar retorted. "You should be more curious about Vienne and her intentions. Why do you have to sell items to them? And why are you stealing documents from the gentry and members of the court? They have nothing to do with your father's debts."

I bit my lip. It was true. At first, I'd been stealing from families with names I recognized: *M.* Gagne, Master Laurent, and Barlow. Now the names belonging to the households were longer and more distinguished: Baron Phillipe Carriere and His Grace the Duke of De Chambray, and so on. But all of that paled in comparison to the reason why I followed Stepmother's orders.

I sighed to dispel the emptiness. Unbidden, a memory resurfaced: Papa's pained face resting against his sweat-damp pillow.

I never should have left him. If I'd only been faster, I could have saved him. Instead of helping, I'd killed him.

"Doesn't matter," I said, squaring my shoulders. "Stepmother takes care of us and we take care of her. I owe her. Without her, we'd be out of our home, starving."

"Vienne is Alemanian. If tensions between our countries continue to rise, the time may come when starvation would be preferable."

I shuddered to think what that would mean.

Now I was ten paces away from the shed. My stomach tightened.

Wordlessly, Shar slipped under my collar. In the shabby corner, movement flickered in the shadows. My mouth went drier than ash.

"*Ma chérie*," a soft and greasy voice spoke.

Suppressing the urge to run, I planted my feet on the dock. Oil leaned against the dilapidated shed, seeming to be made of the shadows themselves. He was a foot taller than me and his angled features caught the light from the waves. He smiled, his canines glossy.

Toad's stocky frame hunched on a box, his hands dangling limply over his knees. He looked like a fish—soggy down-turned mouth and glassy eyes. In all our meetings, he'd never said anything. I shuddered.

"Here are the papers," I said, holding them out even though I was still five feet away from the shed. *This is as close as I get.* My skin was already tight and prickling.

"That's no way to talk to your *bon ami*. It's been ages since we last spoke." Oil's voice undulated.

"It's been a week." My arm started to ache. "And we are not friends, let alone good ones."

"Seems like ages," he cooed, pushing himself away from the shed.

I narrowed my eyes, hoping I looked tougher than I felt. "You'll need to wrap this in oilskin. Stepmother wants it undamaged upon arrival."

Oil glided out of the shadows, his wiry frame creeping toward me. He stopped, and his dirt-stained fingers curled around the parchment. I yanked my hand away, leaving the rolled paper in his hand.

"When will you give me more than paper?"

I pulled my shoulders back and crossed my arms. "When will you take a bath?"

Toad chuckled. Oil gave him a dagger-filled glare. The corners of Toad's wide mouth twitched a bit, but he settled back on the crate, watching.

I held out my hand, demanding the coins they owed. Every muscle ached to run, but I couldn't.

"*Bien sûr.*" Oil smacked his forehead in mock surprise. "*L'argent.*"

Toad shuffled forward and stood to my left, blocking my view of the wharf, and produced a grimy coin purse and handed it to Oil. I flinched. Where had Toad kept it?

Oil held the purse in an outstretched hand and the coins jingled inside. *This is what you're doing it for. Money for your family.*

Keeping my eyes on Oil's face, I reached for the bag.

Suddenly, he lunged, and before I could react, he grabbed my outstretched hand and yanked me toward him. I arched my back trying to keep my face away from his.

He pulled me close.

Stay calm. Don't make this worse. I desperately wanted to raise my knee and drop him to the docks, but that would have repercussions. I still had to do business with Oil and Toad. Until Stepmother said otherwise.

Oil's thumb rubbed the back of my hand. He purred deep in his throat. I pulled away, but I hit Toad's frame and jumped. When had he moved from the crate? The sharp tang of sweat rolled off Oil. His face inched forward. Panic squeezed my heart.

"*Je pense à toi,*" he said. "*Allons chez moi.*" His hot breath seared the skin on my neck.

Stay calm. A strangled cry withered in my throat. *If he does anything more, fight like the Great Beast himself.*

Oil chuckled once, then released both the money and my wrist.

Stepping backwards, I kept my hands by my sides, clutching the coin purse. My skin pricked with hot needles where he'd touched me.

"The oilskin, *crétin,*" I said, jamming my hands in my pockets.

Oil hummed softly to himself, his eyes raking over my face, down to my toes, and up again. I wanted to retch. And to thoroughly bathe in the hottest water Shar could provide.

Oil gestured to Toad, who shifted to the right. He pulled out an oilskin almost as dirty as himself and gave it to Oil. As Oil wrapped the paper in the oilskin, the sleeve of his left arm lifted, revealing a scar in the shape of a D. I bit down a gasp, my body suddenly cold. A brand. The mark of a deserter.

As if he read my thoughts, Oil moved closer. I stiffened. He reached out and touched the end of my braid.

"Maybe one day I'll show you the rest." He winked, then turned and walked down the wharf toward the docks, thankfully away from me. Toad followed him silently.

They clambered down the dock and into a boat. Soon only their angled silhouettes were visible as their slip pulled away from the docks, water splashing as their oars dug into the water.

Exhaling, I put my hands on my knees, my leg muscles shaking. Done. *It's over. They're gone.*

Shar exploded out from under my lapel, her light roiling a violent orange. "Are you all right?" She streaked around me, checking me from head to toe.

I nodded, looking at the dark sky. "I'm f-fine. I'm f-fine." My voice trembled, and I wanted to fly back to Lady Eline's. To Armand. To forget all this.

"Why do you put up with it?" Shar huffed. "He's a slimy, disgusting man, and that shadow of his is no better. Filth comes off of him in waves."

I shrugged again. It was the only thing I could do. I had to do this because I wasn't fast enough to save Papa. Because I should have restocked the pantry. Bought the celandine when I'd had the chance. Now I had to do everything I could to get us out of the mess I'd made. These meetings with Oil and Toad were simply part of my penance.

14

I stood in the middle of the crossroads leading to Lierre or back to the country. Ash covered my hands, the tips of my fingers a charcoal black. I gripped Lady Eline's shoes, now stained with soot.

But I'd only stolen one shoe. And he'd given it to me.

Someone coughed and I looked up. My heart dropped. What was happening?

Papa scowled at me, then he looked down at my hands clutching the shoes. "What have you done?"

I tried to explain, but my tongue swelled to fill my mouth. "I—I was trying to help."

He shook his head, angry and disappointed, and turned and walked away. Toward Lierre.

My heart seized in my chest. I threw the shoes down and raced after him. "Papa!"

He never looked back.

I ran until my lungs burned, but the road stretched away from me.

Something appeared in the distance. A figure.

"Papa."

The distance warped and closed.

Now I knew who it was, but I was moving too quickly to stop.

Oil's spindly arms trapped me in an embrace.

"Mon cher."

I screamed.

Something jabbed me in the back. Hard.

I bolted upright, the mattress creaking against my movement. My bedroom was painted in the dark purple of predawn. Stepmother hovered by my bed, a candle in her hand. She clasped her black wooden cane in the other, the silver raven atop seeming to shriek at me. She was already dressed, the edges of each pleat of her black skirt rigid and unmoving.

My heart slowed to a steady beat. Today, I was glad for training. The masque was less than two weeks away, and the more training I had, the smoother it would go. Plus, it would help chase away the haunting disappointment from Papa.

Stepmother said nothing—she didn't need to. I sat in bed, rubbing sleep from my eyes. Satisfied that I was indeed awake, she glided out of the room, her skirts rustling after her. Aimée stirred but remained asleep.

I dressed, the rough linen scratching against my skin.

I had met with Armand the last two nights—the small talk hadn't been completely terrible. But it was the meeting with Oil and Toad that concerned me. Shame at the memory crawled across my skin. Oil's rough hands pressing against my wrist. The stale odor wafting from his body.

The memory of the incident had been eating at me for two days. I needed to tell someone.

Tell Aimée. She'll listen.

We could come up with a way to deal with those two.

I moved toward Aimée, but a floorboard creaked upstairs and I stopped. The empty darkness beyond the bedchamber door beckoned me, warning me. Better not keep Stepmother waiting.

I pulled my hand back from Aimée, tucking my shame away. *Train now. Tell her later.* Perhaps Stepmother would be in a good enough mood and I could tell her.

Trailing my fingers along the carved paneling, I traced my way through the dark house to the attic, stopping at the warped threshold. The thin light was even weaker here. The door was ajar, and through the crack, I saw Stepmother sitting at the desk, the tortoiseshell lid of the jewelry box catching a thread of light. *She opened the box.* Stepmother held a silver something gently between her hands. The object was oddly shaped and small. It had a thick cream-colored handle and a silver top shaped like some sort of animal.

What is that? I inched forward—a floorboard creaked.

Stepmother slammed the tiny item back into the jewelry box, locking its lid. She grabbed her cane and stood in front of the desk, shielding any evidence the box had been touched at all.

"Enter," she said. Grasping the candle, she stalked to the center of the now web-less room, her cane thumping on the wooden floor. In the center of the room was a single dress-mannequin wearing the strangest training suit I'd ever seen—it was covered in tiny silver bells. A second candle rested on the floor beneath the mannequin, throwing twisted shadows onto the ceiling.

"I thought we'd already covered picking pockets," I said, entering the room.

"Covered, yes. Mastered, no."

Shame at disappointing Stepmother buried the hours of practice last week. I would do better. I had to.

I began to stretch, pulling my arm across my chest, hoping she'd see I was willing to work. Maybe if she saw how much I wanted to help, she'd listen about Oil and Toad.

I eyed Stepmother. *Just tell her.*

She arched an eyebrow. "Yes, Cinderella?"

"It's about Oil—I mean, Oliver." The words crashed against my teeth. "He t-touched me and—"

Stepmother folded her arms and raised her chin. "And this concerns me how?" Her face was as stony as the broken garden steps.

Embarrassment at bringing it up filled my chest. "N-never mind. I was mistaken."

She moved closer, the tightness around her eyes softening. She placed a hand on my shoulder and I nearly jumped. It had been so long since she'd shown me any kindness. "I know you do not enjoy the business with Theodore and Oliver any more than I do."

I found myself nodding.

"But they are a necessity forced upon us by—well, I don't think I have to say it again."

Guilt and shame bored into my chest. I shook my head.

"But this is our last job. People are nervous about Alemania. With our take from the masquerade, we won't have to worry, even if Lierre goes to war against Alemania. You understand, don't you?" Her voice swooped up sweetly, like someone talking to a small child.

Our last job. After, things could go back to the way they had been. We could be a family again. Safe and together. Hope flared in my heart. *Work hard. Save your family.*

"No more complaining about Oil and Toad."

I nodded, but a sour taste remained in my mouth. *Why did you think you could tell her? Tell Aimée.* She could make the dark feeling in my chest go away.

Stepmother walked over to the mannequin, once again all business. She pulled a key from the pocket and placed it in the mannequin's suit pocket. The bells jingled lightly.

"Retrieve the key. Silently."

I shook out my tingling hands, rubbing my fingers over my palm. *It's easy. You're doing this for Stepmother, for your family.*

I bit my lip and slid my hand into the pocket.

A jingling sound filled the room, signaling my failure.

Maybe if I was faster.

Jingle.

Not fast enough.

Jingle.

My fault.

Midmorning light filtered through the attic window when I gave up. "Show me."

Stepmother smiled, like a cat displaying its claws to a bird, and glided to the mannequin. "First two fingers only. Avoid using your thumb so it doesn't get caught on the pocket."

Facile. I should have seen it earlier. I reached in. Still silent. My fingertips brushed cold metal. Slowly I pulled out the key.

Stepmother took the key, her face expressionless, and replaced it in the suit pocket. "Again."

After I mastered the pocket, the sleeve, and the vest pocket, Stepmother finally took the key and placed it on her desk. "*La fin.*"

Curiosity recharged my muscles. We were done? We usually didn't end training until the evening.

"Clean yourself up and get Aimée. We're going to court today."

My eyebrows rose at the "we." As in, me too? To go to court in an actual dress like a real lady . . . could it be? My eyes scanned her face.

"The Grand Council is today."

I whooped and thumped the mannequin and all the bells jangled.

Stepmother backed away as if I were a puddle to avoid. She faced the fireplace, her voice still carrying through the empty attic. "We need another mark," she said matter-of-factly. "*M.* Bontour has served his purpose and poorly at that. Aimée knows how to not sound Alemanian, but she still looks it, and that may be a disadvantage very soon. We need to find another suitor sooner rather than later and move through them quickly. Our next job will be at the masquerade ball, and we need viable escape routes."

"You mean our last job."

Stepmother blinked.

"Our last job so we can go back to normal," I said.

"Yes, of course."

I glanced out the circular window. If I hurried, maybe I could tell Aimée about Oil and Toad while we got ready for court.

Excitement flooded my heart, pushing some of the fear from earlier aside. And I was going to the palace. As a lady and a guest!

Stepmother's face remained impassive, but her green eyes flashed impatiently. "We leave in twenty minutes." She thumped her cane and I raced down the stairs into the kitchen.

Aimée looked up from the cutting board. "What is it? Are the Garde Royale arresting you?"

Her fingers tightened fearfully around the knife she held and I knew then that I could never tell Aimée about Oil and Toad. I shoved all the skin-crawling feelings deep inside. She deserved better than my problems, and I would give her better. I'd make our day at the palace the best she'd ever had.

I plastered a smile on my face as I stepped into the kitchen. "No. We're going to court, and I get to come too."

Excitement bloomed in Aimée's eyes. She scrambled around the table, rattling bowls and silverware. She dragged me upstairs into our room, and after changing into a new pair of white gloves, grabbed dresses from the closet and held them up to me.

I laughed. "Oh yes, the white gloves really make the presentation of the dress more official."

"Never mind, you unfashionable hen."

I stuck out my tongue at her, then allowed a small giggle to escape, her excitement stoking mine. "Perhaps we'll see the gardens? Do you think we could see the map room?" My heart tripped at the thought. Papa had spoken of both so many times, of taking me to the palace. And now it was today.

"Later, later. The pertinent question is this." Fabric swished as she held up more dresses. "Do you prefer blue or green?"

15 ARMAND

Coming to the palace several hours before the Grand Council had done nothing but build my frustration. I rolled my shoulders and sucked in cold air, willing myself to relax. The palace weapons room tasted of metal and wood polish. I ran my hands over the various wooden and metal lances and sabers, eager to use one, to feel like I was doing something. A training session would release some stress. This place was as familiar to me as my own chambers. A place away from the courtiers and politics.

Despite the chilled air in the weapons room, the late morning sun would have heated the gravel-strewn fighting area. The warmth was enough to prevent muscles from becoming stiff, and the shade would be ideal for cooling down. The perfect time for sparring.

The red-tinged fae-image of one of Alemania's lances impaling a border patrolman flashed through my mind and fresh anger roiled in my stomach. I wrenched a saber from the wall and gripped the handle.

"Are you ready yet?" Luc strode into the weapons room and decisively picked a sword, twirling it in his hand. "Still trying to decide how you want to lose?"

"I got a message from Captain Reynaud." I swung the sword across my body. "There was another raid. Three men wounded. If Father d-doesn't investigate, more men will d-die." I raised my sword as if to parry an attack, my muscles taut with anger at Father's chosen ignorance. "If I don't stop this, then I'll be as c-culpable as the raiders."

"We both have suspicions against Sanson. What if this evidence is all for his gain?"

I hated that Luc had so easily voiced my own concerns. I clenched the hilt of the weapon. "F-Father will see. The entire C-Council will see." I turned to face Luc.

I pulled on the leather greaves and bracers. The long sturdy gloves were stiff but gained flexibility as I moved my fingers. I wanted to hide how desperate I was.

"Be careful, Armand."

"I'm always c-c-careful. You should watch yourself today. I need a good fight."

Luc laughed. "Just don't stab me in the back. Who will watch yours if I'm gone?"

I smiled ruefully. "There will be plenty of backstabbing in the Grand Council."

"See you out there."

I hefted the wooden practice saber—it could still deliver heinous welts and bruises. Just what I needed. After the Council, I'd dig deeper into Sanson. After Father finally listened.

I stepped from the weapons room onto the perimeter of the training yard. To my left, limestone steps led to a walkway circling the arena that was filled with dignitaries and courtiers during tournaments.

Taking a few steps farther into the arena, I looked up and stifled a groan. The ladies of the court lined the raised walkway like a swarm of jeweled butterflies. What were they doing here? They tittered and giggled as if at a *grande fête*. I quickly saw what had drawn their attention. Luc was sparring—with his shirt off.

"My, but the young prince is well trained," one young lady said, loud enough that she could be heard a courtyard over.

"Avert your eyes, Camilla. Where is your modesty?"

"Lying under the prince's shirt, I suppose."

The ladies barely stifled their laughter. Their properly demure expressions failed to conceal pink cheeks and wandering eyes.

"He would not flaunt himself if he did not want us to gaze upon his defined and . . . inviting assets. My dear, think of it like admiring an exquisite sculpture—in the flesh."

The tittering exploded and they waved their fans.

I rubbed the back of my neck and stared at the sand. Worst way to start training ever.

I stepped out from under the arch into full view. The noblewomen fell silent. Their skirts rustled in a vibrant synchronized curtsy.

I waited patiently at Master Battaglia's elbow until Luc, with a quick jab to his opponent's shoulder, was declared the victor. The ladies clapped enthusiastically and comments on Luc's physique rained down.

"Put your shirt back on," I said. "It's not d-decent."

Luc glanced down at his trim abdomen. His mouth formed an "oh" and his eyebrows rose in mock surprise. "By the Beast's beard, where did my shirt go?"

I rolled my eyes.

"Spar with me. Or are you afraid you'll be upstaged by your younger brother?"

Murmurs from the balcony swelled.

Luc's alternated flexing his pectorals. A murmur swept through the women.

"Upstaged b-by you?" I said in a low voice, not wanting my stutter to carry to the crowd. "I'll beat you soundly. I am the best." I gave a slight bow. "And I'll d-do it with my shirt on. F-first one to three?"

Luc nodded, readjusting his gloves.

We stood across from each other. Fine dust filled the hot air and sweat rose on my brow. We saluted each other, then fell into our stances, sabers at the ready.

I circled him, my muscles charged with energy. I lunged low, thrusting my sword.

He parried and I swung high. He blocked, then took a risky lunge and thrust, exposing his shoulder.

Ah, Luc's usual. I slashed high, whacking him on the back. *One for me.* A large red welt appeared almost instantly.

He lunged, swinging his sword. From the movement of his shoulders, I knew he was going to parry and then slash high. I raised my sword and smiled when a satisfying crack split across the yard.

Luc nodded, then fell into a complicated series of attacks. All my attention focused on his frame, trying to anticipate his next move. I swung and he ducked, bringing his sword across the ground.

Whack. Pain shot up my leg.

"Point for *Principe* Luc," Battaglia said.

"More than just a p-pretty face, I'll give you that," I said. I raised my sword and attacked with a cross-body sweep.

Our wooden sabers cracked, the blow ricocheting over the arena. A moment later Luc thrust, taking the opening while I dodged. I blocked his attack and returned with my own. Dust billowed from the ground as we circled each other, making the air hazy. Within a few more minutes, each of us had earned another point—Luc by hitting my leg and me by tapping his side. Tied.

I breathed heavily. Sweat dripped from my face. I fell into my stances like they were second nature. I pressed Luc in a smooth and steady offense, satisfied as his defense scattered, his face red and slick with sweat.

Let's see him try to dodge this. I swung and our swords crossed at the hilt and I pushed, driving Luc back several inches. *If I could just complete this move—*

"His Royal Majesty, King Henri," a voice from the balcony shouted.

Father, here?

Movement on the balcony caught my eye. Every courtier on the balcony dipped into deep bows, leaving Father and his shadow, *Général* Sanson, exposed like rocks in a sea.

My muscles stiffened and I lost my momentum. With a sudden burst of speed, Luc jabbed his saber point into my stomach. I groaned and doubled over.

I looked up to the balcony again. Father turned away, utter disdain on his face. Within moments, he had disappeared from the balcony.

Murmurs from the courtiers diminished as the crowd dispersed, the fight complete.

Luc came forward, grinning from ear to ear, and clapped me on the shoulder, oblivious that Father had made an appearance. "That was impressive footwork," he said, his breath coming heavily. "You had me several times. I thought I was done for."

"May I speak with you, Your Royal Majesty?" a voice behind me said.

I turned, my body cold despite the fight with Luc.

Général Marcel Sanson focused his dark eyes on me. Several of his uniform's highly polished decorations caught the morning light, and he practically preened. Along with Sanson's newest promotion had come a new stipend, one it seemed he had spent quickly, judging by the new Hessian boots. The *général's* mouth twisted and he gave a shallow bow.

"You brought the firelance?" It was more a statement than a question. His military medals clanged softly as he straightened. "Your father mentioned how anxious he was to see it."

All my anger from before the bout flooded through me. "I d-did." What was he playing at? He knew I was planning on it.

"By the by, how is tutoring? Must be tedious as *enfer* but it can't be all that hard." He smiled, showing more teeth than was necessary.

"Not t-too b-bad, thank you." My heart tripped as my stutter continued. Blast *M.* Parler. I was stuttering worse than ever.

"You're an inspiration to us all," he said, his eyebrows raising slightly. "I am looking forward to what you have to *say*." He bowed to me and then to Luc, the rings he was wearing glinting in the sun like scales on a serpent. "Until later."

"*À t-tout à l'heure.*" The muscles in my jaw pulled taut. *Soufre,* the Council was going to be embarrassing enough with my stutter, and Sanson was certainly up to something. I was walking into a trap, but I'd already announced the firelance and evidence to Father.

What I really needed was one of the Magpie's spice bombs.

Sanson turned on his heel and glided up the stairs. I glared at his retreating back until he disappeared from sight.

"I really don't like that man," I growled.

Luc wiped the dirt and sweat from his face with a towel, cocking an eyebrow. "Really? I find him rather charming." His sarcasm belied his light-hearted tone.

"I c-could have him executed." I took the proffered towel.

Luc shook his head and clapped a hand on my shoulder. "He's not worth the civil war."

ARMAND

16

Luc and I, now dressed in formal attire, walked into the council chamber, another one of Father's carefully crafted rooms. My lace cravat and high collars threatened to choke me. A lapel pin with the seal of Lyonelle glinted from my chest; Luc's stood out in stark contrast to his muted brown jacket. Thankfully he had replaced his shirt. Convincing Father of the evidence of firelances and its importance to Lyonelle's safety would be hard enough with everyone fully clothed.

Six lunette windows flanked the left side of the room. At the top of the rounded arch was a stained glass window depicting the different city-states that had been absorbed into Lyonelle after King Adam's curse had been broken and he had reclaimed his birthright.

Anger at past kings' oversights—and at Father's—rumbled in my chest. *Calm down, Armand. This is your chance to convince Father to listen. You've practiced for this moment. By the Beast's beard, you even have evidence.*

Generals, counselors, politicos, and diplomats stood in small groups around the room. Several people stopped their conversations to glance at me, then huddled closer together and whispered to each other.

I rolled my shoulders. That match with Luc had done nothing. A storm of stress roiled through me.

Father took his seat at the head of the massive rectangular table in the center of the room, and conversations stopped. Luc and I moved to stand behind Father—a son for either side.

The broken firelance Sanson had given me was resting in a box I had placed on the marble side table. The palace's blacksmith had confirmed the weapon hadn't been made in Lyonelle.

My heart pounded against my chest. This would work.

With medals clinking, *Général* Sanson sat to the immediate right of Father, coiled at his elbow—a place that, as the crown prince, I should have been granted. Feeling my gaze, Sanson turned and gave a smooth smirk.

I clenched my fists to stop myself from punching him.

The room filled with the sounds of people taking their seats. It felt like all eyes were on me. *Once you convince Father, all this will change.* I steadied my breath.

Father stood, formally welcoming everyone to the Grand Council. We started with the usual reports about education and the country's infrastructure. *M.* Ranier wanted to increase the production of books available to the public. *M.* Nadeau wanted to implement a different training program to help condition the new members of the military.

"We are concerned about His Royal Highness taking a holiday during this crucial time."

My jaw nearly dropped. On vacation? Who dared to accuse me of sloth?

M. Nadeau continued. "Trade with Alemania has dropped, but their costs on imports have risen. By almost double. It is more than concerning that the prince is absent. Especially with the upcoming ball."

Father steepled his fingers and leaned forward. "Your concerns are valid, *M.* Nadeau, however, Prince Hermann"—I cringed inwardly at my name—"is not on holiday. I would never allow my son such neglect."

I turned a fraction to Luc and raised an eyebrow. He gave a minute shrug in return. It was backhanded support, but I would take it.

My heart hammered in my chest. It was the perfect lead-in to the border raids.

"*Général* Sanson," Father said to the assembly as a whole, his voice filling the chamber. "Please begin your report on the border patrols."

State your position, clearly and quickly. Lives are at stake. I could do this. I had to.

"Father, b-before the *général* speaks, I have s-something to show the Grand Council."

Father's brow darkened, but he waved his hand for me to continue.

I pulled in a deep breath. I transferred the box to the council table, my heels clicking on the floor. I extracted the dark metal tube and placed it in front of Father. The bent pieces jutted out from the center, tilting it at odd angles. "This is an Alemanian firelance."

The Council members murmured.

Father turned it over in his hands.

Général Sanson shifted in his seat. "Your Highness—"

I moved to stand between Father and Sanson. "In a m-moment, *Général*," I said. He wasn't going to interrupt me.

Father's brows were pinched tighter as he examined the firelance, deep in thought. I clenched my fists behind my back, hanging on to my anxiety. He was considering this. I plowed on. "It was found by *Général* Sanson's men near a village close to the border—Ville de Mensonges. Near the remains of a campfire."

Murmurs surged around the table. As the conversation swelled, my chest expanded.

Sanson stood and smoothed his jacket, then fell into pacing behind me, probably to further bask in their praise. It rankled that he was gaining anything from this. *The important thing is they are listening, Armand. Father is listening.*

Behind my back, Sanson coughed into his hands. "Your Highness—"

"Not n-now, Sanson," I said, my tone almost a growl.

A few other members of the Council shifted uneasily, but I wasn't going to be distracted. I was so close. Father was going to listen to me. *Please let me speak clearly.* "This is the evidence we've been looking f-for."

Near-perfect speech. Hope rose in my chest.

Father looked, scrutinizing me, like he was seeing me for the first time. Finally he was listening.

"Prince Hermann—" Sanson's voice sliced through my thoughts.

Father looked away from me and down at the firelance again, the moment gone.

My nerves grated at Sanson's interruption and I whirled on him. "What is it, *Général?*"

"That," he said, pointing to the tube in Father's hands, "is not a firelance."

Whispers snaked around the council chamber.

Father set the firelance onto the table, its odd angles scratching the surface. "Then what is it?" he growled. He addressed Sanson but looked at me, the respect gone from his eyes.

Sanson stepped forward, not bothering to hide his obvious disdain for me, and picked up the tube. "It's the base of a musket. One of our own."

Anger boiled inside and I whirled on Sanson, my fists clenched.

Luc stepped from behind Father and held out his hands for the object. Sanson obliged, throwing me a smug glance.

Why was he doing this? He had given me this evidence himself.

Then it hit me like a ton of bricks. This was his trap—to make me look ten times the fool. Discredit and then depose me.

"Your Majesty," Sanson continued, turning to address the room. "This is my fault. I had given this to Prince Hermann."

As Father stood, his ornate carved chair scraped against the floor. He placed both palms flat against the table, his large frame all the more imposing. As if by mental command—or perhaps it was fear—each member of the Council sat straighter.

"Grand Council, I apologize for this sideshow." Father's deep tones resounded against the walls.

My chest tightened. "*Général*, you p-presented this to me."

Luc put the object back on the table, then returned to his place behind Father.

"Apologies, Your Highness," Sanson said, addressing me. "It was my mistake. I was too eager to find these so-called firelances." He paused, his expression contrite.

My gut roiled.

Murmured exchanges rumbled around the table. Several of the Council members folded their arms, glaring at me. Panic tightened my muscles. I was losing the battle, but this wasn't over. Even though there were lots of people talking, Father still looked at me. He was still listening. Perhaps I could still salvage this.

Général Sanson turned to address the chamber once more. "After some investigation, I discovered that this was only a broken musket of one of our own. This, however"—he waved and a manservant came forward—"is the *rose authentique.*"

I broke eye contact with Father to stare at the object.

The footman carried an oblong box the length of my arm. He placed it on the table, and Sanson opened it, revealing a long wooden shaft. At the end of the shaft was a metal tube, similar to the one Sanson had presented me but wider and thicker. It had an entry point for a wick. The Alemanian emblem—two crossed swords over a star—and the word "Gerechtigkeit" were etched along the tube. *Justice.*

This was wrong. Everything about the weapon felt wrong, but I couldn't put my finger on it.

Sanson stood and bowed gracefully to the assembly. "Despite the prince's—*ahem*—false claims, this is a true firelance."

Sharp remarks swept through the Council, bouncing off the walls.

I turned back to Father. He watched me like a lion deciding if its next meal was worth the effort. Sweat dampened my palms. *Please,* I mentally threw at him, knowing it would change nothing. *Father, please.*

"Your Royal Majesty, I also have more distressing news," Sanson said. "In the last few weeks, there were reports of deaths among the patrols." He placed a hand on his chest.

Father stood. Sanson's features contorted into a grimace in a show of false concern Father seemed unable to detect.

"Deaths?" Father said, his voice rasping and guttural. His eyes flicked to Sanson then back to mine.

Sanson's face twisted, his eyes tight. "Yes, sire. Burns and . . ." He paused, lowering his voice slightly. ". . . pieces of flesh ripped away. We know now, it is these new firelances."

My skin crawled. I stared at the weapon on the table. These weapons were even worse than I'd thought. The room buzzed. Father spoke, and everyone quieted.

"How many dead?" He asked Sanson, but his eyes bored into mine.

"Seven, sire."

Seven? There were only twenty-four in a border patrol regiment. My head swam. The room exploded into small conversations, each growing louder than the last.

In the chaos, Sanson's features twisted into a small smirk. Every muscle in my body snapped, jolting me into action.

I stepped toward Sanson. "Why wasn't I informed?"

The room quieted, and I could feel Father's eyes on me once more.

Luc leaned around me and pointed a finger at Sanson. "As His Royal Highness is head of the military, you should have reported this directly to him."

Sanson lowered his head, and I pressed my fists to my sides so I didn't punch him.

"My deepest apologies. I did send word to the estate, but it is so far removed from our capital, I'm sure it was delayed."

Lady Eline's was only a thirty-minute carriage ride. Twenty or less at a full gallop.

The Council erupted in more and more heated exchanges. Snatches reached my ears.

"The prince is too removed."

"What is he hiding?"

"Why is the king so trusting of his son?"

As this last comment rose to the surface, I turned to Father. His eyes drilled into mine, but this time he broke his gaze fully and then turned to address the room. A dark silence descended.

"So," Father said. "Alemania has been building new weapons. And using them, apparently."

Sanson nodded. "I know the duties of border patrol fall under the authority of Prince Hermann, but I felt this matter could not wait."

Father turned his gaze to me, his face red, jaw clenched.

My heart stopped. *Soufre,* this was bad.

"Did you know of these firelances?" he asked coldly, quietly.

I glanced at *Général* Sanson. His mouth turned upward slightly. Resentment and jealousy exploded inside me. That snake. This was what he'd been waiting for. For Father to publicly turn on me—his own flesh and blood. This wasn't a trap—it was an ambush.

"Well?" Father's snarl echoed around the chamber.

My resentment at Sanson retreated in the face of Father's anger, and a cold shame burned through me. Though I'd incurred his displeasure and disappointment on more than one occasion, Father had never condemned me in public. Had Sanson gained so much of his confidence that I was irredeemable? I swallowed as another thought occurred to me: Father was so disappointed in me that he no longer cared about the reflection I gave. Father's concern for his respect was my last form of defense against his attacks.

"Did you know of these weapons and attacks?" he asked again.

The vision from the orchard flashed in my mind. Of *Général* Sanson in the woods with a garrison of Lyonelle's border patrol. This must be what the vision meant—that Alemanian troops were attacking Lyonelle's.

"Y-yes."

Out of the corner of my eye, Sanson stood, his arms tight by his sides, looking as indignant as the other diplomats. "You knew?" he hissed.

Everyone's eyes were on me, waiting. Shame and anger at myself burned through me. I nodded slowly. I had known. And I hadn't said anything. At least, not well enough that Father took me seriously. I'd tried. But I could have tried harder. *He who goes well in his own skin goes well with everyone.* The proverb prowled in my mind. I felt less like myself than I ever had before.

"Why is this being brought to my attention now?" Father said, his voice rumbling.

"I t-t-tried t-to." My mouth flopped open and closed like a dying fish, horrible clicking noises coming from my esophagus. "Weeks ago. Y-you d-didn't l-listen."

Général Sanson leaned in closer, whispering, "Looks like the m-match goes to m-me."

"Failure," Father hissed, his words echoing through the room. If he heard the *général*'s words, he didn't seem to care.

"You w-wouldn't listen—"

"Father," Luc said, but he was silenced with a look.

A royal finger pointed at me, then to Sanson. "Listen and learn," Father said. He then gestured to Sanson to continue.

"Several of my sources tell me these firelances are single-shot weapons that can cause moderate to severe damage. They can also be used from a great distance."

Father turned to Sanson. "Are your sources reputable?"

Sanson shrugged, then shook his head. "No, not reputable. But they have nothing to lose so they're as reliable as we're going to get."

The king nodded his approval to Sanson—approval that should have been mine.

I cleared my throat, hoping that my words would be clear too. "You accept the word of g-gamblers and drunks over the word of a p-prince. I have spoken of this before, Father."

Remember.

"You have nothing to say," Father spat. "Drunken ramblings are better than the stupid stutter of royalty."

Each word rained down on me. Anger at his inability to listen to the truth churned inside me. It burned like a red sun, radiating outwards. I clenched my fist so tight my fingers ached.

"I brought you information regarding this situation w-weeks ago. When the deaths might have been p-prevented."

Father thumped his fist on the table. "If you had this information, you should have fought to bring it to light."

A member of the Council shifted in his seat. Luc stood statue-like near the table, a solemn expression on his face.

I hated that this conversation had an audience, that I might have to expose my wounds more, but I was backed against a wall.

"I shouldn't have to fight for your attention. You are my father. You should listen based on that f-fact alone."

"I have listened," he said. "The words you speak confirm you are a mere shadow of the man you should be." Father jabbed his finger in my face. "These deaths are on you." A growl grew in his chest and he waved his hand dismissively. "You'll soon be married, and hopefully you'll produce an heir with some sense in his brain. Then your child will inherit, and I won't be forced to leave this kingdom in the hands of the village idiot."

Shame and fury burned from my face to my feet. I hadn't stuttered at all on the most important truth: he was my father. But that fact hardly mattered to him.

The eyes of the Grand Council bored into me, condemning me.

Luc's eyes were full of frustration, reflecting my own. He nodded slightly at me, then glanced at Sanson, then back to me. This wasn't over yet.

"Yes, you are my son." Father spat the last word. "Thank you, Hermann, for the familial reminder." His voice was smooth on the surface, but his tone belied his true feelings. And it was still projecting perfectly for the entire Council to hear. "Now allow me to remind you of your marriage."

"M-marriage?" I barely kept my voice from cracking from rage. *Soufre.* I shouldn't have been surprised that Father would finish our dispute with a final attack. Crushing defeat was always his tactical approach.

Sanson coughed into his hands.

Father's eyes were hard. "Yes, the masquerade ball. You will announce your engagement."

Between Father's continued dismissals, Sanson's subterfuge, and now Father's open disdain, my head felt like it was being battered against the rocks in the harbor. I hung on to my anger, hoping it would pull me out of this storm.

Father called over his shoulder for Ambassador Layette, who scurried to him and then returned to his seat. Father thrust a paper into my chest. "Choose from this list. These are domestic brides. This will show Lyonelle's strength from within."

I looked at it, drowning in a sea of names. Madeline DuBois, Phillipa Paselle, the Manette daughters, Lady Abigail Forcené. Who were these people? I clenched my jaw to prevent it from falling on the floor. I should have more of a say in the matter. My mind raced to catch up.

"Plus, a wife from Lyonelle will save you the trouble of learning another language. You can barely speak your own," Father said, his voice shredding my remaining defenses. "You have failed abysmally today. You have three days to redeem yourself." He gave me a small wave of his hand. With a final glare, he went back to addressing the Grand Council, who were heatedly discussing the firelance.

I gave a shallow bow at his back.

Marriage in three days?

Father could sink his own ship. I'd have no part of it.

Turning, I strode toward the gardens, the list fluttering in my clenched fist.

ism. 17 cyn

As I swished toward the hired carriage, the coachman tipped his hat. I flexed my fingers, trying to stop the tingles in my palm. Today was going to be everything I wanted it to be. Everything Papa had wanted to show me. The palace, the gardens. We'd be near the imperial marketplace. My blood pumped fast at the thought.

As I climbed into the carriage, gravel crunched underfoot and my skirts rustled. I sat opposite Stepmother and squeezed next to Aimée. Light warmed the carriage and I couldn't contain the smile on my face. But when I saw Stepmother's icy features, I settled into my seat quietly, readjusting the fabric hanging off my shoulders.

"The tension with Alemania gives us no room for unprofitable arrangements," Stepmother said to Aimée, who stared out the window and sniffled quietly. "*M. Bontour est fini.*"

The carriage lurched forward.

Stepmother whirled on me. "Where are your tools?"

I gulped and I tapped my sleeve. "Always prepared." I didn't mention the chess piece I'd shoved in my bodice. Just in case we ran into Luc, although that sounded less likely now.

Stepmother nodded, then turned to the window.

Aimée sniffed, clenching her gloved hands in her lap. Luc had given her the striking cornflower-blue gloves only this morning and they perfectly matched her eyes. Someone had been paying attention.

Landscapes rolled past the window. I tugged at a loose thread on the bottom of my bodice. I partially agreed with Stepmother, but if Aimée and Luc loved each other and got engaged, would it be so bad?

Stepmother's features hardened as we rolled over the bumpy road.

The fields gave way to small tenement houses basking in the autumn sun. A few wild rose brambles lined the road.

Say something, Cyn.

I gave a tiny cough. "Papa said there are over twenty-three varieties of flowers in the palace garden."

Aimée stared out the window, her round shoulders hunched inward.

"He actually brought a new species to Lyonelle. Gifted it to the palace. Do you remember, Stepmother?"

"What did he name it?" Aimée asked, quietly.

Stepmother looked far into the distance, her features softening. This was closer to the woman I remembered meeting when Papa first brought her to the Manette Manor. The black mourning accents on her dove-gray dress no longer seemed harsh. Her eyes caught mine and they were sad and lonely, like mine. I turned my head away, my throat constricting painfully.

"He named it *Tranquillité*. He said it smelled like coming home."

My heels dug into the floor of the carriage. I heard a sniff that could have come from Stepmother, but I kept my eyes trained on the landscape, giving all of us time to once again form protective exteriors.

My excitement at seeing the gardens bubbled to the surface, pushing away the cloud in the carriage. I was going to see the gardens. Find *Tranquillité*. My chest warmed at the thought.

Gradually, houses disappeared and more estates crowded the scenery. Closer to town, shops sprouted from the ground level and the streets narrowed. My heart pressed against my chest. *Almost there.*

After an eternity, the carriage arrived at the palace grounds, the imposing outer brown-and-gray stone wall giving way to a small entrance with guards posted on either side. The driver pulled the carriage in a large circle and then stopped.

My jaw dropped. Our whole estate could fit inside this outer courtyard with room to spare. The inner courtyard must be absolutely expansive. We exited the carriage and the cacophony of the bustling outer courtyard increased. The smells of sunshine and dirt mingled with the horses and leather from the carriage.

"Just wait until you see the inside the palace," Aimée said, pulling me along as I gaped. "The ceiling is covered with paintings of Lyonelle's history and the imperial rose motif is everywhere. The king even has a room full of mirrors."

My skirts rustled as I turned. "Mirrors? So he can look at himself?"

Aimée laughed musically. "Of course not. It's for the sheer audacity of having that many mirrors."

Here I was, thieving to help keep my family alive, and the king had rooms of mirrors for the sake of his vanity.

To the left was the marketplace, and I smiled as the comfortable clamor embraced me. The hours Papa and I had spent here. There was the fabric merchant just where she'd always been, colorful swatches waving in the breeze. Cries of "Pepper!" and "Cinnamon!" crashed against the walls. If I remembered correctly, there was a stall around the corner that sold spicy lion-cakes with candied almonds for claws—Papa's and my favorite.

No more, Cyn. You're here to enjoy your day.

I blinked hard, then linked arms with Aimée. "Show me everything."

Stepmother cut in front of us, blocking our path. Both hands rested atop the raven's head. "Aimée, with me. You," she said, looking at me, "practice."

"You want me to pick locks in the palace?"

Stepmother shifted, gravel crunching under her heel. "Not locks. Pockets. And certainly not in the palace. The market will suffice."

I looked to Aimée in confusion, then back to Stepmother. This couldn't be happening. Maybe this was a test?

"I've had plenty of pocket practice this morning with the mannequin." I was whining, but I couldn't help it. I was one hundred feet away from the palace gardens. "I even brought my lock set. Perhaps I could—"

Venom seeped through Stepmother's eyes, and I knew.

"Yes, Stepmother," I mumbled.

"And find at least three conceivable exit strategies from the palace into the market or outer yard," she said.

My shoulders slumped and I worked a pebble loose from the packed dirt.

Stepmother and Aimée crossed the street, dust swirling in their wake.

"Sorry," Aimée mouthed. Before they disappeared into the palace, she threw a sad backward glance at me. Then they were swallowed by the arched gate.

I ground my threadbare slippers into the hole from the pebble. My nostrils flared, anger burning my blood, and I shook my head. *Petite bêtes!* No. Not today. I would see a beastly imperial rose whether Stepmother liked it or not.

But how to get in? My eyes darted over the walls and gateway. No, not there. Too many guards and I might run into Stepmother. But what about over the wall? A large exotic-looking tree with dense foliage covered the top of the barrier, half of its branches hanging over the palace wall.

A merchant selling woven baskets stood outside his store. I wandered over, running a finger over the thick strands of braided grasses. The man smiled at me, watching me for a potential purchase, but hung back. I nodded at him but continued to move along the edges of his store, showing casual interest. I turned to leave his shop, but not before noticing his shop's lovely and perfectly situated balcony that almost reached the tree in the king's garden. I smiled—perfect. And with the clamor of the marketplace, I could do almost anything and no one would notice.

I'll go picking—just not pockets.

Moments later, I stepped onto the balcony and a patch of green grass beckoned from over the wall. Though the tree blocked some of my view of the garden, no one seemed to be in it. I smiled. This was almost too easy.

Carefully, I eased myself over the wooden railing, my billowing skirts snagging on every splinter. *Robe stupide.* At least Shar had spelled it with the anti-dirt charm. Where were ugly masculine pants when you needed them? The railing creaked louder, and the balcony seemed higher off the ground than before, making the twenty feet seem like fifty. *Please hold. Shar will kill me if I die.*

I looked at the market. Business as usual. It was now or never. My heart fluttered in excitement as I took careful aim and leaped.
Then I fell.

18 CYN

last these skirts. Their weight dragged me through the air. One foot landed on the top of the palace's wall, and a jolt of pain shot up my leg. The other leg trailed behind and for a moment, I balanced like a high-wire walker.

A gust of wind pushed me toward the garden. Yards of fabric tangled in my legs and I teetered backwards, my arms flailing. I leaned forward, pulling with my gut. The tree blocked most of my view, but I saw the garden on the other side with neat hedges and a sprawling lawn. The wall, which now seemed much higher than I'd thought, promised me a broken leg—at least if I fell.

I swallowed. *Just don't fall.*

Then I overcorrected and fell forward, over the wall into the garden. I caught hold of a branch and pain shot up my arms. I bit back a scream.

The bark dug into my palms and I hung like a *Noël d'hiver* bauble. I gritted my teeth, scanning the garden for anyone who might have seen me. Empty.

I loosened my grip on the knobby branch, preparing to drop to the grass. I froze. Beneath me wasn't ground—it was water. An ornamental pond, surrounded by large flagstones and previously blocked by the tree, shimmered merrily in the afternoon sun.

The fabric on my dress cut into my shoulders. I looked at the trunk of the tree and my stomach fell. *Petite bêtes!* The beastly tree's gray roots pressed deep through the water like thick fingers. If I shimmied to the trunk, I'd be worse off than I was now.

An inquisitive duck paddled from under the roots and quacked.

Could I swing to dry land? Not unless I could launch myself fifteen feet.

I kicked my legs up so I could re-grip the branch. My fingers ached. My hands were sweaty and the branch was too wide—I couldn't hang on much longer. I'd have to try it. *Curses.* My dress would get wet and filthy, and there was no way I could hide that from Stepmother. I walked my hands as close to the farthest tip of the branch as I dared, swinging my legs.

One.

Please work.

Two.

Please, please, please.

Three.

I let go and closed my eyes. The air rushed past my face, and I waited for the inevitable splash.

Nothing.

No splash. And my feet were still dry.

I cracked one eye open. The embankment was still four feet away. I looked down. The skirt of my dress poofed out in a perfect bell, creating small ripples in the pond.

The mallard quacked in indignation.

I pressed my hands against my skirts. The silk was completely rigid. What in the blazes was going on? Then it hit me like the edge of the wall—Shar's anti-dirt charm. It was repelling the dirt from the murky pond, but it was doing it so well, I was floating like some ridiculous water lily.

"Beasties." I pushed a tendril of hair out of my face. How could I have been so shortsighted? I'd completely forgotten how close it was to the autumnal equinox. Her spells always went sideways before the equinox.

If I could reach something, maybe I could pull myself to shore. I looked around, spinning. Nothing.

Parfait. Now what? I had to get out of here before someone saw me. It would be very difficult to explain how I was set adrift on the royal pond and avoid being arrested for trespassing.

I rocked my body, using my momentum to get closer to land. One side of my dress dipped an inch in the water, then bounced to the surface. No. Perhaps I could use my toes and paddle to the edge. My knuckles turned white as I reached with my toes and kicked. They barely touched the water. I merely bobbed up and down, tiny waves rippling in the pond.

"Argh. No, no, no."

The duck quacked once more, swam to the edge, and waddled out of the water, slipping between two large rocks. I glared. He made it look so easy.

At least I could rule out "over the western garden wall" as a masquerade escape strategy.

I studied the tree. Maybe I could pull myself back up. I stretched, pressing against the stiff dress, when suddenly a tall figure burst from the palace. I jumped, sending more ripples through the pond.

The young man stormed into the bright sunshine, then squinted at the change in light. I froze. *Please don't look up.*

His angled jaw clenched and his nostrils flared. He stalked across the lawn as if he had chewed Papa's spiciest peppercorns, and he pushed his hands through his dark wavy hair.

Wait a Lierran minute. I knew that hair. But he said he was staying at Lady Eline's!

Armand paced the garden, muttering under his breath, completely unaware of the preposterous water lily floating not twenty feet from him.

My lips tightened and I glared at him. I needed Armand about as much as I needed a visit from the Garde Royale. Could this day get any worse?

I felt as exposed as a deer in a meadow, but I forced myself to remain still. *Don't turn*, I begged, but my heart sank as he stopped mid-stride.

I fluffed my beastly off-the-shoulder sleeves, then, clasping my hands, I smiled as alluringly as I could and batted my eyes, waiting for him to make his move.

ARMAND 19

A stream of curses against Father, the Council, and Sanson was raging through my head when something blue flashed in the corner of my eye.

I stopped in my tracks. I wasn't alone. My anger roiled. I simply wanted to be left alone.

I folded Father's ridiculous list and shoved it into my vest pocket, then I turned. *Confront them as royally as you can. They'll run away and you can have peace and quiet.*

When I saw who was wearing the blue and where they were standing, I blinked, flabbergasted.

A beautiful brunette with glowing olive skin stood on the water. The hem of her bell-shaped dress rested on the surface. She clasped her hands in front of her, and her sharp green eyes pierced me. My breath caught in my throat at her fierce beauty.

I shook my head. *No.* Alluring or not, she had to leave.

I moved forward, stopping where the grass met the rocks.

The woman pushed a tendril of hair from her face—that motion triggered something. *Who is she?*

We spoke at the same time.

"*M-mademoiselle,* as your s-sovrei—"

"When you're done—"

My words died in my mouth. It couldn't be.

She smiled, mischief playing at the corner of her mouth. "When you're done admiring, I could use some assistance." She lifted her hand.

Her voice was a slap to my face. There was only one person who could get herself into such a laughable situation and still act like a queen.

The muscles in my neck coiled. Fate must be mocking me. First Father, then Sanson, then the debacle at the Grand Council, and now this. I wanted solitude, not to discover a notorious thief stealing from the palace.

"Hello, M-Magpie." I'd have to get her out of the castle before someone arrested her. Though, in her current court dress, no one would take her for a criminal. "What were you g-going to steal from the p-pond?"

Her eyebrows shot upward, her smooth skin paling. She played with the trim on her bodice. "Me, the Magpie?"

I folded my arms and tilted my head. "You can change your d-dress as much as you like, b-but you'll never change your saucy mouth."

The Magpie's lips pinched together and something fluttered in my stomach. Blast. Why did she have to be so beautiful? Anger from the day's events fueled an irrational feeling of betrayal by her beauty. I rolled my shoulders, the muscles pinching a nerve. She was supposed to be the person I talked to at Lady Eline's. My cure. Who was this woman? Lady or thief?

How long would it be before she dismissed me like everyone else?

Perhaps she was a spy sent from Father. It made for an elaborate espionage plot, but I wouldn't put it past him. Or perhaps she was like the other courtiers, deceiving me for their personal gain.

She huffed. "Fine, I'll help myself." She reached up, straining for the branch, but it was still two feet above her head.

She quickly abandoned the branch and made swimming motions with her arms. Ripples radiated from her futile attempts and lapped at the rocks along the edges of the pond.

I snorted. If this woman was a spy, I was my father's favorite son.

A duck waddled from behind me, then settled on a rock as if at the theater. Stupid duck.

Fiery darts flew from the Magpie's eyes. "Are you going to help me or not?" If she were on the ground, she would be tapping her toes.

I narrowed my eyes. "You are the most s-stubborn thief I have ever m-met."

"I'm the only thief you've ever met."

By the Beast's beard. I rolled my shoulders back, then stormed away.

"He's leaving." Her strident tones pelted my back. "Of course."

Leaving would be so much easier. I searched under the hedges and found a small branch the gardeners had missed. As I returned, her features softened. I placed one foot against a medium-sized rock for support. I doubted my day could get any worse.

I sighed and held out the stick. "Here."

She leaned forward and grasped it. She started to lose her balance, threw her arms out, and knocked the stick into the pond. Water sprayed everywhere, and an impressive string of salty curses followed.

Inching my foot out as far as it could go, I lifted the dripping stick again and fully extended my arm. Her hands darted forward, grabbing the branch.

I pulled—she yanked.

Soufre! Her skirt still stuck to the pond's surface. Her torso shot forward and she bent in half. The momentum made everything worse. I knew what was going to happen. She was going to fall over and get a face full of ornamental river rocks. She tipped forward and let go of the branch, her arms flailing.

My heart flipped in my chest.

"I've got you." I dropped the stick and lunged forward onto the rocks with outstretched arms. One boot stepped into the pond, water spilling into it. I caught her and leaned back, pulling both her and myself onto the bank. I twisted, shielding her from the rocks, and we rolled onto the lawn. A rock jabbed into my back and I cracked my elbow against another one. Pain shot up my arm. I landed flat on my back, gasping for air.

As her bell-skirt deflated, blue fabric billowed everywhere. Her weight pressed me into the wet grass.

I lifted my head to check that she was all right but saw only cleavage. I jerked my head away, staring at the duck on its pond rock. "Um . . . oh . . . are you . . . er . . . injured?" I removed my hands from her torso.

She twisted back and forth, trying to get up, but whatever she was doing wasn't working. My neck flared with heat, and she let off another volley of curses.

When I tried to help again, I got another eyeful of bosom. I swallowed and averted my eyes. Our bodies seemed to be touching everywhere. "C-can you get up? This is . . . um . . . in-indec-indecorous."

The duck tilted its head and quacked.

Her head thudded against my chest. "I'm stuck," her muffled voice came from within my jacket. Her warm breath passed through my shirt onto my skin. The smell of cinnamon mixed with the mud. Her chest pressed against mine with each breath. *Soufre, help me!*

"Wh-what seems to be the p-problem?" I looked everywhere except at her.

The duck hopped off its rock and waddled closer.

"The embroidery on my dress is stuck on several of your buttons." She huffed. "But I can't undo them when we're squished together."

The duck tilted its head, then nibbled at the grass.

"I think I c-can help," I said calmly. "I'm g-going to hold you up, then you can undo the b-buttons."

"Fine."

While staring at the duck, I slowly lowered my hands and placed them where I thought her shoulders would be.

My fingers brushed soft, warm skin.

"Watch where you put those hands!"

I pulled them away, cracking my elbow on another rock.

"This is a rescue mission, not an expedition."

"I c-can't." I clenched my teeth. This was more difficult than it looked. Once more, I moved my hands to her shoulders. As I felt their soft curve, my mouth dried. Strong ungentlemanly urges flooded my body. I pressed against her shoulders and raised her torso away from mine, my elbows digging into the grass. Her fingers worked at my jacket.

Soufre. Hurry, woman.

I felt a tug and the tension on my jacket loosened. "*La victoire!*" An explosion of rustling blue fabric followed her words.

The duck fled in a flurry of feathers, quacking indignantly.

She brushed off her skirts. Her hair was a mess. I followed suit. Several buttons on my jacket were looser than before, but other than that, we were relatively unscathed. She clicked her tongue at a torn ruffle on her sleeve. I grimaced. No doubt I'd be blamed for the tear. And everything else.

She stalked over to me. I braced myself for the verbal lashing.

"Thank you." Her voice was . . . not mad.

I pulled back, some of my internal tension deflating. "You're w-welcome." I tugged my jacket down and gave a small bow.

She unpinned her hair and it cascaded down her bare shoulders. I tried not to stare at it—or other things.

Tiny flecks of mud sprinkled her cheeks in a bad imitation of freckles, and I resisted the urge to wipe them away. "Here," I said, handing her my handkerchief.

She dabbed at her face, then returned it. With a deft hand, she tucked the end of the torn ruffle into her sleeve, effectively hiding the tear.

"Out of curiosity, how were you floating?" I asked, dusting my pants. *Blast.* A large stain covered both knees on my breeches.

"Shar," she said, talking around the pins in her mouth. She pulled her hair back and then did something with her hands and the pins. In moments her hair was up again as if nothing had happened. "Her charm went sideways but at least I'm not dirty." She frowned when she saw the stain on my pants. She grabbed my shoulders and pulled me close, warmth from her hands. I swallowed, nearly choking on my saliva. "Hmm, maybe we're not close enough."

My throat grew tight as she stepped so close I could see brown feathering along the edges of her deep green eyes.

"Yes, you see?" She pointed to my knees. I looked down. The edges of the stain were fading. "Here." She placed her hands on my hips and twisted my torso until we were lined up as if we were about to dance the Alemanian waltz. Particles of dirt lifted from the fabric. "There," she said, and we both straightened, looked at each other, then froze.

I hadn't realized how close she'd moved, but now that she was a few inches away, a strange feeling flooded my chest. Every nerve aligned itself to her, just like it had when we'd danced the bolero. The memory of her so close, her legs touching mine.

No, Armand. Focus on your pants. On the stain.

A speck of mud remained on her cheek. *Do not brush it away, Armand.*

"It's very nice fabric. Shiangsu silk?"

"M-maybe." *What the flames do I know about fabric?*

The awkwardness stretched thin.

"Now we're even." She backed away and dipped a curtsy, the grass bending away from the bespelled hem of her dress. "Thank you for the rescue."

The Magpie turned to go, and I grabbed her hand. She tilted her head and lifted her brows expectantly.

"I w-want to talk to you." With my other hand, I pressed my fingers against my thumb as all the frustration and complications about Father and the Grand Council jammed inside my brain. Perhaps if I had someone to talk to. Someone who would listen. "P-please stay."

A smile played at her lips. She took my arm. For some reason, this small action felt like a huge leap.

We strolled away from the palace, our feet crunching on the gravel-strewn path. She said nothing but allowed me to lead our conversation, and soon everything—Sanson's deceit, Father's dismissal—came stuttering out. Everything except specific names. Like mine.

"And now my f-father won't listen to my . . . b-business plans." We turned along a path to the right, underneath an arched rose bower.

Shadows danced across her face. "Papa dealt with several people of that ilk. He is your father. He'll come around."

I snorted. *Not likely.*

After the bower, the sun dazzled and we passed a large golden statue of a stag and hart, then turned right along a rose hedge.

"Does your father only trade in t-textiles?"

My tongue swelled. "T-t-textiles?"

"Your father. Here for the Grand Council's domestic business portion. What else does he trade in?"

My steps slowed. In a certain shade of light, Father was a merchant of all trades. I couldn't tell her who I really was. If she knew, she'd disappear and I'd never see her again, and I didn't want to lose the small bit of trust we'd gained. "He t-trades in this and that."

"Well, I highly doubt that a merchant's business is of national importance," she said.

You'd be surprised.

I guided her to the other ornamental bridge. My skin tingled from the warmth of her hand resting upon my arm. "What d-does your father d-do?"

Her face darkened. "He's dead."

The gravel crunched in the silence.

I pulled her arm close, wrapping her hand in mine. A strong desire to protect her surged through me.

Two courtiers were talking along the path ahead. I pulled us into an enclosed grotto on our right. A sculpture of a sleeping griffin was carved into the rock. Weeping willows shaded a stone bench. I led her to sit and she settled on it, immediately picking at her dress.

She was shrinking in on herself, as if she were hiding from something. A place in my chest tightened. I had to help her somehow.

I paced to the griffin, running my fingers over the carved wings. *Cheer her up, Armand. Now.* The title of the sculpture and the artist's name were emblazoned on a metal plaque below the griffin's paws. *Voila*—I couldn't believe it hadn't hit me before. I turned toward her.

"I d-don't know your n-name."

She lifted her head. "My name? To you, *Mademoiselle* Magpie." Light broke through the dark clouds on her features.

I nodded and sat beside her. "That is only your s-stage name. Who is the woman behind the p-persona?"

Her eyes reignited with that impish spark and she pursed her lips. Those tiny expressions made my whole world condense. "I'm narrow-minded, selfish, and prickly as a holly bush."

Her tone was most certainly prickly, though it was more like a porcupine with its quills raised protectively. Why did I feel like this was a test?

I nodded. "Let's t-trade. If I c-can get you to smile, you tell me your n-name." I leaned back on the bench and tapped a finger against my chin. "R-Rumpelstiltskin? No, I'm only joking." She scowled and I held up my hands as I took in her beautiful features. "Perhaps you're Alemanian. Is it Aschenputtel?"

She wrinkled her nose and shook her head, but her posture straightened and she turned toward me. *Keep going, Armand.* Her skirts pressed against the side of my leg.

I rubbed my chin. "Perhaps T-Tivolan. Pentamerone?"

"Beasties, no." She pushed me playfully with her shoulder and leaned closer. Only a few inches remained between us on the bench.

"Aha. Cendrillon. You are Swizzeran, no?" She rolled her eyes and I took a deep breath. "Fabienne, G-Gertrude, Hebsiba, P-Parisa—"

"Stop. I'll tell you if you just stop," she said, holding up a hand and rewarding me with a radiant smile.

"Point goes to m-me, *Mademoiselle* Thief."

Her features softened, her mouth drawing up as her chin dipped lower, her cheeks rosy with a most becoming blush. "You were close. It's Cinderella." Her tone sounded as if a weight had been removed from her shoulders.

Cinderella. Magnifique.

"By the way, what were you d-doing in the middle of the p-pond? Not going to steal much there," I teased. "That's why you're here, isn't it?"

She paused, looking into my eyes, making sure I knew she was serious about her next statement. "I came to see an imperial rose. Papa promised . . ." A shadow flickered across her face. "I've always wanted to see one."

The need to help her swelled in my chest with such force I nearly choked when I spoke. "The rose g-gardens are off limits while my mo—until the m-masquerade." I hoped she took the slip about my mother as part of my stutter. "You actually c-climbed into the only remaining free patch."

She wilted visibly. We completed our loop of the garden and I saw the entrance to the palace. I'd come to the garden seeking solitude, but instead, I'd found something better—someone to talk to. And it had helped, sharing some of the load.

As we crossed back to the pond and its embankment of near-disaster, I spotted something in the grass. While I stooped to examine it, Cinderella continued onward for a few paces. The familiar chess piece poked out of the grass. What was Luc's king doing in the garden? Luc had been gone all day. There was only one other place it could have come from. But how had Cinderella gotten it? I stood, placing the king in my jacket pocket.

"So you pick pockets? What else do you do—fly?"

"Would you like to help me?"

"F-fly?"

"No, help me practice."

The words jumped out of my mouth. "Yes." *Practice witchcraft perhaps*—because that's exactly what this felt like.

She took a step closer, her feet rustling the grass. Her nearness sent my heart racing. What was she doing? She smelled of cinnamon. She was close enough that I could almost embrace her if I wanted to—and I did want to. Very much.

I was in trouble.

And I liked it.

CYN

Picking Armand's pocket would be easy if he weren't so incredibly charming. And handsome.

Armand moved toward me, and I wanted to bite my lip. The garden's intricate topiaries and the patterned walkways seemed to blur and disappear from the world.

My eyes lowered, but I forced myself to look at him. *Never take your eyes off your target.* But *he* was clearly flirting with *me.* This was not covered in basic training. Stepmother had said, "Don't let your emotions get in the way." But perhaps she had been talking about *my* flirting with someone, not the other way around.

These feelings were confusing. I tried shoving them aside—but I wasn't sure I wanted to. Talking with him had been a relief I hadn't known I'd needed. And besides, it was beastly fun flirting back.

Excitement energized every nerve. I gripped my hands to keep them from doing something ill-advised and impulsive. Like running through his hair.

C'mon, Cyn. Do your stuff. I shifted my weight as if to take a step, then twisted my foot awkwardly and allowed myself to trip. Green grass filled my vision as I fell. "Oh dear," I cried.

For the second time that afternoon, he was there in an instant, catching me from hitting the ground. Gently, he stood me up, his strong and steady arms wrapped around me. The hedges and footbridge faded into the background. Just like the balcony had when we'd danced. *Get over it, Cyn.*

A tingling warmth shot up my arms and a genuine blush crept over my face. My heart beat so strong I felt it in my toes. I turned towards the pond and the large ornamental rocks. I raised a handkerchief to my brow and dabbed at it.

"How embarrassing," I said, waving the handkerchief dramatically. "I'm not usually this clumsy."

Armand walked around to face me. His manner changed in an instant when he saw that the elaborate red-and-gold monogram on the handkerchief wasn't mine—it was his. The same handkerchief I had returned earlier when he'd pulled me from the pond was once again in my hands.

As he patted his jacket pocket, his brown eyes widened in surprise. I folded and returned the handkerchief. The sun warmed my shoulders but that did nothing to settle the butterflies in my stomach. He slowly took it from my hand, his eyes flashing with amusement. When his fingers brushed mine, my heart shivered.

I pulled a short golden chain from inside my sleeve. "And your watch chain."

His eyes widened. As the tiny golden links pooled in his palm, they glittered. "Anything else?" he asked, folding his arms. His face was stern but his eyes twinkled.

I'd been tempted by the small lapel pin, but after being stabbed by Luc's, I'd sworn them off.

I shook my head, and he refastened the gold chain to his vest. Stepmother would have been proud of two lifts so cleverly executed.

"Now, Magpie, it's my t-turn," he said.

"What? You, a thief?"

He shrugged. "Perhaps you are not the only one with a secret identity, my d-dear."

A thrill danced over my skin. Had he really just called me that?

I liked it. Almost too much.

"I'd be more surprised if you claimed to be the prince himself."

He started at my jest like he'd been stung by a bee, but he quickly recovered.

"I'd like to see you try," I continued. "If you succeed, I'll take you on as my burglar apprentice."

We were already inches apart after my stumble, but he came even closer. Close enough that I caught a whiff of his delicious cologne. He was now closer than propriety allowed and I found myself following the angle of his jawline. His well-shaped mouth. His lips. Soft, no doubt—and entirely kissable.

I wanted to slap myself. *Get a grip, Cyn. You're the Magpie. Act like it.*

Armand brought his hand close to my face. I wanted to lean into that hand. Feel his warmth.

Then, with a quick twist, he produced the chess piece from behind my ear.

I gasped, eyes wide. My hands flew to my bodice. I turned away from him slightly, glancing down my dress. Sure enough, no chess piece.

"B-but how—how did you . . . Shar said it was safe in my bodice . . . How?" I felt the color drain from my face.

Armand's strong voice rumbled off the garden walls. "R-relax, I found it by the pond."

"The pond?"

He nodded. With a sigh of relief, I felt my legs threaten to buckle.

"I didn't know bodices had pockets," he said. "T-terribly convenient place. Protect your v-virtue and your v-valuables."

Heat crept up my chest and neck. I lunged for the chess piece, but he held it high.

I stepped closer to him, reaching, the tips of my toes digging into the soft grass.

"Who d-did you steal this from?" he asked, holding the chess piece to the light.

"A milkman." My cheeks burned and I held out my hand. "Give it back."

"I'm getting *déjà vu*. No, I'm going to k-keep this as c-collateral for anything else you might steal while in the p-palace." He leaned in closer. "Perhaps a d-dress that fits?"

"My dress fits. Mostly." My blush flared up to the tips of my ears. I groaned inwardly. I'd brought the chess piece all the way from home just to return it.

Home.

The carriage and Stepmother.

They were waiting for me.

Stepmother's sharp features jolted through me like lightning.

What time was it? *Blast it, Cyn. How could you let yourself get so lost in his curls, his smell . . . his mouth? Beasts, you're still doing it!*

I glanced at the sun, then started to back away from Armand. My feet crunched on the gravel walking path.

Concern twisted his features. "W-where are you going?"

Stop messing around, Cyn. Stepmother. You have to go.

"The Council will be done soon and I have to go." Regret tugged at my heart, urging me to linger. My steps slowed. I still hadn't seen an imperial rose, and I didn't want to leave Armand. Being with him was fun. Was this how Aimée felt about Luc? Stepmother could never know—about either of us.

I turned and started walking into the palace. I was sure I would have no trouble getting out. Nobody stopped you from leaving.

Armand's hand grabbed mine again before I'd gone two steps.

"W-wait," he said, biting his lower lip. He looked to the ground, shuffling his feet, then glanced at me. Was he nervous? "The C-Council isn't over yet. M-may I show you something?"

I tilted my head, a smile hiding behind my lips. He was stuttering again. "As long as it's not a jail cell," I said.

He chuckled softly and pulled me into the palace.

CYN 20

He led me into a darkened hallway. *Who does this man think he is, wandering the palace?* Sons of merchants weren't allowed such freedoms, even if their fathers were beastly ministers. Of course, I wandered strangers' houses all the time.

Sconces lit by what could have been residual ancient fairy charms brightened the gloomy hallway, illuminating a floor-to-ceiling portrait. The oversized painting rested in a gilded frame, portraying a king standing behind a seated queen. In front of her stood two young boys, perhaps five and six. The older of the two boys stood ramrod straight, serious eyes hiding under his dark wavy hair. The younger boy with light brown hair had similar features, except his were marked with laughter where his brother's were solemn.

Armand yanked me past the portrait before I could study it any further and into a well-lit room. Intricate yellow-and-white rosette stained-glass windows let in the midday sun. The light dazzled my eyes and I blinked. The dusty, familiar smell of old parchment filled my nose.

Armand waited in the center of the room, gauging my reaction. My stomach fluttered and I opened my hands to steady myself. I was in the royal map room. And it was magnificent.

A beautiful illuminated map of Lyonelle graced the wall facing the entrance. Bookshelves spanned the walls from floor to ceiling, displaying ancient tomes, narrow atlases, and rolled parchment. Pedestals in the center of the room revealed exotic curios. Shallow drawers, identical to the ones in Papa's study, held single large maps. Framed maps filled the remaining wall space.

So much of it reminded me of Papa's study at home. Even the metallic tang of ink mixing with the musty book smell stirred memories. The room was immediately familiar and new at the same time.

My eyes flew from one wonder to the next, my breathing rapid. "I hardly know where to start," I whispered, cutting through the silence.

My gaze fell back on Armand. He stood with eyes alight. "I often come here to think," he said. "And escape. When I was younger, I'd come here and plan t-trading routes, imagining a d-daring adventure. May I show you the room?"

As I took his hand, a tingle dashed up my spine. Armand guided me around the room, explaining each map, most speech defects swallowed up in his enthusiasm.

"The greatest t-tradesmen have planned their routes here," he continued. "Afterwards they present one of their treasures to the c-crown as a token of thanks for use of this room."

"Did you come here with your father?" I asked.

"Y-yes. My father—the merchant," he said, his mouth tightening. "But this room is open to the p-public."

A sharp pang pierced my heart. Papa should have been the one to give me a tour. A strange heat swelled in my throat, and I tightened my grip on Armand's hand, glad that he, at least, had shared special times here with his father.

"I've always wanted to come here," I whispered.

In a way, it felt like I was divided in two. One half was the girl who ached over missing her Papa. And the other was a woman drawn to the kind man beside her. It was odd thinking that. But Armand was a life preserver saving me from drowning in grief. I knew that if I stayed close to him, he could keep me safe.

Armand moved closer and my body felt drawn to his. For comfort? Whatever it was, it didn't matter. I was happy to be swept away in more moments with him.

His gentle fingers took my hand, wrapping it around his surprisingly solid arm again. I gently pressed my fingers, trying to feel through the fabric. He flexed his muscles. He wasn't fooled and I bit back a giggle.

"You must help unload your father's merchandise," I mused. "Are marble slabs part of his wares?"

He tilted his head and a thick lock of hair fell across his forehead. "Anything Lyonelle t-trades in, my father does."

I almost reached up to brush the lock away.

Cyn, control.

I ran my hand up from his elbow, letting my fingers linger. "I'm glad you're such a helpful son."

Armand smirked and—beasties take my heart—two small creases dimpled his cheeks.

While we examined the shelves, his free hand rested on mine. After he pointed something out, his hand always quickly returned to mine. Heat blossomed from the contact, touching my heart and dulling the pain of missing Papa.

Armand led me to a large framed map opposite the one of Lyonelle. In the corner of this new map, Alemania's symbol of three stars and crossed swords blazed from the corner. Armand paused to look at the map, clearly lost in thought.

"Is there something special about this one?" I gently tugged on Armand's arm and he came to himself.

"After his expedition via the Schindler pass, Herr Döbler presented this m-map to us—I mean, to the m-map r-room."

I smiled at his stumble over his last words. My eyes fell on a small unassuming map, overshadowed by Herr Döbler's gift. "Is that *M.* Robinette's . . . ?" I said, leaning forward to examine the parchment. My shoulders fell in disappointment. "No, it is not. It looks to be the refined route."

Armand led me to one of the narrow drawers and pulled out another large sheet of parchment. He must come here often—he hadn't even consulted any of the indices. He laid the parchment flat on a large desk, placing paperweights in the corners to prevent it from rolling.

"This is *M.* Robinette's original r-route." Armand leaned over my shoulder and traced his finger along Robinette's path.

His face was inches from mine. Warmth rose from my neck and burned my cheeks. Surely, he felt my face heating. *Breathe, Cyn. Just breathe.* No, breathing was a mistake. His earthy cologne carried notes of vanilla, fogging my brain.

I closed my eyes and swallowed, then attempted to focus on the map. I followed the dotted trail with my finger. It led over a mountain pass and around a lake. "This is a terrible route."

Understanding lit up his face. "Yes, this was before T-Tradesmen's Bluff, d-discovered by—"

"—Alexander Manette," I finished, trying to keep my throat from constricting.

"The most d-daring merchant."

"But to cross the bluff you have to leave no later than mid-September."

Armand's eyes lit up. "You know of the bluff?"

"It's not actually a bluff," I corrected, tapping the map. "Though there is a bluff along the way. Papa said there was a lake of glacier water he had to cross. It was a vibrant aquamarine, smooth as glass, and clear to the bottom. He named it after his only child."

Armand's eyebrows lifted. "Your f-father?"

"Yes, my father was Alexander Manette." The words hitched in my throat. Pride for Papa wouldn't allow me to say anything else.

My cheeks grew hot again as Armand's gaze rested on my face, and I smoothed the corners of the map, which had begun to curl, to distract myself.

"The g-glacier lake. *Le Lac de Petites Cendres.* That's named for y-you." Wonder filled his voice.

"Guilty," I said, giving him a watery smile. I looked away again quickly, my emotions tumbling over themselves. Maybe coming here was a bad idea. This room had thrown the past in my face like one of my own cinnamon bombs. My feelings inside churned, but I swallowed them back. Why did Papa have to die? Why did missing him have to hurt so much?

"You—you must miss him t-terribly."

"Ugh. *Je suis si pathétique.* Being reduced to tears over a map."

"N-no," he said. He placed his hand on mine and gently caressed it. "I think you m-miss him so much because you loved him so m-much. And that is a beautiful thing."

He hooked his fingers around my hand, pulling it to his lips, and kissed my palm. Warmth from the gentle intimacy and kindness flowed through me. *Armand is here.* Papa's death had left a terrible hole inside me, but Armand was here. And knowing that made it somehow easier to climb out.

"This was an incredible d-discovery," Armand said, motioning to the map. "You must be very p-proud."

"I am." My voice folded in on itself.

Armand's hand caressed mine and he turned fully to look at me.

This is nice, a tiny voice inside whispered. *Having someone here.* I silently agreed.

"You're Alexander Manette's daughter. With all of your knowledge, I would think you would be running his b-business."

I wiped my eyes, sure they were turning red, and Armand offered his handkerchief.

"There were . . . complications with his business." It may have been common knowledge that Papa had passed away, but it was not common knowledge that he'd gambled our savings on the ships that had sunk. I fingered the intricate embroidery around the edges, relieved that my emotions were retreating.

"I steal because I have to," I continued, shrugging my shoulders. We'd have been on the streets within weeks if I hadn't started "collecting" Papa's reneged debts. My thumb picked at the corner of the map, curling the paper slightly. "Stealing gets harder all the time. Especially with Alemanian border disputes."

"Political c-climates aside, stealing is wrong."

"Now you sound like Shar." My ribs constricted. "You're not a hundreds-of-years-old house fairy, are you?" The joke sounded thin even to my ears. Climbing the palace wall had been such a stupid idea.

"There is a right and wrong—the law."

I turned and rested my back against the edge of the table, folding my arms. My warm feelings for Armand from earlier prickled under his adamance.

"There is day and night, but what about dawn and dusk? How would you classify them? Stealing usually *is* wrong," I said, my voice small even to my own ears. I couldn't believe I was letting Armand this deep into myself. "But, there are worse crimes than stealing." I would know better than most.

"How c-can something that is wrong be good?"

I snorted. Spoken like someone who had never broken the rules. His words helped me out of my pity, and I looked him up and down. "I'll show you. Two days from now. We'll meet at Lady Eline's again. Then we'll have some fun."

"As in c-committing a c-crime?" he asked. "In t-two days?"

Warmth flared in my heart at the return of his stutter. How could I have thought it was annoying? It was adorable. I wanted to lean into him. For him to wrap his arm around me, just so I could feel his closeness.

"Afraid?" I asked, poking him in the ribs. "I've already investigated. Just a few guards stationed at the front of the estate."

"N-no, it's n-not that." He paused, his mouth open as he tried to speak.

"Afraid you'll like it?" I asked, folding my arms again, glad my threatening tears had fully retreated. Sparring with Armand was far preferable to wallowing.

"What about our nightly meetings?"

That gave me pause—in light of today, our nightly meetings seemed less obligatory and more amiable. Stepmother's warning about feelings grew fainter.

"I'll still come," I heard myself saying. "And then, let's have some fun." I held up two fingers to indicate the days.

Armand smiled, a smidge of relief obvious on his features. "T-two d-days," he agreed.

His fingers rubbed the back of his neck. His ears were growing red. Was he actually nervous about stealing or was it something else? Looking at me with his warm brown eyes, he took my hand and again caressed my skin. My heart fluttered. *Beasties, what is wrong with me?* This room was playing with my mind.

He tugged at the cravat around his neck. "Shall we finish the t-tour?"

He moved us to a shelf full of books with yellowing pages. As we left the map, I kept my gaze upon it for as long as possible, as though it were my father's carriage leaving on a long journey.

"I was going to show you this p-piece anyway," Armand said, "but now I know it will have special import for you."

I gasped when my attention landed on the shelf. "My father's music box," I breathed. "It's here." My heart rammed against my ribs and my breathing quickened.

"When the trade merchants return from a particularly d-dangerous or profitable journey, they present a gift to the c-crown," Armand said. He pointed to a small portraiture of Papa. The room condensed around this single display.

I pressed my hand to my heart. Papa. He was young and smiling.

Armand spoke, breaking the spell of seeing Papa's picture. "Because of *Monsieur* Manette's accomplishments and exploration in the n-name of Lyonelle, this piece is kept on p-permanent d-display. Would you like to see it?"

I clasped my fingers together to keep from reaching. I nodded, not trusting my voice, as Armand picked up the box.

Precious stones were inlaid in the rich mahogany wood and my fingertips traced the edges of the lid. It was the first artifact my father had brought home after discovering Tradesman's Bluff. I had been young at the time he'd presented it to the crown, but I remembered Papa's pride at being able to do so.

I barely breathed. Stepmother had sold its twin long ago—despite the fact that it had been mine.

Armand gently placed it on the table and lifted the lid. My breath caught somewhere between my heart and my lungs. The outline of the music box blurred as tears stung my eyes. I already knew the first notes it would play—its melody was written on my heart. I had played it every spare moment when Papa was away on his travels.

I missed my papa so much.

Armand gently lifted the box, clearly looking for the hand crank. One of the reasons the box was so valuable was that the hand crank was removable and hidden. Armand's hands slid over the box but found nothing.

"It's under the base," I murmured.

He nodded, quickly found the crank, then fit the shaft into the hole. The tiny gears clicked, then squealed from disuse. Armand winced.

"I'll s-send someone to oil it," he said, rotating the crank a few more times.

I looked at him quizzically. "The son of a trade minister can order the palace staff to do his bidding?"

He swallowed. "S-someone should oil it, I m-mean."

The pull of the music box drove everything else to the background. With the crank replaced, Armand lifted the lid. Delicate notes filled the room, each as sweet as chocolate and, to me, just as bitter. My breath caught again and I bit back a gasp as the loss of Papa mounted inside my chest. Hot tears spilled from my eyes despite the hollow feeling. I'd wept bitterly in the weeks after Papa died, blaming myself, listening to my music box as both a balm and a curse. Maybe if I had actually been there for his last breath, I could have saved him. I'd made the medicine myself. It would have saved him.

The music faded and I sniffled, the noise amplified by the sudden silence. Tenderly, Armand reached over and took my hand, warmth spreading at his increasingly familiar touch, and slowly the hole shrank, the ache dulling and retreating.

Gently, Armand closed the lid and placed the box in my hands. "Please, I w-wish you to have it," he declared.

He was forgetting himself, and I smiled weakly.

"Sadly, it is not yours to give. Unless you'd like to steal it here and now." I turned and replaced the music box in its proper display. The last few notes of the song sounded especially sad, as if the box knew it would not be played again for a long time.

Armand's jaw clenched and his shoulders stiffened. "I m-meant, that I wish I c-c-could g-give it to you."

"Thank you," I said, clutching my hand over my chest, my heart close to bursting. "Hearing my father's song was gift enough."

Aimée sat sullenly in the corner of the carriage. I settled next to her, my skirts filling the rest of the carriage.

"You're fifteen minutes late," Stepmother said. "Did you acquire anything?"

Nice to see you too. But it had been worth every minute. It had felt good to talk to someone and share a part of myself—a relief to tell Armand everything I had. But I wasn't going to tell Stepmother any of that.

"Experience," I said. My emotions were raw and simmering too close to the surface for me to speak of anything that had happened this afternoon.

Stepmother arced an eyebrow. "And the exit strategies?"

Petite bêtes. I should have been looking while Armand was leading me through the palace. "I found at least one from the palace garden."

"The palace garden? How would you know? You haven't been inside the palace, let alone the gardens."

Heat flushed my neck. "There's a tree. With low branches on the outside of the wall. And it looks as if there might be some branches on the other side."

Stepmother folded her arms. "'It looks as if . . .'?"

I shifted, looking down, hoping my expression didn't betray my secret garden rendezvous. "What I meant to say was, I think I found at least one possible exit via the palace garden." Warmth spread to the roots of my hair and I shifted in my seat.

Stepmother didn't respond.

On to more interesting topics. "Aimée, how was court?" I asked, hoping she'd seen Luc and hoping she hadn't. Stepmother might have forced her to spurn him if they had met.

"A waste," Stepmother answered. She thumped her cane on the floor of the carriage, and the driver started for home. "No one paid her any attention. They were too consumed by a sparring session between the two princes earlier this morning."

Aimée sat straighter in her seat. "Actually, a *Général* Sarçon, no . . . Sanson spoke to me."

Stepmother moved to the edge of her seat. A *général* was big news.

"You were speaking with Lord Rallison," Aimée continued. "But the *général* is not the right target."

Stepmother scoffed, leaning back in the carriage, glaring at the countryside. "Aimée, if you are trying to convince me about Luc . . ." Her tone held a warning.

Aimée shook her head vigorously, her features set. "No, Mother. The *général* stared at me for ages, like someone who had forgotten what they were looking for. When he did approach me, he stood inches away, looking at me like I was a ghost. He asked odd questions about where I grew up." She rubbed her arms.

"What did he look like?" Stepmother asked. She leaned forward, her back straight, her fingers clenching onto her cane.

"Friendly sort of face." Aimée shrugged. "A few wrinkles and a scar on his forehead."

Stepmother's mouth pressed into a hard line, her eyes wide. Her face drained of all color. "The left side?" It was more a statement than a question.

Aimée nodded. "Like a spider's web."

My brows drew together.

"No," Stepmother said, and a muscle in her jaw ticked. "Not him. We will choose a different target. Anyone but him."

Her fingers tightened, strangling the neck of the raven.

Aimée glanced at me and I lifted my shoulders. Her guess was as good as mine.

Stepmother spent the remaining carriage ride staring at the passing landscape, her muscles coiled tight, lost in her thoughts. She gripped her cane as though it was her lifeline.

Aimée and I rode in an uncomfortable silence as my thoughts and emotions struggled against one another. I'd trusted Armand with my safety and my name. Was it possible I could trust him with more? What would it be like in two days' time when he came with me on a job?

"How do you think Armand will fare?" I asked, almost to myself.

Shar's light kept pace with Pumpkin's brisk gait. The moon rose steadily, its harvest light making it easy to see Lady Eline's wall approaching in the distance. Shar's yellow light hardened at the edges, her entire being shaking as if holding back the tide. Then, all at once, her light burst into swirls of blue and green, and her voice flooded the countryside.

"Oh, m'lady. I advise against this. It's foolhardy and dangerous. There are supposed to be hundreds of guards. I've even heard Lady Norbette found a three-headed guard dog. You know how paranoid she is."

I snorted and dismounted Pumpkin, tethering him to a tree. "You worry too much." Like a cat on a sinking raft.

My words sounded confident, but doubt fluttered against my chest. Perhaps she was right. The biggest liability was Armand. My fingers tingled with cold as I remembered my first job—I'd been terrified.

Shar squealed. "What if you fall from the tower?" A purple swirl collided with her blue whorls.

Pumpkin turned his back on Shar's fussing to munch the grass.

I held up my hands. "I won't fall. You'll be there."

"But what if you do?" Another swirl of light, then another. "What if you fall and get impaled on the spikes of the outer wall and your mangled body is left for the ravens to feast upon, and Aimée and Vienne are left without a sister or a daughter?"

I stopped halfway to Lady Eline's wall, my face twisted at Shar's gruesomely detailed conjecture. Her light pulsed a dim red.

"Shar, I'll be fine. Look, my lucky star is out."

Shar harrumphed.

"Besides, I'm the Magpie, remember? This is just another job and one step closer to the end."

Shar's light quivered and then steadied itself. I took that as a good sign.

After double-checking my satchel, I took a fortifying breath. *Everything will be fine. It will be fine.* As I climbed over the wall, I hoped the stars were listening.

ARMAND

21

"*Je suis ce que je suis, alors qu'est-ce que je suis?*" The overstuffed orange chair threatened to swallow *M.* Parler's petite frame.

My leg bounced and I tapped my fingers.

"Is Your Royal Highness feeling well?"

"Hmm? Yes. C-continue." I waved my hand, and *M.* Parler's voice faded once again into the background.

The Magpie—Cinderella—was the daughter of Alexander Manette. I reviewed the afternoon of the Grand Council, from the garden to the map room, once again. Her expressions were as clear as if she were standing in front of me. The way a tiny vertical line appeared between her eyebrows whenever she was annoyed. The way her wide eyes took in the map room and its treasures. The way her shoulders pulled together when she had spoken about her father.

Her sadness echoed even now. I wanted to help. To hold her and make sure she never hurt again. But short of moving her into the palace, I didn't see how that was possible.

My bouncing feet stopped. *Soufre. By the end of tonight, I will be a criminal.*

Cinderella's mocking voice floated through my memory. *Afraid?*

I swallowed. Yes. No. But I had to see her again. To impress her, protect her. Be with her. My needs battled my morals and my palms prickled with sweat.

Parler enthusiastically read tongue twisters, but my gaze darted between the sprawling lawn and the balcony, both barely visible from the study. I gripped the armrest, my fingers pressing into the brass nailhead trim.

Somehow knowing her true name made her more real. Also, now that I knew who she really was, would things be different? I shifted in my seat. In the last two nights we'd spoken, they had already been different—and I liked them different.

I stood and took the book from Parler and his face paled. "Actually, *M.* Parler, I *am* unwell."

Without waiting for an answer, I headed to my chambers to change. And get a special something for tonight. I was almost as nervous about this one item as I was about committing a crime.

As I entered my chambers, I glanced at the desk where my surprise lay. *Hmm. Qu'est ce qui c'est?* A letter with the royal seal rested on the nightstand. I picked it up, and the thick paper filled me with dread. I inhaled. *What does Father want now?*

My fingers broke the seal and my eyes jumped to the bottom of the page. It was from Luc. As I read the letter's contents, my relief was short-lived. Frustration filled my throat.

Thought you should know that after the Council, Sanson approached me. He insinuated I should aspire for more than my current station, that I was the better son. Which is complete rubbish—I've always known I was the best. Then he asked where you were because he wanted to inform you of another possible border raid. It was a lovely conversation.

—Luc

The letter fell to the desk next to my gift for Cinderella and I paced the room, filling it with a cloud of curses. As if an incurable stammer, a looming masquerade ball, a betrothal, and an imminent crime-filled night weren't enough, Sanson had to jump into the fray.

My heels dug into the blue-and-tan Eastern rug. The *général* was up to something, but when was I going to solve that problem—before or after my wedding?

Sanson wanted war. The reason was all too evident: power. He had inserted himself so close to Father that if war began, Father would rely on Sanson and, consequently, he would have more power than I did.

I couldn't leave Sanson and Father to tangle us in a war. With those two at the helm, Lyonelle would be sunk before we left the harbor.

The clock chimed. Blast. It was time.

Frustration growled in my chest, and, profaning every saint I could think of, I slipped out of my dinner jacket and donned a green hunting jacket—soon to be my thieving jacket. I grabbed my short sword and fastened the belt, then rearranged the tails of my jacket to conceal it as much as possible. Cinderella would probably not want me to bring a weapon, but I wasn't going to be caught unarmed again.

I pushed all thoughts of Sanson, my betrothal, and the masquerade deep within me. They melted together and lodged between my shoulder blades. Uncomfortable, but they would keep.

My hand grabbed the surprise and I crept down the stairs, carefully skipping the ones that creaked. No need for "clandestine meeting with woman in black" to make its way into Parler's reports.

The doors closed with a satisfying click. As the cool autumn air brushed over me, I sighed. The empty balcony was a welcome sight. The shaped topiaries behind me rustled in the breeze. Within the last week, their green leaves had yellowed. A few fallen leaves littered their pots.

I searched the balcony, but there was no sign of my partner in crime. I walked to the balcony's edge and peered over.

"Hello, Armand."

I jumped, nearly slipping over the railing and almost dropping the surprise.

She stood, arms folded, wearing her usual black attire.

I jammed the item toward her face. She stepped back before taking it, pinching it between her two fingers. My etiquette tutor would have died of humiliation if he had seen me. But Cinderella made me *forget* all courtly tactics with one cheeky arch of her brow.

"Wait, is this . . . ?"

"An imperial r-rose. From the gardens. You said your father was going to take you to see them, so I brought it to you instead."

She turned the stem between her fingers, making the flower dance a pirouette. Then she brought the rose close and inhaled deeply. My heart leaped as her smile reappeared. "You remembered." Her voice was soft, but her features tightened.

Beasts, she was upset. Should I comfort her? My hands hovered over her shoulders. Would a near-to-tears thief want to be embraced?

Her eyes met mine and for an instant, it looked like she was warring with herself. She looked so sad and lonely. My heart pounded in my ears. *She could probably throw you off this balcony if she wanted to.* But before I knew what I was doing, I had pulled her into my arms. She stiffened and then sighed, tension releasing from her frame. She fit so perfectly against me. Her head rested on my chest and for a moment, nothing else mattered.

Cinderella raised her hands and gently pushed away, shaking her head slightly. A tendril of hair fell across her face. I folded my arms, but they still felt empty.

"This—this means a lot to me. Thank you," she said, her voice catching. She looked so downcast; I wanted to cheer her up, even a little.

A joke. Those always worked for Luc. "At least you're wearing s-something that fits," I said. "Anything else hidden in unusual p-places?"

She looked at me like I'd sprouted an extra limb. Not very cavalier, I'll admit. She sniffed and wiped her tears with the back of her hand. She shook her head and stepped back, peering at me as if seeing me for the first time.

"You're not very thief *à la mode*, are you?" She folded her arms and leaned against the balustrade. Her mouth twisted upward.

I looked down at my green overcoat and white breeches and removed the wide-brimmed ostrich-plumed hat off my head. It was the most appropriate thing I owned for thieving. Everything else I had was too royal. "It's d-dashing."

She shook her head and heaved a long-suffering sigh. "A man in hunting getup will be noticed in town in the middle of the night as he's scaling someone's wall," she said, tugging at my coattails. "Especially when he has a beastly sword strapped to his hip!"

I placed the hat on the head of a lion topiary. "How to dress like a thief wasn't c-covered in my education."

"No," she said, waving her hand as if to clear the air. "It's not typical education." She pushed away from the railing and circled me, a finger to her lips. "But you do have to leave the sword here."

I gripped the pommel and shook my head. "I'll leave it with the horses."

As she nodded, her lovely features relaxed. The urge to embrace her returned in full force. Instead, I clapped her on the shoulder.

"Very well. Let's be off, then." I moved toward the balcony's edge and peered over. "We're not robbing the r-royal f-f-f—the r-royal f-family, are we?" That could prove awkward.

"No, some other equally silly aristocrat."

"We're not s-silly," I mumbled.

"What?"

"N-nothing," I said, only slightly grateful we weren't robbing me. *Please don't let it be a distant cousin.*

How were we going to get down? The front door was obviously out. At least I'd had the sense to order the guards to the front of the estate.

Ivy trailed along one side of the wall. That must be how Cinderella climbed up each evening we met. The thick vines tangled around each other. They should be able to support my weight. I hitched my leg over the balustrade, my boots scraping the stone.

"Stop," Cinderella said, holding up her hands and beckoning me down. "You're in no state to go thieving."

"Impossible." I rubbed my hands together. Bits of grit from the railing fell to the tiled ground. "I've been ready for hours."

Cinderella lifted her collar and Shar flew out, zipping around me from head to toe. "That should take care of you," the fairy said, her light a satisfied orange.

"Shar, what *is* a house f-fairy doing on thefts? I thought they just did domestic things." My hands suddenly felt clammy. "And what did you do to me?" I opened and closed them.

"M'lady is the heiress of her family's household," she said as if that explained everything. "And I put a charm on you. Though your looks are charming enough."

"Shar," Cinderella said, her tone clearly a warning.

I turned to wink at Shar, and the fairy's light blushed pink.

"It's a silence charm," Cinderella said. "Which is good, because you breathe loudly."

"I d-do not." I smoothed the sleeves of my jacket. "And yes, I am. Charming, that is. W-wouldn't you agree?"

Cinderella shrugged noncommittally, then climbed soundlessly over the railing and down the ivy.

As I peered over the railing, my nervousness transformed into a babble. "B-beastly useful charm, though," I said, following Cinderella over the balustrade. "I imagine it would come in handy for all s-sorts of things. You could charm the children during a game of hide and seek, or the c-cat for catching mice."

My stomach lurched at how high up we actually were. Broken limbs and bruised bodies came to mind. My broken body.

Shar's light flared pale orange in appreciation, keeping pace with me. "He's smart," she said in a loud whisper down to Cinderella.

"And handsome," I supplied. Shar's giggle helped me ignore the fluttering in my gut. We were so high.

Concentrati sul tuo obiettivo. Master Battaglia's words filled my mind. *Yes, focus on climbing down, Armand.*

I obeyed, jamming my fingers in the space between the ivy and the wall.

"Everything all right?" Cinderella's whisper cut through the night.

I clutched a large handful of greenery. I swallowed. "Y-yes. W-why do you ask?"

I glanced down. This wasn't so bad. Deep breathing helped and soon we passed the second-story windows. Tiny gnats, disturbed from their sleep, exploded from the vines and attacked my face.

Climb. Down.

I needed a distraction. "W-what other charms d-do you use to h-help the M-Magpie?" I asked. I clenched onto the vine, moving my face around to avoid the gnats.

As I struggled against the tiny bug invasion, Shar continued our conversation as if nothing were amiss. "*Le charme attaché* is an adherent. There's a dirt-repelling charm, though it is a difficult season right now, being so close to equinox. My spells can go sideways."

The tiny monsters flew at my eyes.

Shar continued. "Just two days ago when m'lady had to go into town, she claimed my dirt-repellent charm gave her some grief."

"That explains floating on the palace pond," I said. Several gnats flew into my mouth. I spat furiously, hoping Cinderella didn't notice—or worse, was right below me.

"You broke into the palace?" Shar shrieked.

"The guards, Shar," I whispered. I knew guards were at the front of the building, but I still scanned the hedges and garden paths for any movement. Nothing.

At least someone could boss *Mademoiselle* Magpie around.

I passed the first-story windows on my right and looked down. Cinderella stood on the grass, facing up, her hands firmly planted on her hips. A smirk crossed her lips.

I quickly glanced back at the wall to hide my amusement. I liked her attention—even if it was annoyed. The grassy ground beneath my feet felt blessedly firm and horizontal. I pushed my hair from my eyes, hoping Cinderella hadn't noticed my nerves. Or my spit.

Cinderella winked, then shoved me like we were playing tag, then dashed across the lawn. Shar and I followed close behind.

Within moments, my feet landed on the other side of Lady Eline's outer wall. Gallant, already saddled and impatient to be off, stood tethered to a tree beside Cinderella and her horse. I crossed quickly to Gallant and untied the rope. How had she known he was my horse? Of course, this was the Magpie. I shouldn't have been surprised.

"You're a horse thief t-too?"

Cinderella's smile deepened and I saw the stunning young woman from the palace garden. My heart leaped like Gallant over a hurdle.

"C'mon," she said, her beautiful eyes gleaming. "This will be fun."

I climbed on my horse and we galloped off, each step away from Lady Eline's sending my heart beating faster. This was really happening.

+Armand 22

As we stood on the outskirts of Lierre, I looked at the ugliest manor I had ever seen. Its numerous additions made it appear like a child trying to wear every outfit at once. Ornate flying buttress sleeves, complete with a *néoclassique* neckline, competed with its crown, a crooked Lierran gothic tower. The city would eventually swallow the estate and its land but had so far only nibbled at the orchards. The surrounding buildings and alleys shied away from the unsightly structure, as unsure as I of what to make of such an odd chateau. *Soufre.* I knew where we were, and I knew that I'd officially taken my rebellion against Father too far.

"Here?" I asked. "This is Lady N-Norbette's house. She has the fashion sense of a c-confused pea-hen."

Even with the seven-foot barrier of the outer wall, bad imitations of architectural elements from Russiavic, Alemania, and even Delftwijk could be seen jutting from the estate with little logical direction.

Cinderella nodded as she tied up the horses by a tree. "Which is why it's perfect. Lady Norbette's eclectic style ensures no one would notice one of her dresses on another woman. We'll just have to make sure we don't grab anything Alemanian."

I rubbed my chin. "Why not?"

She blinked at me. "The war? People are already refusing to buy Alemanian goods. Imagine showing up to a Lyonelle party wearing Alemanian fashion. We wouldn't steal anything from anyone."

I'd never thought of it that way. The possible war with Alemania was affecting Cinderella's livelihood. My worlds were colliding. "You're certain there are only t-two guards at the front?"

She nodded and held her arms out, giving me a clear "And?"

I shrugged. "You're the M-Magpie." Who was I to tell her how to do her job?

She gave me a wicked smile, and an adorable glint lit up her eyes. "I am. And we're going to have some fun."

I folded my arms as I reexamined the house over the estate's outer wall. Stealing a dress from Lady Norbette's tower was ludicrous. I could simply buy her one. Fifty, if she wanted them.

A noise behind me made me turn. Cinderella charged at me, her full fists trailing ash. *Soufre!* I raised my arms, but too late. Ash filled my esophagus, scratching and burning. I stumbled, my back hitting the stone wall, and I doubled over hacking. I clutched my neck as Cinderella rubbed even more ash onto my ears and neck.

My eyes seared shut, streaming water. "What are you d-doing?" I spluttered.

"Camouflage," she said. Then she dumped the rest of the ash bundle all over my white breeches. "Brought the beastly thing in case we needed to use the *bombes.* Turns out you needed to be less well dressed."

"You enjoyed that," I said, tugging at my now-gray pants.

Her teeth flashed in the moonlight. "Who wears white while they're stealing something?"

"T-trading," I corrected.

"You are smart," she said, winking in appreciation.

I stood a little taller, walking to the outer wall. Father should hear her praise of me. Perhaps he'd change his mind. She was very convincing.

"We should enter here," Shar said, flying toward a remote side of the estate, away from the city's buildings and alleys. The unlit side facing the orchards—the safe side.

I brushed ash from my hair.

"No, we'll be spotted," countered Cinderella. "We should take the most direct route." She pointed toward the highest tower.

I swept my hand through the air in a wide arc. "There will be g-guards on the g-grounds."

"Guards?" Cinderella asked.

"Yes, I've been here b-before," I said.

"Why would you call upon Lady Norbette? Her family isn't in trade," Cinderella said.

Soufre. Think fast. "N-no, they're n-not." I clicked in my throat. "My f-father was looking for s-support for a v-venture of his." Which was true—when we'd come Father had needed backing for new legislation.

Cinderella leaned against the outer wall. "Continue."

"Lady N-Norbette is paranoid and employs several g-guards. With news of the break-ins, I wouldn't be surprised if she's d-doubled her security."

Shar clucked her tongue, turning toward Cinderella. "This is fate punishing you for your misdeeds."

"Shut it," Cinderella said. "Last week she only had two guards at the front. Besides, *if* they see us, I have these." She patted her pouch, which I assumed held spice bombs.

It was only mildly reassuring. "A lot c-can happen in a week," I murmured, eyeing the tower.

"Yes, like willingly breaking the law," Cinderella retorted.

Something I still wasn't sure about. Instead of responding, I sighed and pointed to a high window, refusing to let her get under my skin. "Lady Norbette's room is probably there, in the highest tower."

Cinderella glanced up at the needle-thin spire tower and scowled. "Are you sure?"

The court gossiped about how eccentric Lady Norbette was and how only a fool would want the highest room in the highest tower. Who would want to go up and down so many stairs?

"Did I s-stutter?" That's right—I ventured there.

Cinderella's face darkened. "Of course it is." She sighed. "Shar, we'll need *les charmes attaché et volant*."

Within moments, two strange sensations came over me. First, a wave of prickles swept from the back of my neck to my heels. Next, it felt as though someone were drilling hundreds of holes in my bones all at once. There was a slight pop, and then the feeling was gone. I shook my head to clear the sudden dizziness.

"Now you can climb any wall with ease," Shar said, "and you weigh less than before."

I jumped and landed on the grass. "N-nothing seems different."

Shar's pale blue light rose and fell. Had the fairy just shrugged? "It reduces the weight your muscles have to lift as you climb." She flew closer to my ear, whispering, "It's for making laundry loads lighter going up and down the stairs."

"Fascinating." I flexed my fingers, imagining the possibilities this presented. If my muscles had to work less, imagine what this charm might do on a sword or for an army. "You should c-consider branching out. Fairy for hire. My mother would find c-countless uses for you. Or the m-military, if you're so inclined."

"I'm loyal to the Manette household, thanks," Shar said, her light tinged pink.

Cinderella lifted her collar and Shar zipped underneath it, concealing her light.

We were ready.

The moon was bright and yellow. Terrible cover for us. If Lady Norbette really had doubled the guards, her estate should be swarming with them. My heart raced at the silence. Even though Cinderella had checked the guards at the front, my training still kicked in. Tactically, placing them on the city side of the estate would make more sense. Every nerve was on high alert for guards, staff, anyone. Lucky for us, there wasn't a person in sight.

I tamped down my unease. Cinderella was the most notorious thief and was still at large. That had to count for something.

Minutes later we were over the wall and across the gravel driveway. I hesitated at the base of the tower, remembering the swarms and gnats and the dizzying height from just thirty minutes ago at Lady Eline's. Cinderella, though, didn't hesitate, placing her palms flat against the bricks and scrambling up the side.

My muscles charged with lightning. *Fais-le, Armand.* I gulped and began to climb.

With the help of *le charme volant*, we bounded up the wall. Soon the top of the tower was only twenty feet away, its spire piercing the sky. The wind whipped past me, snapping at my clothes. This was incredible.

I glanced at Cinderella's face—it shone like the moon. Wild joy blazed across her countenance, as if Shar's charm had gone straight to her heart. Whatever darkness that haunted her had been temporarily erased. I felt lighter too, like I'd left all my troubles on the ground.

Cinderella was right. This was amazing. The freedom. The excitement. If you could forget about the stealing part, this was thrill enough to risk jail for.

As we approached Lady Norbette's window, we slowed. I glanced down and the vertigo from Lady Eline's returned. *Soufre.* Never look down. My palms tingled. This was easily triple the height of the balcony.

A thin metal railing surrounded the tower, and I gripped it, my knuckles whitening. *Thank the stars.* Cinderella climbed up beside me, an arm's length away. She ignored the railing, keeping her hands on the wall.

Back on the ground, our horses looked like tiny sausages. My gut somersaulted. *I really shouldn't have done that.* I'd been high before, but never on the wrong side of the railing.

Cinderella tilted her head, a smile playing at the corner of her mouth. "Nervous?"

I managed a grimace.

Suddenly, satisfaction drained from her face, and her eyes widened and she grasped frantically for my arm. Cinderella's feet pulled away from the wall and rose over her head.

"Shar!" she hissed. Her hands peeled off the stones and as she drifted away from the wall, her arms flailed. Shar's pale white light zipped out from Cinderella's collar, circling her. "Oh no. Mistress!" She moaned. "What do I do?"

Cinderella's hair, clothes, and satchel floated eerily, as if she were submerged in a giant pool of water.

My heartbeat pounded in my ears. *Soufre.*

Her fingers were already six inches away from the railing. How high would Cinderella drift before the spell wore off? I looked down and my mouth dried. What if *le charme volant* wore off before she could be pulled to safety?

23

My feet rose above my head and my heart dropped. My braid fell across my face and I glimpsed the ground, seemingly miles away—an endless upside-down landscape ready to swallow me whole.

"Shar!" I hissed again, my hands pulling away from the wall. My fingertips scraped the gritty brickwork, trying unsuccessfully to find purchase.

Shar zipped around me, fairy light buzzing bright orange and yellow. "Should I remove the spell?"

My breath came fast and tight. "No. Too far out."

I glanced at Armand, but he was six feet below my hands. His mouth was agape, as if trying to swallow what he was seeing. He was useless right now.

I grasped at the railing. If I could only grab it. My fingertips brushed the cold metal edge and I sailed past. My body started to rotate in midair, spinning like a lazy windmill.

"No!" My eyes slipped to the ground. Lady Norbette's squiggling garden paths twined like spilled noodles. So high. So very, very high. I squeezed my eyes shut, my heart thrashing in my chest. I had to grab something. But what? There was nothing. I flailed wildly.

Stars filled my view. What if I floated forever? What if the spell stopped? My blood froze. I could fall at any minute.

Something grabbed my ankle and my body jerked. The stars jumped as the horizon tilted in and out of view.

"G-got you!"

Armand clung to my ankle while both of his locked around the metal railing. Apparently, his charms, too, had just gone sideways.

Lady Norbette's sharp spire bobbled in and out of view.

"Don't let go," I said.

"Don't throw any more p-pepper bombs at me and I'll consider it."

I shook my head. "I promise." I reached down and grabbed onto Armand's wrist, which sent me spinning toward him. As Armand and the tower came into my view, hysterical laughter bubbled up in my throat. I bit my lip to hold it back. *Keep it together.* Bless Armand's unrelenting grip.

He released my ankle, and we clutched each other's wrists. My feet floated up again, giving me full view of the ground. The garden and tiny animals wobbled below me.

Shar buzzed around our wrists as though her circling could reinforce our hold.

Armand pulled me close, tightening his leg hold around the railing. I buried my face in his chest, gulping for air. *You're all right, Cyn. Breathe.* His woodsy aroma surrounded me and I giggled nervously. My head felt as light as the rest of me.

"You're safe," he murmured into my ear. "I've g-got you."

He held onto me with one hand. With the other, he reached down and gripped the railing, pulling us until we hovered horizontally over the floor, on the safe side of the balcony. A chartreuse and peach-tiled floor filled my vision, turning my stomach as much as the vertigo had. I swallowed. A cross-eyed mosaic lion stared up at me from the tile. *Who allowed this woman to design her home?*

If the charm wore off at least we wouldn't be scraped off the flagstones— we'd just be dinner for a demented-looking lion mosaic.

Armand hooked his elbow under the railing, then wrapped one leg around the post of the balustrade, reinforcing his hold. We floated vertically a foot above the rail.

I reached for the railing, but my arm wouldn't extend.

"Are you all right?" he asked. "You're sh-shaking."

It was true. My whole body trembled almost as much as my heart.

The tiled lion stared at me with a deranged look on his face. Which eye was I supposed to look at?

"You d-don't look so good yourself," I said, my teeth chattering. Armand's skin was cold with sweat. His dark hair floated and swayed as if held aloft by a breeze.

Shar hovered near my ear, her light a ghostly white. "Mistress, forgive me—it's so close to the equinox, I shouldn't have tried."

Armand, with his arm still around me, rubbed my arm. I nestled into him further and my muscles relaxed.

The lion stared.

"I'm okay," I murmured, forcing a quivering smile.

Armand shifted his arm around me, pressing my head against his chest. His breath tickled my neck, and a tingling warmth burned slowly through my body, strengthening my wobbly muscles.

"Thank you," I said to him. I steeled myself with a deep breath. *Cyn, you've got this. You are the Magpie.*

"Mistress," Shar whispered near my ear. "Do you think someone heard the noise?"

I straightened and strained to hear "Halt!" or "Arrest them!"

Nothing. Perhaps the rumors of Lady Norbette's extra guards had been false. Or perhaps she only employed guards who were hard of hearing—either way, we were fine. We *were* at the far side of the manor, so it was unlikely anyone had heard us, but it always paid to be cautious.

Using Armand's arm as an anchor, I worked my way downward. I clutched at his soot-covered sleeve, walking my hands over his elbow and forearm. A twinge of guilt plucked at my heart as I saw each ashy stain. I gripped the railing, the cool metal chilling my skin. Armand loosened his grip on me but still held tight to the rail. Our feet floated slightly above our heads as we regrouped. Keeping a firm grip on the rail—no need to float off twice in one night—I alternately rubbed each hand on my pants.

Cyn, be resourceful. I chewed on my lip. The lower half of our bodies bobbed gently in the air like boats moored at the docks. I tilted my head and peered beyond my feet at the doorway leading into Lady Norbette's house.

Could uncontrollable floating be useful? Perhaps.

I needed more information. How fast could I rise without the added momentum of a jump? As much as I hated the thought of letting go, I needed to know. I bit my lip. *Beasties.* Here goes nothing. I released my sweat-slick hold on the railing and slowly rose higher.

Armand gripped me again and pulled me back down, leaning in. His lips brushed my ear, sending marvelous tingles over my neck. "Are you c-crazy? D-don't try it again. If you fly away, who will I m-meet with tomorrow night?"

"Do you like spending time with me?"

"Yes, well, who wouldn't?"

I shrugged. "Most people want to arrest me."

In answer, he pulled me tighter, his skin warm in contrast to the chilly night air. He smelled so good. Being in his arms felt so good. His warmth spread through my body.

What was wrong with me? *Must be all the blood rushing to my head.* I pushed away slightly, and he released me but stayed close. The sides of our bodies touched as we floated shoulder to shoulder. I shivered. The dark curls were floating around his face, making him look like a Tivolan sculpture. Was he blushing?

"Well, if holding me close is my reward, perhaps I should let go again." A sly smile crept across my face, and I peeled my fingers from the metal railing one by one.

"D-don't you d-dare." He made a stern line with his mouth, but I could see playfulness behind his brown eyes.

The way he is looking at me . . . Heat flashed through my body, burning away the last of my nervousness.

My one finger hooked around the railing.

Armand glared, but it simply wasn't convincing because the corners of his mouth quirked up. "Okay, Shar," he whispered. "R-remove the charm."

Shar, whose light shone a sickly algae green, began to oblige.

"No," I said.

"I b-beg your—I b-beg your p-pardon."

"No." I shook my head. "Not yet."

Shar froze in midair near my shoulders. "You are crazy," she said. "You could have died!"

The hazy outline of an idea tickled at the back of my brain. I peeked into the darkened interior of the tower and saw several chairs arranged around a mirror and table. A possible antechamber for a bedroom.

Be resourceful, Cyn.

A gray moth, drawn by Shar's light, fluttered by. She shooed it away and the moth settled under the railing of the balcony, walking down, before flying off. *Voila.*

"We can float upside down, inside the house." I locked eyes with Armand and raised my brow. This was probably my most brilliant idea yet.

He opened his mouth, then closed it, his scowl turning thoughtful. When he spoke, it was slowly, as the idea formed in his brain. "If we float upside-down, we'd m-move across the ceiling."

I nodded. The lion mosaic on the floor jumped erratically.

"And there would be less risk of m-making noise," he said. "Or of knocking something over."

"Exactly," I said, grabbing his hand. "And no one would think to look for us on the ceiling."

"The charm has addled her brain," Shar said to Armand. Her light dimmed to a dun yellow. "Don't listen to her."

But I knew a hooked fish when I saw one. Excitement flashed through Armand's eyes. He nodded slightly, tipping his head in my direction.

"Yes. This will be the best heist yet." I smiled.

Shar groaned.

"Shar, scout ahead and see if the ceilings are vaulted." My words poured out as I pointed inside the tower. "We are close to the sleeping chambers, so we can't be far from a wardrobe. If we push off the railing quickly, we'll be inside before we can float too high. We'll crawl upside-down like spiders."

Armand nodded eagerly, his feet rising like a hot air balloon.

"Looks like I'm the only one with any sense left," Shar sighed, her voice flat. "I'll go scout ahead." Her light dimmed to a flat blue and she flew into the open window.

I looked at Armand. "Thank you," I said, after a pause. "For coming—for saving me."

He shrugged. "I understand."

I stopped. He understood what? That not floating off was a good thing?

He must have seen my confusion, because he shook his head and continued. "Why you enjoy stealing. When we were c-climbing, you looked . . ." He paused, glancing over the landscape. "You looked r-radiant."

I followed his gaze. The upside-down neighboring estates and the city in the near distance glowed in the moonlight.

Heat rose to my face. Me? Radiant?

His dark eyes met mine. They really were nice eyes. He took my hand. "I understand," he repeated.

Feelings from when we'd been in the map room resurfaced. Not the sad, lonely feeling about Papa's absence, but the warm closeness of Armand. His thoughtfulness. An excitement spread through me at his nearness, stirring unfamiliar emotions inside of me that I couldn't name. A delicious heat burned where his thumb had been rubbing the back of my hand.

I glanced down at the tiled lion, whose eyes pointed in opposite directions as if he were unsure whether to attack or retreat—so very similar to how I felt with Armand. Shar zipped out of the room, startling me. I pulled away from Armand, slightly confused, every part of me wanting more.

"There's no one here," Shar whispered. The glass door she had opened swung on its hinges, creaking slightly.

"Told you," I said. "Norbette's out shopping, buying more stuff for us to steal."

Armand snorted at my declaration and, still holding on to the railing, gave a little bow. As he dipped his head, his dark hair fell across half his face. He pushed it aside but missed a lock. Something inside me hummed, aching to help him with his hair. So far, the strangest thing about this night was my feelings and how they behaved near Armand.

"Ladies first," he said.

I bobbed, performing an awkward curtsy of my own. Then I pushed off the railing with my feet and sailed over the confused lion and into the room.

24
CYN

My push off the railing was flawless, and it carried me into the middle of the room, where I hovered several feet off the ground. I rose, but only an inch at a time. *Parfait.* My eyes adjusted to the darker interior, and I saw a fainting couch resting by the window, several bookcases, and large armchairs, all accompanied by a dusty smell. This was a reading room, not a bedroom. The room probably got a lot of sun. *Not a bad choice, Lady Norbette.* I nodded in approval.

A panicked voice hissed from behind. "I c-can't stop!"

Armand crashed into me, sending us spinning to the top of the room, our arms and legs wrapping around each other. We bounced against the ceiling before resting on our sides against the cold plaster.

"What are you doing?" I asked, giggling at our tangled mess of limbs. Heat from his body spread to mine and my ears grew warm.

"I p-pushed too hard."

"Obviously," I said. My eyes found his, then darted away again. What was wrong with me? We were doing fine, and then suddenly looking him in the eye was embarrassing? I pulled my arm from under his torso.

"It's impossible to change course midair." His leg was still hooked around my ankle, which he used to pull me closer. "And just so you know," he said, leaning toward my ear, "you do not make a very good c-cushion."

His breath tickled and I bit my lip, stifling a ridiculous giggle. *Beasties!* This sideways charm must have addled my brain.

He untangled our legs, and I tried to catch my breath and pressed my back against the ceiling. I scanned the room. The tops of the bookcases needed to be dusted.

"Perhaps you do not make a very good helmsman." I tucked loose strands of hair behind my ear, but they immediately escaped and floated free.

Shar scoffed at us and flew up to the ceiling, coming between me and Armand. "For propriety's sake," she hissed.

I swallowed. "We should get going."

I flipped onto my stomach and pressed myself against the gritty ceiling like a monstrous insect. Furniture sprouted from the floor overhead, giving me vertigo. My eyes blurred and my head spun. A few deep breaths steadied my nerves, and I crawled over the doorjamb and peered down the hall.

A staircase, opposite the room we were in, led down to another floor. Rooms flanked the stairs on either side.

Armand pulled himself beside me. Shar zipped through all the connecting rooms, checking for people. She stopped at the second door on the left, flashing her light once.

"This way," I whispered, moving toward Shar's signal.

We crawled from the hallway into a smaller room decorated in dark purple, white shells, and driftwood. Shells adorned a framed mirror on the walls and were pressed into every available surface. A particularly ugly vase, covered in striped scallop shells, squatted next to an armoire.

My feet pushed against the doorjamb and I floated toward the armoire. I pressed my fingers into the ceiling and pulled myself into a crouch, setting my feet against the ceiling. I stood and smiled. The shell-studded furniture and the objects on them were now within easy reach for a "trade."

"What are you waiting for?" Armand whispered as he stood behind my shoulder. "G-grab something and let's g-go."

I opened the armoire. The gowns appeared to hang upside-down like a family of glittering bats. The packages on the shelves seemed to defy physics, floating against the top. The smell of stale lavender sachets wafted through the air. I reached past the beaded dresses. I needed something she hadn't worn in a while. Something out of season. I reached farther still.

My fingers brushed something crinkly and folded. I pushed harder, feeling the dress underneath. Ridges of piping or embroidery pressed against my fingers. Perfect. She'd wrapped and stored this away and therefore hadn't worn it in a while. But the gown was still stylish enough to wrap and preserve it from animals and dust. I reached inside the paper with both hands and felt three packages, each separately folded and tied with string.

I pulled the bundles out and set them against the shelf inside the armoire. Night drained each garment of its true colors. I tore the wrapping on one, exposing a light-colored fabric. I threw it aside, startled when it rose up to the floor. *Petite bêtes, you're upside down. Reorient your thinking.*

"What's wrong with that one?" Armand hissed.

"I can't tell the color."

"So? It's a dress. T-take it."

I shook my head. "What if it's pale pink? I'll look sickly."

He snorted in disgust and rested an arm against the wardrobe. "Seriously?"

I arched an eyebrow at him. "Curse fashion, not the fairer sex." I tore the second wrapper.

Shar hissed at the noise.

Oh, pish. The guards of the house would not be alarmed at the sound of rustling paper.

The second dress was also light in color. I tore into the next package. *Please be dark.*

Some sort of deep color lay underneath. A black funeral dress? Beads and sequins glinted beneath Shar's light. No one, not even Lady Norbette, would be so audacious as to wear glitter to a funeral. It was perfect.

I unwrapped the dress, the fabric sliding as smooth as Tivolan butter. I held it up. The dress fell down to the floor, covering my face like a sheet of runaway laundry. Lady Norbette's girth had once been greater than her current figure. And it was not Alemanian fashion. Bless this large woman.

With a nod of approval from me, Shar cast the dirt-repellent charm on Lady Norbette's dress. I didn't want to rely on Shar's magic after the floating fiasco, but what other choice did I have? I'd almost floated away forever for this dress and there was no way I'd allow it to stain. Besides, the dirt-repellent charm should be safe enough, even if it did go sideways like last time.

"We're stealing that?" Armand grabbed the fabric and the tiny beads clicked together. His nose crinkled in distaste.

"Thank you. Finally, someone with some morals," Shar said, finishing her charm.

"What k-kind of a thief are you?" He folded his arms and shook his head, sending ripples in his floating curls.

I shrugged. Wasn't it obvious? "A brilliant one." I swished the dress back and forth, the fabric undulating from me toward the floor. Why did nobody appreciate my genius?

"No wonder items fall out of your b-bodice. You c-can't even c-clothe yourself in a proper d-dress size."

I rolled my eyes. "Puh-lease. This is perfect. I still have two days to alter the gown. With modifications, no one will know it was Lady Norbette's dress, and she would never accuse a young woman with a different figure"—I gestured at myself—"of having stolen her dress. I hope Lady Eline's shoes match, though."

Armand sighed, his fingers tugging at his hair. "All right, you've got your tent. Let's g-go."

"Not yet," I said as I reached into my satchel. "The Magpie always leaves a gift." At least for non-revenge jobs. I pulled out a snuff box. "Would you do the honors?" I handed Armand the box.

He took it and reached into the armoire. Five inches from the wardrobe, he fumbled with the tiny box and it slipped. He tried to recover it, but the box fell away from him toward the floor. He flailed after it but knocked over the ugly vase.

I jumped for the vase, but it tumbled to the floor with an enormous crash.

Muffled voices sounded from below.

I glared at Armand.

"Oops," he said.

"Oops?" I hissed.

"Things usually fall d-down, not up," he said, pointing up to the floor.

Footsteps thundered on the stairs, coming toward us.

Armand's eyes widened. "What d-do we d-do?"

I rolled the dress into a ball and crammed it into the crook of my arm. "Leave, of course." I turned toward the door.

A deep male voice spoke right outside in the hallway. I froze.

"This is where the sound came from," said the gruff voice. "You two, check that way. I'll take this way."

The voices in the hallway cut off our exit through the reading room's open window. *Beasties.* We needed another way out, but we were trapped in this dressing room.

I dropped to the ceiling and pressed myself flat against it. Armand crouched next to me, his features as grim as a soldier about to charge. I placed a hand on his arm and pointed to the ceiling. After a moment he flattened himself as well and I bit back a sigh of relief. The last thing we needed was Armand storming the ceiling.

I motioned toward the door, then mimed walking down the stairs.

Noises from the hallway and muffled thumping in the room next to us told me where the guards were. We crawled out the door and into the hallway. The top of the stairs appeared below me on my left. If we could make it to the stairs, we could pull ourselves down along the railing. Energy jolted my muscles. We simply had to get out the front door, then Shar could uncharm us and we could walk out free as birds.

"Try Lady Norbette's personal chambers," said a voice from the room behind us. "Maybe it's an Alemanian spy."

"Spy? Just because Lady Norbette is daft don't mean you have to be. More likely it was the Magpie. If we catch him, we'll be famous." The voices moved toward the hallway.

My stomach twisted in on itself. *Petites bêtes.* The stairs were only a few feet away. Armand's face was grim.

Their footsteps pounded from deep inside the adjoining room like a hammer on my coffin. We crawled a few more feet to the stairs, but we'd never make it.

I was going to prison. No, *we* were going to prison, and it was all my fault.

Unless they had spears. Then I wouldn't have to worry about prison at all.

More footsteps.

My breath came in short gasps. They would be here any second. *Hide, Cyn!* But where? We were in the middle of a hallway, plastered against the barren ceiling. There was nowhere to hide—nowhere to go.

Then something crazy popped into my mind. If Armand and I worked together, we might get out of this yet.

I pressed my mouth to Armand's ear. "Grab the spear and hold it steady."

He nodded and a calm settled over him, as if fighting was more comfortable for him than anything else.

"Shar," I whispered, and her gray light wavered, wisps floating from the center. "Knock over that suit of armor."

She flew around the suit, whispering a spell. The armor rattled.

The footsteps were right on top of us. I rolled over flat on my back, feeling infinitely more exposed than I wanted to. Armand rolled onto his back just as the suit topped over, gauntlets and greaves spilling into the hallway. Two guards rounded the corner, stopping right below us, and looked up.

"*Bonjour,*" I said.

One guard's jaw dropped, and I screamed, "Now!" Armand and I grabbed the spear from his slack hands and rammed it into the ceiling between us.

The first guard blinked, still unsure of what was happening.

"What the—" the second guard started.

I kicked off the wall and, holding onto the spear, pole-vaulted my feet into the guard's face. His jaw crunched shut and he slumped to the floor. I landed on the ceiling facing Armand, just in time to see him roll across the ceiling away from a jabbing spear. I lunged to help, but in a solid sweeping motion, Armand grabbed the spear from the ceiling and whirled it around his body, thwacking the second guard in the temple with the wooden shaft. The second guard crumpled, his spear clattering against the first guard.

I blinked, staring at the two unconscious guards.

It worked.

Armand grinned stupidly, just as surprised as I was. I whooped, my glee ringing loudly down the halls. "We did it." I reached across the ceiling and grabbed Armand's hand, laughter bubbling in my chest. We were going to walk—or float—out of here free and easy.

Shar circled me, countering her *charme volant,* and I gently sank to the floor. Armand followed, landing softly.

"I c-can't believe that worked," he said, his hands rubbing the back of his neck.

"Me neither. Good work, Shar," I said, lifting my collar.

"M'lady," she said, disappearing beneath the fabric.

I crammed the dress in the satchel and started for the stairs.

As my hand touched the railing, a loud voice shattered the silence.

"You there, halt!"

I turned. A guard pointed a spear right at us.

I smacked my forehead and groaned. There had been *three* guards.

I looked at the stairs and my muscles coiled, willing Armand to see my exit strategy. *Please follow me, Armand.* Without another thought, I leaped onto the stair's banister and, straddling the rail, slid down. The guard's jaw dropped in time with the point of the spear.

This rail had better go all the way down. My eyes flicked up and I got an eyeful of Armand's backside a few feet above me. At least that was one less thing to worry about.

I winked at the guard as we spiraled downward.

He blinked, then lunged for us. I felt more than saw his hand pass over my head.

"You there! Stop!" His voice now echoed down the tower from several floors above us. He sounded very unsure of himself.

Hundreds of stairs spiraled past in a blur. Moments later, I slid right off the banister, landing on my rump, then I scrambled out of the way so I wouldn't be crushed by Armand.

I pressed my hands against the cool marble floor. Moonlight spilled from two large adjoining doors with glass panes from top to bottom.

Echoes of "Halt!" and "Stop!" sounded from the tower we had just come from as the guard thumped down the stairs. Another guard clattered to the landing and raced toward us.

I held my hand out to Armand and pulled him to his feet, energy thrumming through my body.

"*Soufre.*" His eyes shone. "That was amazing!" His cheer echoed in the foyer.

I pulled him toward the front door and into the night.

25 ARMAND

We hurtled from Lady Norbette's main entry steps onto the garden path, making our way to the horses, the gravel crunching under our boots. The spiked perimeter fence was only fifty feet away.

Two turquoise-liveried guards leaped out from behind a statue of a peacock, then crouched in a fighting stance, gripping their spears.

"There they are!" Two more voices sounded to our right.

Another pair of guards, each holding a halberd, stood between us and the horses. Where had they been earlier? I pulled Cinderella, veering left toward the front of the house. The horses could wait. We could lose the guards in the city if we were fast enough.

We sprinted down the driveway, and I turned right onto Rue Principale, heading deeper into Lierre. The smaller houses near Lady Norbette's quickly transformed into leaner city buildings. The transition from large manor to crowded city was jarring, and I pushed my mind to catch up with my feet.

Thundering footsteps followed us into the city.

Within minutes, houses stacked on top of each other sprouted on either side. A few minutes more and we could lose the guards in the maze of alleys. I guided Cinderella left toward the wharf, down Rue de Poissons. The houses here leaned on each other for support. We'd be safe there.

"Halt!"

The guards' shouts roared between the houses.

Soufre, those guards were closer than I wanted. We had to lose them.

Rue de Quai. *Turn left.*

Clay walls built between wooden framed houses closed in on us. My fingers tightened around Cinderella's hand. Was this Rue de la Perte or Rue de la Confus?

My feet slowed.

We darted left.

No. Dead end.

Right.

What street was this?

I growled. You'd think as beastly prince of the country, I'd know Lierre's streets better.

The guards' voices sounded closer than ever. My legs burned. Cinderella's breathing rasped between the alley walls.

Bile filled my throat. *C'était mauvais.* If Lady Norbette's guards kept at it, the Garde Royale would get involved. A horrific vision of Father glaring at me in shackles flashed before my eyes.

"We have to hide." Cinderella bent over, her ribcage heaving.

I turned to her. "Don't you have a plan? You're the Magpie."

She glared daggers. "My plan was 'don't get caught.' Now we've got a small army after us." She hooked her hands behind her neck and paced, her skin glowing from sweat.

An even worse thought appeared, this one of Cinderella bent over the chopping block. Father would execute her faster than I could stutter an explanation. Barbs of cold fear shot through my body. I couldn't let that happen.

"Halt," several guards called. Their shouts sounded farther away, as if they'd turned down a different side street. I could only hope. My mind raced. *A plan, Armand.*

"C'mon." I waved her toward another street. Rue de les Déchets.

A sour taste filled the back of my throat. A dingy inn squatted between two tall buildings with a cramped alley hanging on its side. Foul odors wafted from the dark corridor, where bits of refuse peeked from the shadows.

The door to the inn opened and light spilled into the street. A beefy man with shoulder-length stringy hair and a filthy cravat stumbled toward us. "Thanksss, Charlie," he called back into the inn.

Shouts sounded from a few streets away. The guards could be here any moment.

Suddenly a terrible idea came to my head—it would give me a splitting headache, but it might work.

I pulled us to a stop just after passing the inn. Cinderella leaned over, panting.

"What . . . are . . . you . . . doing?" she said. "Let's go."

"I've g-got this," I said, rubbing the stitch in my side. I ran to the horse trough. Cinderella followed and folded her arms. I washed off as much ash as I could.

The drunkard squinted at us, rubbing his eyes.

"How is washing your face going to help?" Cinderella said, gesturing to her own face and clothes.

I turned to her. "Punch me." Water dripped from my hair onto my green jacket.

"What?"

"Punch me," I said again.

"Halt!" It sounded only a street away.

My heart pounded.

The guards' footsteps thundered from the other side of the buildings behind the inn.

I ran toward the beefy man. He swayed unsteadily. I grabbed onto his coat and shook him. "*Ta m-mère est une vache s-stupide!*"

Cinderella gasped and her hands flew to her mouth.

The greasy man's eyebrows rose and he blinked.

"Don't talk about his mother that way," Cinderella said, shoving me.

The man's face contorted in rage. "Don't insult me cows that way."

As he pulled back his thick fist, I closed my eyes. This was really going to hurt.

The punch rang from my jaw to my ears. I shook my head and pressed my hands against my sides, ready for more. I tasted blood.

The man staggered and managed to smash his other fist into my eye. *Oui, that would do it.*

The man pulled back for another punch. This time I ducked, then pulled my arm back and let loose. One punch square on his chin. He crumpled against the wall of the inn.

"Have you gone mad?" Cinderella grabbed at my arm. "You're bleeding. What was that for?"

"Plausibility," I said, licking my lip. I shrugged off my jacket and threw it into the alley. I stumbled, still dizzy from the punches.

The split lip had been the easy part. This next part would be worse. The smell from the alleyway only intensified the throbbing in my head.

I pulled off my cravat, shoving it into the shadows. Then I yanked on the laces of my shirt and ruffled my hair. I slapped as much ash off my pants as I could.

Shouts carried from the other side of the building.

I turned back to Cinderella. "You trust me, right?"

She glanced down at the unconscious man, her forehead wrinkling. "I did, but now I'm not so sure."

The guards were close, their boots pounding the road. Energy jolted through my body.

"*Soufre*, woman. Yes or no?"

"Yes."

She will hate you for this.

"Then I'm really sorry," I said.

"For what?"

"For this."

Then, I heaved her into the most disgusting heap of offal known to man. I wasn't sure what they served at this inn—from the smell, I didn't want to sample any of it. Whatever it was, I had just pushed the Magpie directly into it.

Cyn

Armand hooked his hands under my arms and lifted me in the air. It only took a moment for me to realize what he was doing, and then I was up to my knees in filth, trying not to fall face-first into the muck.

Why, oh why did I say yes? This was a really disgusting way to stop us from getting arrested. And it still didn't make sense!

I scrambled on the slick mess and a foul smell assaulted my senses, threatening to bring back my lunch. The decaying food created a humid miasma, and I stepped on something large and round. I threw my arms out for balance. As I did, I stumbled and fell headlong into the trash.

The dress flew past me into the filthy alley. Shar flew after the dress. I hoped she could re-charm it before it landed.

I rolled over, glaring up at the man who had shoved me—my partner in crime.

Shar returned, her light a sick green, and rested on my shoulder.

"Stay d-down," Armand commanded, pointing at the waste, his features twisted with worry.

The sound of footsteps echoed into the alley. My heart pounded.

Armand looked wild eyed for a moment, then staggered out into the street, holding his head and moaning.

"This way," shouted a guard.

I ducked into the filth and pulled some sort of mildewed fabric thing over me and Shar.

A mouse's tail brushed my face. Its owner clung to my skin, working its way through my hair. A scream built in my throat. *You are the Magpie. This is nothing.*

Muffled voices filtered through my rising horror. There was shuffling, and then the voices moved farther away. I think. It was hard to tell sitting in the middle of a pile of garbage.

Just a few more minutes of hiding and then Armand was going to get an earful.

"Inviting him was a mistake," I whispered. "As was using your magic."

Shar's sickly light sharpened at the edges. "He is protecting you."

I opened my mouth to respond when the door to the inn scraped open and a stocky man shuffled out. Keys jangled from a belt on his waist. I held my breath. Through a hole in the fabric, I could see the squat man looking my way, a large bucket shining from his meaty fist. I swallowed. This was bad. Where was Armand?

The man turned and raised his arms. With a grunt, he hefted the pail, then emptied its contents in my direction. A wide spray of muck arced through the air. Most of it landed near me, but several large blobs landed on my fabric-covered head. I squirmed as liquid seeped through the cloth and the mice scrambled to find a drier spot in my hair. This stuff made my pile of trash look like a paradise. I almost stood up for the guards to arrest me. *I'm the thief—take me now.*

Liquid dripped on Shar. Her light bobbed under the weight and then righted itself. My heart softened. Her light, flaring magma orange, burned away all the refuse before deepening to dark scarlet.

None of this was her fault.

It was Armand's.

The cloth was pulled from my head, and Armand stood there. He had a split lip and was covered in some of the ash from earlier, but he was squeaky clean compared to me.

How I hated it.

The smell hit his nostrils and he gagged. "They're g-gone. Thankfully." He pinched his lips together after each sentence.

I stood, and bits of liquid and garbage sloughed off me. What had possessed me to even consider bringing Armand, let alone think it was a good idea? That map room must have cast a spell on me. I mumbled several curses under my breath, searching for the dress. *There!* A few splatters had hit the front of the dress, but they rested on top like oil on water. I sighed, my muscles shaky with relief.

"Shar, you're brilliant."

Shar's crimson light softened around the edges.

I turned and pointed at Armand. "You!"

Armand

26

My apology died on my lips.

Cinderella stood amid the trash, palm-sized patches of her black clothes gray with slime. She pushed strands of wet hair from her face and a mouse dislodged itself, plopping onto the heap and then disappearing. I shuddered.

She scowled and pointed, aiming between my eyes. "This is all your fault."

"I t-told the g-guards—" The words pushed against the roof of my mouth. "I t-told the g-g-guards—"

No, no, no. My tongue swelled around the words.

"The g-g-g—"

The cracked plaster walls of the alley seemed to loom over us.

Her nostrils flared in anger. I pressed my fingers against the dingy walls of the inn. *Apologize. Get the words out.* "I'm sorr—" Memories of reading aloud in Father's study jammed into my mind.

Cinderella glared. The same as Father.

The muscles in my neck coiled, and I could feel the bridge between my brain and mouth collapsing.

"I'm so—" Words ballooned in my mouth and my mind crumbled. Soon it would be too late.

My mouth froze and the horrible clicking appeared. "I'm so—I'm so—I'm so—" *Beasts*. I sounded like a deranged parrot. And in front of *her*. I'd done all this to be with her. And now she was going to leave.

Cinderella stepped forward, her feet crunching against the ground. She placed her hand on my arm.

I closed my eyes. Heat burned up my neck. Father's demanding growl ripped through my brain. *Just say it. Do it!* My breath cut through my chest like a knife. I couldn't. She'd come to mean more to me than just someone to talk to. More than a friend. Which was why her leaving would hurt so much more.

I balled my hand into a fist and pressed my knuckles into the wall. The gritty plaster cut into my skin.

When I dared to open my eyes, Cinderella's face filled my view. I looked into her eyes, waiting for the insulting words that I knew were coming.

"It's all right." Her fingers squeezed my arm, the pressure firm.

I blinked. The storm of anxiety in my chest slowed.

"It's all right," she repeated. Her green eyes were as calm as a morning meadow.

I lowered my fist from the wall and pressed it against my side. My neck muscles uncoiled and I forced my shoulders to relax.

She smiled, then gestured for me to continue.

I closed my eyes and took long a long, slow breath, controlling the muscles in my stomach. *Slow and steady.*

I opened my eyes.

"I'm s-so . . ." I shifted my weight, bouncing on my toes. Embarrassment at having to do this in front of her crawled over me. I'd only ever bounced in front of Luc, but this was important. She needed to hear this. Even if she did leave after. "I'm sor—"

Her warmth transferred through my hand and melted my tongue.

"I'm s-sorry."

My feet stilled and I exhaled. The whole world seemed to expand, as if everything breathed with me.

"I'm sorry too." She chewed on her lip.

My eyebrows rose.

She nodded. "Almost floating away forever, stealing and getting arrested . . . the garbage. I was upset, and I'm sorry." She motioned toward the garbage and then herself. "I'm not that dirty and it's nothing a little water won't fix. Can't even smell it anymore."

A detached feeling came over me and I nodded. This was completely different. As I processed her words, I came back to myself bit by bit. I'd expected anger and rejection. Not patience. Not acceptance. She hadn't even mentioned my stutter.

The alley and its contents disappeared. Lightness filled my chest and it felt like Shar's *charme volant* had lifted the world off my shoulders. I grabbed Cinderella's hand, wanting her to know how much her acceptance meant to me. She returned the pressure with a gentle squeeze of her hand, and I brushed the remaining pieces of trash from her clothes. Her smile was soft and kind. Dirty alley or not, it was a good feeling.

The inn's door banged open and I jumped. Light washed over us. The innkeeper stood in the doorway, raising a bucket. From the smell, it was easy to guess what was inside.

"No!" I leaped between him and Cinderella, my arms raised. The innkeeper dumped the bucket's contents onto me. Liquid spilled into my open mouth, down my neck and back.

"Next time, don't stand in me way," the innkeeper grunted. He disappeared, plunging the alley into darkness again.

My body shuddered and I bent over and retched. My lungs swelled and I managed to spit the garbage out of my mouth.

I used my sleeve as a napkin, then turned to look at Cinderella. Hopefully nothing had gotten on her. She rested a hand on the wall of the alley, bent at the waist. Her shoulders shook. *Beast's beard, she's going to be sick.*

She straightened and covered her mouth with one hand.

One moment. She was laughing. She tried—unsuccessfully—to hide a smirk.

She stepped forward, her mouth twisted. A giggle escaped her lips and she bowed. "Your Majesty," she said.

My heart banged against my chest. *Majesty?* She knew. But how?

Her eyes twinkled and she stepped forward again, pulling a lumpy crown-shaped melon rind off my head. She held it out for me to see.

I breathed. *Ha. Très amusant, universe.*

She clutched her side, then leaned against the wall as another wave of giggling seized her.

I straightened and bowed. Might as well play the part. "I fear we have overstayed our w-welcome. Shall we c-continue our *fête* elsewhere?" I offered my arm, though my fingers ached to touch hers again.

She dipped a curtsy and fanned her face with her hand.

"M'lady, shall we r-rescue the horses?"

We walked away arm-in-filthy-arm, the gown swishing from the crook of her elbow.

27

We crept back to Lady Norbette's, avoiding the main streets. A couple of guards stood near our horses, but with Shar's help and a few well-aimed spice bombs, Armand and I quickly retrieved our mounts. With the dress secured in Pumpkin's saddlebag, we left Lady Norbette's. My thumbs, sticky with drying liquid, rubbed Pumpkin's leather reins.

"Let's get c-cleaned up." Armand flexed his fingers, and crumbs of gray stuff flaked and fell onto the street.

I glanced down at myself, lifting my arms away from my side. "You don't think we could start a new fashion trend?"

He guided Gallant closer, leaned over in the saddle, and sniffed me. "A new c-cologne p-perhaps." He laughed, then pressed his heels to Gallant's side. We trotted away from the city, back toward Lady Eline's.

I took the opportunity to study Armand from behind. His hair may have been matted with trash, but it was easy to see that he cut a dashing figure. Images of him dressed in his best for the Grand Council flashed through my mind. Good thing his father traded in textiles. They did look good on him.

Armand placed both reins in one hand and prodded his swollen cheek. He looked at me, grinning. That strange flipping sensation fluttered through me. *Beasties.* Even with a split lip and purple eye, he made my heart summersault in my chest.

I grinned back. I'd never met anyone like him before. He was determined, committed, and extremely thoughtful.

Cyn, what is wrong with you? You are acting like a moonstruck, lovesick debutante. Stepmother warned you about letting emotions get in the way.

I'm not a debutante, I argued with myself. *And no, this isn't love or anything like it.*

No one had ever treated me like he had. He'd been through a lot tonight, and none of it had been for himself. It had all been for me.

What if he had gotten arrested? What would I have done then? My insides knotted.

I told myself to shut up and urged Pumpkin ahead. His hooves clipped along the road as we kept to side streets. Clumps of trees peeked through the thinning rooftops.

My gaze shifted to the moon itself. *Beasties.* I still had a meeting with Oil and Toad tonight so I could drop off Lord Carte's map, and I'd be late. Again.

Shar's chastisement from last week filled me with remorse: *Those houses had nothing to do with your father's debts.* My frown deepened. It was true. Papa had no argument with Lord Carte. In fact, he valued his friendship and skill as a cartographer. But Stepmother had insisted I steal the map. I looked at Pumpkin's saddlebag, half-expecting to see a hole burning in its side.

As the cobblestone street turned into a dirt road, the clipping of the horse's hooves changed to a dull thud and the distances between the buildings stretched.

Armand slowed Gallant's steps and pulled alongside me. "Penny for your thoughts," he said.

Looking in his deep brown eyes, all of the events from the past week condensed into one question.

"Why do you want to cure your stutter?" I shifted toward him. "I don't think you need to."

Armand's eyes remained fixed ahead.

As cedar, ash, and wild cherry trees lined the road, the last of Lierre fell behind us. Moonlight dusted the trees silver.

"My father—m-my father—" As he struggled with the words, Armand blinked hard.

Pumpkin's steps thudded.

"M-my father doesn't approve of my s-stammer. Says it's b-bad for b-business."

"Bad for business?" I asked. What kind of father puts his business above his son's emotional welfare? "Change your business."

"C-can't," he said grimly. "In my line of work, good articulation means g-good b-business. I need to c-cure my speech."

"I don't think"—my fingers rubbed the rough leather reins, knowing that my next words might push him away—"I don't think I can cure your speech."

His features softened as he regarded me. Heat flashed in my cheeks and I tucked my hair behind my ears.

"Probably not, but I c-can be myself with you, and that has m-made it easier to b-bear. I'll have to f-find another c-cure. Besides, you're far more enjoyable company than the w-warlock my mother hired to cure me."

"Warlock? I didn't know there were any in Lyonelle." My cheeks grew warm at his words. *I can be myself with you, and that has made it easier to bear.* At least there was no way he could see my blush underneath all the congealed trash.

"There's at least one. And b-besides"—Armand shifted in his saddle—"You're much p-prettier than him."

"That's not saying much," I said, motioning to my matted hair. "Besides, don't warlocks have beards?"

Armand kicked Gallant, pulling in front of Pumpkin, and he stopped in the center of the road. I pulled on Pumpkin's reins and cocked my head to one side. Was this another joke?

Armand placed his hand against his chest and seemed to peer into my very bones. "You're right. That wasn't much of a c-compliment, but this is: I have never met another woman like you. I don't think I will ever again." The corner of his mouth crooked up. "You, Cinderella Manette, are simply the m-most bewitching woman I have ever met."

This time, my face burned like a brush fire. What could I say to that?

A tiny sigh came from Shar and I turned to the right. Her rosy glow said it all. I nodded my head as emotions swirled in my chest like the leaves on the road.

"Tha—tha—" My tongue refused to cooperate. "Thank y-you." I croaked the sticky words out.

Armand's smile only deepened, causing my ears to burn.

He clicked his tongue and pulled Gallant to the left as we continued along the road. Snatches of the harbor were visible through breaks in the trees.

What was wrong with me? There were no emotions in our friendship.

No, something about that thought didn't sound right. *Relationship?*

I pressed my heels into Pumpkin's side and glanced to the right. The tips of several masts pierced the sky. An unfamiliar schooner was moored in the fifth pier. Papa's *Marigold* should have been there.

As I turned, I caught sight of a dingy shed on our right, and my body tensed. Oil and Toad. I shuddered at the thought of my upcoming meeting with them.

I twisted in my saddle, my face like stone.

Armand coughed. "That was the most f-fun I've ever had at Lady Norbette's."

"Fun?" I said, scoffing. "You think almost floating off into the night, being chased by guards, getting assaulted by a drunkard, and getting drenched in trash is fun?"

"The life in p-peril bit was exciting." He waggled his eyebrows. "I can see why you'd keep doing it."

Shar turned a muddy brown. "Don't encourage her."

I snorted and continued looking at the road. Why was I doing it? It was exhilarating, but tonight had been a close brush with the guards. Armand had almost been arrested. Seeds of uncertainty grew in my mind.

We rode in silence, passing a stone marker. *Deux milles à Lierre.*

"Thieving is fun," Armand said, "but you can't c-continue this forever. Would your father really want this?"

The back of my throat tightened. Papa. Guilt over the thefts churned in my stomach like a pile of worms in the sun.

The road curved and sliced through a meadow. Dried grasses hissed in the wind.

"It's not that simple," I said. Memories of the cold and hungry look in Stepmother's eyes surfaced. She had always said the masque was going to be the last job. But on some level, deep down, I think I'd always known she'd been lying. And it was my fault again. I was too good at my job.

"Of course it is," he said, simply. "You just stop doing it."

I snorted. We crossed a small bridge that spanned the creek, marking the halfway point between Lierre and Lady Eline's.

"And how would we get food on the table?"

"We?" he asked.

Hazel and oak trees closed around the road and the meadow fell behind us. He pulled Gallant to the side, avoiding some low branches.

"My sister and stepmother." I shook my head. I couldn't believe I was telling him this. But if I couldn't trust a man who had taken trash in the face for me, who could I trust?

"You c-could be a m-milk m-maid."

"We don't own any cows," I said, ducking under another set of branches. A sharp cedar smell cut through the night air.

"A lady's maid," he said.

"I'm lower aristocracy."

"You could be a washing m-maid taking in laundry."

"That's a lot of maids," I said. "And much more back-breaking than floating on someone's ceiling."

Armand pulled Gallant in a sharp left, then dismounted. In the distance, the spires to Lady Eline's pierced the treetops. I pulled Pumpkin to a stop and dismounted as well. Armand motioned for me to follow, then walked deeper into the forest, leading Gallant. Where were we going?

Did it matter as long as I was with Armand?

I tugged on Pumpkin's reins and hurried to catch up, Shar keeping a silent pace beside me.

"What would you be d-doing if you weren't stealing?"

That question hit me like a blast of steam from an oven. What would life would be like? Me at court, dancing and flirting outrageously with anyone who happened in my path.

Armand snapped his fingers. "You should go into trade. You'd be g-great at it."

I nodded in agreement. "Father and I used to spend hours in the kitchen—him quizzing me on the difference between green and black cardamom and when was the best time to harvest pink peppercorns. But in order to make money, you have to spend it. Knowledge, I have. Money, I don't."

Soft undergrowth dampened the thudding of the hooves, and twigs snapped beneath our feet.

Armand nodded. "Hence the stealing."

The memories resurfaced and I sighed, trying to ignore the ache. Thoughts of what Papa would want filtered through me, and suddenly I needed Armand to understand. "It is fun." *Mostly.* "But being the Magpie was never part of my plans."

As Gallant followed Armand, moonlight speckled his dark coat like spilled milk. Armand glanced over his shoulder.

"Three years ago," I continued, "Papa sent his ships to Alemania full of end-of-season mercantile. One carried Alemanian spices and furniture— for Stepmother. But there was a storm. All of his ships sank except for the one he was traveling on."

The trees grew tighter and the night seemed to darken. I hardly noticed where I was stepping. I shuddered, remembering the *Marigold* as she limped into harbor. Father had needed help off the boat. He'd looked hollow.

"Papa died . . ." I swallowed, the truth deep inside, tears strangling my words. I wasn't about to tell him what I'd done. "He died a few weeks later."

I rubbed my arms, trying to fight off a sudden chill as I remembered Father gasping for breath in his bed. His hands were so cold.

Armand stopped his horse and turned to look at me. "I remember," he said, his face tight. "All the merchants hung black from their stalls. The marketplace was s-somber for weeks."

I stopped next to an oak tree and swallowed again, pressing my fingers into the rough gray bark.

After a moment, Armand and I continued walking, and I was grateful he hadn't pressed the conversation. He seemed to instinctively understand how to help me. Quiet moments here. Gentle words there.

Pumpkin stepped on a branch and the crack snapped my thoughts into place. Armand not only helped me—he lifted me up. Like in the map room. He'd been more than a life raft, keeping me from sinking into grief but also somehow calming my storm. He gave me these quiet moments to myself, and it was easier with him. How did he do that? How did he make me feel better, safer?

The woods became dense, the mellow smell of autumnal decay filling my nose. Armand stopped and tethered the horses to a low-hanging branch. He took my hand, and his warmth flared over my skin until I felt my pulse in my fingertips. Being with Armand felt like being home.

The trees cleared, revealing a small pool. Reflections of the forest rippled on the surface.

"My b-brother and I w-would swim here when we were y-younger." He gave Gallant a pat on the shoulder. "I'll get a fire going. Why don't you wash f-first? I'm sure you're anxious to get c-clean."

Shar bobbed in agreement and made a sniffing noise, approving his sense of propriety, and her light stabilized to its neutral yellow.

I nodded. I couldn't stand my own smell anymore and I refused to meet Oil and Toad covered in muck. Besides, I didn't want to leave Armand just yet.

Shar flew over the surface of the pond with tiny ember-like sparks dripping from her fire-orange light. They sizzled when they hit the water. "I can't spell this water warm, Mistress. Better be quick."

My lips pressed into a thin line. I placed my shoes by the bank. My clothes needed a wash as much as I did so I waded in. *Petite bêtes!* Was there ice in this water? I raised my hands over my head and stumbled over a submerged tree root. I sucked in quick breaths. *Just do it, all the way under. Un, deux, trois.* I dunked my head and thrashed around, scrubbing everywhere to release the filth. I shot out of the water. Grime and tiny bits of trash floated on the surface.

My soggy, freezing clothes added fifty pounds, and I slogged toward the small crackling fire Armand had started. I lowered myself onto a log. My teeth chattered like an insane squirrel. Shar flew over me, bespelling my clothes, her light a fuzzy glowing peach. Steam rose from the fabric and I sighed. My frozen muscles thawed and I settled on my log seat.

"My t-turn," Armand said, taking off toward the pond. As I caught a whiff of his trash-ruined clothes, my nose wrinkling. *Phew.* We really did smell bad.

Moments later—thanks to Shar and the fire—my clothes were merely damp. I stretched my hands toward the fire and sighed. Armand's words from earlier about stealing turned over in my mind. *Not steal?* Impossible. How would I get my family out of debt?

Behind me, Armand splashed into the pool, yelping like a startled dog. Splashes came in intervals as if he were submerging and then breaching like a whale.

Armand exited the pond. Soon after, he stumbled into view, his hair streaming rivulets. "*Soufre,* that water is c-cold."

He turned toward a tree and lifted his shirt, his honey-colored skin peeking through, and I blushed. Was he really going to undress? He wrestled to get out of the wet fabric and wrung the shirt before hanging it on the branches.

Shar froze and stopped her drying charm mid-spell.

By the Beast's beard! Rounded muscles rested on arms connected to powerful shoulders. His torso looked like it had been chiseled out of marble. The artist had even included battle scars for authenticity. My eyes widened and my blush burned from my hair to my heels. He'd been hiding all of that underneath his shirt? I sighed. I should have dumped trash on him sooner.

Armand cleared his throat, sitting on a log to my right. His wet body glowed in the firelight. He rested his elbows on his knees, then turned to me and winked.

My eyes fluttered and I sat up straighter. *Stop staring!*

I grabbed a stick and began poking the fire. I stared at the logs. They were nice logs.

Shar flew over to Armand, her light a girlish pink. "Can I warm you up?" she asked softly.

That little traitor. I shifted on my log to see him better, even though a knot dug into my thigh.

Armand glanced at me. I made sure my gaze never wavered from his. *No, I wasn't looking at your chiseled, blush-inducing body.* The corners of his mouth turned up, and my heart exploded into thousands of butterflies. *At least, not much.* I pulled my poking stick from the fire, only mildly surprised to see it in flames.

"N-no. I'm f-fine. Attend to Cinderella." Was he stuttering or just cold?

Shar's light dimmed slightly, and she reluctantly returned so she could finish drying me off.

I tossed the stick into the fire, where it was rapidly consumed.

Armand edged closer to the flames, and it was impossible to think about anything else anymore. I tried to catch glimpses of the way his skin curved around his muscles. I was pretty sure Shar was doing something similar, because she circled lazily, her light still pink. Eventually, his teeth stopped chattering. He leaned back from the fire, his body relaxed.

"What's on your m-mind?"

Erm.

You.

Play it off, Cyn.

I clasped my hands together and leaned forward. "You're right," I said, now bone dry. Shar hovered nearer the fire. Armand leaned back, stretching his long legs before him. "I can't steal forever. But I can't see a way out."

Armand's golden face filled with concern and something else I wasn't quite sure of. Something intense—and it was all directed at me. A thief, a liar, and worse. I shifted uncomfortably, and the knot jabbed into my leg.

"You could always g-get arrested," he said.

"On purpose?" I asked.

"That's a terrible idea," Shar said.

"Or you could run away and join the Anivoli performing troupes," he said.

Shar snorted at the thought.

"How could I leave my home?"

"What if s-someone asked you to r-run away with them?"

Shar's light drained of color.

My head jerked up. "What?"

"What if someone—what if s-someone asked you b-because they had f-fallen—f-fallen in love? With you?"

I stared. Was this a joke? Then a heart-stopping alternative occurred to me: Was he offering? Because he was in love with me? The butterflies exploded inside my chest. I kind of hoped he was. Life with Armand wouldn't be so bad. Actually, it sounded pretty good. I was stunned at how comfortable that idea sounded.

Was my solution sitting right in front of me, wearing a fat lip and a black eye?

Impossible, Cyn. He doesn't really know what you are. He's being nice.

As I looked at Armand, he sat perfectly still, waiting for my answer.

Shar's white light remained frozen in the air.

The knot dug deeper. I pressed my toes into the dirt. It was an incredibly generous offer, but I couldn't allow Armand to sacrifice his future for chivalry's sake.

I opened my mouth, searching for the words.

Armand's brows rose and he shifted.

My heart gave a flutter, and I hoped humor would deflect the question. "Well, he'd have to be handy in a bar fight," I said.

"A b-bar fight?"

"If I'm going to run away with someone, he'd have to know when to duck. I wouldn't want his pretty face to get damaged; otherwise, what's the point?"

Please don't feel rejected.

Armand moved closer, his shoulder inches from mine. His grin deepened, the shadow of a beard speckling his chin.

Breathe, Cyn.

"So you think I'm h-handsome?" he said.

My blood thrummed in my ears, his question filling the small space between us. *The most handsome man I've seen.* He nudged me with his shoulder and I dropped my eyes. Why did he have to take off his shirt to dry? I wanted to run my fingers over his skin to see just how much the fire had warmed it.

I licked my dry lips. "No more than most," I lied, looking away. Beasties, was the fire getting hotter?

He moved even closer, his thigh touching mine, and tiny bolts of lightning shocked my body. His gaze dropped to my lips. My breathing grew ragged and my thoughts clouded over. I leaned toward him. Then my gaze shifted over his shoulder.

A light bobbed in the background. A lantern.

The Garde Royale had found us.

Jolts of energy charged my body. The light came closer. My muscles tensed. Where was my satchel? *Stupid Cyn. You left it with the horses.* Another light joined the first, bobbing a few feet next to it. They had brought a full squadron. Beasties, we were in trouble.

"Get down," I hissed, throwing myself at Armand. My hands slammed onto his bare chest and I pushed. He fell backwards over the log with me on top of him, his skin emitting the heat it had absorbed from the fire.

"This is a bit forward, but I d-don't mind," he murmured, his eyes soft and sultry.

Argh. I crammed my hand over his mouth.

Moss and dead leaves surrounded his head. Woodlice scurried along the forest floor.

"Quiet." I brought my mouth to his ear. "Lanterns."

As his eyes widened, his jaw clenched. I removed my hand.

It took me a moment to realize that I was pressed against his sculpted chest in a most unladylike position. I bit my lip and turned my head to stare at the log. His personal scent mingled with the smell of the fire. *Beasties, slopped and rinsed and he still smells incredible.* My blood raced through my hyperaware body.

Shar's voice came close to my ear. "I'll investigate," she said. I nodded and her light darkened and she zipped away.

Please hurry. I took another breath. He smelled so good. I wanted to lean down and relax into him.

Armand's chest rose with each breath. *Petites bêtes,* he was so much more distracting when his body was pressed against mine.

Don't make it awkward, I thought, licking my lips, avoiding eye contact. My fingers began fiddling with something—until I realized it was his chest hair.

"Sorry," I mouthed. My face flushed, threatening to light my hair on fire.

He chuckled, a small puff of air tickling my ear. Apparently, imprisonment wasn't that big a deal for him. What was taking Shar so long?

Was he feeling as awkward as I was? I looked into his gaze.

This was a mistake. His rich brown eyes were far from awkward. They were filled with the same intense emotion as before, pulling me closer to him. My lungs stopped. His hands pressed gently into my back, then moved to encircle me, grasping onto my shirt. His chest stopped moving as I felt him hold his breath. His lips parted, soft and inviting. I bit the corner of mine and inched lower. Maybe being arrested wouldn't be so bad . . . if we . . .

"It's only a couple of wild fairies—"

I jumped at Shar's voice.

"—possibly gathering for the . . . equinox . . ."

I looked over my shoulder and my face twisted in a grimace. Her light was two feet over my head.

It flared white, then darkened to a deep rose. Her voice wavered and her outline rippled. "Umm . . . I'm going to . . . double-check." She whizzed back into the forest and nearly hit a tree.

I scrambled off Armand and straightened, pushing my hair out of my face. My legs were unsteady and my brain refused to work. *What is happening to my body?*

Armand stood up. "Are you feeling all right?"

Bits of twigs and leaves were stuck to his skin. My fingers tingled to smooth the dirt off him. "N-no . . . I mean, yes." Beasties, I was stuttering nearly as bad as Armand a moment ago. "Y-yes, I'm fine." I took a step or two backwards and nearly tripped over the log Armand had been sitting on.

"Log." I smiled like an idiot and swung my arms around my body. Abruptly, I turned away from Armand to the fire, pretending to warm my hands, hoping he didn't see my blush. *Cyn, tu es un idiot. "Log"? What is wrong with you?*

Armand walked to the tree where his clothes were hanging. I rubbed my hands, then glanced up, hoping to catch one last glimpse. I sighed. *Beasties.* He'd already put his shirt back on.

Too bad I didn't have time to dunk him again.

Time.

I groaned. *What time is it?* Late enough that I knew Oil and Toad would be waiting. But this time, the thought of meeting them didn't bother me as much as it had in the past. Something had become very clear to me in the last few hours, besides the fact that Armand was devastatingly handsome.

I was done. Done thieving. Done being the Magpie. I had something very important to tell Oil and Toad. Something I knew they wouldn't like.

I quit.

I hated leaving Armand even if I was going to see him tomorrow. We'd spent hours together and somehow it still wasn't enough. He was like some beastly magnet. Curse these feelings. They were complicated.

I jammed my feet into my shoes, lacing them up before I changed my mind and stayed with Armand for another hour or two.

"I have to go," I said, wincing at how abrupt it sounded. "I have to be somewhere."

Armand stopped putting his boots on. "N-now? This late? Please t-tell me you're not off to rob s-someone."

I shook my head and laced up my other shoe.

"Where is Shar?" He swept his arms wide, indicating forest.

I chewed my cheek nervously. "Gone. Probably swept up with the other fairies and the equinox." Each year she disappeared around this time for days until the equinox was over. I yanked the laces tight, then sighed. I'd have to meet those two without her. Not that she had ever shown herself to Oil and Toad, but having her tucked under my collar always made me feel safer.

"Then let me c-come."

I jerked my head up as he stood. "I'm not thieving. I don't need your help. Nor your protection." I placed a hand on my chest. "I'm the Magpie, remember?"

Armand shook his head. "I'm still c-coming." A mulish look crossed his face.

"This isn't a good idea," I said, folding my arms.

"I insist."

I pinched the bridge of my nose. He'd probably follow me if I refused. "Fine. But you have to do what I say." I jabbed a finger at him for emphasis. I was really going to regret this.

He nodded and doused the fire, the sharp smell of smoke filling the air.

A shiver coursed through me in the fading heat. *Perhaps it is a good idea for him to come along. Safety in numbers.* Perhaps there was another reason, but beasts if I was going to admit it.

I walked back toward the horses and untethered Pumpkin, my stomach hard as dried peppercorns. Even though this would be my last meeting with Oil and Toad, and even with Armand coming, I still had a bad feeling about this.

28 Cyn

When we arrived at the dock a short time later, the brine and smell of fish assaulted my nose. I shook my head. *I can't believe I'm doing this.* There were so many things wrong with this meeting. First, I'd brought Armand. Stepmother would kill me if she found out—which she wouldn't. Couldn't. Second, I was about to tell two of humanity's foulest creatures that they were out of a job.

It has to be this way, Cyn. I nodded, agreeing with my inner voice, seeing the logic unfold. If I told Stepmother first, she'd never allow me to quit. But if I broke the first link in her chain, she'd have no choice but to follow suit. First tell them, then tell Stepmother.

I dismounted, then rummaged in the saddlebag. My knuckles scraped against the rough sides as I pulled out a medium-sized leather tube. Armand climbed off Gallant, his eyes darting nervously around the docks. I shoved Pumpkin's reins in his face.

He tied both horses to a sun-bleached hitching post. "Why do I g-get the feeling we're not buying fish?" His voice echoed over the wharf.

"Quiet." I felt along the leather stitching until I found the buckle. Just needed to double-check its contents.

He pulled his brows together in a deep scowl. "You said—you said this w-wasn't another theft. You're not r-really an Alemanian s-spy, are you?"

I fumbled with the buckle. Blasted thing.

Armand held his hand out so he could help open the tube.

I shook my head, working at the stubborn fastener. "It's not a theft. And I'm not a spy. Be serious. But this is as far as you go."

"Here?" He pointed to the ground.

I looked up and shook my head. "No, not there." I pushed against his right shoulder, nudging him six inches closer to the horses. He rustled a clump of coastal grass. "Here. Wait here."

He rolled his eyes. "You c-can't be serious."

I nodded and returned my attention to the buckle. *Ha.* I popped the lid open and slid the rolled map from the felt-lined interior. "I'm not making the same mistake twice. If you come, we'll be covered in garbage within the hour."

I unrolled the map, the parchment crackling, to reveal Lord Carte's magnificent illuminated map of Lyonelle. In the corner, a golden lion's paw and red rose glinted in the moonlight.

Armand moved from the clump of grass to stand behind me. "Nice m-map. We won't d-discuss what you're g-going to with it." He moved to face me and placed a hand on the top of the map, lowering it. "I'll risk g-garbage." He remained stone-faced and crossed his arms tightly across his chest. "This isn't the safest place even d-during the d-day."

"No." I drew a deep breath and released it slowly. I rolled up the map, then returned the tube to the riding bag. "You." I pointed first to Armand, then to the ground. "Here."

Without looking back, I marched to the wharf, clutching the paper. As I stepped onto the wooden dock and stalked to the usual meeting place, the air cooled and the waves lapped beneath my feet. I held out the papers, not waiting for Oil to separate from the shadows.

"I'm out," I said.

Oil glided from the darkness, Toad following closely behind, both of them stopping to form a human wall.

"Who's he?" Oil asked, jerking his chin in Armand's direction.

"None of your concern," I said. "But this is: I'm out."

Toad's face remained placid. Oil sneered. "Out? That's a laugh."

"You heard me," I said, holding the papers out farther. Why didn't he take them? I could be gone already, done with him and his living shadow forever.

Oil stepped closer, the rotten boards creaking under his feet. Pumpkin whinnied in the distance. Oil glanced over at Armand near the two horses. "Is he a guard?"

I dropped my arm and snorted. "Why would I bring a guard to a meeting where I could also be implicated?"

Oil circled me, smelling of stale tobacco and spit. Each pass brought him closer, like a noose tightening around my neck. *Don't move, Cyn.*

He stopped, his face inches from mine.

"Why bring anyone? Don't you trust me?" Oil's lip curled, his voice slick like film on water. "Of course you do," he crooned. His hand reached up, and the back of his grimy fingers slid across my cheek. "It's why you keep coming back, isn't it? You can't get enough of me," he whispered.

I stiffened.

Oil's sneer deepened at my reaction. His eyes slid from my face to my feet then back up again. He kept one hand on my face while the other moved toward my hand with the parchment. His fingers curled around the map, brushing my skin. He pulled it from my hand and, without looking behind him, passed the document to Toad. My skin crawled.

"If this really is our last meeting, let's make it worthwhile," he said, inching closer. His hand fell from my face, clenching my arm. I leaned back, pushing against his chest, gasping for air.

A pair of strong arms dropped around me from behind, pulling me away, and then someone stepped in front of me. Armand's dark hair and broad shoulders blocked Oil and Toad from my view.

I growled. I *told* him to stay by the horses.

$\mathcal{A}$RMAND 29

"Leave. Her. Alone." The uneven planks pressed through the soles of my boots.

"Who are you?" the thin one asked, licking his lips and then peeling them into a jeer. The stocky one merely shifted. "How do you know she doesn't like it?"

My muscles quivered and rage pounded through my veins. Who was I? Their beastly sovereign, that's who. I clenched my jaw so hard my ears rang. I knew what I had to do. The tricky part was doing it without Cinderella noticing. If she found out, I could lose her. My stomach knotted at the thought, but it would be worth it if it meant keeping her safe.

My heart pounded as I planted my feet and broadened my chest. As she tried peeking around me, I shifted, blocking her view. *Don't watch this next part.*

The blade hissed as I pulled it from the scabbard and raised it in a formal salute. By the Beast's beard, the weight of the weapon felt so good in my hands, and it took every ounce of control not to slice these two to ribbons. With my other hand, I pointed at the cross guard, where the blade sprung from the open mouth of a roaring lion. "Do you see these?" Then I pointed at the pommel displaying a rose in full bloom. The symbols of Lyonelle. The *royal* symbols of Lyonelle. I snarled through my teeth and advanced. "You know what this means, d-don't you?"

The stocky man stumbled backwards. The slimy one's eyes narrowed, his gaze flying between me and the sword. Recognition slackened his features. "No. It can't be."

"Leave," I growled. "Now."

Those *deux crétins* fell over themselves as they ran down the dock, stumbled onto the street, and disappeared into the night.

I sheathed my sword and surveyed the empty harbor. *Parfait.* No one else was here and those two were gone. Hopefully for good. Cinderella was safe—that was all that mattered. Those foul creatures would never touch her again.

I turned, placing my hands on her shoulders, then her arms, checking for injuries. "Are you okay?" I asked, gently gripping her shoulders. "They d-didn't hurt you?" That thought sent rippling waves of fear and fury through me. "Have you dealt with them before?"

"I'm fine," she said, flinging my hands away. Then she turned back to shore, stomping her feet so hard I was surprised she didn't punch a hole in the dock.

I blinked. What was happening?

My stomach dropped to my toes. She must have seen the royal crest. She knew and was furious I had lied.

I caught up, my feet sinking in the soft sand. She fumbled with the saddlebag and I placed my hand on top of hers. She whirled, her eyes full of fire.

I raised my hands above my head and took a step backwards.

"I told you to stay here, by the horses. And you didn't listen."

"He—he—he t-touched you," I said.

"I didn't need your help. I had it under control." She turned back to the horses, the tall grass rustling. She growled at the latches on the saddlebag.

"Under control like a brushfire. I p-protected your honor," I said, stepping closer.

She rolled her eyes and lowered her voice. "I'm a thief. I have no honor. Besides, what would you have done if they hadn't run away? You could have gotten hurt." She turned to me and pointed to my sword. "You're the son of a merchant! Not the Garde Royale. Do you even know how to use that thing? You could have poked your eye out. Or mine."

I placed my hand atop the pommel and barked a laugh. Master Battaglia asked that same question every day during training.

A furrow lined her forehead. *Soufre.* If she glowered any deeper it might become permanent.

"You could have gotten hurt." Her voice was softer than usual.

Warmth burned through my chest. She cared. About me.

I leaned against Pumpkin, resting my elbow against his saddle. "Better me getting hurt than you. And t-trust me. I know how to use a sword." I pointed at the tip. "The pointy end goes into the other man."

She cocked a brow. *C'mon, Magpie. Work with me, not against me.*

"I can't believe they ran away simply because you told them to," she said, shaking her head.

"Really? You expected more from two moral bastions?" I scoffed and waved a hand in front of my face. "They're n-not even hygienic."

She gave a quick laugh and turned toward me. A dimple sank in her cheek. My heartbeat increased and a sigh escaped. I loved her changing moods. Her fight receded to the background, but I could see it in her eyes, always at the ready. She was perfect. Her stance relaxed, and she glanced beyond my shoulder to the docks.

"*We* weren't hygienic forty minutes ago." She shifted her weight to one side and tilted her head. "Maybe you do know how to use that fancy sword," she said, her eyes drifting to my weapon. I moved to shield the royal markings.

"I'd be happy to give you another d-demonstration sometime." Like against Luc. He owed me a rematch. And I'd strongly consider removing my shirt if it meant she'd look at me the same way she had earlier tonight.

Her sassy mouth quirked as she turned her full attention to me. I swallowed—I was in trouble. As she edged closer, my thoughts blurred at the edges. She was inches away. My throat went dry.

"Maybe you're just more formidable with your righteous anger. Stutter or no." She placed her hand on top of mine and fire burned up my skin.

I pulled back. Had I stuttered? I tried to remember. "I—I—" I opened my mouth to retort and all my words crushed together.

Her eyes danced. "And it's back stronger than ever." She untied the reins of our horses, handed me Gallant's, then winked. "And it's adorable."

My heart tripped and I shook my head to clear it. My stutter. Not only okay, but adorable. I pursed my lips. Not the manliest of terms, but I could live with adorable. Heat bloomed in my chest and my pulse throbbed.

She thought I was adorable.

I mounted Gallant and settled into the saddle. If she liked me with my stutter, maybe I didn't need a cure. Perhaps Father couldn't accept it as readily as she had, but could he accept it eventually? Could I? Uneasiness churned in my gut.

She turned Pumpkin away from the wharf, toward the edges of town.

I took a last glimpse of the harbor. The sharp masts of the navy jabbed like bayonets in the sky. Unbidden, the vision of the fairies superimposed upon mine. Instead of a peaceful scene, I saw flames engulfing the ships.

I shook my head to clear it. *One disaster at a time, Armand.* I pulled Gallant around. Cinderella was already twenty feet down the road, Pumpkin walking steadily toward the country.

"Where are you g-going?" I asked, kicking Gallant to follow her.

"Home," she said.

I stared at her retreating form and pulled Gallant to a halt. Was that it? My mind raced for excuses to stay together. I could say Gallant had thrown a shoe. No, she'd leave me anyway. Perhaps I could pretend to be sick. Not believable enough. I thumped my fist on my leg. If Shar were here, she'd be on my side.

Cinderella suddenly stopped and pulled Pumpkin around, regarding me. I leaned forward in Gallant's saddle.

"Are you coming with me? There might be bandits."

Beast help the bandits who came upon her. "I thought you d-didn't need any h-help."

Her mouth quirked up. "I don't." She tilted her head. "But I would like your company."

I grinned and it felt like my face was going to split. I probably looked like an idiot. I kicked Gallant forward, pulling even with her. "Lead the way."

Cyn

I didn't believe for a minute that Armand actually knew how to use that sword, but he did look incredibly dashing brandishing it around. I was almost disappointed when we made it home with no other incidents.

Since when had I blushed so much like a lovelorn debutante, and why did my breath catch in my chest whenever he was near? Had it started before or after I'd seen him with his shirt off? Images of the map room and garden filled my head. Another sigh escaped my lips. It was before, definitely before. He was kind, brave, and thoughtful, and my heart raced as I thought of his almost-proposal. Was this what love felt like?

The full silhouette of the Manette manor against the sky interrupted my thoughts. On the second floor, a light flickered from one room to another. Was Shar back?

Twenty feet from the entrance, Armand slowed. "I n-need to g-go." His voice was tight. The leaves rustled as he and Gallant backed away. "See you t-tomorrow. Last night of the deal."

Then he pulled on the reins, turning away from me.

How could he leave so easily when it felt like he was taking a part of me with him?

I absently led Pumpkin into the stables and removed his tack, then grabbed a brush.

My heart lurched at Armand's words. Tomorrow was the last night of the deal. What were these feelings boiling through me? Alarm at their strength pulsed in sync with my racing heart. Was this what Aimée and Luc felt? I swallowed. Beasties. This was awful.

I ran my palm against the bristles of the brush and my skin prickled. All his soft looks and quiet words tumbled into place. How had I not seen this happening? Maybe I hadn't wanted to see. Then another, more frightening thought crossed my mind. Was I in love with Armand?

No, that's impossible. You're not falling for him. Besides, he wouldn't want you if he knew what you were.

Don't let your emotions interfere with a job. And I had a pressing, important, and terrifying job still to accomplish: telling Stepmother I was done being the Magpie.

Pumpkin shifted on his hooves away from my aggressive brushing.

You know what you need to do. I pressed the heel of my hand against my forehead, then stood and slapped the brush down on a ledge. I gave Pumpkin a few apples and carrots then walked out of the barn as confused and apprehensive as ever. I sighed. My feelings about Armand would have to wait. One thing, though, could not, and the thought of facing it filled me with dread.

How was I going to tell Stepmother that I was done with the Magpie?

30

Don't stop until you talk to her. Do it now!

My legs froze two steps from the top of the attic stairs. A sliver of yellow light escaped from under the door. I pressed my fingers into the stair rail, the ridges on the grainy wood indenting my skin. *What will Stepmother say?* My stomach twisted and my skin went cold. I wished Shar were here. Or Aimée. Beasts knew I needed all the encouragement I could get.

I straightened, let out a long breath, and pushed the door open. A wave of heat enveloped me and I squinted against the light. A roaring fire crackled in the hearth on my left, filling the air with the smell of cedar wood. The corners of the room remained dark despite the fire.

Stepmother stood near the center of the room, her hand resting on the small jewelry box still in its usual position on the edge of the desk. The sleeves of her indigo dress trembled slightly as she breathed. Where was her cane? My muscles tensed. The screaming raven had always made me nervous, but seeing her without it made my skin prickle. She stood unmoving, then she turned and peered down her nose at me, as though I was something unpleasant she'd stepped in. She beckoned me inside.

All my instincts screamed at me to leave. The air inside the attic stung, biting the inside of my mouth.

Run. Something is wrong.

I took quick breaths. Beads of sweat rimmed her face, but her expression was cold as marble.

As I entered the room, my nerves charged. Did she know about Aimée and Luc? I inched closer, every muscle in my body coiled.

The sharp smile that cut across her face raised the hair on the back of my neck.

Step.

The floorboards creaked and Stepmother shifted her weight.

Step.

Run!

I was halfway to Stepmother when the door to the attic slammed shut. I whirled to see Toad blocking the door and Oil leering at me from next to it. Panic seared through my nerves. What were they doing here?

Behind me, I could hear Stepmother moving, limping slightly without her cane. My back felt very exposed.

"I heard you quit." Her accent clipped her words short, her voice as bitter as vinegar.

Oil's soft laughter prickled my skin and I groaned. I should have known they'd come straight here—to tell Stepmother.

My heart pounded. *Out, get out.*

Stepmother moved to the side of the room and stood between her desk and the roaring fire. "Grab her."

On my left, Oil advanced, a wicked grin on his face. As he rushed me, his arms outstretched, I crouched to attack. A feral growl tore from my throat and I charged, ducking under his arms. Before his momentum carried him past me, I rose and swung my elbow, aiming for his face. A satisfying crunch followed and he fell to the floor. Oil howled, and blood poured from a broken nose.

The floorboards on my right creaked a warning as Toad strode forward, swinging his thick arms. If he caught me, I'd never get away. I circled, placing the door at my back. I glanced around and back. The door was ten feet behind me.

On my left was the fireplace and Stepmother.

If I ran for it, they'd be on me by the time I touched the doorknob. *Weapon, I need a weapon.* The jewelry box on the desk might work, but Stepmother was still too close.

Toad stalked closer, his glassy eyes fixed on me. He moved from the middle of the room, guarding any routes of escape.

Oil stood, blood pouring from his nostrils. His open-mouthed smile made me want to crawl out of my skin. He wiped his face with his sleeve, smearing red.

Stepmother glided closer to the fireplace. I turned to Toad, who was now only four feet away. With Stepmother on my left, Toad in front, and Oil on my right, there was no way out of this, except behind me.

The door was so close—only six feet away. I wiped my sweaty palms on my pants.

Toad held his position near the desk while Oil closed in on my right side, forcing me closer to the roaring fire. My head pounded and sweat broke out on my skin. Just a few more feet to the left and I could lunge for the door.

I felt something happening on my left before I knew what it was. Time slowed. Stepmother's hand dove near the fire. I ducked at the movement, then I caught the gleam of the cane in her hand. Holding onto the end of the cane, she raised its raven head across her body and swept down behind my legs.

My back hit the floor and my head cracked on the wood. Ringing filled my ears.

"Hold her," Stepmother said, her voice cold and impassive.

I rolled to one side but Toad and Oil surged forward. Toad's meaty hands pinned my shoulders to the floor. I pulled with my stomach and kicked my feet high, aiming for Toad's head. He moved his head to the side.

Oil licked his blood-covered lips.

My heart hammered. *No, no, no.*

Oil leaned down and reached for my feet.

"Don't touch me!" I screamed. I pulled my legs to my chest, then kicked at his face, hitting his nose a second time. He shrieked and fell.

I kicked up again, aiming for Toad.

Air whistled above me just before a bone-shattering crack exploded in my shins.

Pain ripped through me and I howled. Toad pressed against my shoulders, forcing my back to dig into the floorboards. I pulled my legs up again but slower, fighting gravity.

Another whistling sound as Stepmother's cane thudded into my stomach. I curled in agony and more pain shot up my legs. I coughed and gagged.

With both hands, she drove the heavy head of the raven into my chest. My hands formed claws near my throat, trying to stop the air from escaping, then I turned my head to the side and retched.

Oil grabbed my legs and pinned them to the floor while Toad's hands moved from my shoulders to my wrists. He stretched my arms out, holding me tight. Oil's lips curled wolfishly and my heart screamed for escape. Heat from the fire pressed down on me.

My voice tore from my throat. "Please, please don't. You don't have to do this," I whimpered at Stepmother's back.

She stared into the fire. Panic and fear distorted my mind, making the flames seem to grow and spill from the hearth. She turned, her eyes burning with bitterness and hate, her face a calm mask of indifference.

Tears streamed down my face. "Why?" I cried. "Why would you do this?"

"Did you think you could leave? It's your fault we're in this mess. Your fault your father isn't here. You owe me."

My breath came in ragged gasps. Oil and Toad held me silently, their weight pressing me into the dirty floorboards, numbing my limbs.

"You are mine," she hissed. "You always have been. Perhaps you need a more permanent reminder."

She crept closer, her feet falling soft on the dingy floor. The fire burned behind her, hiding her face in shadow.

"The G-Garde Royale," I stammered. "I'll tell—"

"I'll turn you in for the lying thief you are," she said.

Betrayal burned through me, and I closed my eyes.

The memories of Stepmother's kindness—her teaching me to waltz, her crying over Papa—they all shattered in one instant, leaving only darkness. All the tears, sweat, and blood I'd shed training for her, for our family. I'd loved her because Papa had loved her. Loved her because she had loved me.

"Who do you think they'd believe? A thief or grieving widow?" She towered over me, her mouth a hard, unforgiving line.

My heart sank into a black pit. No one would believe me. Especially if Stepmother told them she'd caught the Magpie stealing from her.

Oil laughed.

Stepmother turned back to the fire. Only then did I notice the shaft of her cane protruding from the flames, the raven's head buried deep in the fire's heart.

"I'm going to give you a permanent reminder that you belong to me."

Stepmother pulled the end of her cane from the fire and held it in front of my face. The screaming head of the raven glowed angry and molten red. The heat radiating from it made sweat flow down my face and mingle with my tears.

"No." My muscles trembled.

Stepmother pressed the heel of her shoe into my wrist, holding it in place. As she ground her heel in deeper and forced my hand open, splintering pain lanced up my arm.

No. I couldn't close my fingers.

She lowered her cane, its hungry mouth screaming for flesh. I thrashed, straining every muscle to escape, but Oil and Toad held tight as Stepmother lowered the cane.

"Wait. Stop!" I screamed. "Stop!"

Stepmother regarded me coolly, the glowing metal bird inches from my palm.

"You need me. For the masque. And—and I need my hands." I gasped for breath. "How can I—how can I steal if my hands are burned?"

She paused a moment before she spoke, her voice bright with false emotion. "Of course. You are so thoughtful. Your hands are essential to your work."

Relief surged through my body as she pulled the cane away, my skin cooling with its distance.

"But where, if not your hands?" she asked quietly.

I shook my head, sobbing.

Toad shifted his weight, his slack features hovering over my face. Sweat streamed into the creases under his chin.

Stepmother leaned down and gripped the collar of my shirt. She pulled, tearing the fabric to expose my chest. Toad's jaw slackened and both he and Oil leaned in, their eyes lingering on my skin like hungry wolves.

Shame burned through me almost as hot as the fire. A familiar sickening sensation followed, deepening the wound, whispering that this was all my fault.

"Remember, you deserve this," she hissed.

I nodded. For what I did to Papa.

"This will suffice."

She lowered the still-red bird over my left breast, over my naked skin.

"No!"

Using both hands, she pressed the cane over my heart.

I screamed, the pain ripping me apart. The sickly sweet smell of burning flesh—my flesh—reached my nostrils.

Through my agony, a voice inside murmured, *This is your fault. You deserve this.*

Yes. My fault.

Then everything went black.

ARMAND 31

The chill crept through the apple orchard in the blue dawn light. I raised my sword and leveled it at the nearest tree. Father's latest missive, along with a practice speech he'd sent, fluttered weakly, run through with the end of the branch. The letter's words hammered at my head.

Sanson reported a contingent of Alemanian soldiers may have entered Lyonelle. Je ne permettrai plus. I have doubled the guards around Lierre. It is a shame Sanson must pull his weight and *yours.*

I sliced the practice speech and letter until tiny ribbons of paper fluttered to the ground. I pressed the heels of my hands against my eyes, then winced. *Beast's beard, my black eye.* I kicked at a clump of dried grass. Paper exploded from it like dandelion fluff. I was a failure.

I rubbed my neck and turned to face the direction of the Manette estate. It was only a few miles away, but I wanted—no, needed Cinderella here. Part of my heart tugged toward her and my body had to follow. She had done nothing to cure my stutter, but why did my stutter not bother me as much when I was with her?

I had to talk to her. I took a step then stopped. I gripped a branch, leaning against it, and exhaled. *Snap out of it, Armand. She is probably still asleep.*

A warmth burned through my chest. What was this feeling? Love? I picked up one of the torn pieces of paper and shredded it further. Bits of parchment fell like snow. Whatever was between us was different than anything I'd ever felt before. When I was with her, my stutter didn't matter. When I was with her, I was free.

I propped myself against the tree, the bark cutting into my back. How could I convince her I needed her by my side? My jaw tightened. I had to show her how much she meant to me, but how?

The answer was as obvious as an arrow hitting a bullseye. *You love her. Marry her.*

But how?

I'd subconsciously been thinking these thoughts and it only surprised me a little as they rose to the surface. My thoughts circled each other as I paced between the trees, kicking at loose clods of dirt, considering my options. Removing my shirt had been a shameless attempt to impress her, and I couldn't very well propose seminude. Could I?

"Ha!" Luc's voice rang in my ears as he leaped from behind a tree, making me stumble.

"*Soufre.*" As I pushed him away, I stepped on several fallen apples, nearly slipping again.

Luc slapped his knee. "Sorry, Armand. I couldn't help myself."

I straightened my jacket, my heart still racing. "D-don't do it again."

His smile disappeared as he looked at my face. "What happened to your lip?" He stepped closer and his eyebrows shot up. "Is that a shiner?"

My eye was thankfully already yellowing. "I had a rough n-night." I lifted a boot and grimaced at the grass and mushy apple stuck to it.

Luc smirked. "Apparently so."

I scraped my boot against the base of a trunk and the sour tang of rotting apples filled the orchard. "What are you doing here?"

Luc leaned against a tree and folded his arms. "I was going to visit my country lass, and as it is nearby, I came for your advice."

"On what?"

"Women."

"Ha. What m-makes you think I've g-got them figured out?" I straightened and walked between trees, turning away from the house. This would be a terrible conversation. I jammed my hands into my coat pockets, surprised to find the chess piece there. *How did that get in there?* I pulled it out and fiddled with it.

Luc trotted to my side, then stopped short and pulled my arm. He took the wooden figure. "Where did you get that?"

"Would you believe I s-stole it from s-someone?"

Luc paused, his brows tight. "Actually," he said, "I would. Did she have dark hair and green eyes?"

Now it was my turn to heave a sigh as Cinderella's face surfaced in my mind. "Yes, and a bewitching smile and a razor-sharp t-tongue."

"Seems like she stole something from you in return," he said, his tone smug. "What will Father say?"

I stopped in my tracks. It wasn't hard to guess. He'd say it was disgraceful that the crown prince would dare consider marriage, let alone lose his heart, to such a woman. Lower, fallen aristocracy, no less, and a thief to boot. Reformed thief, but still.

I lifted a shoulder. "Beasts if I care." I was surprised to find that it was true. I *didn't* care what Father said. I would fight for Cinderella no matter what. Provided she'd have me, of course.

Luc stepped forward along the path, continuing our walk. I snatched the nearest apple from the tree and bit into it, the tart juice stinging my split lip. I grimaced.

"How did she s-steal the chess piece from you?" I tossed the apple aside. "How would the Magpie ever have g-gotten c-close to you, let alone to pick your pockets?" I stopped walking as a horrible thought occurred to me. I turned to him, a muscle twitched in my cheek. "Wait, have you been leaving offerings like the other c-courtiers? Hoping the Magpie would pay you a visit?" A flood of jealousy surged inside. He was trying to steal the Magpie right out from under my nose.

Luc held up his hands, backing away. "Wait, the Magpie? You're in love with the Magpie?" He backed up into the low-hanging branches behind him.

I advanced on him, my fists balled as a wave of vehemence swept over me, surprising me with its intensity. "Are you in love with her too? What about your c-country lass? Are you leading her on as well?"

Laughter escaped Luc's lips and he pushed me back gently. The branches swayed as he pushed them aside and stepped onto the path. "Relax, Armand. You've got it all wrong. When I lost the chess piece, I was visiting my betrothed . . ." Luc sighed as he continued. "My sweet, golden angel, *Mademoiselle* Aimée." He looked so lovesick my stomach twisted.

His betrothed? My sudden rush of jealousy subsided. There was no way he was courting two ladies at once. He was helplessly in love with Aimée.

The sun rose higher and warm orange light fell on the orchard, cutting through the trees.

"C-congratulations on your betrothal," I said, clapping him on the back, completely relieved he had no intentions toward Cinderella.

"Thank you." He beamed. "After a rather unfortunate accident involving an exceedingly muddy pond, Aimée and her sister helped themselves to the contents of my pockets." He stopped and rubbed his chin thoughtfully. "Cinderella Manette is the Magpie?"

I nodded. "She's been helping me with my speech." Or showing me how to accept my speech. "More or less."

"Which means . . . ?" Luc said.

"Aimée is the Magpie's stepsister," I finished.

Luc whistled.

"Those Manette sisters . . ." I said wistfully, seeing Cinderella's beautiful face in my mind. I rolled the chess piece between my fingers.

"Yes." He nodded. "Aren't they wonderful?" Pink and orange morning light settled on his unfocused, slack-jawed face. He looked like he was about to be sick—and liked it. Was that how I looked when I spoke of Cinderella? Even if it was, I didn't care.

A fish jumped in the pond and Luc shook himself awake. He picked up a pebble and skipped it across the water's surface. "So you stole something from the Magpie?" He bent down, searching for another rock.

The memory of Cinderella's horror-stricken face as I'd shown her the chess piece resurfaced. "More like her bodice g-gave it to me."

Luc froze, his arm pulled back for another throw. "You know what? I don't want to know. But please tell me how it feels being in love with the kingdom's most wanted thief? Father will have your hide."

"Both our hides," I said. "Obviously you have no q-qualms about being in love with a thief."

"Accomplice," Luc corrected, throwing another rock. A few ducks quacked and swam to the other side of the pond. "I think Aimée was put up to it. The Magpie too."

I nodded in agreement. Heat flashed in my chest at the thought of someone forcing Cinderella to steal. And deal with that oily *crétin* and his *gros ami*. I tamped my anger down. "But by whom?"

Luc shrugged. "Your guess is as good as mine."

We continued walking silently, both at a loss. By now, we'd passed through the trees and were at the edge of the dense woods that bordered Eline's orchards.

I turned to Luc. "I'm not g-going to have to guess who forced them into this mess. I'm going to ask Cinderella tonight. Then I'll p-propose."

Luc's eyebrows shot into his hairline. "Nothing says 'I love you' like cold accusations."

I folded my arms, scowling at him. "What do you think I should do?" If there was anyone who could come up with a harebrained scheme that was likely to succeed, it was Luc.

He shrugged, then clapped me on the back again. "I came to you for advice, remember?"

I put on my most princely face. "Well, I am the firstborn. And as your p-prince, you will cede to my wishes. Advise me."

He scratched his chin. "What have you done so far? Probably nothing more than giving her a flower."

"It was an imperial r-rose, to be exact," I said.

"*Très bon.*" Luc nodded approvingly. "But this has to be something more."

"M-more?" What more could I do? I had broken the law, risked arrest, and had trash dumped over me, but I didn't think those acts counted as romantic overtures. "So what do I do?"

Luc's shoulders rose. "Beasts if I know."

I grabbed my hair and groaned, looking heavenward. Luc started toward the house and I followed. I was almost out of time. Showing up shirtless was sounding more and more appealing.

Close to the house, one of Lady Eline's laundry maids brought in the washing from the line. Several orange-colored napkins flashed in the sun. I grimaced. Lady Eline must have had extra fabric from reupholstering that repulsive chair.

Then an idea snapped into place like a perfectly thrust saber. I grabbed Luc's arm, still staring at the orange napkins. Yes, this would be perfect.

"C-can you do me a favor?"

Luc nodded, though slowly. "As long as it's not arresting Aimée."

I shook my head, my eyes boring into his. I had to make sure he knew this was important. "Can you help me set up something t-tonight? For Cinderella?"

He grinned, rubbing his hands together. "Knew you'd figure it out. I'm in."

I nodded. "Good. And do some digging on the M-Manette sisters for me." Perhaps if I found out why Cinderella was forced to steal, then I could find out how to help her stop—preferably before she was arrested. "You must find out what's really going on. Between t-tonight and t-tomorrow's preparations for the masquerade, I won't have the time."

My excitement grew the more I spoke. This could work. With Luc and I working together, this could actually work.

"Look into any thefts before the Magpie showed up. Particularly ones connected with Alexander Manette's trading partners."

Luc nodded. "Anything else?"

My eyes narrowed. Knowing why she stole was only the first step. Getting her out of the mess was something else entirely. "Yes. Since you're digging, I'll also need you to look into Sanson. I think he is t-trying to start a w-war with Alemania. F-find d-documents, l-ledgers. There must be something."

"War with Alemania? Wouldn't put it past him." Luc barked out a laugh. "It's about time someone looked into him. I'm only upset no one has done it sooner. But what does he have to do with the Manettes?"

I shrugged. "Maybe nothing."

"Or everything," Luc said. "Either way, he's dirty."

"You'll have to lie," I said.

"Gladly."

"And probably gamble."

"Happily."

"And most likely get sloshing drunk."

Luc clapped his hands together, a wicked glint in his eye. "When can I start?"

"Right away. But come back here late tonight and tell me what you've found out."

Luc rubbed his chin. "You certainly don't give a man much time. Looks like it will have to be a quick visit with Aimée."

I clapped him on the back, preparations galloping through my head. "My idea for Cinderella tonight won't take long. I'll just need a few things."

My heart raced as I outlined my plan to Luc. Tonight I was going to get answers—for better or worse. At the very least, it was going to be interesting.

32 CYN

Images swirled in my mind. Oil's face. A screaming raven. Toad's dark eyes . . . and Stepmother, dancing in the fire. The smell of burnt flesh hit my nostrils. Turning to one side, I retched.

I sat up and leaned against the wall behind me, my head pounding.

Where am I?

Late morning light filtered through the circular window, and the attic stretched before me like an empty field. The door leading downstairs seemed miles away. Stepmother's long desk sat ten feet ahead of me and to the right.

The smell of cedar pushed aside the smell of burning meat. Where was it coming from? Why did it smell like that?

Lightning pulsed from my shoulder and I gritted my teeth as the pain built on itself. Every muscle throbbed. I leaned forward and took deep breaths. Flashes of memory came to me. Oil and Toad pinning me down. Stepmother's cane. Screaming. So much screaming. Then it all came thundering back.

Stepmother had burned me—branded me.

As I reached for the nape of my shirt, my hands shook. The blood-soaked fabric had dried with my skin. Dark rust colored the edges. I moaned through my clenched teeth and gently peeled the shirt away, gasping as it pulled at my skin. As I exposed more of the wound, air hissed through my lungs in heavy breaths and my forehead beaded with sweat. Almost there.

Je l'ai fait. With a final tug, the shirt came free. My muscles turned watery with relief. I lifted my face, staring at the wooden support beams above me. I'd look at the damage in a moment.

I laughed at the ceiling, though I wanted to cry—to curl up in a tiny ball and sob.

But I couldn't. I needed to dress the wound before it became infected. I knew all too well what could happen.

I looked at the burn, and tears streamed down my face. My skin was dry and cracked with bloody red crevices that had ripped open when I'd removed the fabric. Though the entire area was swollen and puffy, the face and outline of the raven could easily be seen. A giant blister had formed, surrounding the seared skin, looking like a pale pink worm under my flesh.

I rubbed my face with shaky hands. My mouth was dry, my tongue sluggish. *Water, I need water.* Groaning, I pressed my back against the wall and stood up, my legs wobbly. I cried in pain as the weight of my arm pulled my skin tight. My right hand cradled my left elbow and I hugged my arm close, hunching my left shoulder to relieve the tension on the wound.

I would never get the wound cleaned on my own. I needed help. Lavender and frankincense, if we still had any, would ease the sting and help with healing, but they were in the kitchen, three flights of stairs down. My skin went cold. I'd have to get there myself.

Where was Shar? She should have come back from the forest already. Did she know what had happened?

Tap, tap.

What now? I turned to the circular window a couple of feet away from me. A pumpkin-orange light bobbed by the window, lazily looping and then knocking against the glass like a trapped honeybee, trying to get out.

I closed my eyes and groaned. Shar. She must have come home at some point last night.

"Shar." My voice croaked out of my throat.

Tap, tap.

"Shar." I lifted my left arm toward the window and winced as pain shot through me.

Tap. Tap, tap.

Her light flared at every hit. Beasties. The equinox was tonight. She didn't even recognize me.

My legs shuffled to the window and I reached for the latch. Stuck. As I leaned harder, sweat broke out on my face, and my head and shoulder shrieked in protest. The latch gave way all at once, and I thumped against the wall and bit back a scream.

Shar flew out into the late morning air, drunkenly looping her way toward the forest.

I leaned against the wall and waited for the room to stop spinning. Who could help? Armand would, if I could somehow get word to him. Longing filled me with a desperate, aching hunger. I wanted him, wanted his arms around me. I wanted him to scoop me up and tell me he could make it all better. Like in the garden. The map room.

Suddenly, shame burned through me, so intense that I gasped and cowered from myself. If he saw this wound, he would know. No one who killed their own father deserved any kind of love.

I cradled my arm. Who else could I ask? Aimée? She was either asleep or with Luc by now. Not Aimée. I didn't want her to know what her mother had done. I would have to take care of myself.

The door was only twenty feet away, but the attic seemed to stretch into infinity and I trembled.

As I pushed off from wall and almost fell. Pain ripped through my head like shrapnel from a *bombe fumigène*. Support. I needed something to get me across the room. I needed Stepmother's cane. Oh, the irony.

My eyes scanned the room for anything that could help. The mannequin from my practice sessions rested a few feet to the left of me and still wore the jacket of bells. It would work—if I could only reach it.

One hand pressed against the wall for support, I pushed off and stumbled forward, then fell against the wire frame. The bells' bright sound filled the room. Fire roared up my arm and I bit down, tasting blood. I had to be quiet. I wasn't going to give Stepmother, wherever she was, the satisfaction of knowing how much I hurt.

I inched toward the door, using the mannequin as a crutch. *Why didn't we add wheels to this thing?*

After several agonizing minutes and dripping in sweat, I leaned against the door, my chest heaving. *I hate this attic.* Before Papa died, I'd hardly ever come here. Now it seemed the place in the house I visited most frequently. I abandoned the makeshift crutch by the door and crept down the stairs.

After an eternity, I stood at the threshold of the kitchen, my throat dry as sand. Water. Where was the water? My vision throbbed with each heartbeat. I needed a drink. I stumbled into the kitchen and knocked over the broom and some pots. They clattered to the floor, the noise pounding nails into my head.

Footsteps sounded immediately from the hall. *Stepmother!* Fear shoved my pain back, chilling my skin. I had to hide. The room's outline blurred. I lunged, banging my hip on the table, and fell into the corner, pulling myself into a tight ball. I rocked back and forth, sobs choking my throat.

The footsteps came closer and I whimpered.

She had found me.

A hand touched my back, and I flinched.

"Cyn?" a gentle voice asked.

The soft call of my name pierced my fear. A warm hand touched my knee and I started, then looked up. *Aimée.* She was dressed in her bedclothes and her hair was a halo around her worried face.

Relief dissolved everything, and I held her, choking on fresh tears.

She stroked my hair. "You're safe." Her delicate hands gently rubbed my back, spreading warmth. "I'm here."

My chest shook, and the pressure of her solid arms slowed my breathing, and I nodded. Safe.

Finally, I took Aimée's gloved hand and stood, my legs trembling. I released her hand and leaned against the kitchen wall for support.

Aimée's gasped, her round eyes wide, and she reached for my shoulder. Her hand hovered, unsure of what to do.

"What happened?" she whispered.

"It's nothing," I gasped, weakly trying to shield her from my burn.

"*Ma sœur*, you're hurt."

"I'm fine," I croaked. The room swayed and my knees buckled.

Aimée caught me before I fell, then helped me to a chair at the table. I eased my arm onto the table and sighed, my skin no longer pulled tight. Aimée sat in the chair opposite, her brow pulled into a tight line.

"Let me see," she said, her normally gentle voice tight.

I turned to cover my shoulder, but she put a hand on my leg and leaned forward. I was too weak to do anything other than submit. I leaned back against the chair, the top of the backrest jabbing into the base of my skull. She lifted a corner of my shirt. Her face paled and she hissed at the familiar outline of the burn. Her features hardened with a grim understanding, and she gently placed the remains of my shirt back over my skin.

"Tell me what you need," she said.

"Lavender," I croaked. "Frankincense. Almond oil." The fact that she didn't ask any more questions was as much a relief as anything. "And water."

She retrieved the water first—which I guzzled so fast I nearly choked—and then rushed into the pantry to make the ointment.

As I instructed, Aimée mixed the liniment, then brought it to the table with more water and clean linen. I watched as if in a trance. She stirred the ointment, somehow managing to keep her gloves clean. I filled my lungs with the cool kitchen air and soothing herbal smells.

Aimée lifted the fabric to clean the burn, her chair creaking, and I bit my lip and looked away. She applied the ointment, pressing the clean linen to my skin, and I groaned as the pain intensified and then cooled.

Just breathe, Cyn.

Aimée's gentle touch released the last knots in my muscles, and I slumped in the chair, closing my eyes. I was safe, for now.

Aimée dipped her chin to her chest. "She wasn't always like this. After James died. She changed."

My chair now creaked as I sat straighter. What had happened to Stepmother that had made her like this?

Aimée continued but avoided looking me in the eye. "After we came out from hiding in the woods, we returned to the house. It was nothing but charred stones. Mother searched for hours, but they were gone." Aimée's voice trembled like aspen leaves. "When we left, Mother was clutching a jewelry box she'd found."

That's what rested on the desk in the attic.

Aimée's feet scraped the floor as she leaned forward and dipped the cloth in more ointment. She gently dabbed it on my shoulder.

"We came to Lyonelle and struggled. We worked so hard sewing and mending, but I knew it wasn't enough. Soon, Mother would go out at night with nothing. But each morning it was like we'd had a visit from *Père Noël*. Blankets, clothes, then jewelry and paintings." Aimée's forehead wrinkled as memories played out in her mind.

That sounded too familiar. I sipped at my water, my brows drawn together. I was just like her. Revulsion snaked through me, making my burn pound. *We are the same.*

"One night I woke up scared. Nightmare." Her tone was stoic, but strong emotions rippled just below the surface. "I lit a candle." She shrugged her shoulders. "And I saw the box, sitting under her bed."

I sat up again in my chair as much as my shoulder would allow.

"I was just going to see what was inside and put it back. Promise." She gave a weak smile. "Inside was a piece of burnt wood from the house, Father's wedding ring, and a blackened silver rattle—James's rattle." Her voice broke. "Mother came back and found me, crying and holding the rattle."

She shivered, even though the room was warm. The hairs on the back of my arms rose.

"She screamed and grabbed my hand . . . the one that was holding the box," Aimée said, her voice halting. "And she pulled me to the fire and . . . put my hands in the coals."

I gasped, my chest aching at the sudden movement.

"I screamed and Mother came to herself, but . . ."

Aimée pulled off her gloves. She set them next to the mixing bowl, then held out her hands for me to see. I held one carefully with mine. The skin on the back of her hands was pocked and her palms glistened, tight and shiny from spotted burn marks. I cringed at the old wounds.

"Aimée," I breathed.

"Mother kept saying she was sorry." Aimée put her gloves back on and continued to apply the ointment to my wound. I sat back in shock.

"She's not herself," she continued. "Hasn't been since your father died."

I nodded. Stepmother had been happy—with Papa, as a part of our family.

As Aimée picked off a scrap of fabric, I moaned. I certainly used to be happier. Before this burn, before stealing, before Papa died.

But since I'd met Armand, things had become better. I'd had someone to talk to. Someone who could make me laugh. He was intelligent, determined, and adorable. He had a great heart—a heart that might be mine. Could his tenderness even be love?

I dismissed the hope as soon as it came. He wouldn't—couldn't—love me if he knew what I'd done.

He'd been wrong. I couldn't leave. There was no way out. Daughters who murdered their fathers didn't deserve to be free. I belonged to her.

Aimée replaced her gloves and stoppered the almond oil, offering me a tiny smile. "I'm not saying what Mother did was right. I only wanted you to understand. And to say thank you."

I eyed her ruefully. "Thank you?" *For getting us into this mess in the first place?*

Aimée smiled, lighting up the room. "For keeping us going. You'd probably face the Great Beast himself to save our family."

As she replaced the bottles on the shelves, they clinked together and I sighed in relief, the lavender relaxing my muscles. How was I supposed to go to the ball and do whatever Stepmother wanted me to do when I was burned so badly?

Tears pricked behind my eyes again. I banished them with the back of my hand.

I moved to stand.

"You're not going anywhere," Aimée said, gently but firmly pushing me back into the chair.

"But my chores. I'm meeting Armand tonight. The ball is tomorrow, and I need that shoe."

"You'll feel a lot better if you're rested," Aimée said firmly. "I'll do the chores."

"You?" I lowered my chin and leveled my gaze at her.

"Me."

"You've never milked the cows or tended to the animals," I said. The very thought of Aimée feeding the chickens was as unbelievable as the idea of mice turning into horses. I pressed my cool glass of water to my forehead, savoring the chill, then took a sip.

"Well, it's a good thing I'm betrothed to a milkman."

I choked and droplets sprayed over the table. "Really?" I pressed my lips together. *This complicates everything.* Stepmother would never approve, and she'd take it out on me.

"Yes," she said, her hand on her hips. "And I can see you thinking this is your problem. It's not. I'm a big girl. I'll tell Mother."

I eyed her, my jaw jutting out.

"When the time is right," Aimée said, her eyes toward the floor. "Maybe after we're married."

My eyes narrowed to slits.

Aimée glanced at me, then threw up her hands. "*Ça, alors*, I'll tell her after the ball." Her tone was only mildly annoyed. "Now you rest. Luc is on his way." She poured several more cups of water, lining them up in front of me. "So you don't have to pour them yourself. Let me take care of you for a change."

I sighed in relief. Someone watching out for me? That would be nice. Nicer still if it were Armand. I imagined him pouring me water, his brown curls falling over his face. Then, resting my head on the back of the chair, I closed my eyes.

33

Cyn

I woke with a stiff neck. In the dim kitchen interior, I saw evidence of Aimée's touch. The floor was swept, the dishes were clean, and a pile of apples, onions, and potatoes sat at the end of the table, waiting to be cut. A plate of bread and cheese and a pitcher of water rested on the table within easy reach. The smell of lavender and almond oil lingered in the air from the bowl of ointment on the table. A fresh pile of linen lay neatly folded next to the bowl.

I gritted my teeth and straightened in my chair. My fingers curled around a cup. I brought it to my lips, gulping greedily. After emptying two more, I licked my lips, then stretched for the cloth. The skin pulled tight across the burn and I hissed. I blew on the blister but stopped as the raw skin prickled with pain.

Footsteps clipped across the floor and I turned.

Aimée rushed to the table, quickly changing my bandages. "No, no. *Autorise moi.*"

"Where is she?" My voice scratched and I pressed chapped lips together. Still so thirsty.

"She said she was conducting business." Aimée gently dabbed at my shoulder.

"Business?"

She shrugged.

Something moved outside the kitchen door leading to the yard and I half-turned before my skin caught. Pain surged and sweat formed on my upper lip.

Aimée's hands pressed against my arm. "It's only Luc. I told him to wait outside."

I nodded and my nerves uncoiled. I didn't want anyone to see me like this.

"There." She finished by wiping a few drops of spilled ointment from the table. "Now, eat." She pointed at the plate.

As if on cue, my stomach grumbled. I grabbed a fistful of bread and devoured half of the loaf. Aimée grabbed a couple of apples and whisked out the door. I leaned back in my chair and closed my eyes.

Just a quick rest, Cyn. You still need to meet Armand.

I started awake, my head pounding like Pumpkin's galloping hooves. Stars peeked through the kitchen window. I perched on the edge of the chair, then stood. The room swam. I stumbled to the door. I rested my back against the kitchen doorframe, the cool autumn night bathing me in soothing fresh air. I sucked it in as deeply as the burn would allow.

The moon was already high in the purple sky.

Petites bêtes. I'm going to be late. My black clothes were not only dirty with ash and stubborn bits of trash that hadn't washed off in the creek, they were also now dank with sweat and blood from last night. I also needed a sling for my arm. Shame burned through me, reigniting the burn. I covered my shoulder with what was left of my shirt collar.

I needed that shoe. And I needed to see him one last time.

My heart throbbed as if it, too, had been seared by Stepmother's cane. I clenched my hand against my leg.

As I shuffled to the stable, evidence of Aimée and Luc's hard work throughout the day was everywhere. The yard was clean, the leaves gathered, and from the smell of hay permeating the air, the chicken coop and goat pen had been cleaned.

I froze. Did they remember Papa and Maman's trees? I bit my lip. Cedar trees were particularly susceptible to snow if they weren't properly prepared. Maybe I could do that myself, though it would cost me precious time. Still, I needed to see Maman and Papa.

I shuffled down the path, kicking up tiny clouds of dust with each step. Something was wrong. There was more open sky than there should have been. *Where is Maman's tree?* My heart fell into my churning stomach. Why couldn't I see it?

Air rasped in my chest, and I ran to where the trees should have stood— trees that weren't there.

"No, no, no!"

Maman's tree lay across the path, angry cuts gouged deep in the trunk. I placed my palms against the rough bark. *No.* My palms tingled with sweat. *Where is Papa's tree? Where is Papa?* My breathing shallowed.

I stumbled around the cedar, and a strangled cry escaped my throat. Papa's sapling was reduced to a ragged stump stabbing up from the ground.

Ugly pain and sobs wracked my body. Last night's fire. In the attic. It had smelled of cedar. Stepmother had used Maman's tree for the fire and left Papa's tree to die.

I wrapped my arms around my body, trying to hold my heart together. I stared at the broken sapling stump. I pressed my fingers over its jagged edges, hoping to feel something different than I saw. *Maybe I can fix it. I can still save them.* Splinters dug into my fingernails.

I collapsed onto my side, twigs and leaves digging into my body. My burn throbbed with renewed pain, but I didn't care. Maman and Papa were gone.

I pushed myself into a sitting position, the burn on my shoulder scream- ing for me to stop. I curled against Maman's tree, hugging my knees. *I did this. I never should have quit the Magpie.*

If I'd saved Papa, things would be different. Before his last trip, he'd asked for my help. He'd told me I was responsible for the house. And I'd ignored him.

A breeze swept across the path and I shivered in the cold. Nothing. I had nothing. Everything had been stolen from me. Father, the music box, my honesty . . . and now the trees.

I remained sitting on the cold dirt for a long while.

By the time I pulled together enough energy to go into the barn and use the mounting block to climb atop Pumpkin, the sky was a cold, impassive blue. As if sensing the need to be gentle, Pumpkin held still.

As I lifted my leg over the saddle, I bit my lip, sucking through my teeth. My skin pulled, bringing tears to my eyes. I let them fall. I tapped my heels to Pumpkin's side, and slowly, we made our way toward Lady Eline's.

Armand

34

As I paced by Eline's outer wall, my heart rammed against my ribs. When I'd left, Luc had been putting on the finishing touches for my surprise tonight. Aside from the fact that he'd smelled as if he'd been mucking out stables, he'd set up everything perfectly.

I pressed the wrinkles in my cranberry-colored velvet evening jacket, then fiddled with the golden trim. *Stop, Armand. She cares about you. She'll forgive you for lying to her for the entire time since you met.*

I kicked at a lavender bush. *If she doesn't kill me first.*

Someone hissed from over the wall and I froze. "Armand."

I was at the wall in three strides and pressed my hands against its cold face. "Cinderella, is that you?"

"Who else would it be?" the voice snapped.

My heart soared. It was her.

"Can you climb over?" she whispered.

"Why can't you c-come over here?" I frowned and looked down at my jacket and vest. I had tried on four different vests before settling on this one embellished with the royal motif and golden thread. It would be ruined if it snagged on anything. And I looked so good in it.

"Are you coming over or not?" Her sharp voice cut through my hesitation.

"I'm coming." I sighed and gathered a handful of vines. *Apparently, we don't care about stealth anymore.*

I dropped to the other side, jarring my heel bones as I landed.

She was leaning against Pumpkin at an odd angle, her arms hunched awkwardly around her left side. "Do you have the shoe?"

I stepped closer, waving my hand vaguely. "It's somewhere . . . else."

She closed her eyes, then shook her head. Her skin glistened in the moonlight. Was that sweat?

She unwrapped Pumpkin's reins from the tree. "I don't have time for this. I was crazy to even come." She turned to leave and Pumpkin followed behind. "The shoe is yours."

My stomach dropped. That was it? No goodbye? I opened my mouth, but nothing came out. I swallowed. *No.* She couldn't leave—not yet. The shoe. The surprise. I needed to tell her who I was. And how I felt.

I jogged to catch up and took her by the left hand, pulling her backwards. "Cinderella, I—"

She screamed and fell to her knees, her right hand flying to her shoulder.

Her cries melted my bones and tears streamed down her face.

I dropped next to her. "I'm so—I'm sorry!" I hovered, not daring to touch her. "What happened?"

Her cries melted my bones and tears streamed down her face. Her face was contorted in pain, her body trembling.

I inched forward with my arms wide. "Let me see," I said, softly. I moved beside her slowly, as if she were a spooked horse.

Pumpkin tugged at his reins, and Cinderella let them slip from her hand.

As I shifted closer, a stale tang like an afternoon in the sword training yard drifted from near Cinderella. Why did she smell of sweat and blood?

I peered across her shoulder. Her shirt was torn near the collar. I pulled her hand away. The soothing smell of lavender combined with the sharp scent of frankincense filled my lungs.

My chest tightened and anger flared. I knew those smells.

A corner of linen peeked through the collar of her shirt. "M-may I?" I held my breath. *Please say yes.* After what seemed like an eternity, she nodded. Gently I lifted the covering, then I bit down a curse.

"Who did this?" I whispered, my voice shaking with anger. "Was—w-was it those—was it those—those m-men from the wharf?" My fury burned my tongue.

"Yes . . . no. Sort of," she said, her lip trembling.

"Where are they?" I said, my jaw barely moving. How dare they touch her again, especially after they knew who I was! First, I'd have the Garde Royale arrest them. Then I'd tear them to pieces with my bare hands.

Her face screwed tight, and she leaned forward to stand. "Stop worrying about me. This is the last night. Where's my shoe?"

"You're b-burned and b-bleeding! Why are you worried about a b-beastly shoe?"

She winced as if I'd struck her. She spoke through gritted teeth. "Do. You. Have. It."

"Yes—no. I told you. It's somewhere c-close."

"This is the last night of the bargain," she said, her voice sharp. Pumpkin raised his head and flicked his ears toward the sound. Cinderella lowered her voice to a hiss. "You're supposed to have the shoe."

She glared daggers, then turned and shuffled away, still clutching her arm.

No. If I didn't stop her, I could lose her forever. There was still so much I wanted to do with her—to say. And something very important I needed to ask her. Even if I stammered through the whole thing.

"S-stay," I called after her retreating form.

She stopped, her back toward me. Her body caved in on itself, and the need to protect her, to hold her close, flooded through me.

In a few strides, I caught up with her. "P-please. You n-need to rest." I placed a hand on hers. "And I have s-something for you."

Her eyes searched my face. Could she see how I felt? How could she not? A few feet separated us, but every nerve in my body longed to hold her. I stepped forward, closing the distance between us. I brushed a wisp of hair from her face.

"For m-me, it s-stopped being about our bargain a long time ago."

Her features softened, and I sighed. A good sign. I stepped closer and cupped her face in my hand, caressing her cheeks. She exhaled and leaned into my hand. How could so much strength be in such a small frame? She may not admit it, but she needed me—just as I needed her.

"I have s-something for you. In the orchard," I said, gently placing my arm around her. I wanted to scoop her up in my arms but I didn't want to hurt her further.

She nodded and together we shuffled toward the orchard.

Cyn

After he shows you . . . whatever it is, you have to take the shoe and leave. I nodded to myself. *Shoe. Leave. Shoe. Leave.*

Armand offered me his arm.

Except he was here. This was our last night. And I was going to take whatever time I could with Armand. I would at least have that.

I wrapped my arm around his, pressing my fingers into his red-and-gold jacket. His hair curled around the nape of his neck. *Petite bête*, he looked good.

As we walked into the apple orchard, the smell of dirt and fruit filled my nose. My shoulder ached, but Armand's body moved with mine, and I wanted to lean into his arms and never leave. And it hurt. Why did he have to be so wonderful?

We ducked beneath waxy apples ready for harvest. The night was as silent as if it were under one of Shar's charms. A dim yellow light flickered between the trees. *Perhaps she did have a part.*

We crossed through the trees toward the light until we stopped in a clearing between the orchard and the woods bordering Lady Eline's land.

When I saw the glade, my mouth hung open, and what lay before me dulled my pain. By the light of several candles, a sumptuous meal waited. Breads and jams surrounded a tray of cold meats and cheeses. Two orange sitting pillows lay next to plates and cutlery. A tea service had also been set. Recently. Steam rose from the spout of the teapot.

How had he known? Papa and I had shared many autumn picnics to celebrate the end of the trading season, the time when he was home to stay. I rubbed Armand's velvet sleeve between my fingers. Armand had somehow peered into my heart, seen the broken bits, and set out to mend them one by one. I waved my hand in front of my face. What was it about Armand that reduced me nearly to tears?

I took in one final detail of the picnic and gasped in delight. Lady Eline's other shoe rested on an orange sateen pillow, glowing in the candlelight.

Armand bowed and gestured for me to sit. With his help, I managed it with minimal pain. He took my hand and tiny fingers of lightning shot through me.

"Thank you," I whispered. Emotions, both warm and confusing, stirred inside my heart. This was wonderful. What was I feeling? Did it matter?

Armand dished out some food, and as the warm nourishment hit my stomach, I sighed again. *Délicieux.*

The moon cast an ethereal light, weaving a dream I never wanted to wake up from.

35 ARMAND

The food was terrible. I was so nervous, everything turned to sand in my mouth. I gulped down the strawberry jam and sharp creamy goat cheese, then choked on the tasteless mush. I hacked into the pumpkin-orange napkin. *Soufre.* I'd be dead before dessert if I didn't tell her soon. All it would take was a few short words: *I am the prince. I lied. Would you like a royal pardon? Good. Now tell me who hurt you so I can execute them.*

Just say it. I cleared my throat.

Cinderella reclined on her side, one of the pillows supporting her wounded shoulder. Her black clothing stood out in stark contrast to the orange linens.

"I'm a ly-ly-ing . . ."

Cinderella's fork stopped halfway to her mouth. Her brows knit together. "You're a lion?"

I wrung a napkin in my fist. *No, I'm a lying beast.*

Why was it suddenly so hard to talk to her? I had to tell her who I was, but the words wouldn't come. At least not whole. I opened my mouth to try again.

"Look," Cinderella whispered, pointing to the sky.

My eyes followed her finger and I saw several stars looping lazily in the sky. No. Those weren't stars. These lights were closer. Much closer. They were about the size of my palm and a pale yellow—like Shar's light.

My heart stopped. The fae. They were back. *Another vision?* Images of the navy ships on fire swam in my mind. I'd long ago discerned that Cinderella was the woman in my arms. And even if she wasn't, I wouldn't dance with anyone else.

I looked back at Cinderella. Her face glimmered with excitement. "I've never seen so many."

I stood and helped her to her feet, careful not to disturb her shoulder. Her scream from earlier echoed in my mind, and my spine crawled.

We stood, the tips of our fingers brushing against each other. First one light, then another gathered, coming from all directions. I raised my brow. Lady Eline didn't have any house fairies. But still they came, swooping and fluttering, always in the same direction—toward the woods. Their combined light glowed like a golden moon from within the trees. I bent down and blew out the picnic candles. The light of the fairies intensified in the new darkness.

What were they planning?

The fairies flew over us, disappearing into the forest beyond Lady Eline's property.

"Where are they going?" Cinderella's gaze followed them.

More fairies flew into the woodland. None spoke as they drifted past, and I was pulled to them like a fish on a line.

I turned to take Cinderella in, absorbing every detail. Her hair was rumpled. Her clothes—dirty, torn, and old. I could see the trails her tears had made on her smudged face. She was radiant.

Too bad I had to ruin everything. *Tell her now, before something happens with the fairies.*

"I'm a l-l—"

"Let's find out," she said, her eyes shining. She held out her hand.

Her hand slid into mine—fitting like a missing puzzle piece.

Cinderella pulled me out of the orchard and into the forest.

My gaze darted from the trail of glowing fairies to the forest floor and dried leaves crunched under my feet. My shoulder throbbed, a steady reminder tying me to her. To Stepmother.

Cyn, you have to tell him goodbye.

This can't go on. I pressed my lips together.

More lights flew overhead, leading us deeper into the forest.

After this. Just let me have a few minutes more.

We left the picnic behind, and instead of the sweet tang of cheeses and fruits, the damp scent of earth filled my lungs.

As we walked, our fingers knit together, and my world condensed. The trees grew deeper and denser, throwing off purple shadows. Streams of moonlight spilled through the branches. More than once, Armand saved me from falling, and he apologized as I winced at the pain. Thankfully, the fairies continued to gather, and their shared light increasingly illuminated the forest floor.

A large dancing glow shone ahead in a clearing. We turned a corner and soft yellow radiance welcomed us. Fairy light glimmered against my skin like gold dust. Although my burn was covered, the light penetrated the fabric, cooling the angry wound.

After my eyes adjusted, I looked up and around the clearing, then gasped. My fingers tightened around Armand's hand. I thought Shar was the only fairy left in Lyonelle. The mass of lights tonight said otherwise.

Hundreds of fairies gathered in the glade, each gleaming various shades of lemon, sunflower gold, or tangerine. Each small light was part of a dancing couple, each pair spinning and swooping in a giant aerial waltz, and a rhythmic humming filled my bones. Was it fairy music? Then it hit me. *They're celebrating the autumnal equinox.*

I scanned the fairies for Shar's familiar light, but I knew I'd never find her. Each glimmer was nearly identical to Shar's and I'd never had to pick her out of a crowd before. I had no idea there were so many fairies remaining in all of Lyonelle.

As we entered the glade, the lights slowed, hovering above our heads. What were they waiting for?

Armand grabbed my hand, looking around nervously as if expecting an attack. His voice was tight. "Cinderella, there is s-something I have to t-tell you b-before anything else happens."

What did he think was going to happen?

"I'm the pr—I'm the p-p—"

He closed his eyes and bounced on his toes.

"I. Am. The. P-prince."

"What?" I blinked. "No, you're not. What are you joking at?" The prince was a muscle-headed sword jockey. He was joking, wasn't he?

I looked at Armand's serious face. Wasn't he?

"I am." He stood straight, pulling his strong shoulders to attention. That's when I saw it. The truth was everywhere. In his clothes, his bearing.

I closed my eyes. The music box in the map room he'd wanted to give to me. "No, no. You said you were the son of a merchant. Your father trades in textiles." I dropped his hand, backing away. "He works for the king."

Armand took a few steps forward, his hands out in apology. "My father is the k-k-king. My full name is Hermann P-Paul de Lyon. But I prefer that those I c-care for—who c-care for me—c-call me Armand." He closed his eyes and took a deep breath. Words streamed from his mouth in a flood. "I wanted to t-talk to you and I was worried you wouldn't c-come back if you knew who I was."

I pressed a hand to my forehead. He'd lied. About who he was. It felt like I was floating away from Lady Norbette's tower again, except this time, no one would catch me before I fell.

"You're the prince? Why did you lie to me?"

His shoulders fell, all royal posturing gone. He spoke simply and honestly. "You literally c-called me the 'stupid prince.' I've been the stupid prince my whole life. I didn't want to be that p-person. I'm n-not. You helped me see that."

Everything scrambled in my brain like eggs over a skillet. He'd lied to me. But he was the prince. This was terrible. It only confirmed everything I'd been about to say to him. Him. Me. This would never work.

I backed away, my heart throbbing through my burn.

"Cinderella?"

Had he faked all the looks we'd shared? *Stupid Cyn.* How could I have let myself get so involved? Care about him so much? Feelings twisted in my chest, and I wasn't sure if I wanted to run, hide, or fall into Armand's arms and never leave.

"I l-love you and I want to m-marry you. If you'll have m-me."

I snapped my head to look at him. Something inside me recoiled like an owl from the sun. Stepmother's voice whispered from deep inside. *You know what you are. Who could love a murderer?*

"I can't."

He stepped forward.

"I can't be with you. *I'm* not that person." *A princess?* "Besides, how could you understand me? You're the prince. Heir to the kingdom. You know nothing of starving, of being mistreated." My shoulder screamed in pain. "Of wanting something so bad you can taste it through your fingertips."

Like I wanted him.

Armand pulled my chin upward until I was looking into his face. His eyes were full of tenderness—for me. *You don't deserve this.* But oh, how I wanted it.

"No, I d-don't know about starving or stealing. I've only ever wanted to be a g-good ruler. To p-please my f-father." A dark look slid across his features, and he removed his hand from my face to clench his fists. "But I d-do know about being m-mistreated. About wanting something so m-much, you'd give anything for it."

He lifted his hand back to my face, his touch so tender it glided past my defenses.

Grief ripped through me and my heart turned to lead. I looked away. The forest glowed all around me, but the light inside me faded.

I looked into Armand's dark shining eyes and my heart fluttered. I could see everything—his kindness, his gentleness. He was gazing at me as if I were perfect—the answer to all his problems. My chest tightened. What if he could see into my soul? His eyes exposed me—a common thief. A murderer. I didn't deserve him.

End this now, Cyn.

"But someone born in an ivory tower could never understand someone like me."

A look of hurt slid across his brow, and he turned from me. It felt like he was pulling my heart right from my chest.

"C-can you show her, please?"

I cradled my arm. Who was he talking to? The fairies?

Several came closer, their lights shimmering to gold.

"Show her the t-truth like you showed me the future. P-please."

Hundreds of fairy lights sparkled gold, and that's when they swarmed.

36 — Cyn

The fairy lights blazed around us and I buried my face in Armand's chest. "Armand, what is happening?"

"I d-don't know. This is different than before."

My shoulder burned as if the brand were searing more of my flesh. A scream tore through my body, and Armand pulled me close. Pain ripped through me—his embrace was the only thing keeping me together. Suddenly, the pain subsided, leaving me hollow. An immense silence filled my ears.

I opened my eyes and soft white light filled my vision. Fear spiked in my chest. *Easy, Cyn. This is fairy magic and Shar is involved. It will be okay.* I took measured breaths and exhaled slowly.

Where am I? Where is Armand? I felt him still holding me, and even though I couldn't see him, I knew he was there. He was in me and all around me at the same time. Somehow, I knew Armand was experiencing the same thing I was.

Blurry shapes formed in the center of the light, and I blinked. A small boy, dark-haired and serious, came into focus standing near a desk. Armand snorted at what was obviously the image of his younger self.

A seven-year-old Armand tugged on a white-and-red tunic and shifted from one foot to the other. A man with brown hair and a close-cropped mustache stood behind an imposing desk in the center of a study. Several other well-dressed children sat at desks and chairs. The man, clearly the instructor, leaned forward, his fingers tapping on his folded arms. The real Armand recognized the scene unfolding before him. I could feel his grim determination to see this through. Were these his memories? What was bad about school? He probably had the best tutors.

"It is the k-king—" the boy Armand said, choking on his stutter. The boy's eyes screwed shut and his mouth gaped. Clicking sounded from his throat.

I really didn't want to believe Armand. What did he know of suffering? But despite myself, my heart softened.

Young Armand took a shaky breath and tried again. "It is the k-k-king—"

Another boy sneered. "Cat got your tongue?"

The old insult stabbed at Armand—my Armand. I felt him shrink inside himself, his pain throbbing in his chest.

I scowled at the tiny bully.

"Show her m-more."

Images shifted and the colors changed. From outside the memories, I pressed my fingers into the back of Armand's hand.

A candlelit ballroom appeared. Another young Armand, now around twelve, shifted nervously in blue formal wear. His gangly limbs jutted out at odd angles, and his hands moved from his vest to his hair, then back to his vest. He walked toward a red-haired young lady and her friend.

I knew the instant Armand recognized the scene because his heart pulled away, wanting to hide from these memories. Instead, he leaned into them, opening them wider like a wound needing to be cleaned. The young girl's outline sharpened and I felt his voice inside me, heavy with golden magic. *You need to understand.*

"C-Catherine," the young Armand said.

The young woman turned. Her beautiful features hardened and her eyes narrowed slightly.

"W-would you—w-w-would you—d-dance—"

She leaned forward, cupping her ear. "P-p-pardon?" she said, over-enunciating. "I c-c-can't understand you." Tiny flecks of spit sprayed with each of her consonants. Catherine giggled again, whispering to her friend.

As I stared at the crushed young Armand, my chest tightened around my heart. His feelings of worthlessness and failure seeped through the memories. The real Armand shuddered in my arms. These still hurt, I realized. I had been wrong.

It's okay, I soothed. *You are so much more than this moment.*

"Show her my f-father."

More flashes as the scene shifted.

A study came into focus, lavishly decorated. Rich green velvet curtains flanked the windows, and a cream-and-green medallion rug covered the floor. A fire burned in the hearth, warming the room. A man with graying hair and luxurious robes stood at attention, facing the corner. He clenched his hands behind his back. A woman with worry lines etched into her features had her arm on the man's shoulder, clearly trying to console him. The king and queen.

Armand, his hair longer than he wore it now, sat in a chair by the fire. He had grown into his limbs, but he didn't quite have the frame of an adult. He must be fifteen or so. There were glimpses of the strong, caring Armand I knew.

"He hasn't been cursed, Mathilde," the man said. "He's simply slow."

The real Armand winced at the words, and anger flared deep in my soul. How dare he. His own father.

The woman gasped. "Henri, do you really think so?"

Henri turned to face Armand. I recoiled at the disgust plain on his face. "What else could be the matter? The boy can't even clearly say our titles."

Armand's self-loathing stained his memories like oil on paper. Nobody should make him feel this way, not even the beastly king.

King Henri turned back to his son, and the young Armand quailed inwardly but raised his eyes to face the challenge. My pride swelled.

"Just be calm," Henri said to Armand, handing him a paper with words gouged into the parchment.

The adolescent nodded, swallowing audibly.

"Think about what you're going to say. Then just . . . say it."

Armand's memory opened his mouth to read from the paper, but no words came. He was blocked. Only a garbled hiss came from his mouth.

His father growled, then stalked from the room, but his comment still sounded clearly. "Worthless."

Years blurred by with people laughing at him, ignoring him, and—how I hated this—patronizing him. Day after day of his father's judgement and his mother's frantic pity added layers of hopelessness and despair to Armand.

The bright white light returned, blurring the memories, and then everything faded. I opened my eyes and found myself in Armand's arms, real and trembling. The glade still glowed with the fairies' golden magic, and a wind rustled through the grass.

Armand's features were tight with pain from the memories. He dropped his gaze and turned his face away. "So you see, I d-do understand a little. I know what it feels like to be m-mistreated. Overlooked." He swallowed. "Abandoned."

I'd been wrong, so very wrong about Armand. How could I have been so stupid?

He rubbed one arm, and despite standing several inches taller than me, he looked so small. My heart ached to erase all the pain and self-loathing. I took a step closer and dipped my head into his line of sight. None of this changed what I was, but I couldn't leave him like this. I loved him.

I paused. I did, and knowing that made everything more painful. But I had to help him in this one last thing. I couldn't erase the past, but maybe I could ease it—make him see himself the way I saw him.

I explored the magic surrounding us and found the connection tying us together. A golden thread glittered between us. I poured all my love into the thread. It pulsed, growing wider and stronger. Strangely, the more love I gave, the more I had to give. So I gave. I poured my respect, admiration, and pride for him through the thread. *Please believe me. Can't you feel my love?*

He opened his eyes and breathed. "Cinderella—"

"I'm sorry," I said. "I was wrong. But this—we—" I moved my hand between us and it felt like I was sinking back into life before Armand. I would drown and he wouldn't be there to save me. But he couldn't.

I pushed away from him and walked out of the circle of light into the glade. The dark forest was a sea of black pulling me under, and I struggled to see. To breath. I blinked, getting my bearings. I had to go, but I was so tired. So tired of fighting against the truth. Hiding who I was. What I'd done. Exhaustion weighed me down.

"Where are you g-going?"

I looked back at Armand. The golden magic swirled behind him. Images from my past swept across the magic, rising and then fading like golden ghosts. Stepmother, Aimée, and Papa.

Stepmother's voice snaked into my heart. *He won't love you. Can't.* I wanted to fight them, but it was too much. I couldn't. But there was no one who could.

Armand took my hand again, and at his touch, golden sparkles circled up my arm. My pulse raced as his eyes drifted across my face, settling on my lips. He leaned down, his breath tickling my face. His eyes seemed to ask, *Is this okay?*

I wanted it to be, but I was just so tired. I put my hands against his chest in a halfhearted push. Armand paused, his dark lashes lifting. "I l-love—I l-love you, Cinderella."

I felt the words slipping from my lips, and I was unable—unwilling— to stop them. "I love you too."

I couldn't keep hiding from him. I wanted him—I wanted to be loved, to belong with someone again. He needed to know. Then this could all be over. I could go back to Stepmother. *Back to where I belong.*

Shar's voice came from the magic, smooth and calm. "Mistress, you have to face this."

"We can't be together," I whispered, barely audible.

Armand grabbed my right hand, his calluses rough against my skin. I dropped my eyes. I pressed my fingers against his knuckles. The words didn't want to come, but I knew they had to. I had to open the wound. Had to share it.

Maybe he could help.

"Please show him."

The fairies' golden light surrounded us.

"We can't be together, because I'm the one who killed my father."

Then everything exploded.

ᴀRMAND

37

She killed her father.
She killed her father.
The words flew in my head like a volley of arrows.
No.
Each one missed their mark.
Impossibile.
Colored images from Cinderella's memory blurred together, painting a small bedroom. Exotic trinkets rested on shelves and a nightstand. A man lay on his bed, his eyes closed, his breathing shallow. The four-poster bed's drapes surrounded the man like mourners at a funeral.

Cinderella recoiled at the images, and through our connection, I felt her despair. *It's okay, I'm here.* She trembled in my arms and I pulled her closer, as if I could shield her from her past. Nervousness snaked through my stomach.

Two young women surrounded a bed—I easily recognized Cinderella's figure, her brown hair cascading down her back. As she crouched by the bedside, tears glided down her face. The second girl's flaxen hair hung limp, her frame weighed down with grief.

The man's skin was as yellow as the candlelight. His face was sunken and sharp. Even through his illness, the familial resemblance was strong. This was Alexander Manette.

"I'm sorry, Cyn. I can't—can't stand to see him . . ." the young blonde girl said, wringing her gloved hands together.

"I understand," Cinderella whispered, then turned back to her father.

The second girl choked on a sob and left the room. Her weeping could still be heard through the door.

Grief rolled from the Cinderella in my arms and I staggered.

"It's all right, Papa," the young Cinderella said. Her hands slipped under her father's. "Stepmother is coming with some medicine. She's mixing it now, the one from your list—"

An older fair-haired woman entered the room, carrying a bowl of herbs. Her rich green gown looked out of place. She set the bowl on the side table, pushing aside other bottles of ointments and medicines. The woman retreated from the bed and pressed her fingers to her temples, her eyes glassy. I'd seen that look on men haunted by cannon fire in the military hospital. Her stepmother. I pressed deeper into Cinderella's memory for her name. There. Vienne Manette. I burned this memory into mine.

"See, Papa. She is here."

He stirred in his bed, wincing in pain. One didn't need to be a *médecin* to know that this man was dying.

In the memory, Cinderella's tone was pleading. "You'll get better." I recognized her fear and hope—I felt the same each time I spoke to Father. Fear flooding my chest, but hope rising above.

Vienne dipped the cloth in the ointment and began daubing it on *M.* Manette's forehead. Grassy aromas filled the air, driving away the staleness.

Young Cinderella's body tensed as the odors hit her nose. "What is in that ointment? It doesn't smell right. You've mixed the ingredients wrong."

"I followed the recipe." Vienne stood and clutched the bowl to her chest. "We had everything but celandine."

Cyn stood upright, dropping her father's hand. She walked to the bowl and leaned over it. She inhaled and shook her head. "He needs the celandine." She gestured to the mixture. "It's the only thing that activates these other herbs."

Vienne's face turned a ghostly white. "There isn't any. You stocked the pantry yesterday, didn't you?"

Horror jolted through the memory.

"I did." Cyn licked her dry lips. "Except for the celandine."

Vienne's knuckles whitened against the rim of the bowl. "Your father put you in charge of the pantry. He told you to maintain it. Resupply if needed."

Cinderella's fingers trembled against her lips. "He did. I did. I mean—I tried." Her eyes darted, pleading, from Vienne to her father. "The king had bought almost all the celandine . . . the prices were exorbitant."

M. Manette moaned on the bed, his forehead slick with sweat.

Her stepmother's eyes hardened, glittering with anger.

"Vienne." His voice croaked. "*Je suis . . . je suis désolé.*" He inhaled and then coughed.

"Alexander." Vienne choked as her shoulders fell. She shoved the bowl of ointment onto the side table and it clinked against several other uncleared mixing bowls. She dropped to her knees by his bed.

Vienne twisted the red blanket, her glance darting from her husband to Cinderella.

M. Manette's eyes searched the room. "Cinderella," he whispered. "C-Cyn."

Cinderella moved to stand next to her stepmother and gripped his hand, burning with fever. "I'm here, Papa." Young Cyn's heart fluttered in her chest. Mine ached for her.

His cheeks lifted in a weak smile. "*Mon . . . trésor,*" he wheezed. Deep, rattling coughs wrenched through his chest.

Cinderella's tears streamed down her face. "Papa," she cried again.

He coughed and then choked. His thin frame doubled over in spasms.

Vienne wrenched Cinderella's hands away from her father's. Cinderella stumbled back, frowning.

"Go," Vienne hissed. "Save him."

"But—but, I want to be here," she whispered. "For him, when he—" Her voice clenched.

"You know what will help. It doesn't matter the cost. Go. Now!"

Cinderella squeezed her father's hand. "*Je reviendrai. Je promets.*"

Then she flew out the door of the bedroom, past the young blonde girl weeping on the stairs and the dull blue light hovering above the girl's shoulders. Drops of blue fell from the light. *Shar.* I inhaled, their pain burning my throat. The real Cinderella trembled in my arms.

The memory flashed to Cyn galloping on her horse toward Lierre. *Faster, faster.* She pounded on a heavy wooden door, deep in the market quarter of the city.

A head poked from the uppermost window, hair sticking up at odd angles. "Stop that banging," the man slurred, wiping away sleep from his eyes. "We're closed for business."

"*M.* Maurier, I need celandine."

The merchant's tiny eyes narrowed, then grew sharp as he took in Cinderella. "*Mademoiselle* Manette. I knew you'd be back." He smiled, showing all his canines. Starving dogs gave that same look before attacking.

"I have money," Cinderella said, hefting a bag clinking with coins.

The man's eyes gleamed in his round face. I already knew I wasn't going to like his response. "First you insult me yesterday afternoon, in front of the rest of the market, and now you rouse me from my bed."

"I . . . I apologize. I was w-wrong. *Monsieur.* The root."

"My price just tripled. Perhaps you should bang on the palace door. The king has more than he can spare." Then he moved to shut the window.

"Yes, I'll pay it."

The hand at the window paused, then disappeared.

Guilt sliced through me. Father had bought it all. I held my breath, praying the man would reappear at the front door.

The front door squeaked on its hinges, and his craggy frame darkened the doorway. Relief washed over me and the young Cinderella.

"Should have asked for more," *M.* Maurier grumbled, dropping the celandine into her hands. She wrapped her hands around the bulbous yellow root and shoved her money purse against *M.* Maurier's chest.

Cinderella scrambled back on her horse, leaving behind nothing but a cloud of dust.

The vision changed. Cinderella was scrambling through the pantry, throwing herbs into a bowl with the root. She wiped her eyes. Dittany, dogwood, milkweed. She mixed the poultice, letting her tears fall. She clutched the bowl to her chest and scrambled up the stairs.

As she burst into the room, she froze. Vienne stood by the window, her back to *M*. Manette. Cinderella's gaze flickered between Stepmother and her father.

Her father's face was waxy and pale.

He was dead.

Vienne didn't turn around. Her voice came as if from far away. "He called for you before he died."

Pain like glass shattered between me and the real Cinderella. Her legs gave way and I held her close.

The young Cinderella shuffled toward the bed. She placed the bowl on the nightstand, next to Vienne's, where it clinked against the others. She stared into her father's still face, then picked up his hand. It was warm, no longer burning from the fever.

"I'm sorry, Papa," Cinderella whispered. "I'm so sorry."

Vienne stalked toward Cinderella, avoiding looking at her husband's body. A cold fire burned in her eyes. She leaned down and hissed.

"He's dead because you weren't the obedient daughter you should have been. He's dead because you weren't fast enough." Vienne's venom dripped into Cinderella's heart.

Cinderella looked up at her stepmother. *No, it's a lie.* But the young girl nodded, and my body went cold.

Vienne abandoned the room and didn't look back. I focused on the closed door. Cinderella's weeping was the only sound.

"*Je suis désolé, Papa.*" She wept over his body. "*C'est de ma faute.*"

My chest constricted at the injustice. *It's not your fault. It was simply his time.* Anger at Vienne burned in my blood.

The images crashed into each other. *Cinderella isn't in control of this.* The fairies' magic swelled.

Cinderella was sweeping the already spotless bedroom floor. *This will help,* she thought.

Vienne sat at her vanity, her fingers pressing into the edges of an inlaid jewelry box.

"I've finished," Cinderella said. Vienne blinked rapidly, as if coming out of a trance, and gave the floor a scrutinizing glance.

There's nothing wrong with the floor, I thought.

Bitterness laced her tone when she spoke. "You have certainly finished this family, Cinderella."

Cinderella's shoulders fell and she looked at the tidy floor. "I'm sorry."

Vienne turned from the mirror. "I'm sorry, Cinderella, but you can't really understand what you've done."

The vision hurtled to Cinderella training in an attic somewhere. Yarn snaked around the room, and there were bells tied to each strand. Sweat glistened on Cinderella's brow. Vienne loomed by a desk. A bell tinkled and Vienne's face tightened.

"Again," she said.

The Cinderella in the memory panted, her heart pounding, then stood and began again.

My fault. My fault. My fault. I could feel it with each beat of the memory.

The real Cinderella's breathing shallowed. I pulled her to my chest.

A darkness exploded between us, throwing us back. *Cinderella,* I screamed with my mind.

Cold pressure battered my temples, as if I'd dived deep into the Lierran harbor. I opened my eyes but saw nothing. I groped in the empty, icy blackness. *Where was Cinderella? Are we still in her memories?* My instincts told me we'd gone deeper.

Then I felt it. She was pulling on the darkness around her, trying to crush herself.

No, Cinderella, stop!

But she fought against me, wanting to be crushed.

My pulse thundered in my ears. Her guilt would destroy us both.

Coldness pierced my skin. *I deserve it*, she whispered. Next to me, Cyn shivered and pulled herself tighter.

The golden thread pulsed and quivered feebly. I licked my lips. I had to help her, but how?

Tell her the truth, a voice whispered.

"I saw your courage, Cinderella. Vienne was scared and hurt so she blamed you. She was wrong." I leaned in close, whispering into her heart, "It's not your fault." The boulders froze. "It never was."

The connection between us flared, growing stronger. She hesitated, unsure of herself, and her shoulders uncurled a bit.

"He would never have blamed you." I placed my hand on her arm, and this time it was the boulders that trembled. "*Tu sais que c'est la vérité. He would want you to be happy.*"

The thread between us brightened and the shadows retreated.

I reached for her and the thread blazed. I closed my eyes as golden heat washed over me.

The damp smell of cedar and the forest floor filled my lungs. Wind rustled through the leaves. I opened my eyes.

The real Cinderella was in my arms, her face pressed against my chest.

We were in the glade again. The fairies, now tiny lights once more, hovered in their colosseum formation. The two iridescent lights in the circle floated in the center and it felt like every fairy eye was on us. My skin prickled.

I gave a deep bow. The fairy lights bobbed, then rose up through the branches and disappeared into the sky. The magic was gone, but something inside me burned in my chest like molten gold. My bond to Cinderella was still there, pulsing with every heartbeat. Somehow, I knew it would always be there.

Cinderella pulled her head from my chest. I leaned in closer and brushed that stubborn tendril of hair from her face. Warmth poured over my head to my toes. By the Beast's beard, she was beautiful.

She rested her hand against my face and I lowered mine to hers. "*C'était incroyable,*" I whispered.

Something inside pulled me toward her. Everything inside me oriented to her like a compass.

I closed the distance between us and did something I'd wanted to do for a long time. I leaned in close, waiting. Did she want this as much as I did? She looked at me through her lashes and pressed her mouth over mine. My skin radiated with a sudden heat that pressed through me to my bones. Her kisses came soft against my lips, and I savored her taste. As she pressed her lips against mine, I groaned, and her body melted against me. The warmth between us increased, like a taste of cayenne pepper on my tongue. I tangled my fingers through her hair and she sighed. Her body pressed against my arms, my chest, and my hips, each point sparking with fire.

I pulled away gasping and rested my forehead against hers. I exhaled, my breathing shaky. Hers was as ragged as mine. The air was heady and my heart was pounding like cannon fire. I ached. It was so much to take in, and at the same time, I craved more.

I rested my palm against her cheek, my fingers weaving through her hair. Amazement at this night, at her, coiled inside.

A few fairies looped in the night, weaving between branches and leaves. A small breeze kicked up dry leaves, which rustled by our feet.

Happiness that I felt first in my fingertips spread and exploded from my chest. I wrapped her in my arms and spun her around, whooping into the night. Cinderella squealed and buried her head in my shoulder.

A voice inside my head made me freeze. *Stop, Armand! She is injured!* Quickly I set her down and backed away.

"I'm s-sorry, I'm so s-sorry," I said. "I f-forgot." I rested my hands against her back, guilt crawling through my bones.

Her brows crossed and she tilted her head. "What for?"

"Y-your shoulder." I pointed at the torn fabric. The frayed edges of the fabric fluttered against the blood-stained bandage. "I must have hurt it." The last part came out more as a question. I stepped closer.

She frowned at me, then at her shoulder. "No. You didn't." She pulled at the dressing away, then gasped. She turned to me and lowered the fabric, exposing the skin just below her shoulder.

"How—how . . . ?" It was healed. There was no charred flesh, only a pearlescent scar. I leaned closer and then pulled back, hardly believing. "They healed it." I lifted my fingers to the pinkish skin. Its outline looked familiar.

"Not completely." Her shoulders pulled together and she made a noise in her throat. "It left a scar. Why couldn't they heal me completely?" She turned, digging her feet into the forest floor.

I followed her, the dry grass rustling against my legs. "N-no. This is a p-part of you. It shows what you've b-been through." I thought of my father and the scars no one but I could see. Cinderella turned to face me. "N-never apologize for who you are." I ran my fingers along the length of her jaw. Those words lifted something in my chest, almost as if we were floating away again.

"You're right." She examined her shoulder. "It was a raven, but now it looks more like a . . . like a . . ." She ran her fingers over her skin, pulling it tight.

"M-magpie." Chills shot down my spine. The bird's outline and plumage pattern were clearly visible, layered over Cinderella's skin tones.

She truly was the most beautiful woman I'd been blessed to behold. I wanted to hold her forever. I took her hand in mine and pressed it to my lips. "*Mon, belle pie,*" I murmured.

She smiled, then stood on her toes and pressed her lips against mine. She tasted of cinnamon. Her fingers pressed into the back of my neck and she sighed. Heat burned from her fingers through my body.

I deepened the kiss, and she returned it with as much as I gave. I moaned in my chest, my fists grabbing onto her shirt. Ungentlemanly feelings radiated through my body and I steeled myself, forcing them under my governance once more.

Steady, Armand. Ask her.

I inhaled the cool night air. "Earlier, y-you said you c-couldn't see a way out of stealing. Of being the M-Magpie." I licked my lips, my throat suddenly dry. As they came, my words rolled over, polishing themselves. "I once—I once asked, 'What if s-someone asked you to r-run away with him?'"

I paused. Her face shone, beautiful in the moonlight. My chest tightened as if to keep my heart inside. This was what I wanted—what I needed. I just couldn't believe I was doing it here. Now.

"I'm asking you, r-right now. Will you r-run away with me?" The *r* stuck behind my teeth, but she didn't even flinch. My heart thundered against my chest. "Because I have fallen in love. With you." My insides tripped over themselves.

She pressed her hands against her mouth.

"In the memories, your father called you his t-treasure." My throat thickened and my body felt as if it would split apart without her close. I pulled her to me, cradling her head in my hands, and whispered into her hair, "And now you are mine."

Nervousness stuck in my ribs, and I pulled away and fidgeted with my jacket's buttons. "I don't have anything to give you as a sign of my affection. I honestly didn't think I'd be doing this tonight." I chuckled, then choked.

Cinderella's face broke into a look of pure happiness, and warmth flooded my body. *Tell her now; she already loves you.*

"We could always 'trade' for a ring from Lady Eline," she said, a mischievous twinkle in her eye.

"Those d-days are behind you."

She glanced down at her scar. "Yes, they are."

I unfastened my lapel pin. It was the only thing I had. "I'd be honored, Cinderella Manette, if you'd attend the ball t-tomorrow night wearing this." I handed her the pin, the miniature lion and rose crest glinting in the moonlight. "I have s-something I'd like to ask you and an announcement I'll n-need to make if you agree to my question."

"Didn't you already ask?" she asked, mischief in her eyes. "We're supposed to run away together, remember?"

"Something a little more p-permanent. I'm sure you already know what my q-question will be, but I'd like it to be official," I said. "I'll be looking for this"—I said, pointing to the pin—"Lady Eline's shoes, and you at the masque t-tomorrow."

She took the pin and pulled two edges of her torn shirt collar together. She fastened the pin and covered her scar, though the wings of the Magpie peeked through. I wanted to kiss those wingtips. Heat pulsed through my core at the thought of my lips on her skin. Instead, I lifted her hand where a ring should have been and kissed her fingertips. *Slowly, Armand. You do not need to do everything tonight.*

"The masque? Of course, I'll be there," she said. She lifted her chin and nibbled on her lip, knowing exactly what it would do to me.

I groaned inside myself. The flirt. I loved it.

"See you tomorrow," I said, huskily.

She smirked, then stood tall and poised. "Of course, you'll be easily recognizable." She then curtsied deeply, her eyes never leaving mine. "Your Royal Highness." Then she whispered, "You liar," smiling mischievously, still curtsying.

A tentative laugh escaped my throat. She stood. I rubbed the back of my neck, then dropped my hands and bent at the waist. "Thief."

She turned and walked toward Eline's orchards. The undergrowth crunched under her feet.

I filled my lungs and exhaled, the cool air lifting weight from my bones. She finally knew. A fairy drifted above my head, following the breeze.

Cinderella called back and held out her hand. "Coming?"
I smiled.
She knew, and she didn't care.

38

My feet pressed against soft grass. As the moon dropped below the trees, it outlined the world in silvery light. Our midnight picnic soon came into view. Every detail was highlighted in the soft moonlight, just as we had left it—the half-eaten food, Lady Eline's shoe leaning slightly into the pillow. Except everything was different. Armand's fingers laced through mine and the world felt right. I inhaled, memorizing the pressure of his hand in mine.

Armand gave my hand a final squeeze and then began stacking the plates and silverware. I dropped down to help.

"Let's g-go to Lady Eline's. I'll have her staff prepare a r-room—"

I rested a plate against my thighs. "I still can't believe you're the beastly prince." I groaned and smacked my palm to my forehead. "Not even close to being the son of the trade minister." I shoved him.

Armand fell off balance, a sheepish grin plastered across his face. "Father does oversee the minister for d-domestic and foreign trade. So in a certain light, I am." He gathered the bread and rolls into their basket. "My brother agreed it wasn't technically a lie."

"I'd have said the same thing, but . . ." I pressed my knuckles against my head. "You told your brother?"

"In my d-defense, he mostly figured it out himself."

"Smart brother. Aimée is like that too." I reached for a napkin, the buttery fabric sliding against my hand. "Oh, and don't worry about preparing a room for us. We won't need one tonight."

Silverware clattered against the plates and a bread roll wobbled across the blanket. My gaze lifted to see Armand frozen with his mouth agape. Even in the dim light, it wasn't hard to see his deep blush. What was that all about? "'We' won't n-need a r-r—When you say 'we,' you are not p-proposing you and m-me—you are referring to you and your s-sister, because I—I . . . m-marriage . . . p-proper . . ."

A room! Cyn, you're an idiot. Now it was my turn to blush. "No, I mean, not that we need one, of course. Although, if after tomorrow, you ask what I think you will and then you and me, we'd be . . . woohoo . . ." I tugged at the front of my shirt, pumping cool air around my torso. *So hot all of a sudden.* "I—I still have to get Aimée." I twisted the orange napkin in my hand. *Armand and I. Alone together.* As wild fantasies of what sharing a room might be like filled my head, I bit my lip. *No, Cyn. Focus.* I blinked hard, then swallowed. Gray sky lightened the horizon. "It will be nearly dawn by the time I can get her out of the house."

"It's not safe. You c-can't g-go back."

"That's exactly why I have to." I stood, leaving the crumpled napkin at my feet. "I have to get Aimée before Stepmother finds out I'm not there." Even though my shoulder was healed, it felt like the raven's head was still pressed into my skin. I rubbed it. What would Stepmother do to Aimée if I wasn't there to protect her?

Armand pressed his lips into a hard line, then sighed. He pushed the plates aside, grabbed the shoe, and stood.

"I'll be at the p-palace—" He choked, as if he wasn't comfortable saying that word. He fiddled with the shoe and rotated it once, then twice. "—helping prepare for tomorrow night. If you n-need anything, please send word."

Fingers of warmth stretched through me. *Incroyable. Is this what it feels like when someone cares about you? This is nice. Really nice.*

I stepped close and rested my hand against the side of his face, his stubble prickling my palm. Moonlight silvered the edges of his curly locks. I threaded my fingers through his hair, then shivered. *Enfin.* It was every bit as luxurious as I thought it would be.

"I'll get Aimée and meet you back at Lady Eline's. You go back to the palace and work on a royal pardon. *Facile, non?*"

Armand's eyebrows pulled tight, but he nodded. "*Facile.*"

I darted in, giving him a quick peck on the lips. I didn't trust myself to linger longer than that. I might never leave. "You're cute when you're worried."

I snatched the shoe from his hands before he could argue, then raced into the remaining night, welcoming the shadows.

I crept into the still-dark household. Everything was where I had left it. The moon shone through the lead-lined window, the shadows crisscrossing the floor as they always had. The stair railing, polished through years of use, slid smoothly under my palm. Yet everything was also new. This night— Armand and I—had changed everything. Even my black and torn training clothes felt unfamiliar on my skin. I easily made my way to Aimée's and my room.

"Aimée," I whispered, shaking her gently.

The faded patchwork quilt shifted and she mumbled, rolling over. Ugh, we didn't have time for this.

"Aimée, wake up," I said, shaking her a bit harder. "We have to go."

Her eyes slowly fluttered open. "Go?" she murmured. "Are you going to be arrested?"

She needed a spark to light her fire. I reached behind me and held up the shoe. The violet morning light caught the sequins and set them glittering softly.

Aimée sat up, rubbing her eyes. *Yes.*

"It's beautiful." She took the shoe, turning it in her hands.

"And no, I'm not going to be arrested. I'm about to be pardoned," I said, whispering. "Royally."

She blinked and pushed her hair back.

I took the shoe and placed it on her bed, then moved to get the valise from her closet. We had to hurry. Quickly, but quietly.

"Cyn, you shouldn't be doing this. Your burn."

"Long story." I moved the valise to the bed. "There was magic; I'm better. Armand is the prince. Get your things."

Aimée got up and started to gather some of her gloves. "You can't be serious!"

I shoved some shoes into the baggage, then grabbed Eline's. "Tomorrow at the masquerade, he'll be looking for this." I pointed to the pin.

Her eyes widened.

"And these." I waggled the shoes before cramming them into the bag. "Hurry, Aimée. We can get everything later." I looked at my hand mirror, ribbons, and other small items resting on the vanity. Unimportant. We had to go.

"Aimée, time to go. Aimée? Aimée?" What was taking her so long? We had to go before Stepmother woke up.

A floorboard creaked from the door and I whirled. Stepmother's figure filled the open doorway, her cane back at her side. The morning light caught her cream-colored morning dress, and it glowed like fire.

Every part of me screamed to run, but I wasn't leaving Aimée.

I grabbed the heavy mirror, gripping the handle in my fist. "Aimée, run!" Silence.

Satisfaction curled in the corner of Stepmother's mouth. Cold dread washed over me.

"Aimée?" My voice sounded far away.

Toad was behind Stepmother, but where was Oil?

Then I saw him. His arms coiled around Aimée's chest and hips like a giant serpent. He kept his eyes on me and buried his nose in Aimée's hair, inhaling deeply. Anger burst in my body as if Stepmother's cane burned again on my chest. *How dare he touch my sister.*

Stepmother pulled the lace at her neckline. "I was going to send Oliver and Theodore for you, but this saves me the trouble." Her fingernails clicked against the raven's head and she lifted her shoulders.

"Let her go." My body shook. *Out. I have to escape. We have to escape.* My eyes darted from the window to the door, my mind racing through every conceivable strategy. Each idea was more impossible than the last.

Stepmother crept into our room, her cane ticking against the floor. "You don't have to give me the pin now, but it will save time. And you don't want anything else on your conscience."

Aimée thrashed in Oil's arms, her hands clawing at his. "Cyn, you can't—" He shifted his grip from her shoulder to her throat, his fingers curling around her neck.

Anger raked through me. I hated that Stepmother was right. I was like a fly hitting itself against the window. But I couldn't—wouldn't—leave without Aimée. And Stepmother knew that. My body burned at the knowledge that she knew me so well.

"Theodore, bind Cinderella's hands," Stepmother said, stepping aside to allow Toad into the room. "She will behave."

Toad smiled, his wet lips looking like stretched earthworms.

"S'all right, little cat," Oil cooed. "Theodore ain't gonna hurt you."

Toad wrapped rope around my hands and its fibers jabbed into the inside of my wrists. His solid footsteps thudded against the floor, and his musty body odor filled my lungs with each breath. I glared at Stepmother, hoping she could feel the hate burning from my eyes.

Stepmother arced a brow. "Oliver, please bring my daughter to the attic." She glared at back me. "In case this gets messy." Stepmother leaned down, and sharp citrus from her morning toilette hit my nostrils. "And so there will be fewer ways for you to escape." Flecks of her spit landed on my cheek.

Blood rushed through my ears and panic sparked through every nerve. Not the attic. Air jammed through my chest. A calm satisfaction crept over Stepmother's face.

Breathe, Cyn, breathe. Don't let her in your head.

We moved to the hallway, the sun peeking through the upper window, and I blinked. Stepmother moved up the stairs and Aimée and Oil followed. Aimée struggled against Oil, but he held her closer.

"You should stop struggling, Aimée. We're going home." Stepmother's smooth voice pooled through the air.

"What do you mean? This is our home," Aimée whispered.

"This stopped being our home when Alexander died." Stepmother scowled at me. "What do you think all the thefts were for, Cinderella?

You're smart. Certainly you noticed they were no longer from merchants owing us money. You've chosen your path every step of the way."

I reddened. I had noticed. But I'd chosen not to care.

Shar's words echoed in my head: *At least someone is asking questions.* Anger flooded around me.

She's right, Cyn. It's not as if she bewitched you.

My heart spun as another voice rose inside. *You are simply the most bewitching woman I have ever met.*

Power rushed into my soul and burned away my doubt. Yes, I hadn't cared, but that was then. And now I had Armand. We had each other. Together, we could do anything.

I lifted my chin.

Stepmother's needle-sharp laughter stabbed into my skin. "You never could put your emotions aside. The 'determination' playing across your face is pathetic."

My jaw hardened. The floorboards groaned under our weight. We were almost there.

Stepmother's bloodless lips pressed together. "I was simply going to turn you over to the authorities for all your thefts once we reached the border, but now I can turn you over as the prince's assassin."

What was she talking about? "The prince is alive."

Stepmother's fingers wrapped around the attic's doorknob. "For now." The sun blazed at her back through the window, throwing her face into darkness. "I made a deal with Alemania. If we weaken Lyonelle, they will grant us lands, titles, wealth—anything we want. And, Cinderella," she said, fixing her cold eyes on me, "what better way to weaken a kingdom than to kill the prince?"

My stomach dropped into my feet. *Armand. No.* I thrashed against Toad. His thick arms constricted in response, pressing the air out of my lungs. I wheezed and blackness crept into my vision.

Stepmother plucked the lapel pin from my shirt. The torn fabric opened. Her eyes fell on the magpie-shaped scar and she hesitated, as if unsure whether to strike or flee. Then she pulled back her lips, showing all her teeth. Her gaze roved back to the pin and she rolled it between her fingers. "Yes. This is perfect."

Stepmother turned back to Aimée, who recoiled as far as she could within Toad's grasp. Stepmother smoothed Aimée's hair. "Don't worry, *mon chère fille,*" she cooed. "All you have to do is give this back to the prince."

Aimée's face froze in disbelief. "Return this to the prince. That's all?"

"Yes," Stepmother purred. "Just be sure to prick him with it when you do."

Aimée's eyes darted to mine.

My eyes narrowed. "Why?"

"Lyonelle has caused me enough pain," Stepmother said, her eyes tight. "It's earned a little bit of its own."

*A*RMAND

39

My hands shook and ink splattered all over the parchment, filling the air with a subtle metallic tang. For some reason, writing this letter made me more nervous than *M.* Parler's tutoring methods. I groaned and leaned back in the chair. My agenda looked like I'd tried to murder it. "Obtain royal pardon for the Magpie" now seemed to read "Pardon the Dogpie."

I raked my fingers through my hair and stared at the painted ceiling in Lady Eline's library. On one panel, a young man sat deep in thought while reclining against a tree. Another panel depicted a young woman with a quill in her hand in a meadow. Who wrote in a meadow?

Epaulettes and military decorations made it impossible to relax. How could I? Today I would announce my betrothal, find Cyn at the masque, convince Father and Mother that my fiancée was not the true criminal, and pardon the dogpie—I mean Magpie. I crumpled the paper, throwing it across the room.

I abandoned the desk and stalked to the window. Lady Eline's library was one of the few rooms that faced the front of the house. Where in the beasts was Luc? After the best night of my life, why did today feel like a fraying rope? Doubts ripped at my defenses. But I was different. I'd changed. Right?

I pressed my fist against the morning-chilled window. *Maybe I can be the ruler I want to be, stutter or no.* Cinderella certainly thought so.

Hope lifted my chest. My stutter was a part of me, and that didn't affect who I was, but there was still that lingering doubt. What about Father?

No, I could rule Lyonelle—stutter or no.

Lady Eline's drive remained empty. *Blast it, Luc.* I stood by the fire, rubbing my hands together, fighting the growing fatigue. I yawned and rolled my neck.

Morning light stole through the windows, making the gold trim around the ceiling shine. In a few hours it would be noon, and I had to be at the castle by one. I hoped Cinderella and Aimée would arrive quickly. *She'll be okay. It's Cinderella.* She was the most capable woman I had ever met. If anything came up, she could handle it. With her burn from last night, those *deux monstres* would think she was still incapacitated.

Fury shook my bones at the thought of Cinderella's wound. After the masquerade, I would hunt *les cretins* down.

I rubbed my hands together. Had Luc discovered anything helpful? The corner of my mouth twitched. Actually, it wasn't necessarily a matter of whether or not Luc could do things—what mattered more was whether he could do them without burning half the kingdom down.

Footsteps sounded in the hallway. And voices. Someone was singing. Loudly. And off-key. "*Amie*, raise your glass. *Faites attention*, don't spill it . . ." Giggles interrupted the song.

I stood and turned from the fireplace, tugging my shirt into place.

From behind the door, a second voice hissed. "Your Royal Highness . . . You must be quiet."

"You cannot silence *me*." As he roared the last word, Luc burst into the library, followed by a harried footman. His shirt was undone and his hair was wild, as if he'd been sailing through stormy seas the entire night. The smell of sour grapes flooded the room. Luc puffed up his chest, then deflated. He leaned against the door with his eyes half-closed. The bottle of wine in his hands sloshed a few drops on the rug. The footman grimaced at the stain.

"Presenting His Royal Highness—"

"Thank y-you. That will be all."

The footman quickly retreated.

Luc took another swig from the bottle.

Soufre. Getting anything useful out of him was going to be a monumental task.

I walked closer to Luc and bent down into his line of sight. His eyes widened when he saw my face.

"Armie." He hiccuped. "You're here." He took a few steps into the room and swayed like he was on a ship. I caught him under the arm. He exhaled his stale and sour breath in my face and I coughed. Did espionage require this much alcohol?

I shook him by the shoulders and stood him up. "T-tell me what you d-discovered."

Luc grinned. "You don't smile enough. You're always so—*hic*—" He frowned and his brow furrowed in concentration. "Ser—seer—yes—"

"Serious?"

"Yesss. Alwaysss. But you'd be proud of me. Seer-us-lee proud of me."

I rolled my eyes. "Let's sit d-down. Then you talk." I half-dragged him around the couch, but he pushed me away and swayed—the invisible ship Luc was on was apparently going through some rough seas.

I lunged forward and gripped him under his arms before he capsized. "I've g-got you." I pulled the bottle out of his hands, setting it on the side table. If he was this intoxicated, how could Luc have gotten anything of value from the *général*?

"T-tell me about Sanson." I tossed Luc onto the settee. His head flopped on a yellow velvet cushion. I pulled a chair from near the fire and set it next to Luc and sat, and waited.

His eyes drooped. He'd pass out in a moment. "I was drinking with that slimy, snakey snake Sanson." His eyes closed and didn't open.

I lunged and shook Luc's shoulders. "What d-did you d-discover?"

"He'sssssssss baaad." Luc giggled, his eyes remaining shut. "But I got him. He told me everything. And he really doesn't like you," he said, waving a swooping finger in my general direction. He flopped it against the floor with a thud.

I could have told him that myself.

"T-tell me what he said," I growled, sounding more like Father than I cared to admit.

Luc rolled onto his side and nestled deeper into the pillow, then gave a tiny snore.

"Luc."

His breathing grew heavy.

"By the Beast's beard, Luc!"

A footman knocked, then entered the room. "Your Royal Highness, the carriage is waiting to take you to the palace."

I nodded. "I'll be down shortly."

Luc gave a loud snore and drool spilled onto the pillow. I doubted Lady Eline would appreciate that.

Cyn

I hadn't envisioned myself spending the morning tied to the support posts in the middle of the wretched attic, but here I was. Aimée was tied to the adjacent beam, a fact which gave me little comfort and mountains of anxiety. But at least we were together. By midday, the room was stifling and my arms were numb. The skin on my wrists was raw from struggling against the ropes.

My brain hurt from all the possible escape routes I'd schemed. None of them worked. *Where is Shar?* I knew I wouldn't see her until after the equinox, but by then it would be too late.

Toad sat on crates, arms on his knees, mute and staring. Oil paced near the fireplace. Stepmother had disappeared shortly after we'd been "safely secured."

"Don't worry, Cyn," Aimée said, shifting against the pillar and tucking her feet under her nightgown. "We'll get out of this."

Oil chuckled. "You ain't never leaving here."

Even though he was across the room, Aimée turned away from his gaze. I glared at him, a growl escaping my throat.

Oil made a scoffing noise, then fell back to pacing.

I thumped my head against the beam. What time was it? Stepmother, the pin fastened to her lapel, had been gone for hours. She came to check on us— or on Oil and Toad—occasionally. But she had been gone for most of the day.

An hour after lunchtime, Stepmother entered the attic, dressed in her finest black gown with dark-green trim. A golden raven-shaped brooch glittered over the place where her heart should have been. She pointed at Aimée. "Come. You need to get ready."

Stepmother gestured at Toad, who lumbered over to Aimée and untied her from the post but kept her hands bound. He pulled Aimée toward the attic door.

"Aimée," Stepmother said, her soft voice carrying easily in the near-empty attic. "Understand that you will do as I say, or I'll kill Cinderella." The ice in her voice left little room for doubt.

"You wouldn't actually kill her?" Aimée asked, her eyes pleading.

"Me? No. But Oliver would."

Dread as cold as glacier water washed over me. I had to get out of here. I had to save Armand. And Aimée. And besides returning the lapel pin, how was Stepmother going to involve Aimée in killing the prince? My pulse hammered through my scalp and my mind raced. How could you bring down a kingdom with a lapel pin? Blood magic was the obvious answer, but it had faded from the kingdom centuries ago.

"Aimée, don't do anything you'll regret," I said, watching Aimée's face twisted with fear.

Stepmother turned, her eyes cold. "We're simply going to a ball, Cinderella. We will return shortly after midnight." Her eyes narrowed to slits, freezing my heart. "Oh, and if by some miracle you escape or cause trouble, Theodore will kill Aimée."

Those words stabbed through my heart.

"She's your own daughter," I said. "You can't!"

Stepmother crossed the room and grabbed my collar. Vengeance burned in her eyes and she yanked me toward her, pulling me against the ropes. A sharp, tangy aroma burned my nose. What was that smell?

I held my breath, leaning away.

"None of this is *my* fault. *Tu te trompes.* You had to involve Aimée," she hissed, like a snake ready to devour a mouse. "And given your miraculous recovery and newfound moral confidence"—she pulled my collar down, revealing the pearlescent skin—"I can't trust you."

She let me go. I slumped.

"Keep an eye on her, Oliver. I'll be back after midnight." Stepmother turned on her heel and with a flick of her fingers signaled Toad to follow. They both left the attic, Toad lugging Aimée behind him.

"It'll be okay, Aimée," I called out, though I couldn't see how. I thumped my head against the pillar again. It was my job to protect my sister. How was I going to get us out of this?

Toad reappeared a few minutes later, taking up his usual perch.

"Back so soon?" Oil asked, scratching his ear. "Didn't want yer help getting ready for the masque? Or did the lady not want you close because of yer smell?" He cackled at his own joke.

Toad shrugged.

We waited for an hour. Sometimes Oil paced. Sometimes they played cards. Toad always lost. Oil always cheated. Toad didn't care.

It was early afternoon when Toad stood from his crate.

"Don't forget to move the boats to the southern docks," Oil said.

Toad turned and grunted.

Oil stared pointedly and repeated himself. "Don't forget to move the boats."

Toad waved a hand in acknowledgment, continuing toward the attic door.

"Farther south," Oil called. "Don't want it burning with the rest of the navy."

Toad's footsteps thudded down the stairs.

"Where is he going?" I asked, raising my chin in the direction of the door.

Oil's mouth twisted, showing his yellowing teeth. "To create a distraction." His eyes turned on me. "It's a lot of work, taking down a kingdom."

Taking down a kingdom? Fear for Armand pressed against my chest and I couldn't breathe. *Think, Cyn. What clues do you have?* Not only was Armand in danger but the entire kingdom as well. *You can't lose him, Cyn.*

I tugged at the ropes and only succeeded in rubbing my wrists raw. I had to get out. This wasn't how I had planned to spend my day at all.

Oil's eyes raked over me and my skin prickled. When I looked away, he chuckled, and I tried not to think about how we were the only ones left in the room.

ARMAND 40

I leaned against the tufted green and gold cushions of the royal carriage and rubbed my eyes. Mother had mentioned the royal carriages were being made *en vogue*, but this wasn't fashion. It was an assault on my eyes. Every inch of the interior bloomed with pink roses, ostrich feathers sprouted like ferns, and the whole thing reeked of paint. It looked like a mad *pâtissier*'s nightmare.

Soufre, I need more control in my life. I just needed to believe that I could, as Cinderella had suggested. I could believe. I brushed a feather away from my face. *No, I would.*

I leaned as far as I could out the window and inhaled the briny air. I glanced to the right. Several Royal Navy ships rested in the harbor. Their red-and-gold flags snapped in the wind.

If word doesn't come by noon from Lady Eline's about Cinderella and her sister, I'll ride back out myself. And drag Luc to the pond if he doesn't tell me what I need to know. For now, I had to survive Mother's fussing and endless preparations for the masquerade tonight.

Despite my growing confidence, nerves still attacked my brain. What was Sanson going to do? With an increase in guards, would he try for a coup?

A dense flock of blackbirds circled the mast of one navy ship, then curled back, billowing in the wind.

Wait, no. Birds don't billow.

I squinted and leaned forward. Smoke. Tendrils of black were curling above the docks. Energy burned through my body, racing against my fear.

Fire.

I thumped on the roof of the carriage. "To the d-docks!"

The carriage veered left and within minutes I was out, standing on the edge of the harbor wall. Three of the five navy ships were on fire, one already engulfed in flames. Blazes danced across the decks of two other Royal Navy ships, the *Sirène* and the *Vengeance de Rois*. Fire spread from the bow to the figurehead, far from the galley or sleeping quarters where fire would be kept. I swallowed the dry air—these fires had been deliberately started. Was it the Alemanian patrol Sanson had reported? Anger snapped through my bones. Whoever had started this would pay.

"*C'est en feu . . .*" a voice next to me whispered. The carriage driver.

I gripped the man's shoulders. "Go to the c-castle. Get C-Captain Durrett. F-fire at the docks."

The driver's eyes were wide but he obeyed.

Heat ignited my throat but cold fingers of dread slid through my chest. The vision from the fairies blazed before me, but the smell of the ash and the heat tearing at my skin made it worse. So much worse.

Hundreds of people scrambled on the embankment, their shouts cutting through the air. Several horses screamed and pulled at their harnesses.

"Sir, we need assistance," a man in a naval uniform shouted. Soot and ash covered his face and clothes.

"The prince is here," another man shouted. "He will help." Was that Captain Durrett?

The heat from the fire rolled in waves, forcing us to retreat.

Men from the navy swarmed me and I took a step back.

"Sir, your orders."

I can't do this.

"Sir," Captain Durrett said, his face dirty with grime. "Sir, your orders."

The docks echoed with hundreds of footsteps pounding back and forth.

"C-Captain, get three t-teams of m-men. V-volunteers will be org—will b-be or—"

The heat pressed against my skin and the screams of people and animals hammered my brain. The wall to my words slammed down.

Not now.

Captain Durrett and the others waited.

Get the civilians out of danger.

"V-v-volunteers—"

The clicking sound came from deep in my throat.

Cinderella's voice rose to my mind. *Why do you want to cure your stammer? I don't think you need to.*

I glanced at the grimy faces of the soldiers desperate for me to lead them. I swallowed. I had to bounce my words. *Soufre. They will laugh. You'll never lead.* Fear roared in my chest as loudly as the flames on the ships.

Per la vittoria devi farlo. Signore Battaglia's words roared in my mind. For victory. For them.

I can do this.

I rose to my toes.

"V-volunteers will be—"

Bounce.

"Organized in a b-bucket b-brigade—"

As I bounced out my words, the fire roared behind the men, but they stayed. Waiting.

"But k-keep them off of the d-dock and away from the fire."

Captain Durrett nodded and without hesitation turned and waded into the crowd of people shouting my orders.

Bounce.

"I'll lead f-from here on the embankment." Confidence calmed my thoughts. From my vantage point atop the harbor wall, the battle against the fire was easier to navigate.

"Focus all your efforts on the *Sirène*," I shouted to Captain Durrett, who stood on the stairs leading to the docks. "If it c-cannot be c-contained, save the *Vengeance*."

The captain nodded and barked the orders to his men.

A loud crack sounded from the deck of the *Sirène* and the mizzenmast tilted toward the *Vengeance*.

"It's going to fall!" I shouted. "Get back!"

Men scrambled across the deck and over the sides of the *Sirène* and *Vengeance*, jumping into the water to escape the falling mast.

With an explosive crack, the mast broke and crashed onto the deck of the *Vengeance*.

I surveyed the damage. At least the tip of the mast wasn't on fire and spreading to the *Vengeance*. But it would. The fire was creeping from the base of the fallen mast toward the other ship.

That's when I heard someone shouting for help from the center of the fire. I scanned the *Sirène*, but that had been evacuated well before the mast had fallen.

"*Aide-moi!*"

Where was it coming from? Not the *Sirène*. There! A sailor was pinned under the *Vengeance's* topgallant sail. And the fire was advancing from the *Sirène* to the *Vengeance* like an enemy army. Captain Durrett was organizing men to board the *Vengeance* and remove the mast, but they would have to climb up and around the embankment and onto the adjoining dock.

I raced along the embankment, stopping between the two ships. It was a twenty-foot drop to the frothing sea.

"*Aide-moi!*"

I scrambled out of my coat and sword belt. "Hold these," I said, thrusting them at a nearby soldier.

I leaped from the embankment, hot air ripping past me, and plunged into the sea. Saltwater stung my skin as I swam to the *Vengeance*. Fallen ratlines hung in the water and I hauled myself onto the deck. The fire spread across the deck and the heat was like a weight on me.

Men's screams from the docks filled my ears and the fire.

The sailor beneath the beam pointed behind me. "*Fais attention!*"

I turned and saw the *Sirène's* foremast and topsail streaking through the air. I threw myself aside and rolled across the deck. Yards of heavy fabric cascaded down, suffocating me. I had to get out.

"*Aide-moi,*" the man wailed.

I pressed against the deck, straining under the sail's weight, then collapsed. *Crawl, Armand.* Arm over arm, I pulled myself to the edge of the sail, throwing the fabric over my head. *Free.* I inhaled the hot air, then I raced to the man and pulled against the crossbeams. My muscles strained and I heaved. The man groaned for a moment and then stopped as the beam lifted six inches.

"*Je suis libre!*"

I dropped the beam and it thudded to the deck. I hooked my arm beneath the man's torso and we stumbled onto the gangplank then onto the docks.

"*Merci,*" the man murmured.

I clapped the man on the back and nodded. A medic rushed to my side but I waved him off. "H-help him." The medic turned to the sailor, pulling him away from the fire.

I pushed my dripping hair from my face, then ran back to my vantage point on the embankment and took my things back from the waiting soldier. My eyes scanned the furious activity below. As people scrambled along the docks, an organized chaos emerged. *Bien.* I might actually save the Royal Navy.

A rider and horse pulled to a stop nearby and the blond-haired man dismounted. I recognized his self-assured stance. Sanson. As if this disaster needed another one.

"You," I said, pointing to Sanson. "Organize a second b-bucket brigade and g-get some men to move those ships." I gestured to the right side of the wharf. "If the wind shifts, they are in d-danger."

He stared at me. "Those are merchant vessels."

I stepped forward and grabbed Sanson's coat, my hands charged to throttle him. "Do it."

Heat scorched my back.

Sanson's eyes narrowed to slits. If he defied a direct order, he'd face treason. The question was if he'd risk it so openly. My hand fell to the pommel of my sword. His eyes flicked to my weapon, then he turned and began shouting orders at the merchants.

Captain Durrett ran to my side. "Two fires are under control and the third is nearly contained, Your Royal Highness."

Men still crawled all over the harbor, but the activity was receding.

"Thank you, D-Durrett." I clapped the man on the shoulder, then focused on the wharf. "Be sure the m-men drink plenty of water, and p-provide an extra meal as well."

"Sir." Durrett raised his chin, looking behind me. "His Majesty has arrived."

I turned and saw Father astride his horse, conversing with Sanson, whose eyes flashed like a lion watching his prey.

A wagonload of water barrels arrived and men swarmed around it, quickly forming a line.

"K-keep up the good work, Durrett."

The captain bowed, then took his leave.

There was no sense in delaying the inevitable. I wiped my brow, then strode toward Father and Sanson. Father glared from his mount.

"Why did you dispatch the palace guards?" Father's pristine garments made him look out of place in the ash-covered harbor.

"I'm s-saving these ships."

"You couldn't save a paper boat from a bathtub. Sanson organized the bucket brigade."

I bristled but held my tongue.

"You have left the palace's defenses weakened. You always were a stupid, worthless boy. This has just proved it." Father peered at the harbor and sniffed in disgust.

Sanson stared at me unapologetically, basking in Father's directed wrath. The snake. My patience crumbled to ash like the ships below.

"As c-crown prince, one of my duties is to oversee the military. This matter c-clearly falls under my jurisdiction. It is wise to split our forces and wiser to help our p-p-people." Another wagon full of supplies rumbled behind me. I waved at the harbor. "If this were an attack on the p-palace, we still have the army here to p-protect us. If it is from a foreign entity, we'll need to salvage our n-navy so that we can protect Lyonelle against future threats. I c-can and will save Lyonelle and I will d-do it in the way I see f-fit!"

Father's mouth flapped open, but he snapped it shut. His horse stamped his hooves and Father blinked, as if trying to see me clearly.

"About time you did something for the kingdom," he said. "Be sure you don't mess up your speech tonight," he warned, turning to leave.

Not the warmest response, but at least he had listened.

The fairy vision flared in my mind. Sanson holding a torch and the boats burning. The fires could still have been caused by the Alemanian border patrol, but I wouldn't put anything past Sanson. Why in the blazes hadn't I wrangled Luc for the information when I'd had the chance? I shook my head. Perhaps Father would listen to me this time.

"Father, one m-more thing." I trotted to catch up to him. "I know you t-trust Sanson, but Luc has news that Sanson is involved in underhanded d-dealings against Lyonelle." I made sure to keep my voice low enough for Father's ears only but loud enough to be heard over the general clamor.

"Does he have proof?" Father growled.

Maybe I had bitten off more than I could chew.

"Y-yes." *Luc, you had better not make a liar out of me.* "I'll know m-more as soon as Luc g-gets here," I added.

"Be certain you are taking one step forward, not two steps back," he rumbled, then he kicked his heels to his horse and galloped off.

I couldn't believe it. Father hadn't dismissed me. It wasn't the complete victory I was hoping for, but neither was it a defeat. Perhaps Cinderella was right.

Soufre. Next time I asked Luc to gather information on a suspect, I'd have to take into account how long his hangovers were. Beast's beard, when would he get here?

Would Sanson commit arson to get his war? If so, it wouldn't be long before Sanson deposed me.

CYN

By the time afternoon came, my arms were numb and sweat dripped from my temples. As the oven-like attic heated, the smell of dust and mildew intensified. Oil sat at the desk, his legs kicked up as if he were on a picnic. I shifted and the corners of the pillar dug into my skin.

I hadn't seen Aimée or Stepmother, but I'd heard shuffling below—most likely preparations for the ball. I was probably safe from Oil while they were still here. Exhaustion dug into my bones, but there was no way I was sleeping. Not with Oil ten feet away.

I blinked, and he chuckled. My eyelids grew heavier with each blink.

I woke up, gasping.

Oil sat on the same crate as he had when playing cards with Toad. I swallowed, my throat dry. At least he hadn't tried anything.

Russet-colored light permeated the attic. Even though the sun had set, the attic still remained warm. How long had it been? Anxiety tingled through my blood, burning away some of my body's aches. What about Armand? Had the masquerade already started? Was he still safe?

The door creaked and Toad walked in, followed by the smell of ash and brine. Where had he been?

"It's done," he said, his voice as dull as his personality.

I raised my eyebrows. *So he does talk.*

"And?" Oil asked.

Toad didn't change his expression. "Moved the boat."

"Good for you, Theodore," Oil said. "Glad to see you have some sense."

Toad grunted.

"Her Ladyship wants to see you downstairs," Oil said.

Toad's thick shoulders brushed the doorframe as he passed through.

A few minutes later, a carriage arrived, crunching the gravel beneath its wheels. Oil moved toward the window, and the maroon light from the window seemed to bend around him into the room. Even the light didn't want to touch him.

"*Un, deux . . .*" His raspy voice scraped against the floor. "In the carriage." My stomach twisted with each word.

The harnesses jangled and the horses pulled away, the driveway falling silent. Stepmother, Aimée, and Toad were gone.

"*Et trois, et fait.*" He brushed his hands together as if to show his work was done.

We were alone.

Oil smiled at me, showing his sharp teeth.

My stomach rolled. I pressed myself against the wooden post, its sharp edges cutting into my back. My lungs tightened with each breath I took.

He stood smoothly, wiping his hands on his thighs. "Now that it's just us, how about we get to know one another a little better?"

All of the past midnight exchanges, all of his unwanted touches filled the room. He stalked forward, grabbing the jewelry box from the table, turning it in his hands. The contents rattled inside, setting my teeth on edge.

"Watch it," I said.

"Or what?" Oil stalked forward until he stood above me. His cheeks were sunken like rotten fruit.

I struggled against the ropes, my wrists burning from the pressure.

His voice scraped past his teeth. "You really love the prince?" He crouched on his haunches, just out of reach of my legs. He picked at the box's inlay with his fingernail. Stale tobacco and greasy odors washed over me. "You stupid girl. Why would you want the prince when you could have me?"

I kicked at him, but he only smiled. My skin crawled. My defenses were shed as easily as pieces of clothing. I said the only thing I could think of.

"He'll come for me." My stomach twisted with worry. Come for me? *I* needed to find *him*. But what had Stepmother planned?

Oil laughed. "He'll have a hard time doing it if he's dead. Her Ladyship poisoned the pin." He rested the jewelry box on his knee and pulled his thumb across his neck. "He dies before the stroke of twelve."

My blood turned to ice.

"Besides," he crooned, "he doesn't really have feelings for you. How could he love a lying little thief like you?"

How could he love me? I had no idea, but he did. And I loved him too. The golden thread was still there, tying us together. Yes, I was a lying thief, but I was *his* lying thief. Armand's. I searched my heart and found the steady glow of light.

Oil picked at the box's tortoiseshell inlay with his fingernail.

"You're pathetic," I spat.

He dropped the box and tilted his head.

I thrashed against the ropes.

"I like to think I'm more than that. You've said goodbye to me twice now, but we just keep seeing each other," he said, his voice slithering over my skin. "I was right—you can't get enough of me."

My insides crawled with disgust. I glared daggers, hoping he couldn't see my fear. "Stay away from me," I snarled, bracing myself.

Oil lunged like a snake and stepped on the hem of my right pant leg, trapping it.

"I'll take what I want."

"If you do, she'll kill you." Even as I said it, I knew he could kill me and be gone long before Stepmother returned from the ball. My breath scraped my throat raw. This was bad. So very bad.

Oil laughed. He crouched at my feet, and his hands wandered over my ankles, then lifted each foot, pulling off my shoes. I twisted to kick him with my left leg but couldn't reach.

He reached over my head, his fingers stroking the side of my hands. "These must hurt from the ropes. *Autorise moi*," he said, his voice honey-slick.

I closed my eyes, but I could still feel him near me. When his hands touched the skin on my wrist, I whimpered. He turned to look at me, his eyes wild and hungry. He leaned forward until his face was inches from mine. My stomach clenched as his sour smell washed over me, and I pressed my head against the beam.

"You don't smell like apples and cinnamon like you usually do." His breath dampened my face. "I don't mind—much."

My breath came in shallow gasps.

No, no, no.

Behind him, the attic window exploded. I screamed as a fireball the size of a pumpkin burst through the window, scattering glass over the floor. Oil stood and backed away, his fists clenched.

Fear and relief swirled inside my chest.

The golden fireball landed in the small space between us, and an invisible force threw Oil backwards. The tiny sun pulsed twice and expanded in size. A burning yellow radiance filled the whole room.

A woman stood at my feet. Dressed in the night sky, her dark hair shone with the coldness of oncoming winter. A terrifying light blazed within her.

Oil shrank back.

The woman stood between me and my attacker and she raised a graceful hand. When she spoke, it was to Oil.

"You!" The woman's voice was soft and sharper than an imperial sword.

My heart stopped. I knew that voice, but I had never heard it laced with so much power and justice. Usually, it was dripping with sarcasm.

"Shar?" The word creaked between my lips.

She turned and I gasped. Her magnificent face glowed as if she'd swallowed the moon.

Oil raised his arm and cowered.

Shar waved her hand and my ropes fell away. Her silver gleam cooled the scratches and welts on my face. Blood rushed through my arms again and I stood stiffly, rubbing my wrists. I leaned against the pillar, never taking my eyes from her.

"You shall not harm m'lady, *créature immonde.*" Shar's voice thrummed with magic.

Anger twisted Oil's face and he charged.

Shar's light burst from her, burning white.

I squeezed my eyes and turned away.

"N—" Oil's wail hardened, then stopped.

The light burned through my eyelids, then all at once, it faded.

I blinked away the spots. When my vision returned, Oil stood, his arms thrown over his face, transparent and blue.

I gasped. She'd frozen him? I stepped closer, avoiding the remnants of the shattered window. I extended my fingers to touch his shirt, then snapped them back.

Not frozen—crystallized. Shar had transformed him into glass.

She turned to face me.

I winced at her beauty. *Please, don't glassify me. I'm sorry for everything wicked I ever said.* "Thank you, Shar." I gave a deep curtsy.

She beckoned me closer. I inched away from the pillar, stopping a few feet from her. She raised her hands and her long fingers danced in the air.

Golden sparks crackled around me and gathered along the seams of my clothing. I gasped as my tattered and filthy training clothes transformed. The golden light concentrated around me, smelling like damp earth and spiced cherries. The pain from my wrists disappeared, and the light continued to condense. Warmth wove into my clothing, soothing my skin. Fabric tightened around my torso, and threads wove themselves together. As my hair rose and twisted into elaborate braids and curls, the magic tickled the nape of my neck.

"Shar," I breathed.

My old clothes were now an elaborate gown. Intricate beadwork dusted the deep azure bodice and skirts. Large pale silver and green magpies danced along the silk amid trails of ribbon and lace. As I caressed the intricate folds of iridescent fabric, my skin glowed as if dusted with starlight. I inhaled

Shar's magic, pressing her light into the darkest corners inside of me. I was free.

I lifted the yards of fabric and my toes peeked out from the hem. I smiled. Now, where were my shoes? *Ah, voila.* They glinted in the Shar's light near the discarded ropes. Since when did shoes glint? I walked over and prodded them with a toe. I don't know what I expected, but they seemed safe enough. I bent over and picked them up.

Glass. Each scuff and scrape had been transformed, cutting across the smooth surface like frosted ice. But would they still fit? I slipped them onto my feet. They felt the same, if a little colder. I winced as I stood on both glass shoes. *Please don't shatter.* Gently, I took a step forward. Nothing. I looked down at my feet and watched the shoes as I took another step. They bent and moved exactly like the leather they had been.

"How is this possible?" I spoke to Shar but stared at the shoes, transfixed.

My mind flashed to Armand.

"Armand is in danger. Can you help him?" I raised my palms to her, not caring about the tremble in my voice.

"Yes, he is, but I cannot give him aid." Her outline fuzzed at the edges, and my heart fell.

"But your magic . . . the equinox . . ." My arms fell, heavy at my sides. "You turned Oil to glass. There must be something you can do."

"My magic is limited." Her form wavered again, becoming more like mist each moment. She gripped the skirt of her gown and her brow tightened, as if she were concentrating. Her outline solidified.

Everything inside me froze. Armand was going to die. *No, Cyn, he's not. Because you're going to save him. No matter the cost.*

"But how do I help him?" My eyes darted around the room. "Stepmother is going to poison him I'll need an antidote."

She raised a brow, her tone matter-of-fact. "You have to know which poison she used."

My mind raced. What poison could Stepmother make from our pantry? *Think, Cyn.* When Stepmother had come into the attic, something had been different. A smell. What was it? Tangy and sharp, like burnt almonds. Everything clicked in my head, and my heart filled with dread. "*Venenum noix.*"

Shar nodded. "You have the ingredients for the antidote."

Hope blossomed in my chest. I could save him—if I was fast enough.

"Remember, you have until midnight, m'lady."

Terror at losing Armand clawed at me. I pressed my lips together.

"Save him," Shar whispered. "Save Lyonelle."

A light from Shar's center flared and the stunning woman disappeared. When my eyes adjusted, I saw a dim, tiny, palm-sized light drifting toward the floor. I caught her and gently placed her on the window sill so she could rest.

"Thank you," I whispered.

As I raced down to the kitchen, my glass slippers clacked against the wooden stairs. *Make the antidote. Go to the castle and save Armand. Then save Aimée from Stepmother. And, hopefully, rescue the kingdom in the process.*

There was no rest for the reformed wicked.

41

ARMAND

Something was off and had been all day, like an itch I couldn't put my finger on. Where the blazes was Luc? Where was Cinderella?

Music from the mirrored ballroom echoed faintly into the hallway, and the walls hummed with energy from the hive of the court. The murmur of hundreds of courtiers and visiting dignitaries buzzed in my ears.

I gripped the hilt of my sword, pressing my thumb against the rose pommel. *Just a few moments more, Armand. Look for the lapel pin, then you'll see her.* I still couldn't believe I had proposed last night. It seemed like forever ago.

My hands felt as if they were in a furnace. I ripped off the gloves and threw them against a side table. My bright-red waistcoat, embroidered with tiny lions prowling along the hem, constricted with each breath. I raised my golden half-mask and looked down the empty hallway for my stupid brother. Mother and Father stepped into view. Still no Luc.

Originally, Luc had chosen a plain black mask. "Why gild the lily?" he'd said. I'd switched the plain one for another that better suited his personality. It was in his room along with the chess piece. *Serves him right.*

Mother's hand on my arm brought me back to the present. "It's time to go, Hermann dear," she said. "The receiving line is ready for us."

Servants opened the curtains and we stepped into the ballroom. The rustling fabrics of hundreds of partygoers hissed as each bowed and curtsied.

I stepped onto the receiving dais, taking my place beside Mother.

Halfway through the reception, a silver donkey mask stepped into my peripheral vision. I was so worked up, I nearly strangled the ass on the spot. The donkey, dressed in golden breeches and a brown striped jacket, began bowing as if it had been there the entire evening.

"*Soufre*, where have you b-been?" I asked my mule-faced brother. "Sleeping, no doubt, you j-jack-faced knave. There was a fire at the harbor and I saved the Royal Navy. Sanson is still a s-snake. And you've been napping."

The herald thumped his staff on the floor and continued to announce the ambassadors. "Ambassador Kenji from Jaiponi."

Luc placed a hand on his chest. "Yes, the fire. You're such a good prince, risking life and limb for Lyonelle. By the by, someone switched our masks, brother." He bowed to Ambassador Kenji.

I curled my fingers into claws. Perhaps I could wring the answer out of him.

Father glared over Mother's head in our direction. I pulled at my cravat and returned the ambassador's bow, then gestured for him to join the masque.

"Well?" I said, keeping my voice low.

"You'd be surprised what one can accomplish in a few hours before a masquerade," Lucky said, standing upright and straightening his jacket. "I hope you don't mind, but I've taken some liberties."

I bowed to a duke and duchess, the herald's voice fading into the background.

"As though I c-could stop you," I hissed under my breath. "But when have I ever minded your tricks and pranks? Or d-ditching me to frolic with Aimée? Or when you ate all the pies and b-blamed it on me?" I paused and inhaled deeply to settle my nerves. "Did. You. Get. It?"

Luc lifted his donkey mask and dramatically scratched his brow.

"The p-proof about Sanson," I hissed.

"Didn't I say as much last night? I thought I did, though I really can't remember."

"And?" I asked, my hand tight on my sword. This masque was two minutes away from becoming a murder scene.

"It will be taken care of—tomorrow. Sanson *is* an urgent matter, but not with a party tonight." He winked. I growled inwardly and forced a smile at the next pair of dignitaries.

As they moved down the line, I opened my mouth, a string of curses at the ready. "You 'arranged things'? What did you d-do?"

He placed a hand across his chest in mock offense. "And ruin the surprise?"

I turned. "You're going to t-tell me or I'll—"

"Lady Vienne Manette and daughter."

My chest tightened. *Daughter?* There were supposed to be two.

"Aimée." Luc beelined toward the blonde young woman in blue.

She seemed to be trying to sink into the floor. Her round shoulders hunched and her eyes stared at the ground. Even through her feathered swan mask, her eyes looked anxious. Next to her stood Vienne, perfectly matching Cinderella's memories of her. Aimée gave Luc a wan smile. This was the laughing country lady Luc was betrothed to?

The muscles in my neck coiled. Where was Cinderella?

My scalp tingled. There hadn't been any messages for me at Lady Eline's or the palace. She would have sent word if she'd needed me.

I looked again at the Manette women. They wouldn't have arrived separately from her. My chest tightened—something was off.

"Henri, the dance," Mother said to Father behind me. "The most important guests are already here."

She led Father onto the dance floor, marking the start of the ball. I turned to ask about Cinderella, but Luc had already pulled Aimée onto the floor, joining the growing number of dancers.

Where was Cinderella? Worry clawed at my muscles.

As my eyes scanned the crowd, a set of granite gray ones caught mine. Vienne Manette stared, her face like carved marble. I shivered. As couples strode past her onto the dance floor, she stood apart, clutching a large black cane topped with a screaming silver raven.

Anger flared in my stomach. I knew that shape. The last place I'd seen it was seared into Cinderella's flesh.

Vienne inclined her head slightly in the tiniest of nods.

The urge to wrench the cane free and break it in half roiled through me. Instead, I returned her nod, then scanned the crowd for Luc and Aimée. I could feel Vienne's stare drilling into my back, and my skin crawled.

Luc's donkey ears bobbed above the crowd. If anyone would have answers, it was Aimée.

I pushed through the dancing couples. Tigers, dogs, and even dragons waltzed around the room.

"May I c-cut in?" I asked.

Luc pulled Aimée tighter. "It's rude to cut in before one full dance." He gave an exaggerated pout. "Bad form."

"It's also b-bad form to refuse a royal request." I offered my hand to Aimée but glared at Luc.

"Is it a royal request? Maybe I should make some of my own," Luc's eyes twinkled. So he hadn't told Aimée who he was.

I narrowed my eyes. Over Luc's shoulder in the distance, Vienne still stared like a spider waiting for a fly.

I leaned in close to Luc and removed my mask. "I am the p-prince," I said. "D-doesn't get more royal than that."

Aimée's eyes went wide, perhaps at Luc's impertinence, and her face drained of all color as she curtsied. My eyebrows rose. Some people did react oddly around royalty, but Aimée's reaction was more severe than most.

"Are you?" Luc asked. "Just checking. You never know who could be royal at a masque," he said. "I could be royalty and no one would be the wiser."

"Luc," she hissed. "Bow."

"Oh, right," Luc said, executing a sloppy bow. "Bow for royalty and all that."

"You're a royal p-pain in the a—"

"Language!" Luc said. "And at a masquerade." He waggled his finger, then he turned, heading toward the food table.

Aimée's frame stiffened. She took my hand hesitantly, and I led her through the dance. *Where should I start? Your sister's a thief and I love her.* Something glittered on her shoulder. An ornate lapel pin. *My* lapel pin.

I froze. A couple bumped into us, and I pulled Aimée close.

"Where d-did you get that?" My voice climbed higher. "Where is she?"

Aimée's eyes were pinched, her chin tight. She unfastened the lapel pin.

"I believe this is—y-yours." She trembled, her teeth chattering violently.

"What is wrong?" I grabbed Aimée's arms. "Is it Cinderella?"

Her gloved fingers pinched the exposed pin and she extended her arm. Her gaze darted to someone standing near the wall. Vienne leaned forward, licking her lips.

My scowl deepened. Something *was* off. But what?

I reached for the pin. Aimée's hands trembled.

The pin hovered inches above my palm.

"No, Aimée!" a voice shrieked.

The next moment, an iridescent avenging angel with brunette hair and a leather satchel slammed into Aimée and knocked her back.

The rhythm of the waltz pounded in my chest. Aimée held the pin between her fingers, and her arm extended, the point aimed at Armand. I raced across the ballroom floor, my breath catching in my chest.

I lunged for Aimée's wrist, knocking us both away from Armand. Blue lace and silk frothed around me. "Let it go," I growled, pressing my thumb at the base of her wrist. A few people gasped and stepped back.

"Aimée, it's me," I hissed.

Her eyes widened. "*Ma sœur.*"

She stopped and opened her fingers. The pin fell to the floor.

"Cyn?" Her eyes searched my face. "You're all right?" She gripped my arms as if making sure I was real.

I pulled her into my arms. "I'm here, it's okay."

She embraced me, sniffling into my shoulder. I released a shaky breath into her curled hair.

"Aimée, are you all right?" a man's voice asked. Luc wove through the couples, a cup of punch in each hand. "What's wrong?"

Aimée rushed to Luc's side and I turned, looking for Armand. He should have been right behind me. Glittering colors swirled as the masked partygoers waltzed around me. The mirrored walls added to the confusion.

I had stopped her in time. I had.

Armand is safe. But where is he?

A thud sounded behind me.

I whirled around. Armand lay curled on the floor, his dark brown curls spilling around his contorted face. My heart stopped. Armand clutched his wrist, a long bloody scratch covering the back of his hand. His body twisted and his eyes rolled into the back of his head.

"Armand!" I screamed, dropping next to him. I had been too late.

"*Mon frère!*" Luc fell to the floor beside me.

"Brother?" Aimée exclaimed.

The music stopped. As Armand writhed on the floor, guests pulled away. Stepmother clasped her raven-shaped brooch in her palm. When she spoke, her words pierced the cloud in my mind. "Always have a backup plan."

Beasts. She'd poisoned her own pin as a backup.

Stepmother's eyes glinted as she stepped back and raised a finger, pointing it at me. "She has poisoned the prince!" With a rustle of fabric, she disappeared into the throng.

I tore open my satchel.

Faceless voices murmured from the crowd.

"*Le prince.*"

"Murder!"

More guests joined the growing circle around us.

Armand twisted on the floor. My stomach coiled with every convulsion.

"I can help," I whispered. My fingers flew over the packets. "I can help." Where was that antidote?

Got it! I pulled out the smooth glass vial. Dark green syrup sloshed inside.

Armand's shaking increased. He only had minutes left. Less, depending on how much poison had gotten into his blood.

I leaned over Armand, moving my hand to his mouth, ready to uncork and tip the liquid. He just had to drink it.

Gurgling came from deep in his throat.

"Arrest that woman," a voice boomed.

Fear pooled in my ankles. I knew that voice from Armand's memories. The king. I turned to see him scowling and pointing at me.

Liveried arms wrapped around my waist and yanked me from Armand's side. The vial dropped, clinking to the floor.

"No! Let me go!" I kicked and pulled, but the guards dragged me away from Armand. His convulsions slowed, and dread thundered through my heart.

A scream ripped from my chest. "I can save him. I can save him!" I kicked at the guard and one of my glass slippers flew into the air.

"Let her go!" Luc punched a guard, laying him flat.

Guests shrieked. The other guard released me.

"Hurry," Luc shouted.

I fell to the floor, searching for the vial. Where was it? Sweat stung my face. Was it broken?

"*C'est ici.*" Aimée's gloved hand thrust the vial in my face.

I crawled to Armand, clutching the antidote. He merely twitched, which was worse than the convulsions. His skin was white, his lips purple. I flipped the cork off and tipped his head back, shoving the contents of the vial into the back of his throat. Acrid fumes filled the air.

"Work." A drop of the green syrup sat in the corner of his lips. I lifted his head, hoping the antidote would reach his stomach faster that way. "Please be okay." *Please let me be fast enough.*

Within moments, the twitching stopped, and Armand's body lay still.

"No, no, no, no," I moaned. I placed my hands on his chest, as if I could reach beyond his ribs and heal his heart. "Armand, please. Don't leave me."

"*Mon fils!*" Queen Mathilde rushed forward. As she threw herself over Armand's body, the feathers on her gown trembled.

"The prince is dead," someone whispered.

"*Mort?*" Another voice asked. "*Impossibile.*"

The struggle between Luc and the guards stopped.

I stared at his body, not really seeing it. I hadn't been fast enough. Again.

Soon Armand's hands would grow cold. His cheeks and lips would turn blue. Just like Father. I stood and placed the heel of my hand on my forehead. *Dead.* The walls and floor seemed to switch places.

I wasn't fast enough. I turned away. My breaths came quick and I tugged at the trimmings along my neck. Everyone else seemed frozen in time and I alone was living this nightmare. Armand's body. His mother crying. Luc expressionless, a shirtsleeve torn. Even the two guards were frozen.

I backed away and my heartbeat pounded in my ears. My fault, my fault. My hands pressed against my collarbones. I wasn't fast enough. Wasn't fast enough.

A voice screamed in my head. *No!* Anger erupted in my body. This wasn't *my* fault. This was *hers.*

She had done this. All of this.

Stepmother.

My fists clenched and blood seared through me. She'd let me believe that I'd killed my papa. All her lies, her betrayals, and my pain—everything condensed into a burning rage. My breath seethed in my chest.

I banished my tears with the heel of my hand. I hadn't been fast enough to heal Armand, but I would have justice.

I would find her and make her pay for everything she'd taken from me.

I charged after her, shoving guests aside.

As I reached the top of the palace steps, the brisk night air cut through the humidity of the ballroom, chilling the sweat on my skin.

"Guards, arrest that woman." The king's voice echoed from inside.

Roi fou.

Clattering boots followed the king's command.

I raced down the steps.

Be resourceful, Cyn.

The guards' voices carried through the doors and into the night. They were close.

Lead them to her. But where had she gone?

Then it hit me and I barked a laugh. I knew exactly where to go. Oil himself had told me.

My feet crunched on the gravel and I searched for Pumpkin. I found him munching on some imperial roses.

I leaped onto his back, my dress billowing over his flank.

Guards shouted from the top of the stairs, their armor clinking on the marble steps. "Halt!"

My heels dug into Pumpkin's side as I turned away from the palace and toward the wharf.

Time to catch an assassin.

My skin tasted the wharf long before we reached its southern side. The brine sharpened with each breath I took, urging me forward. Ash mingled in the air, carried on a warm southerly wind, a tribute to Toad's handiwork.

I pulled Pumpkin to a stop at the top of the docks and frantically searched the piers.

Movement to my right, fifty yards away, caught my eye. Stepmother struggled to drag a skiff to the water.

I see you.

I dug my heels into Pumpkin, thundering toward her.

Stepmother froze, her boat still several feet from the nearest mooring. She sank into a low crouch, her muscles tense. The raven from her cane glinted in the moonlight.

I dismounted Pumpkin and approached her warily, making sure I kept out of her cane's reach. But I didn't have to catch her. Just keep her talking.

"Your raven brooch was your backup, wasn't it?" I asked. "You murdered the prince."

"Murder?" she spat. "It was justice."

"Justice for what? The prince never did you any harm. You killed him. The man I loved." Where was the Garde Royale? Of course, the one time I wanted the guards to catch me and they were nonexistent. The wind was still and even the waves crashing against the docks faded.

"It was a Lyonelle border patrol that burned my house," she said. "My home, my family. Lyonelle stole my son. It was only fair I steal one of theirs as well."

The rational side of me understood her grief—and the crushing need for justice. The pain of losing Maman, Papa, and now Armand burst through me, shredding my control. "You took everything from me!"

"*Non, ma belle-fille.*" Stepmother's features twisted hideously, venom spewing from her eyes. "You killed the prince and your father. This is only the fruit of your labors."

Her words crushed me like boulders, and I closed my eyes, hot tears spilling down my face. Guilt. Familiar. It would be so easy to accept it again. I inhaled and remembered Armand. Leaning close. Us sharing the same breath in the grove surrounded by fairies. The gilded thread.

I'd given grace to Armand and I'd accept his grace for me.

No. Not ever again. I pushed the guilt—her words, her lies—away. The truth powered through me and I stood firm, my voice ripping through my raw throat.

"You're wrong. I didn't kill Papa. He was sick. But you stole what little time I had left with him." Tears continued to spill down my face. "It was all your fault. All of it. My only mistake was listening to you."

Hooves drummed down the walkway, stopping behind me. I didn't turn to look even though I heard someone dismount. Probably the captain. I stepped backwards so I could keep him and Stepmother in my sights. The rest of the guards remained in a line on my left, blocking the nearest exit to the wharf. No doubt other soldiers blocked other possible escape routes.

The man who stepped down was in military formalwear. Clearly, he had come from the ball and was important, if the medals on his jacket meant anything. He had a large scar bursting from his temple. His pale blonde hair shone in the moonlight.

He stepped forward, pointing at us. "In the name of the king, you are both under arrest."

"Arrest *her*," I said. "She's the one who poisoned the prince."

Stepmother's face was ghostly white, her eyes transfixed upon the captain, or whoever he was. She glided forward, coming even with me. I stepped back to avoid her, but she passed me in a trance, all her attention on the man.

"You," she said, her finger shaking as it pointed. "I know you."

"I am *Général* Sanson," the man said, obviously uncertain of where this was going.

"You were in the border patrol years ago, assigned to the Dascht region," Stepmother said, more in accusation than statement. "In Taurig."

My brows fell in confusion, but my muscles stayed ready. What was going on here? How did Stepmother know this man?

"Yes," Sanson nodded, though clearly shaken by the statements.

"Four years ago . . ." Stepmother said, her gaze unfocused, as if seeing something else.

He remained perfectly still.

"You burned a manor house," she continued. "Baron Sauer's." Her hands dove into the folds of her dress, into her pockets.

The man paled, stepping backwards, but Stepmother crept toward him, completely ignoring me.

The other guards shifted nervously in their seats, their mounts stamping on the dock.

"Sir?" one of the men asked.

"The baron died in that fire," she pressed, her voice dripping with hate. "You went searching for the baroness and child in the woods, but you never found them."

The man turned paler.

Stepmother stalked closer, like a cat approaching its next meal. They now stood only a few feet apart.

"Sir," the guard repeated, his voice tense.

"Did you know there was also a baby inside that house?" Stepmother's accent clipped against the cobblestones. She glided to the man, stopping an arm's length away.

"How—how can you know that?" he said, the medals on his chest clinking as he shook under Stepmother's cold fury.

"Because I was there. You killed my son. *Mein baby!*"

Stepmother pulled her hands from her pockets, raising them high over her head. A few of the Garde Royale moved to intervene, but they were too far away. The man threw up his hands to block her attack. She slashed downward, dragging her raven pin from his fingers to his wrist.

The second-in-command unsheathed his sword and pointed it at Stepmother's chest.

Général Sanson held up his hand, studying it, and the guard lowered his sword.

The *général* laughed, grabbing Stepmother's arm, then he examined the wound. A deep scratch sliced through his wrist, trickling a drop of blood. "A scratch? What harm will that do?"

Her lips pulled back from her teeth. "Plenty."

He snorted, then pushed Stepmother toward the waiting guard. She didn't struggle.

The *général* laughed again, then stopped, his face pale. He staggered backwards and clutched his arm as he fell to the ground. Convulsions racked him, more violent than Armand's had been. He pulled in ragged wheezing breaths as his skin purpled. Bloody froth filled his mouth and his eyes bulged.

As the *général* lay on the ground, I could only see Armand. I closed my eyes. The *général*'s chest rattled as he rasped for air. In less than a minute, he was still.

"*Für Gerechtigkeit*," Stepmother hissed.

"Arrest them both," a man from the guards yelled.

Hands grabbed me, but I continued to stare at the *général*'s body. He was dead.

Just like Armand.

"By the Rose and Claw, you are under arrest . . ."

The guards grabbed my wrists and tied them behind my back, their voices fading into the background.

I was going to prison.

But Aimée needs you, a voice inside my head whispered.

She has Luc. He will take care of her.

The guards pulled me away from the body.

Who will take care of you? the voice whispered.

Armand is dead. It doesn't matter what happens now.

The guards slung me over one of their horses and I didn't resist. Out of the corner of my eye, I saw Stepmother thrown across the dappled gray horse next to me.

She didn't struggle either, and the serene smile across her face chilled me to my bones.

43

Armand

Everything hurt. When had Gallant trampled on my chest? *Inhale.* Pain. *Exhale.* Pain.

I blinked. Red damask curtains on a four-poster bed came into focus. My bedchambers.

Intense morning light poured through the window, making the drapery, the intricate Eastern rugs, and the unlit candles glow. I blinked hard at the painted hunting scene repeating itself around the ceiling of my room.

I sat up, but fire shot from my left arm to my shoulder. The room tilted like I was on a sinking ship, and I fell back. Pain pulsed in my hand, pounding out my heartbeat. An angry purple welt rose on the back of my hand. Yellow pus seeped from the swollen wound. How had I gotten that?

"You're awake," a voice said. I knew that voice, but it had never sounded so serious.

Luc sat in a chair by the window, his hair tangled and his clothes rumpled. Dark circles underscored his eyes. He crossed the room and sat on the edge of my bed.

"What . . . happened?" I croaked, raising myself up. Luc propped several pillows behind my back.

"Poison," he said, matter-of-factly. "Aimée was going to poison you with a pin, but Cinderella stopped her in time."

"Aimée? Your f-fiancée. So you d-do want the throne." I exhaled the last words, then blinked hard. Talking was exhausting.

Luc chuckled softly and some of his tension eased. "She didn't—poison you, that is. But *Madame* Manette intervened and gave you that nice scar."

I prodded at the back of my aching hand, and Luc continued. "Cinderella gave you an antidote, so don't expect too much sympathy. You've only been asleep for two days."

"T-two days?" I pressed my hand against my head, trying to remember the masquerade. I had danced with Aimée, hoping to find Cinderella. Then Cinderella had tackled Aimée. A few moments later, something had scratched my hand. Then pain. Immense pain. After that, nothing.

Luc poured me a glass of water from the pitcher on the side table.

I took it, gulping down its contents. As the water woke me up, I sat a little straighter. "Cinder—Cyn. Where is she?" My heart leaped against my ribs.

"Prison. Aimée, too."

"Prison?" I slammed the cup on the side table. Pain pounded my head and I pushed the heel of my hand to my temple.

"Actually, the whole family. Vienne, Aimée, and Cyn are all under arrest for the assassination of the prince."

"Whose assassination? M-mine?"

"Don't let all the attention go to your head," Luc said, chuckling.

"Stop joking, Lucien." I rubbed the wrist below the scratch, then lay against the headrest. I was exhausted.

"Relax, Armand, they are safe enough. Besides, you're getting ahead of the story. Don't you want me to tell you about Sanson?"

I fell back in the bed. It felt like my lungs couldn't catch enough air.

"Trust me, you're going to want to hear this." From the side table, Luc produced a bowl of broth and a loaf of bread. He tore it into smaller pieces and dunked one into the cold soup, then offered it to me.

"Talk fast," I said around a mouthful of bread. A sheen of sweat formed on my skin just from the effort of sitting up. I took another large bite.

Hopefully, after a quick meal, I could storm the prison and get Cyn out of there.

Luc pulled the armchair to the bed and smiled, as satisfied as a fat lion. "I went to Sanson's house. After I let loose a few slanderous remarks about you, about being lost in your shadow, and how terrible it was being your brother, and how you always take the biggest piece of birthday cake even if it's not your birthday—"

"Luc," I warned. I finished off the soup and motioned for more. It wasn't much, but I did feel some strength returning.

"After all that, Sanson warmed right up to me." Luc offered me a plate of cold-cut meats and I tucked in. "A few drinks later, I casually mentioned dethroning you."

I choked on some chicken and all the muscles in my torso ached. "T-traitor."

Luc shrugged. "In any case, Sanson revealed his plan to stage another attack on the border. Water?" He held out the pitcher and refilled my cup, then settled back into his seat. "Turns out, for the last ten years, Sanson has been attacking citizens of Alemania living along the border."

I spluttered, droplets spattering on the sheets. "*Impossibile*," I said. "Alemania has been attacking us for at least eight years. We were retaliating."

Luc nodded. "Exactly. But what you don't know is that neither country was responsible for the initial attacks."

I pressed the cool cup against my temples. The food and water eased my headache, but Luc's explanation was making it worse. "Luc, I've been poisoned. Tell it straight. Or I'll execute you for treason."

Luc chuckled, pouring me another glass of water.

I wanted to splash it in his face, but instead, I growled for him to continue.

"Ten years ago, Sanson started looting and burning Alemanian estates. When tensions between our countries rose to a certain point, he stopped. Alemania was happy to avoid war, so they ignored the fact that one of their border patrols was missing."

Sanson had captured an entire Alemanian border patrol and no one cared? I set the tray of food aside. My chest burned as Luc continued.

"Sanson used the Alemanian uniforms and began looting and pillaging Lyonelle's estates and villages along the border. He recently began the rumor that Alemania was developing new weapons. Each time tensions would rise, Sanson would lay low and work on gaining political power."

A bitter taste filled my mouth. I'd known Sanson was a poisonous snake, but I hadn't known to what extent. I should have seen his treachery sooner. "People d-died in those attacks, Luc. Alemanian and Lyonelle citizens alike. This is m-murder."

"Yes," Luc agreed.

"T-treason," I said.

"Definitely," he said. "Oh, and Sanson bribed the blacksmith to lie to you about the firelances. Sanson fabricated both weapons." Luc was as calm as if he were on Lyonelle's most relaxing beach.

I absently rubbed my arm. The fairy vision of the Alemanian symbols. That was what had been off about the firelance Sanson had presented—the emblem. During the last year, Alemania had absorbed two new city-states and changed their national symbol to include three stars instead of one. Of course. How had I not seen it?

Anger rose in my chest. What was Luc doing here, acting as nursemaid if Sanson was still walking free? If only I had the strength to throttle him— both of them.

"What are you waiting for?" I said, gesturing for the door. "Arrest him."

"Can't."

I snarled. "*Soufre*, why not?"

"He's dead."

I kept my eye on Luc, placing the cup on the table. "D-dead? How?"

"Vienne killed him. Poisoned him with her brooch. Or possibly your lapel pin. But oddly enough, no one suspects you of killing Sanson, even though I always thought you were the most likely candidate. I guess writhing on the floor after being poisoned has its advantages."

I sat back so hard my head thumped against the headboard. Vienne killed Sanson. I took a sip from the cup of water on the tray.

"But you ought to take it easy," Luc said, tapping me on my right hand, spilling water onto the bedsheets. I glared at him as the cold water seeped through.

He stood, growing serious. "I'll get Father."

I sat as straight as I could against the pillows.

"Show him in." I held the *sh* sound like it was the waves against the seashore. *It doesn't matter, Armand. You stutter. You will for the rest of your life. But it doesn't define you.*

Luc walked to the door and paused. "I overheard him say that you always fight for what you believe in. That you had more guts than the entire family combined."

Luc left.

I swallowed, and not from thirst. Had Father really said that? Had he finally realized that there was more to people than what lay on the surface? That there was more to me?

It didn't matter what Father thought of me, though, but it did matter what I thought of myself.

Despite wanting to sink back into the pillows, I remained straight. Poisoned or not, I would present Father with a strong front.

I flinched when Luc popped his head back in, losing my grip on the cup and spilling the remaining water onto the sheets. I glared at my brother.

"By the by, he won't believe me that the girls had nothing to do with your poisoning. Father has the whole Manette family lined up for execution tomorrow."

"Execution?" I roared.

Luc vanished again, his footsteps retreating down the hall.

Soufre. I wasn't going to stay here for a chat with Father. I was going to drag him to the prison and make him pardon the Manette sisters then and there.

I swung my legs out of the bed, then stood, swaying and gripping the bedpost. How could Father be so blind when the truth stared him in the face? I would make him see the facts. Cold air blew over my legs and I looked down. I wore nothing but a nightshirt. I would save the Manette sisters, but first . . . I had to get dressed.

I had only just managed to pull on my breeches when Father and Mother burst into my room. I rested on the edge of the bed, still gripping the post. Mother wailed and threw herself over my lap.

Luc came in again, shrugged at Mother's antics, then sat, lounging in the armchair.

"My poor, cursed baby," she said. "Stammering . . . poisoning . . . assassinations!" Her shaky voice rose with each word. I grimaced inwardly. A few weeks ago, I might have agreed with her. I was a different person now. Because of Cyn.

I patted her gently on the back as she choked on her hysterics. "It's more than I can bear." She rose and crossed to the other side of the room, her handkerchief fluttering across her face. She looked at me through watery eyes.

"M-Mother, I've been poisoned. Not broken."

"Oh. Yes, I suppose that's true." She gulped, blinking hard. Her lower lip quivered, but she gave a weak smile. She squeezed my hand, then stood behind Luc, much calmer now.

"Father," I said, attempting to rise so I could bow.

Father waved me down, a pained look in the corner of his eyes. My gaze searched his face. *More guts than the family combined.*

"Glad to see you are awake," he said, his voice softer than I'd heard it in a long time.

"G-good to see you, sir."

Luc, who was comforting Mother, raised his eyebrows.

I squared my shoulders. "Father, Luc said the Manette family is in p-prison."

His face hardened. "It's where assassins belong."

I chuckled, then hacked as the effort proved too much for my lungs. Mother wailed quietly from the corner.

"The Manette sisters are no more assassins than I am. What's more, F-Father," I said, "is that I love *Mademoiselle* Cinderella Manette." I glanced at Mother. "I was going to announce our betrothal at the m-masquerade."

Father's features hardened further, his hands forming fists.

"And I love *Mademoiselle* Aimée," Luc added from the corner.

Father whirled on Luc, growling. Luc smiled sheepishly, then redoubled his efforts to console Mother.

"I'll not have my sons married to those criminals," Father said, turning back to me. "One of them the Crow, or something. The Garde Royale searched the house of *les criminelles* and found a hoard of stolen goods. All of the Manettes are without a doubt involved in murder, either directly or by association."

The Crow. Father didn't even pay attention to his own court's gossip. Anger thrummed in my chest. "It's the Magpie," I corrected. "And she s-stole only because she was forced to."

"Crow or Magpie, life in prison is the best she can hope for." Father smacked his fist against his palm.

I shot Luc a look. *Tell him before Father does something stupid.*

Luc made a face that said, "Do I have to?"

I gave a small nod and motioned to my injury, making what I hoped was a pitiful face.

Luc sent me another long-suffering look, then approached Father. "We've been over this," he said, then told Father everything we had learned about the Manette family.

"And, Father, I love her," Luc said at the end of the explanation.

After several more arguments and a few shouting matches about Luc's feelings for Aimée, Father grew uncharacteristically still. His stiff shoulders lowered an inch, just like they had in the Grand Council meeting before Sanson had interrupted with the supposed firelance. A detail flashed in my mind. I smiled. *Voila, la solution.*

I stood, using the bed frame as support, then jabbed a finger at Father. "She's on the l-list."

He turned and blinked at me. "Pardon?"

"You said I could choose a b-bride, provided she was on the list and from L-Lyonelle."

Father scowled but unfolded his arms.

"The M-Manettes. They were on the l-list." My words spilled from my mouth, and I didn't care as my stutter chopped the words to splinters. "D-don't let . . . D-don't let recent events sway your earlier f-feelings, Father. T-trust them. T-trust me."

I stared into Father's eyes. *I'll fight like the Great Beast for this.*

"*Soufre,*" Luc whispered from the corner.

Mother's fit of nerves waited for Father's response.

"Still," Father grumbled. "I'll not have it."

"You don't have a choice." I moved to the center of the floor and squared my shoulders. "I'm the c-crown prince and I choose Cinderella. We will m-marry as soon as possible." I kept my face steady, but power roared in my chest. I'd done it. I'd said exactly what was in my heart, and by the Beast's beard, it felt good.

"Marry as soon as possible?" Father asked, his shoulders fully relaxing. He remained expressionless, but his mouth twitched.

"Yes," I said, clasping my hands behind my back. "We w-will with or without your b-blessing. But I'd prefer it all the same."

He pressed his hands behind his back. "I supposed you'll be wanting me to give her a royal pardon?"

"I won't s-settle for less," I said, standing tall.

"You may not settle for less, but I am king."

"And I am your son."

Father's features started to soften at the edges. "It's not worth starting a civil war over," he grumbled.

"No, it's n-not." I stared, making sure he understood that if I had to start a war for the woman I loved, so be it.

"Me too," Luc echoed, sensing victory.

My words hit their mark. Father's shoulders lowered completely. I exhaled, my feet relaxing into the thick rug.

Father leaned in closer and rumbled in a low voice. "I'm not surprised it took nearly dying for you to speak up."

"P-perhaps it took my nearly d-dying for you to be willing to l-listen."

Father pulled his head back, and Mother squeaked in the corner.

I tensed my muscles, prepared for a battle, but instead, Father chuckled. "We rulers of Lyonelle have been a stubborn lot, through and through," he said. "I'm glad you've finally learned your lesson."

"Lesson?" I asked.

Father walked over and placed a hand on my shoulder. "Unfortunately, it doesn't matter what you say, but it does matter you believe in yourself. I'm proud of you, my son."

Proud? My heart soared at his praise. It was everything I'd wanted from him—but his words weren't as satisfying as I had thought they would be. What surprised me more was that I didn't need them. And it felt good to not need them.

Father moved to the corner and continued to grumble. He turned and spoke to Luc and me, the usual gruffness back in his voice.

"In the interest of peace and Lyonelle, I submit," he said. "Marry your *jeunes filles*, but don't come crawling to me when they rob you both blind." This time there was a definite upturn of Father's mouth.

Luc laughed and clapped Father on the shoulder. "Thank you, Father. You'll love Aimée."

Mother's arms flapped like a startled chicken. She bounced on her toes, nearly hopping to the window. "Oh, a double wedding! We'll have to hurry if we're to have the boys married by the first snowfall." She scampered to Father, grabbing his hands and wringing them between hers. "Isn't it wonderful, Henri? Both our boys married. I've got so little time. Would it be gauche to use the masquerade decorations as wedding decor?"

Father huffed and left the room with Mother chasing after him.

Luc turned to me. "Brilliant speech," he said.

I rested my torso against the bedpost, as tired as if I had just finished an afternoon of training with Master Battaglia. "It was p-pretty good, wasn't it?"

Luc tossed something and it landed in my lap. I picked it up. The chess piece? A grin split across my face.

"Saving your b-bride from execution is a pretty big favor, isn't it?" I said. I moved to the bench at the foot of the bed.

Luc waggled a finger at me. "I knew all this attention would go to your head."

He walked over to my dresser and pulled a shoe from the top drawer. It appeared to be crafted out of ice. He handed it to me and I held it up, light reflecting from its surface. Gooseflesh rose on my arm. Not ice, but glass. A glass slipper?

"Cinderella lost it while fighting the guards."

"She wore this?" I asked, running my thumb over its surface. "Wait— she d-did what?"

"She saved you with an antidote, but the guards assumed she was killing you." He shrugged. "I imagine one foot of hers is terribly cold." He rubbed his hand over his mouth in a poor attempt to hide his smirk. "Plus she's been walking in circles in her cell," he said. "Lopsided, you know."

He hobbled around the room in imitation and I laughed, waving him toward the door.

"Go g-get your *chérie* out," I said.

Luc hobbled toward the door. "You want me to get Cinderella out too?"

"No, I'll do it m-myself."

He nodded. "Glad you didn't die," he said.

"Me t-too," I said, leaning on the bedpost once more.

Luc bowed, then left the room, his footsteps racing down the hall.

I took a deep breath and shuffled after him.

To the dungeon.

ARMAND 44

I stopped to catch my breath for the fifth time. I rested against the cold stone wall on the stairs that led to the dungeon. Despite the chilly air, sweat beaded my forehead. Being poisoned was beastly awful. My eyes followed the curve of the stairwell. Relief washed away some of my fatigue. Almost there.

The door to the dungeon clanged open, and Luc and Aimée crowded the stairwell. Aimée wore her masquerade gown, now more gray than blue. Despite this and her stint in prison, complete with grimy face and matted curls, she managed a dignified curtsy.

"Your Royal Highness."

Luc pulled at her hand, but she remained in her curtsy. "See?" he said to Aimée. "He's fine. No harm done."

With her free hand, Aimée slapped Luc hard on the stomach. He grunted, then rubbed where she'd slapped him. She was going to fit right in.

"Please forgive me." She bowed her head again to me.

I lowered my hand and helped her to her feet. "Of course. It's what family does, is it not?"

She looked up in surprise. "Y-yes. It does."

"I hear congratulations are in order for you both," I said. "Well, at least for Luc. He's obviously marrying above himself." I wrapped both hands around hers and frowned. "My condolences, Aimée."

"Thank you." She looped her arm through Luc's. "I'm inclined to agree with you, especially after I discovered that he lied to me our entire courtship."

Luc picked at his sleeve and gave a huff. "Says the accomplice of a thief. Besides, many women would think a prince in disguise is romantic."

Aimée rolled her eyes. "I was referring to your name." She grimaced. "Lucien simply doesn't suit you." She pursed her lips together. "It's incredibly stuffy."

"I didn't have anything to do with it." Luc folded his arms in a dramatic pout.

Aimée turned to me, her face twisted, as if she were debating something. In a quick motion, she wrapped her arms around me and hugged me tightly. Luc raised his eyebrows, as caught off guard as I was.

"Thank you," she said, "for saving Cyn. Since she met you, she's been happier."

I returned her embrace. "I have too." That was the truth.

Luc shifted closer to Aimée and wrapped her fingers around his. They started up the stairs, but Aimée paused several steps up and turned back to me.

"You know, every night when Cyn was out stealing, I was always terrified she'd land herself in jail. I'm so grateful she ran into you instead."

I nodded. The feeling was mutual.

"I truly am relieved to see you alive and well, Your Highness," she said. "I hadn't heard any news since our arrest."

"You mean, Cinderella thinks I'm dead?" I asked.

Aimée's fingers knotted together. "I haven't seen Cyn. Is she all right?"

"Aimée was in a different section," Luc said. "I think *Mademoiselle Cinderella* is in the second block."

I nodded. If no news had reached Aimée, it probably hadn't reached Cinderella either. She must think I had died.

I had to get to her, but I hesitated. Stumbling past prisoners and Vienne was not a satisfaction I wanted them to have. "I'll have to use the mask," I said, rubbing my chin.

"The interrogator's mask?" Luc turned on his stare, one eyebrow arched. "You're up to something. What are you planning?"

"Nothing for your eyes." I waved them on.

Luc chuckled, his voice bouncing off the walls, then pulled Aimée up the stairs. Their whispers and giggles echoed off the stone. They were clearly anxious to celebrate their reunion more privately.

After two more rests, I entered the second block of rooms. Four cells lined each side. It was dank and dark. A few torches burned on the wall. Water dripped somewhere. I shivered down to my bones. Cinderella had been here for almost three days? I wasn't going to make her wait a moment longer than she had to.

An interrogator's mask hung on a hook next to a heavy ring of keys. As per Father's regulations, every jailer had to wear a mask during interactions with the prisoners. Father said it kept the jailor impartial. It was perfect for slipping through the jail to find Cinderella.

I grabbed the mask, placing it over my head. The fitted leather half-mask rested over my eyes, and a long swathe of coarse fabric covered the lower half of my face. My breath filled the mask, making moisture cling to my skin. It felt like I was suffocating. *Soufre.* Father thought these were a good idea? Even though the mask had large eyeholes, I could hardly see anything.

As I shuffled into the cell block, my fingers curled around the glass slipper. I gripped a torch in my other hand. I pushed the torch toward each cell as I passed but was disappointed whenever I didn't see a flash of Cinderella's olive skin and green eyes.

My eyes darted to my left. Vienne sat in a cell, her back ramrod straight. Her cold eyes bored into mine. Anger roiled inside and I forced myself to walk forward. Let Father deal with her.

The cells on either side of her were empty. The third cell on the right, however, held a beautiful brunette woman. My breath caught somewhere between my ribs. Two days in the dank prison had done nothing to dull her splendor. Her azure gown glittered, scattering stars over the cell. Behind my mask, I smiled. Shar must have spelled the blazes out of that dress.

The fairy currently hovered in circles over Cyn's head. Was Shar pacing?

I placed the torch in an empty sconce. My arm ached with fatigue and I dropped it to my side. When I caught my breath, I fumbled with the keys. They jangled loudly as I fit them into the lock.

Cinderella stood, her eyes flashing fire. All rational thought was washed away by the flood of heat through my body. *Soufre!* I had completely fallen for her if one look alone could reduce me to this.

"What do you want?" she barked.

What did I want?

Her.

She raised her eyebrows, and I was reminded of the night we met. Thank the Beast, she didn't have any cinnamon on her this time.

Cyn

This jailor was an idiot. He stood statue-like, immobile, his hands resting against the bars of the cell. What was he staring at?

"*Monsieur* Interrogator?"

He shuffled closer, tugging his tailored jacket into place. I snorted at his pristine attire as though it had been designed to entice a confession from me. This man was careless too. The keys hung from his belt, taunting me to grab them and make a run for it. It would be so easy to pull him against the bars, grab the keys, and open the door.

"Mistress, the keys," Shar whispered in my ear.

One word from me and I knew she would help. Excitement flared, tingling my fingers, and I rubbed them together. It would be tricky, but I could probably even lock him in the cell before he raised an alarm. But the wave of excitement crashed down abruptly at my next thought: where would I go?

Armand was dead.

"We'd never make it out of the palace," I whispered back. Shar's light dulled to gray and she returned to her pacing.

The man held up my missing shoe, resting it in the food slot between the bars. His voice wheezed over the floor. "I'm here to . . ."

"I'm not an assassin, I'm a thief," I said, leaning against the cold iron bars on the cell door. "I told you before, I was trying to save him. That ruttish, pigeon-livered pignut of a king refuses to see that." I picked at the rust on the bars.

The jailor barked a laugh, then coughed. "Those are treasonous words, Magpie."

"Treasonous? You should hear all the words I don't say." I tapped a finger against the side of my head.

He shook his head. "*Au contraire.* You're making this harder on your-self," the jailor rasped, tucking the shoe behind his back, and entered the cell. "And me." He hissed as if in pain. "Stubborn thief."

"How dare you call m'lady a thief!" Shar hissed, her light sparking crimson. "She exchanges items of unequal value without permission."

"Y-you've got this all wrong. *C'est moi, Armand.*" The jailor leaned against the stone cell wall. "Help me. These masks are t-terrible."

"Armand?" A storm of hope, fear, and relief exploded behind my ribs. *Impossible.*

Shar's light brightened the cell, shifting between hopeful yellow and pink pastels.

Taking two strides forward, I reached up and pulled off the mask. Armand's handsome, beautiful face smiled back at me.

"You are a terrible jailer. I could have escaped a dozen times." My voice cracked and tears streamed down my face even as I teased him. *He's here.*

Shar broke into hysterics, her light dripping golden sparks.

The joy of him being here and alive filled my heart until it felt like I would burst. I wrapped my arms around Armand, breathing him in. He smelled so good. Of course, after two days in this stinking cell, anything would smell good.

I pulled back and kissed him, gently at first. He responded, his lips mov-ing to my jaw and then tickling behind my ear. Shivers prickled my skin from my neck down my back. I swallowed, my breath catching in my throat. *More.* Kissing him wasn't enough. I wanted to hold him, make him a part of myself so he could be with me always. This desire surged through me with such intensity that it crashed through the rest of my control. I moaned and pressed my lips against his, pushing him against the cell wall. *Petite bêtes,* I couldn't get enough of him. My fingers pressed against his body. My lips alternated between kissing his lips, kissing his neck, and nibbling on his ear.

Instead of matching my kisses, Armand's briefly intensified but mostly remained gentle and soft.

Who wanted gentle at a time like this?

"I need a b-break. T-to b-breathe." He eased away from me.

"Breathing is overrated." My chest heaved and I swallowed. "Kiss me."

He chuckled. "You're such a n-nag. Kiss me, kiss me." He rested his head against the wall of the cell, gulping for air.

What? No more kisses right now? I pulled away and folded my arms. "Perhaps instead of marrying you, I should marry the spare. Where is Prince Lucien?"

I'd expected to get a rise out of Armand, but he just shook his head. "You'll have to f-fight Aimée for him."

I crossed my brows. "Aimée? Why would I have to fight Aimée? She's betrothed to Luc. Not that it matters, if we're to be executed."

"Yes, well, Lucien always did hate his n-name," Armand said, resting his hands on his hips. "Shortened it to Luc."

"Luc is a . . . a prince?" I pressed my fingers to my temple. "Why didn't you tell me?" I poked Armand in his ribs and he winced.

"Gently, *mon amour*. I've been poisoned. I should b-be resting." His chest deflated with a cough. "But I had to see you. T-to rescue you."

"Oh," I repeated. My fingers twisted over each other. Dark circles ringed his sunken eyes and I cursed myself for not seeing it earlier. I had been so relieved, I forgot that *Venenium noix* left its victims weak for months. I stepped closer, noticing his labored breathing. I needed *menthe poivrée* and lungwort. Swizzeran *menthe poivrée*. That would help clear his airways. Concern twisted my stomach. He also needed food. I moved to my small table and picked up my untouched bowl of gruel and offered it to him.

"T-tempting, but I'll pass."

I replaced the bowl. He gripped the bars on the cell door for support. "And I'd better say this quick before I pass out."

"Pass out?" I gulped, then wiped my sweaty hands on my dress. I dropped into a ready stance. I'd have to catch his large frame—somehow. *Protect the head, Cyn.*

"Cinderella Manette," he gasped, as one knee gave way.

I rushed forward, arms stretched wide as he sank down. *Don't pass out, Armand, you idiot.*

He grabbed my hand, clasping it between his.

"You are . . . the thief of my heart. Will you . . . m-marry me?"

I straightened and blinked. He wasn't fainting? What was happening?

Shar dipped down and whispered in my ear, glowing a rosy red. "Mistress, he's proposing."

I blinked again. Here? I looked around the dingy cell. Now? "But didn't you already ask me?" I said. "With the lapel pin?"

Despite my confusion, my heart burned with the molten gold light, filling me to my fingertips like it had in the glade.

He bit the corner of his lip. Heat tickled my skin.

"This is official," he murmured. "Yes or n-no?"

He was here and he was mine. Really mine. How did I get so lucky?

"Mistress, it is impolite to keep royalty waiting," Shar said.

"Yes," he said, his voice strained. "And I don't think I can r-remain like this much l-longer."

My heart thrummed in my chest.

"Yes," I said. "A thousand times, yes."

He pulled the glass slipper from behind him, and I raised my foot. The shoe fit perfectly.

Armand pushed himself to his feet, failing to fully stifle a groan. His chest heaved and his face drained of color. He rested against the cold stone wall of the cell once more.

I stepped closer, leaning against him, marveling at him. His nearness, his proposal. My thoughts swirled, bumping into each other and jumbling together. I lightly placed my head on his chest, still giving him room to breathe. Listening to his brave, compassionate heart—one that beat for me—I sighed. I was home.

Gradually, his breathing and color returned to normal, and he wrapped his arms around me, pulling me close. He was my everything. Who else had his courage and kindness? Or his stutter. And here he was offering me all of himself. Promising me all his time, his love. His kisses.

He pulled away and lowered his forehead to mine, his hands cupping my face. When he spoke, his voice was husky with emotion.

"*Mon trésor.*"

His chin tilted and his lips touched mine, soft and gentle. The kiss was achingly sweet and when it ended, my breath caught in my throat.

Armand took in the dazed look on my face, a smirk teasing the corners of his mouth.

Two can play at this game.

I grabbed his collar and pulled him in close, my lips parted. I stopped centimeters before our lips touched, our breath mingling.

"Just allow me to b-breathe every once in a while."

"I promise."

He laughed, then closed the remaining distance between us, stifling a moan from deep within.

My body melted and a fire roared inside. I lost track of everything as kiss after kiss left both of us breathless and more than a little dizzy.

"Ahem," a voice interrupted.

We pulled away and looked up to the source of the voice. Armand's dark eyes struggled to focus.

Shar floated overhead, her light a fuzzy pink. "Congratulations on your betrothal; however, public exhibitions of affection are not for polite company," she said, as her light swirled all different shades of pink.

"You haven't s-seen anything yet," Armand said, mischief filling his eyes.

Shar blushed a deep scarlet.

I slipped my hand into Armand's and pulled him out of the cell, a brilliant sun rising in my heart.

"I, for one, can't wait."

Acknowledgments

We often find ourselves standing on the shoulders of those who have offered guidance and encouragement. This small bit of text is only a shadow of the light and support you've given me. *Stealing Cinderella* is the second novel I've written, but it was the first good one. These people have played a pivotal role in my creative writing and for that, I am eternally grateful.

Peggy Urry: Whose friendship and offer to join a writing conference was the first step on a journey that has changed my life in so many ways.

Karen Adair: Her relentless support and keen sense of story were the driving forces to submit a small 500-word snippet into the Beginning of Book contest. One that I actually won! Her encouragement and enthusiasm propelled me forward. And for that, I am profoundly grateful.

Janette Rallison: The first published, legit author I met who took me seriously despite my utter newbie status. Her attention and genuine interest in my ideas made me start to believe in myself. Because if Janette takes me seriously, then maybe I should too.

Sheryl Khanna: Your submissions and encouragement through trad-publishing. It's not with the Big Five, but thank you for helping me get here.

Jennifer Stewart Griffith: Thank you so much for reading *Cinderella* and offering so much writing advice, help, and support. You are an amazing writer and friend and I think of you often. Thank you for taking me under your wing.

Ruth Olson: Thanks for continuing to push and encourage. And for never saying, "I told you so." Though you have been more than justified on more than one occasion.

Soquel Baumgardner: You are invaluable in your support and friendship and story sense. End of story.

DWENT: You deserve all the tacos.

Suzanne, Kayla, and Emma: Thanks for taking *Cinderella* and polishing her up. She really shines and it's thanks to you.

And to all those big-timey agents who ghosted and rejected me . . . you suck. (It feels so good to say that). But also your rejection helped me push myself to be a better writer. So thanks.

Of course, a huge thanks to Colby for encouraging me and for the help and support. The late nights and ups and downs (see above). He's been with me for all of it. Thank you.

Lastly, my kiddos. Who think I'm way more amazing than I actually am. I hope you all get to follow your dream. Even for a little.

And to anyone whose names may not appear here but who have offered their support, feedback, and encouragement in various ways. Your contributions have not gone unnoticed, and I am grateful for each and every one of you.

ABOUT THE AUTHOR

Rebecca Gage writes to see if dreams really do come true and if happily ever afters exist (they totally do). She has had several incredibly awkward first dates and has also dreamed of being Batman, joining the X-men, and completely decimating her enemies and drinking their tears (she still dreams of this). She holds a BA in English teaching from Brigham Young University and lives near Denver, Colorado, with her husband and four children. She enjoys baking, drawing, writing, and her family.